EARL DERR BIGGERS
TELLS TEN STORIES

BY

EARL DERR BIGGERS

British Library Cataloguing-in-Publication Data
A catalogue record for this book is available from the
British Library

Contents

First Published In The Saturday Evening Post, Aug 18, 1928

First published in The Saturday Evening Post, Feb 3, 1923)

Earl Derr Biggers

Earl Derr Biggers was born on 26th August 1884 in Warren, Ohio, USA.

Biggers received his further education at Harvard University, where he developed a reputation as a literary rebel, preferring the popular modern authors, such as Rudyard Kipling and Richard Harding Davis to the established figures of classical literature. Following in their footsteps upon graduating, he himself began a career as a popular writer, penning humourous articles and reviews for the Boston Traveler.

In 1913 he produced his debut novel The Seven Keys to Baldpate which was well received by the critics and public alike. George M. Cohen bought the theatrical rights to this work and it was eventually adapted into seven feature films, the first in 1915 and the last in 1983. Biggers compounded this success with his next two novels Love Insurance (1914) and The Agony Column (1916) and continued with his magazine contributions as well as writing plays. He enjoyed hits with the plays A Cure for Curables, which had a two year run in New York, and Inside the Lines, which ran for 500 performances in London.

While on holiday in Hawaii, Biggers heard tales of a real-life Chinese detective operating in Honolulu, named

Chang Apana. This inspired him to create his most enduring legacy in the character of super-sleuth Charlie Chan. The first Chan story The House Without a Key (1925) was published as a serialised story in the Saturday Evening Post and then released as a novel in the same year. Biggers went on to write five more Chan novels and all were licensed for movie adaptations by Fox Films. These films were hugely popular with several different actors taking the lead role of Chan. They were even a success in China where the appeal of a character from the country being the hero instead of the villain appealed to film-goers. Eventually, over 40 films were produced featuring the character.

Biggers only saw the early on-screen successes of Charlie Chan due to his death at the age of only 48 from a heart attack in April 1933.

MOONLIGHT AT THE CROSSROADS

First published in The Saturday Evening Post, Oct 7,
1922

"YOU lie, Hilary," said the woman in the deck chair. She looked very lovely but a bit weary in the light of the dying sun. Behind a jeweled hand, she stifled a little yawn. "You know you lie."

"My dear Isabelle, isn't that rather unfair?" The tall, distinguished-looking man stood with his back to the rail, his hands thrust deep into the pockets of a tweed coat. His thin, handsome face was calm; though he stared down at the pale-gold hair, the violet eyes of a famous beauty, he appeared unmoved.

A famous beauty, yes, he was thinking, but a beauty past her noontime. Too bad that even the loveliest flowers must fade.

"Unfair? I think not," the woman answered. "You were always a liar—I see that now. That wonderful time at Mentone?"

The man shrugged. "Why go back to Mentone?"

"Why not? I believed you then, because I wanted to believe. But now I know—when you said there was no other

"Isabelle!" He knelt by her chair, but she looked away, down the deck, at a middle-aged man who stood by the rail, idly swinging a monocle over the side and staring off to where the sun dipped down into a sea as crimson as his own complexion. "Isabelle, if we must go back to Mentone, let's go back to the happiness of those weeks—the perfume of the roses, the pale moon in the star-decked sky, those warm nights on the terrace."

"Sir James!" called the woman. The man down the deck galvanized into life. "Sir James enters on the word 'terrace'" she explained.

"Ah—er—ah—yes—pardon me," remarked Sir James, arriving promptly. "I was admiring the sunset."

He stuck the monocle in his eye and was suddenly an actor. "Er—er—ter-race." He clattered his feet on the spotless deck. "I come in. My line, old chap. Here you are, like two love birds, and so and so and so, ending—"

"Just a moment." The tall man had risen quickly to his feet. "I—I don't understand. According to my part"—he took a rumpled roll of manuscript from his pocket—"I have a scene here—a rather good scene—"

The woman sighed wearily. "That stupid fool of a Nixon—he gave you the original part. The scene you speak of was never played in the London production. Mr. Thatcher can tell you." She glanced at Sir James. "He was with me in London."

4

"Quite true," agreed Mr. Thatcher, dropping the monocle. "The scene was struck out at the first rehearsal, old chap—the first rehearsal at which Miss Clay appeared, I mean. I enter on the word 'terrace.'"

The tall man smiled. "I see," he said. "A corking good scene for Hilary, I thought it. He recalls to her all that they meant to each other at Mentone; for a brief moment he has almost won her again. She is very nearly in his arms."

"I'm sorry," said the woman coldly.

"My one chance in the piece," persisted the tall man.

The woman's eyes narrowed, her mouth hardened. "The scene is out," she said. "You understand that, Mr. Wayne?"

"Naturally," bowed the man. "Naturally, it's out."

Her eyes flashed. "Just what do you mean by that?"

"You are the star," he replied. He paused. "Your word is law." He took out a pencil and scribbled something on the script. "There, the scene is out. And doubtless it won't matter particularly—in Australia."

Two young people came suddenly upon them—a slender girl with sleek, bobbed, coal-black hair, an English boy with rosy cheeks and frank gray eyes. They stopped. "Rehearsal?" cried the boy. "I say, did you want us?"

"No," said the star. The couple moved on; the girl called back over her shoulder, "Isn't it a glorious evening?"

The three by the rail looked after them. "All their evenings are glorious," Wayne remarked gently. "Their days

5

too. They're going to be married in Sydney, they tell me. And young Mixell was about at the end of his rope when this engagement offered. You see, Miss Clay, what happiness your tour is bringing to others."

The woman shrugged. "Happiness, you say? I wonder. It happens that I was married once, myself. Happiness, perhaps, for a little time." It was characteristic of her that though she was speaking now of her own experience, what she said still had the ring of lines from a play.

"Ah—er—yes," said Wayne. "But to continue—let me get this right. Isabelle, if we must go back to Mentone—and so and so—warm nights on the terrace—"

Mr. Thatcher restored his monocle. "Here you are, like two love birds. Frightfully silly line, that. I always hated it. I don't suppose I could say— "

The ship's clock spoke sharply, four times. Passengers were appearing on deck with that air of bright expectancy those on shipboard wear as the dinner hour approaches.

"Six o'clock," remarked Sibyl Clay. "We may as well drop it. I must dress, even for one of these beastly dinners." Her face lighted suddenly with a charming smile. Swinging about, Wayne saw the cause. A good-looking, tanned man of thirty-five or so was drawing near. "Come here, Mr. Maynard," continued the famous star. "I am very, very angry with you. You have neglected me all day."

The newcomer obeyed. He was flattered, as any man would have been. "I was punishing myself," he told her, "for my sins."

"What tiny, unimportant sins they must be," said Sibyl Clay.

"On the contrary," he answered, "I have to-day endured the ultimate in torture. I'm sure you gentlemen agree?"

"Quite," said Thatcher. Wayne merely smiled.

"Rather nice evening," Maynard remarked. "A sample of our Hawaiian climate. I hope you're going to like Honolulu. It's my home town, you know."

"I shall love it," the actress promised.

"You're stopping over, I trust," ventured Maynard.

The lovely lips pouted. "Hardly at all. So stupidly arranged—my tour. I should like to have played in Honolulu, but we spent nearly a week in Los Angeles, and now we must hurry on to Australia at once. They're so eager for me over there. Isn't it sweet of them?"

Maynard seemed disappointed. "Then it's only between boats?" he inquired.

"Yes," Wayne told him. "We land at ten Tuesday morning, I believe. The boat from Vancouver comes in at two and sails for Sydney at ten that night. We shall have only twelve hours in your Honolulu, Mr. Maynard."

Maynard shook his head regretfully. "Not enough," he said. "Twenty-four hours—and none of you would ever leave us. But twelve—why, you'll have hardly a taste of our moonlight!"

"Sit down—do," urged Sibyl Clay, "and tell me about your moonlight, Mr. Maynard."

The tanned young man dropped quickly into the chair at her side. She looked up at the two members of her company.

"Our rehearsal will be resumed to-morrow morning in the lounge. We'll take this piece from the beginning."

Wayne bowed. "By the way," he said, holding out his part, "it seems rather useless my learning lines that are no longer in the piece."

"See Nixon," advised the woman sharply. "He will give you the part as Bentley played it in London." Her eyes went back to Dan Maynard's face, their expression altered magically.

"I've heard so much of your Hawaiian moonlight " she began.

Norman Wayne and Thatcher strolled off to a distant part of the deck. Wayne's mouth was set in rather grim lines.

"So that scene's out," he said. "I might have known."

Thatcher nodded. "Of course," he replied. "A selfish little beast, this Clay woman. I've played with her—I know. But one doesn't rise to the heights without a bit of trampling, old chap."

"I suppose not."

"Rather surprising—her mention of her marriage. He wasn't a bad sort—her husband, I mean. She killed his spirit, squandered his money, tossed him aside like a flattened orange. Oh, she's been on the make, my lad. You'll have very little opportunity I was surprised when you took the engagement, a bully good actor like you."

"Oh, one wants a change. I've always hankered to take a look about, down yonder. The South Seas—they fascinate me. Travel and see the world, I thought. I presume your reasons were quite different. You've been in Australia before, you said."

"Started there," nodded Thatcher. "No, I'm not precisely going for the ride. But engagements are none too plentiful at home, you know."

"We've all learned that," admitted Wayne. "Rather rough time for the artist. Ah, yes, whether our sweet star fancies the role or not, she's a great philanthropist. A year in repertoire in Australia—it's a life- saver for some of us. For instance—"

He nodded toward a little old lady who approached at a rapid gait. "And how's our Nellie to-night?" he inquired as she came up.

A beautiful smile appeared on the lined old face. "Keen as mustard," said Nellie Fortesque. "Working again. Bless you, I thought my run had ended for ever. Working, and the weather's perfect, and my tired heart has stopped jumping about. I don't think I've ever been so happy."

"Wayne here," remarked Thatcher, "has just discovered that his best scene is out of our opening piece."

The old lady tapped Wayne on the shoulder.

"Don't you care," she comforted. "Don't you worry. You'll play second fiddle, my boy, and a very soft music at that. We all will. But what of it? We're working. And if our star is a little touchy, can you blame her? Australia for a year—it makes us happy, but it makes her sad. She's passed the hilltop; she's coasting down. Poor child! I was on that hilltop once myself. But I mustn't stop here chatting. I'm walking two miles before dinner."

She went on down the deck, and Wayne smiled after her. "It's added ten years to her life, this engagement," he said. "It's rescued Harry Buckstone at the very door of the almshouse. It's given young Mixell and that girl their chance to marry. It's showing me the world. Odd turn, isn't it, that so notably selfish a woman should be the instrument of so much happiness? ... Well, I must go below."

As he passed Sibyl Clay's deck chair he saw that she was leaning very close to Dan Maynard's broad shoulder and talking in a low voice. Wayne smiled. The great star was playing Juliet again—Juliet, so young, so fair, so innocent.

* * * * *

THE Pacific, an ocean of many moods, was still beneficently calm the following morning. They gathered in the lounge at ten o'clock, as happy a group of players as one could have found on land or sea: Wayne, studying an amended part; Thatcher, gay old Nellie Fortesque, the veteran Harry Buckstone, the two young lovers, a few quiet Britishers who had minor roles in the plays Sibyl Clay was to offer to Australia. The sun poured through the port-holes; the creaking ship plowed westward toward the East.

"Feeling younger every minute," Nellie said. She smiled at the girl with the bobbed hair. "Look out, Zell, my dear, I shall be asking for your roles by the time we reach Sydney."

"They're yours without a struggle," said the girl. She spoke to the old woman, but it was at the boy she looked.

"I may even try to take Tommy away from you," warned Nellie humorously.

"At that point," said the girl, "the struggle would begin."

"Living's cheap in Australia, they tell me," remarked Harry Buckstone. "Compared with London, I mean. We shall be able to lay by a bit. I shall try, at any rate. Starting rather late, but I realize it now. Laying by a bit—that's the great idea."

Nixon bustled in; he was a little cockney, always flurried and rushed. Not only did he manage the stage but he was Sibyl Clay's business manager as well.

11

"'Morning, everybody. Bit of all right, this weather, what? I've had a radio from Sydney. We open there the third of October—the day after we land—with Isabelle. Six months in that city alone—that's the promise, if all goes well. And after—Melbourne, Auckland—there's no limit, the way I see it. Sibyl Clay's a big name down there. We may not go home for two years, at least."

"Two years?" Tom Mixell looked inquiringly at the girl. "Would you like that, dear?"

"Why, Tommy," she said, "I'd love it! Home's wherever you and I are—after this."

Sibyl Clay came in. She looked fresh and cool in a marvelous blue gown that matched her eyes. With her came Dan Maynard, good-natured, genial. "I've invited Mr. Maynard to watch us rehearse," the star explained.

"If you people don't mind," said Maynard. Amid a little chorus of polite reassurance, he took a chair near the door.

"Shall we start?" said Miss Clay graciously. She rehearsed the plays herself. "Zell, my dear—Tom—you two are on at the rise. We'll say this is the stage, the exit to the garden over here. Now your first line, Zell dear."

They had never seen her more considerate. A little later poor old Harry Buckstone fumbled a line; he fumbled it again and again. Worried, Thatcher watched the star's expressive face. He looked for an explosion that would rock the boat. But Sibyl Clay was infinitely patient, amazingly sweet and kind. The actor who had been with her in London was at a loss to explain it—until his eye fell suddenly on Dan Maynard, intently watching in the background. They rehearsed until one o'clock and the man from Honolulu remained to the end.

After luncheon Norman Wayne sat in a chair outside his stateroom, a pile of books by his side. Maynard came along, stopped. "You look rather literary," he remarked.

Wayne laughed. "Reading up on the South Seas," he explained. "A part of the world that interests me hugely—always has—those lonely islands away down there at the jumping-off place."

Maynard dropped into a chair. "Not quite so romantic as the authors make them out to be," he suggested.

"You've seen them then?" Wayne asked.

"I've run down there occasionally."

"Lucky devil!" said Wayne. "I suppose they are touched up a bit in the stories. Still, environment has its effect, and there must be something in these tales, after all. A forgotten beach beneath the palms—a few white men in a land meant only for the brown—hot sun, hot blood, hate, greed, revenge. A violent landscape would naturally breed violent deeds."

"Oh, yes, of course. Strange things have happened in the South Seas." Maynard lighted a cigarette. "By the way, I was very much interested in your rehearsal. A charming woman, Miss Clay."

"Yes—charming."

"I recall seeing her act five years ago in London. Never dreamed I'd meet her some day."

"A great favorite in London," Wayne said; "for—for quite some years," he added, with meaning.

"And so sweet and unspoiled, despite her big success."

"Absolutely," agreed Wayne, who was a gentleman.

"Must be a great privilege to work with her," suggested Maynard.

"One learns constantly." Wayne thought of the lines missing from his part in Isabelle.

"Sorry you're not going to stop longer in Honolulu," Maynard went on.

"We all regret it," answered Wayne. "You were born there, I believe you said?"

"Oh, yes."

"In business there?"

"Well, in a way. Look after the interests my father left—a few sugar plantations, a trust company."

"Some one told me your name was quite well known in Hawaii."

"I guess it is. My grandfather came there as a missionary."

"You're not—you're not married, I take it?"

Maynard laughed. "No. Unlucky that way—or lucky, however you care to put it."

He rose and tossed his cigarette over the side. "I live in bachelor comfort in a big house on the beach. Speaking of that, I'd be honored if you and Mr. Thatcher would dine with me to-morrow night. Let's make it early—six- thirty—since you're sailing at ten."

"Very kind of you, I'm sure."

"I hope to persuade Miss Clay to come too."

"I'm sure she will. Speaking for myself, I'll be delighted."

"Then that's fixed," said Maynard. "I'll leave you now to your lurid literature."

He went on down the deck. The afternoon drifted lazily by. At eight that night Wayne came upon Nellie Fortesque, seated beside Tom Mixell and the girl in the shadow of a lifeboat on the after deck.

"Come and join us," said the old lady. "It's night, and the moon is shining, and we're all in love. We're planning our future. It's wonderful. We're all going to be married in Sydney—at least, these children are. We're going to save our money and go back with full pockets and take London by storm. How does it sound to you?"

Wayne smiled ruefully. "Sounds beautiful—for the children. You come away now, Nellie. They want to be alone."

"Oh, no!" cried the girl. "Nellie, don't listen to him!"

But the old lady stood up. "Oh, he's quite right. I was just stealing a little of your happiness—you have so much, my dear." She and Wayne strolled down the deck.

"Beautiful—for the children," said Wayne. "But for—"

"Nonsense! You're a mere boy."

"I'm forty-five, Nellie."

"Think of me. I'm seventy-two—seventy-two, and sailing off into the moonlight—the Hawaiian moonlight they say's so dangerous. Oh, well, I've had my fun. And now I'm safe—secure—for another year at least. That's something at my age. Bless you, it's everything!"

"It's something, even at forty-five," Wayne agreed. They stopped by the starboard rail. Through a long silence they watched the waves moving restlessly in the white path of the moon. From the lounge came the sad, plaintive strains of a Hawaiian melody. Wayne looked at the woman beside him.

"I remember you, Nellie," he said gently. "I was just a youngster—you won't mind my saying it? I remember— at the old theater in York—how beautiful you were. Your Viola—"

"Dear boy." Her voice broke. "Those were great days— great days for Nellie. If I'd only saved something for the future; but I thought youth lasted for ever. These children think that too. I'm glad they do."

Another silence. "I think I'll go below," the woman said. "To-morrow will be an exciting day. Good night—and thank you for remembering."

"Thank you for the memory," said Wayne.

Alone again, he moved aimlessly about the ship. On the upper deck, at a corner of the wireless operator's cabin, he heard low voices. One he recognized—a magic voice that had held thousands enraptured in the London stalls. He paused for a moment; he was a gentleman, but he lingered.

"Yes, it's quite true," Sibyl Clay was saying. "I've had everything I wanted out of life. Every one has been so good to me. Fame, applause—the top of the heap, always."

"It must have been a great satisfaction to you," came Dan Maynard's voice.

"Oh, it has been. I've loved it—reveled in it. That's why I think it's so very strange—"

"What is so strange?"

"There must be something in the air out this way—I don't know—I can't explain it. I only know that if you were to come to me to-night and tell me that this boat would never reach port, that my career was ended, that I'd just go sailing on through eternity over a sea like glass, I—I wouldn't mind, Dan. Not with you aboard."

Wayne lingered for Maynard's answer. When it came, the voice of the Honolulu man was calm, unmoved. "It's the tropics," he explained evenly. "You're just on the edge, but they've got you already. Wait until you see Waikiki.... By the way, I want you to come to dinner at my house to-morrow night."

"That will be thrilling—dinner with you."

"Wayne and Thatcher are coming too."

"But " There was disappointment in that magic voice.

"I've already asked them," Maynard went on. "And that reminds me, I promised Thatcher I'd join the two of them for bridge this evening. He said I must bring you—for a very charming fourth."

"But it's so much nicer on deck." Wayne could not see, but he knew that pout of her lips. "Can't we stay here?"

Maynard had risen. "A promise is a promise," Wayne heard him saying.

Norman Wayne slipped away. When, a few moments later, he entered the smoking- room, the three of them were already at a table. Thatcher was dealing the cards.

"I much preferred the deck," Sibyl Clay said. "This stuffy old room But men are all alike. They have no appreciation."

"On the contrary," said Wayne, "I'm thrilled to the depths. There's a drizzle in London, no doubt, and little pools of water in the dark alley that leads to the stage door. But to-morrow we shall stand in the Honolulu sunshine."

"At the crossroads of the Pacific," added Maynard.

"At the crossroads," repeated Wayne. He glanced at his hand. "I make it two hearts," he said.

* * * * *

AT nine the next morning the boat from Los Angeles came to a stop in Honolulu harbor. The air was warm and moist and heavy, uncooled by any breeze. The little group of players gathered at the rail, and with that keen interest characteristic of British tourists the world over, stared at the unfamiliar scene. Beyond the water-front, unromantic and commercial, they saw the white tops of buildings, like islands in a sea of brilliant green, and still beyond, blue peaks against a cloudless sky.

Nixon moved among them, worried as always. "You'll have to look after your own hand luggage," he admonished. "I'll have your trunks aboard the Princess Irene as soon as she comes in. Don't forget, we sail at ten sharp, and for God's sake, don't any of you miss the boat."

A gleaming limousine with a Japanese chauffeur was waiting for Dan Maynard, and at his invitation Miss Clay, Wayne and Thatcher rode with him to the Alexander Young Hotel. There the three players engaged rooms for the day.

"You'll be comfortable here," said Maynard. "I've just told the clerk to take special care of you. I'd like to have you at the house, but I've been away for months, and no doubt things are rather upset there. However, I'll have everything running on schedule by dinnertime. And if you don't mind, I'm going to call for you all at two o'clock and show you round a bit."

Sibyl Clay nodded. "You're too good," she said. There was a noticeable lack of enthusiasm in her tone.

For three hours that afternoon Maynard motored them about the island. His high spirits at being home again were contagious. He was no longer a boy, but his manner was boyish and charming, and Wayne found himself liking the man more and more the longer he knew him. No host could have been more gracious. They saw and they admired, and when the Honolulu man set them down at their hotel at five, he told them that his chauffeur would call for them in about an hour.

Wayne dressed with care, then repacked his bags and rang for a bell-boy. It was a bit after six when he descended to the lobby. He settled his account with the smiling little Chinese clerk and directed that his luggage be piled near the desk.

"I'll call for it later this evening," he explained.

"Yes, sir," agreed the clerk. "It will be very safe."

He went over and, lighting a cigarette, dropped into a wicker chair. Women tourists turned to stare at him, and no wonder. A leading man on the London stage for many years, he had in his day set many feminine hearts to beating faster.

Thatcher appeared, his face more crimson than ever above his white shirt- front, the eternal monocle in his eye.

His luggage, too, came with him, and when he had paid his bill, he strolled over to Wayne.

"Clay's late as usual, I see," he remarked.

As he spoke, the great star stepped from the elevator. She had made good use of her brief time, Wayne thought as he looked at her. Well into the forties, he knew that, but marvelous are the possibilities of make-up when intelligently applied. And well she understood the virtue of the perfect costume. About her pale chiffon dinner gown she had wrapped a Spanish shawl, as flamboyantly colored as the Honolulu scene.

"I believe the car's outside," said Wayne, rising.

"I am ready," answered the star. He looked into her violet eyes and saw a great general going into battle.

Beautiful, yes, Wayne thought, but unkind of the setting sun to be so hideously bright in the limousine. Did she realize that she had passed the hilltop, that she was coasting down, that her days of fame were numbered? Of course she did. Hard lines on that lovely face, tired lines. At a candle-lighted dinner table, however, they would not show, and under the Hawaiian moon Anything could happen under the Hawaiian moon.

They rolled along between rows of tall coconut palms, over the lowlands, past rice fields and taro patches, and came presently to Waikiki, with its huge hotels and its vast rambling houses. Through a gateway and along a drive that skirted a garden all crimson and gold, and so up to Dan Maynard's big front door.

Maynard was waiting in his living-room, a great apartment furnished in expensive native woods, with greenery everywhere. One side of it was open, save for a protecting screen, to the white beach. About the whole establishment there was an air of wealth, security. To these gypsies of the theater it was a new environment, and their hearts stirred in a mild envy. What would it be like, to have a home, to stop all worry over money, engagements, to sit here by the murmuring surf and feel that disaster could never reach them?

Maynard was looking at Sibyl Clay with keen admiration. "You're wonderful," he said. "My poor house has never had such a visitor before. Hundreds of people here would have been thrilled to meet you, but I'm being very selfish."

"I'm glad you are," she smiled. "I shall enjoy the memory more. Just you and I—and Waikiki."

Wayne and Thatcher felt rather out of it, but cocktails restored them. The Japanese butler announced dinner.

The quick tropic dusk was falling. Wayne's premonition came true—the table was candle-lighted, and in that kindly glow the great Sibyl Clay was young again; young as Juliet, and as lovely. The silver of the Maynard family, famous for generations, sparkled no brighter than her violet eyes;

the linen was no whiter than her slim, girlish shoulders. Again Wayne had the feeling of a general going into battle, fighting—for what? For security, perhaps; for peace and safety; for a new sort of happiness in this strange corner of the world.

Wayne found it difficult to take his eyes from her face, and seemingly Dan Maynard was in the same predicament. The Honolulu man saw, sitting across from him at his own table as though she belonged there, the most strikingly beautiful woman he had ever met. A sort of intoxication seemed to sweep over him; he talked faster and faster, stories of the islands, tales of his forebears' early adventures. Sibyl Clay had never been known as a good listener, but she listened now; she led him on, she smiled upon him. Intoxicated—he was all of that.

"Ah, but you're not the first, my boy," Wayne thought.

The perfect dinner ended at last, and they retired to the drawing-room for coffee. Wayne took his cup and strode to the screen. Beyond, in the scented night, he saw the white parade of the breakers, line after foamy line in a sea of molten silver.

"Always wanted to visit this spot," he remarked, coming back into the room. "The crossroads." He sat down. "I've been thinking to-night—each one of us stands at the crossroads at some time in his life. I stood there myself once, long ago—twenty-five years ago. Yes, I was at the crossroads, and one word—one little word—decided my course for ever after."

"How was that?" asked Thatcher, putting down his cup.

"Twenty-seven years ago, to be exact," Wayne went on. He glanced at his host and Sibyl Clay; they appeared to be interested. "I was a boy of eighteen at the time, born and reared in a strict household in the cathedral city of York—in the very shadow of the minster, in fact. My father was a stern hard man; he dominated us all, my mother—all of us. His hardness had already driven my elder brother from home. And I, the second son, his last hope—I wanted to go on the stage.

"You can imagine his horror at that. The theater was the house of the devil, he said, and he meant it too. He ranted and stormed, but—well, a traveling troupe came our way; they were doing Gilbert and Sullivan in the provinces. There was an opening in the company and I ran away from home in the night."

He looked at Maynard. "My dear sir, you can never appreciate the life I got into. For a short time all went well; then the houses fell off. We didn't play to the gas. Our salaries stopped, our pitiful luggage was seized for hotel bills, we ate but rarely. Somehow, we struggled on. I had never dreamed such misery could exist in the world. We managed to reach

Dublin, and there my resistance gave out. I wired a friend for money to go home.

"I got back to York on Sunday morning—they were ringing the minster bells. It seemed like heaven to me. I was sick and weary. I wanted no more of the theater; I had been cured of my madness. For a time I was afraid to go to the house, but along about noon my courage returned and I went.

"I entered the little drawing-room. My father and mother were sitting there, reading. For a long while I stood just inside the door. They never looked at me. Miserably unhappy, I went to my room, freshened up, came back down-stairs. Again I stood there, a young boy, hungry for sympathy, for a kind word. Finally my father looked up. His eyes were stony and cold.

"'Well,' he said through his teeth, 'have you had enough of the theater?'

"'No!' I cried. Just one little word, sharp with anger and bitterness. Mind you, I had been at the point of forswearing the stage for ever. I was at the crossroads. One kind word, one friendly look—But at that tone in my father's voice, something broke inside me. 'No, no, no!' I fairly shouted, and went out of that house for all time. I borrowed money to get to London. More misery, more heartbreak—but there was no turning back now. I dropped our family name of

Harkness. I became Norman Wayne, an actor, and—and here I am."

Maynard shook his head. "Poor little kid," he said pityingly. "It was cruel—cruel. Tell me, have you ever regretted—"

Wayne smiled. "Sometimes," he said. "Sometimes I've wondered, if my poor mother had spoken Oh, well, what's the use? It's all over now."

Thatcher was thoughtfully swinging his monocle on its black ribbon. "By the way," he began, "you say your family name was Harkness?"

"Yes. Naturally, I dropped it. I wanted no more of my father, not even his name."

"Years ago," continued Thatcher slowly, "I knew a chap named Harkness. A Yorkshire man he was too. It was in the South Seas."

"In the South Seas?"

"Yes. I told you I'd been out there, you know, as a young chap. This Albert Harkness—"

"Albert?"

"That was his name. I knew him rather well. We were alone for some months on the island of Apiang, in the Gilbert group. As a matter of fact, I was the last white man to see him alive."

Wayne got slowly to his feet. "You were the last white man to see old Bertie alive?" he repeated. His face had paled.

"Why, yes. You knew him?"

"He was my elder brother, the one my father had driven from home before I left."

"Not really?" Thatcher was silent for a moment. "Odd, isn't it? We've traveled all the way from London together—I never dreamed Of course, my name is a stage name too. If I'd mentioned sooner that I was Redfield—"

"Redfield?" said Wayne. "Ah, yes, Henry Redfield. You were with my brother on Apiang?"

"Precisely. We were traders there."

"And he died—of a fever?" Something in the man's voice brought a brief, electric silence to that room.

"Of a fever—yes," said Thatcher. "I buried him myself. We were alone among the natives, save for a Chinese cook."

Wayne sat down. "Ah, yes," he said. "So you are Redfield. You knew old Bertie. We must have a talk about this, my friend—a long talk."

Sibyl Clay had risen; she stood tall and fair and shining. Dan Maynard felt a little catch in his throat as he looked at her. "All very interesting, I'm sure," she said. "But, Mr. Maynard, the time is going so quickly, and you have promised to show me Waikiki in the moonlight."

"Of course," cried Maynard, leaping up. "You fellows seem to have something to talk over, so if you don't mind—"

"By all means," agreed Wayne, and Thatcher nodded.

Maynard held open the screen door and Sibyl Clay went out. The night was magic, and filled with the odors of exotic plants, flaming with the crimson blossoms of the poinciana trees. They heard the breakers whispering on the beach. Side by side, very close, they walked together down a shadowy path.

Maynard was dazed, bewitched. Thirty-five, rich, powerful, women had been near him before; they had tried to win him, but in vain.

Always he had guarded his freedom, his independence. But now—he was not so sure of himself now. Many women, yes, but never a woman like this before.

He led her to a bench under a hau tree, some thirty feet from the house. Out toward the reef twinkled the lights of Japanese fishing boats; just above the horizon hung the Southern Cross. A cool breeze swept in from the sea, and the hau tree dropped a yellow blossom in her lap.

"Is it what you expected?" Maynard asked.

"It's wonderful," she answered softly. "I know now—I understand—why people come and never want to go away. Life must be beautiful here—and old age always round the corner—the corner one never needs to turn."

"I was born in that house," he told her. "I learned to swim in these waters. It's home, and I love it."

"I love it, too," she told him. "I'm seeing it for the first time, and I adore it. How happy you must be here. But— you are alone. Surely nights like this— How does it come that you live here in this paradise alone?"

"It may be," he answered, "because I've never met a woman I cared to ask to—to share it with me."

She was very close. "We must find that woman for you. Tell me, have you ever thought—what sort of woman—"

The cool breeze touched his face. He hesitated, drew back a little. "Promise me," he began—"you'll be going home one of these days—promise me that on your way back you'll stop over for a longer stay."

She shook her head. "No, I shan't go home this way. It's all arranged. When the Australian tour is ended, we return to England by way of Suez. Around the world, you see."

"Then," he said, "this is your only night at Waikiki."

"Yes. Just once in a lifetime—at the crossroads."

"It's a wonderful night, for me at least," said Maynard. "I shall remember it always. But you, when you're back in London—"

London! She shuddered inwardly. It was true, what they whispered about her—she knew it. She was through. The thought of London appalled her—new faces, new favorites,

Sibyl Clay forgotten. But, of course, Dan Maynard must not suspect.

"Yes, London will be glorious," she said brightly. "They'll give me a marvelous welcome home; they were all so sorry to see me go. And Australia—there's a big triumph waiting there, I know. But even so—"

"Yes?"

"It's just as I told you last night on the boat. Something has happened to me, something very strange. I don't care about my career any more, Dan. I don't care about Australia, or even London."

"Sibyl," he cried—his voice trembled—"do you mean that? Because—"

He stopped. From his drawing-room came the sharp crack of a revolver, followed by the crash of breaking glass.

* * * * *

DAN MAYNARD leaped to his feet and ran along the path to the house, while Sibyl Clay followed more slowly at his heels. As they entered the drawing-room, the Japanese butler, badly frightened, appeared from the hall.

Maynard gasped in amazement as he looked about that usually quiet and peaceful room, for he saw the marks of a terrific struggle. Chairs were overturned, rugs were displaced. Indeed, the struggle was still going on. In the center of the room Wayne and Thatcher fought desperately for possession of a pistol held in Wayne's right hand. In another moment

Wayne broke away; he raised the pistol and pointed it at his panting antagonist. But Maynard was too quick for him. He leaped forward, and after a moment of brief effort, wrenched the weapon away.

"For God's sake," he cried, "what does this mean?"

Wayne staggered back against a table. His face was deathly pale, his mouth twitched convulsively, his eyes were blazing. "I'll get you, Redfield," he muttered. "I missed that time, but I'll get you yet."

"What does this mean, I say?" repeated Maynard. He slipped the revolver into his pocket, and going over, laid a hand on Wayne's arm. "Pull yourself together, man. Tatu"— he turned to the butler—"whisky-and-soda, quick."

The butler went out. Wayne sank weakly into a chair.

"I—I'm sorry, Mr. Maynard," he said. "I broke your window. I'm afraid I'm a rotten bad shot. I owe you an explanation and an apology. In—in a moment, please." He buried his head in his arms.

Sibyl Clay came and stood before him. Her eyes were cold; hard lines had appeared about her mouth. "What is this silly melodrama?" she demanded. "Come, speak up!"

"Just a moment," Wayne repeated.

"Take your time," said Maynard. "And try to calm yourself, if you can."

A long silence. The butler appeared with a tray. Maynard himself poured a drink and offered it to Wayne. The actor's hand trembled as he reached for it; the glass tinkled against his teeth. At a safe distance, Thatcher, his face verging on the purple now, watched with a wary eye.

"Yes," said Wayne slowly, "I must explain. I told you I was interested in the South Seas, Mr. Maynard. I was interested because of my older brother, who ran away from home several years before I did. For a time he drifted about down there, and finally settled down as a trader on the lonely island of Apiang. His partner was a man named Redfield— this creature who calls himself Thatcher. The same man; he doesn't deny it. You heard him yourself."

"I do not deny it," said Thatcher. "We were together on that island, Bert Harkness and I."

"On that lonely island, the only two white men for miles around. Some sort of feud grew up between them—"

"It's a lie!" cried Thatcher.

"Until finally this swine shot poor old Bertie in the back."

"A lie, I tell you!" Thatcher shouted.

"Shot him in the back, like the yellow coward he is, and then reported poor Bertie had died of a fever."

"Mr. Maynard, I appeal to you," said Thatcher. "The man is mad. What proof has he—"

"Proof enough," cut in Wayne. "You thought you were safe, didn't you? You forgot that Chinese cook. You thought he didn't know, but he did, and two years after, he told the whole story to a missionary named McCandless. The missionary wrote it all to me."

"This happened a long time ago?" inquired Maynard.

"Over twenty years ago," Wayne told him. "When I heard the true story of Bertie's death, it was too late. Redfield had disappeared utterly. The earth had swallowed him up. But I've been waiting. That's why I took this engagement. I've been waiting, and now, as luck will have it, I meet Redfield in your drawing-room—and I'll never leave him again, not until I've paid him back, not until—"

"Ridiculous!" said Sibyl Clay. "In all my life I've never heard anything so ridiculous. Mr. Thatcher, I'm sure Mr. Maynard will furnish you with a car. Go to the boat and wait for us."

Thatcher stood up. "Pardon me," he said, "I'll do nothing of the sort. This idiot has called me a coward, but I'm not, and I'll not run away like one. No, we'll have this out here and now."

"I'll get you, Redfield," muttered Wayne. "I'll get you, I promise you that."

"Try it!" sneered Thatcher. "I'm an older man than you, yet I'm not afraid. Try it, but look out I don't get you!"

"In the back," said Wayne. "A shot in the back—that's your specialty."

"You lie!" Thatcher cried.

"Just a moment," pleaded Maynard. "Wayne, I thought you were a sensible man. Suppose you do get him, as you say. Think of what it will mean."

"I've got to get him," said Wayne pitifully. "Poor old Bertie—we were more than brothers. The only member of my family I ever loved. Why, when we were boys—"

"Rubbish!" cried Sibyl Clay. Her face was drawn, old. Maynard looked at her in wonder. He brought forward a chair.

"Sit down," he said.

"Why should I sit down?" she demanded.

"You seem rather tired, that's all," he answered gently. For a long moment their eyes met. Sibyl Clay was a great general, but she knew when her campaign was lost. She dropped into the chair.

"Now let's talk this over quietly," Maynard said. "I can understand how you feel, Wayne, old man. Naturally, in the moment of meeting this chap—of recognizing him, I mean—you lost your head. But you must calm down. I like you; you're a good fellow, and if you take the law into your own hands like this, you know the end. Your whole life wrecked, and what will you have accomplished?"

"An eye for an eye," muttered Wayne stubbornly.

"Nonsense! That's archaic. Besides, if you'll pardon my saying so, your evidence seems a bit flimsy."

"It's all of that," put in Thatcher. "I remember now—I had a row with that Chinaman about his wages after Harkness died. This absurd story of his is the Oriental idea of revenge."

"Precisely," said Maynard. "You hear, Wayne? That's quite likely—"

"Chinese don't lie," objected Wayne. "We all know that."

"Do we?" said Maynard. "Most of them don't, that's true. The Chinese reputation for truthfulness is built upon a pretty solid foundation. But there are about half a billion of them, and there are black sheep in that race as in all others. I speak from experience. I haven't lived all my life in Hawaii without knowing the Chinese. Why, my dear fellow, I could give you examples—"

"For instance," said Thatcher eagerly.

Maynard sat down. "A good many years ago," he began, "we had a house- boy— "

Sibyl Clay interrupted. "Now," she said bitterly, "I suppose we are to have your life-story too."

Maynard regarded her coolly. "I am trying to avert a catastrophe," he said. "Kindly remember that." He turned to Wayne. "This boy of ours was very young—twenty, I think—a Cantonese and a splendid servant. He became obsessed with some fancied grievance and we let him go. He went away and spread the most fantastic lies about us.

35

We had to drag him into court in the end. He broke down and confessed he had been trying to save his face." Wayne listened stubbornly. "What I'm trying to get at is, if one Chinese would do that, another would. How do you know that in this instance—"

Wayne shook his head.

"You mean well, Maynard. But this man is guilty; he's guilty as the devil. Look at him!"

"I see no evidence of his guilt," protested Maynard. "On the contrary, I see several things that point to his innocence— and so would you, in a calmer mood. For example, he was under no compulsion to tell you he was Redfield."

"Precisely," cried Thatcher. "If I'd killed poor Bert, do you think I'd have revealed myself to his brother?"

"You thought you were safe," said Wayne. "You never dreamed that Chinese knew what was going on at Apiang."

"Even so," persisted Maynard, "I think he would have remained silent. Wayne, will you take my advice?"

"I promise nothing," answered Wayne.

"That missionary is still alive?"

"He was a few years ago—living in Sydney."

"Sydney—your next stop. And the Chinese?"

"He was in Sydney too."

"There you are. Remember, there are courts to settle this sort of thing. Let the matter rest for the present. Admit like a man that your evidence against this chap is hone too good. When you get to Sydney, investigate; learn how that story has stood the test of time."

"A splendid idea," cried Thatcher. "Give me a chance. I'll help with your investigation. I'll prove your story is rot, and I'll prove other things. That brother of yours—you think he was a saint. Well, he was a dirty blackbirder."

Wayne leaped to his feet. "You liar!" he cried. "You contemptible liar! Shoot a man in the back, and then besmirch his name!"

Maynard got between them just in time. Sibyl Clay sighed wearily. "Will this never end?" she said.

"He'll apologize for that!" Wayne shouted.

"Yes, yes, of course he will," said Maynard. "Come on, Thatcher, you didn't mean it."

"Oh, didn't I?" Thatcher stood glaring through his monocle. Somewhere in the distance a bell tinkled. "I meant every word of it—a blackbirder! What's that beside the things he's accused me of here to-night?"

The butler entered. "Telephone ring for Miss Clay," he announced.

The woman followed the butler out. Maynard went to Thatcher and spoke in a low voice. Thatcher stepped toward Wayne.

"Very good," he said, "I apologize. I withdraw what I said."

Wayne nodded. "I've got a beastly temper," he murmured. "I inherited it. I'm sorry."

The actress returned, walking slowly. "That was Nixon," she remarked, in a dead tired voice. "It's twenty-five minutes before ten, and he's frantic. He's picked up our luggage at the hotel. We—we had better go." She looked at Dan Maynard.

"Of course." Maynard went to the hall, and they followed. He gave the men their hats and sticks; he wrapped the Spanish shawl about Sibyl Clay. "The car is just outside." In the drive, he turned to them. "I'm taking you down myself. Wayne, get in front with me. Thatcher, you ride in the back with Miss Clay."

Kalakaua Avenue was deserted, an ideal speedway, and Dan Maynard's idea appeared to be speed. They tore on through the brilliant Hawaiian night. As they went, the Honolulu man talked in a low voice to Wayne. In the rear seat, Sibyl Clay sat haughty and aloof beside the erstwhile Sir James. She was thinking of London, despairingly.

Nixon was pacing the dim pier shed, a man distraught. "Well, you nearly missed it, didn't you?" he cried. "Every one's on board but you. In heaven's name, get on!"

"Thatcher," said Maynard, "I've had a talk with Wayne. He's going to make an investigation down in Sydney. Until then, there's a truce between you."

"Thanks," said Thatcher. "That suits me perfectly. I'll help with the investigation, as I promised."

Maynard stood with Wayne's pistol in the palm of his hand. "Do you carry this about with you all the time?" he asked.

Wayne nodded. "For the past few weeks—yes," he said.

"I think I'd better keep it," Maynard suggested.

"I fancy you had," Wayne agreed. "Thank you for what you've done—and good-by."

He followed Thatcher up the gangplank.

Maynard turned to Sibyl Clay. He felt a little pang of regret as he saw her white face. "Better reconsider," he said. "If you'll come back this way—"

She shook her head. "No," she answered wearily. "There are some moments, Dan—they come once, and never again. This was my only stop in Honolulu." She held out her hand. "Good night."

"Good-by, and good luck," said Maynard gently.

The plank was drawn in as she reached the deck, and a few moments later the big ship crept from the pier. Slowly it drew away from the harbor lights, swung round and headed for Australia.

* * * * *

AN hour later Norman Wayne stood in a friendly shadow near the prow of the boat. A pipe was between his teeth, and he was staring at the dim shore-line of Oahu.

A short, stocky man came creeping out of the dark, slowly, silently. For a moment he stood at Wayne's back, unperceived. Then he stepped to the rail at Wayne's side. They looked at each other. Neither spoke. The stout man took out his own pipe and began to fill it.

"You're a damned good actor, Wayne," he remarked softly. "I've always thought so, but I was never surer of it than I was back there to-night."

"Thanks," said Wayne. "I give every part my best. My one rule of life. We weren't a moment too soon with our bit of melodrama, old chap."

Thatcher nodded. "I know. I saw it in her face when they came in."

"I've been suffering a few moments of remorse," went on Wayne. "Are you quite sure we did the right thing?"

"Of course we did. It's just as I told you this noon. I know Sibyl Clay—selfish, utterly selfish. She'd have hooked that chap in another moment—married him to-morrow, probably. And what would have become of us? A lot she'd care. The tour would have ended before it began. She'd have thrown us all over, stranded us nine thousand miles from home, all our hopes smashed—poor old Nellie, Harry Buckstone, the two kids—oh, we did the right thing."

"I was thinking of Maynard."

"Ah, yes, Maynard. A fine chap. She'd have ruined his life, just as she's ruined others. Yes, young Maynard was very near to taking the wrong turn at the crossroads to-night. But we dragged him back. He'll be grateful to us in the morning."

Thatcher lighted his pipe. "We'd best be careful," said Wayne, glancing over his shoulder. "Mustn't act too chummy until I can pretend to dig up new evidence at Sydney and tell Sibyl Clay I was wrong."

"Of course." Thatcher started to move away. "You added a few details to the scenario we worked out at luncheon," he said.

"Naturally. The excitement of the moment, you know. Yes, I had several inspirations."

"There was one in particular I didn't much care for," Thatcher continued—"that about my shooting poor old Bertie in the back. I wouldn't shoot any man in the back. You know it."

"Nonsense!" said Wayne. "I've read more South Sea stories than you have. Men are always shot in the back down there. And if it comes to that, I didn't like what you said about Bertie—a dirty blackbirder."

Thatcher laughed. "You don't mean you've actually got a brother named Bertie?" he inquired.

"Certainly I have. He's a bookseller directly across from the Mitre, in Oxford." Wayne looked up at the star-strewn sky. "How he would enjoy a tour like this. Poor old Bertie has never been out of England in his life."

SELLING MISS MINERVA

First published in The Saturday Evening Post, Feb 5, 1921

BILLY ANDERSON was an automobile salesman. He had a method all his own. It was much the same method the ancient minstrels must have used in peddling poetry. It involved little mention of differential, transmission and other grimy points about a car. Instead it was all mixed up with the everlasting stars, the pounding surf, the misty mountain tops. Romance adapted to business, Anderson called it.

His environment, being Southern California, helped a lot. The climate played a gentle accompaniment to his fervid story. There is something in the air of that wonderful state, no doubt of it—a mild, soothing influence that makes poets of retired wholesale grocers. Hard-boiled widowers from Iowa farms come out to spend a pleasant winter—and not a cent more than they can help. They end by marrying again at the age of seventy—and hang the expense!

Anderson foraged up and down and in and out of the big tourist hotels, interviewing prospects. The psychology of salesmanship was his middle name. He sized each prospect up. Nine out of ten, having shut their roll-top desks far to the east, were ripe for the romance talk. That was the talk they got.

On a warm and sunny morning late in January, Billy Anderson sat on the veranda of the Maryland Hotel, in Pasadena, opposite Mr. Henry G. Firkins, of Boston. Mr. Firkins was rumored to be a prospect. He looked like a good one.

"Now, if I was trying to sell you a Requa car in your home town back East," Billy was saying, "I'd probably use another method. But this—this is California, and buying a car in California is different from buying one anywhere else. Do you know what the difference is?"

"Well, it's a long haul," said Mr. Firkins. "I suppose I'd have to pay more freight."

"No, no!" protested Billy. "It's not a question of freight. It's a question of—romance."

"Romance?"

"You've said it! Romance! Mr. Firkins, what man or woman in this workaday world is too worn with care and worry not to be able on occasion to succumb to its thrill—its glamour?"

"I don't know. Name one."

"I can't! And let me tell you, you don't have to open the covers of a magazine to meet up with it—not for a minute. There's plenty of romance everywhere, even in the everyday business of selling automobiles. Provided, of course, you look for it."

"Son," said Mr. Firkins, "I don't get you."

"What I mean is this," smiled Billy Anderson: "When I sell a man a Requa car out here in California, I sell him not merely a perfect piece of mechanism; I sell him revel and all the romance that goes with it. I sell him thousands of miles of smooth California roads; the roar of angry surf on the rocks below Monterey; the cool silent depths of Topanga Canon; the crumbling, eloquent walls of San Juan Capistrano. I sell him the hush of a great redwood forest; valleys green with alfalfa fields; the sharp airs and vast panoramas of Sierra summits. Do you get me now?"

"I think I do," admitted Mr. Firkins.

"I want to show it to you, with all its allure and invitation," Billy warmed up. "I want to create a picture, not of a wonder-full piece of mechanism but of all the ownership of that piece of mechanism will procure for you out here in God's country."

He stopped, for Mr. Firkins was staring at him coldly, appraisingly. Could he have made a mistake in his man? On rare occasions that happened. Certainly there was little answering gleam in the Firkins eye. Billy Anderson started in on another tack—regretfully. His was never the soul of a mechanic.

"Of course, I don't want you to think I'm neglecting the other side of it," he said. "From a mechanical standpoint, the Requa is a masterpiece. I'm sort of taking it for granted you know that"

"I ought to know it," answered Mr. Firkins surprisingly. "I've had the Boston agency for the Requa the past fifteen years, and I sell it in a number of small Massachusetts towns as well."

Billy Anderson deflated rapidly.

"I didn't know that," he said limply. "It makes me look rather foolish. We'll be glad to fix you up with a car while you're out here. Can I make a date for you with the boss? And I'm sorry if I've wasted your time."

He stood up.

"Wait a minute," Mr. Firkins said. "Sit down. You haven't wasted anybody's time. Tell me, how long have you been handing people out the line of talk that you just gave me?"

"Oh, about three years."

"Does it work?"

"Nearly always. Women have a lot to say about the selection of the family car—and that talk gets them. The men I go up against are here to relax—to have a good time—yes, I generally hook them too. There was only one man in the state of California sold more Requas than I did last year," he added proudly.

"U'm!" Mr. Firkins frowned. "You admit, then, that it's pretty easy?"

"Like selling candy to an infant."

"Yes? Well, we never get anywhere in this world along the easy route. Aren't you about ready to tackle something more difficult?"

"You mean—"

"From what part of the States do you come?"

"I'm going to surprise you," laughed Billy Anderson. "I was born right here in Pasadena, twenty-three years ago. Yes, sir—a native son. Examine me closely. You may never meet another."

"Ever been East?"

"Yes: but I didn't like it."

"What part of the East did you visit?"

"Denver," said Billy Anderson seriously. Mr. Firkins smiled.

"How would you like to come to Boston and work for me?"

"Boston!" repeated Billy Anderson. "I get a shiver down my spine. And I see snow—big piles of it."

"You're psychic," said Firkins. "I admit the snow. But I'll make it worth your while. And a young man like you ought to strike out and see the world."

"I've felt that way at times," Billy admitted. "I did try Honolulu. Easy, too—selling cars. But not so easy to get them over after you've sold them. The steamship company has a nasty habit of leaving your consignment on the San Francisco pier."

"Nothing like that in Boston," suggested Mr. Firkins.

"I know—but quite aside from the climate, isn't Boston a bit chilly? I mean, wouldn't my wild free manner sort of scare 'em to death?"

"That," smiled Mr. Firkins, "is exactly my idea. We're too conservative out there. I want to get things stirring, bring in new blood."

"You want me to jazz up the Boston trade?"

"You've—er—said it," Firkins replied. "I'll be going back in about six weeks—suppose you go with me. I don't know what you're getting here, but I'll start you at five thousand. What do you say?"

"It has an appealing sound to it," Billy admitted. "And I am in a rut here, I know. Yes, I'll take you."

"Good! Give us a trial at any rate. If you don't like it—well, California will still be standing."

"'Till the sands of the desert grow cold'—and then some!"

* * * * *

SIX weeks later Billy Anderson called on Mr. Firkins for his final instruction. He was full of enthusiasm for the task that lay ahead. Mr. Firkins announced that he was returning by way of Canada, but that he wanted Billy to go East by the direct route.

"My boy," he said rather sheepishly, "I'm going to start in by playing a mean trick on you."

"Yes? Go ahead."

"There's only one of my agencies that has never made good. Before you come to Boston I'm going to ask you to stop off there and try your hand for a few months. Did you ever hear of Stonefield, Massachusetts?"

"Never! What sort of a place is it?"

"It's a city in the Berkshire Hills, and it's two sorts of a place: On one side of the main street, a hustling factory town; and on the other, a group of ancient Brahmans still fighting the Civil War. Anything modern they regard as a slap in the face. They still ride about in carriages drawn by an almost extinct creature called the horse."

"I don't believe it," said Billy. "Not in this day and age."

"You will believe it—when you see Stonefield. It's the toughest job in your line in America. I'm ashamed of myself, but I'm going to ask you to tackle it. The leader of the codfish aristocracy is an old friend of mine—Miss Minerva Bluebottle. I believe she came to Massachusetts on the Mayflower—or it may have been her great-grandparents."

"You want me to sell Miss Bluebottle on the Requa?"

"I want you to try it. The rest of them follow her like sheep. Get her into one of our cars, and you'll sell forty more. But—don't be optimistic. I don't believe it can be done."

"Oh, I don't know."

"I do. And here's a tip: Don't be too generous with large talk about California."

"Why not?" Mr. Anderson was thunderstruck.

"Because, though there are many places where a California booster doesn't make much of a hit, I don't know of any spot where his talk will fall flatter than in the Berkshires of Massachusetts. The people there don't do any vulgar boasting, of course; but they happen to know that God spent the whole seven days making their corner of the world—and left the rest of the job to novices."

"Some one ought to tell 'em different," suggested Billy.

"They're pretty deaf," smiled Firkins. "I'll give you a letter to Miss Minerva. If you can sell her you're the wonder of the age."

"I'll sell her," announced Billy firmly.

"I wonder," mused Mr. Firkins. "It'll be worth watching anyhow. Out here you're regarded as irresistible. I know myself that Minerva Bluebottle is immovable. When an irresistible force meets an immovable body, what happens then?"

"The cross," smiled Billy Anderson, "will mark the spot where the immovable body once stood."

* * * * *

BILLY ANDERSON landed in Stonefield early one April morning. April—in California! A riot of blossom and bloom, with the warm sun beaming down. But April here, in this grim eastern state! Sad, dirty piles of snow along the curb, and a wind that cut like a cruel word sweeping down from the hills. Billy shivered, and searched his heart for the gay confidence that had been his when he left Pacific shores. Had he been reporting his analysis he would have been forced to write, "Confidence—no trace."

He had a sort of breakfast at the leading hotel. The fried eggs were stone cold. What is more depressing than a cold fried egg? Billy went out and found what seemed to be the main residential street. A mild little citizen was approaching.

When they were opposite each other, "Say, listen!" cried Billy.

This is the usual form of address in the genial West. But as far as the mild little man was concerned, it might as well have been a bomb. He jumped violently, and nearly lost his eyeglasses. Billy Anderson was conscious of something wrong.

"I beg your pardon," he said, remembering that form of interruption from stories he had read about the effete East. "I'm looking for the house of Miss Minerva Bluebottle."

"Ah—ah—that's it—directly across," said the citizen.

He hurried on. He was flustered all day. He had been spoken to by a strange man!

Billy Anderson looked at the house on the other side of the street. He saw a stern, forbidding type of domicile, left over from another day. It was painted a serviceable but ugly dark brown. Billy crossed the street and accosted a tall lean Yankee who was sweeping the front walk.

"Work for Miss Bluebottle?" he asked the man pleasantly, offering a cigar.

"Yes," said the sweeper, suspicious of everything, cigar included.

"What's your name? What do you do?"

"Name's Carleton Webster. Been with Miss Minerva over forty years. Tend furnace in the winter and drive her carriage in the summer. Say, what you doing—taking the census?"

"No," laughed Billy. "I've just dropped in from California—to sell Miss Bluebottle an automobile."

Something flitted across Carleton Webster's sallow, jaundiced face. It must have been meant for a smile.

"Make it an aer-e-o-plane," he said. "Just as much chance."

"A tough baby, eh?" Billy inquired.

"W-what?"

"I say—she's hard to sell?"

"I don't know what you mean," said Mr. Webster. "But I kin tell you, she hates all these newfangled inventions like pizen."

"Well—of course, the automobile's pretty recent. Hasn't really proved itself, I imagine. Look here—no reason why you and I shouldn't be friends. Buy yourself a box of cigars like the one I just slipped you." He handed Carleton a ten- dollar bill.

"No," said Carleton, shrinking back. "I can't take it. It wouldn't be right. An' besides, Miss Minerva is peeking out round the parlor curtain."

Billy Anderson looked. The curtain fell angrily into place, and in another moment the front door opened. A tall woman, dressed in black, with a fine white coiffure, stepped out on the porch. She walked like a West Point cadet, only straighter. At the edge of the porch she paused and sniffed the air through thin, aristocratic nostrils. It was evidently just the air she had expected—the clear clean air of the Berkshires, eminently satisfactory and correct. It had her approval, what more could it want?

"Carleton," she said in a crisp cool tone, "come and look at the dining-room fire. It is smoking again."

"Yes, ma'am," answered Carleton, and hurried up the walk.

Once more Miss Bluebottle sniffed. Was it possible that some foreign substance was contaminating the good Berkshire air? Undoubtedly, for a strange young man stood on the sidewalk. She did not give the young man a look, but her whole attitude, as she poised there, accused her servant of an imperfect sweeping of the walk. The young man should have been gathered up with little old last year's leaves.

Billy Anderson stared for one frightened, apprehensive second. His heart sank.

"Massachusetts—there she stands!" he muttered, and turned to find his office as local representative of the Requa car. Later that morning he wrote the first of his letters to Miss Minerva Bluebottle.

Miss Minerva found that letter by her plate the next morning when she sat down to breakfast beside the cozy fire in her dining-room. She had entered the room in quite a lively frame of mind, and had even smiled a greeting at her niece, Eloise, who was already at the table. Eloise was the only daughter of the one improvident Bluebottle, who had long ago squandered his substance in riotous Boston and passed to the great beyond. For ten years, in Miss Minerva's household Eloise had played the part of charity child. She was a tall girl, with wistful, appealing eyes and beautiful hair. She might have been very pretty, but Miss Minerva had long ago talked her out of it.

"Only one letter—"

Miss Bluebottle took it up. The name of the Requa Automobile Company on the envelope brought a frost into her steel-gray eyes. With her lips one firm straight line, she began to read. It was rather pitiful, Billy Anderson's attempt to inject a little romance into salesmanship in New England.

She skipped, reading only the lines that seemed to leap out at her:

"Came all the way from the Coast. Want to interest you in the Requa car. Will be selling you a wonderful piece of mechanism, but not that alone. How about a little romance in your life? Selling you more than a car. Selling you the far hills when the green leaves first peep out. Selling you the vast panorama of the Lebanon Valley—the high ribbon of the Mohawk Trail, where once the Indians crept along. And the hills in autumn, all red and orange and brown—like the old- fashioned crazy quilt on your grandmother's bed."

At this point Miss Bluebottle gasped, and tore the letter into bits. Too bad. The last part was the best. "The poor fool!" she said fiercely. "What's the matter, Aunt Minerva?" Eloise asked. "Wants to sell me an automobile—and talks about my grandmother's bed."

"Sounds interesting," smiled Eloise. "Impertinent!" cried Miss Bluebottle.

Her niece observed that she was breathing rapidly. The cameo set amid pearls on her breast rose and fell angrily. Eloise knew it was a cameo set amid pearls, though she had never seen it. Twenty-seven years before, on the death of her mother, Minerva Bluebottle had covered her rings, her pins—all her jewelry, in fact—with crape. This crape she had never removed, just as she had never ceased to wear gowns of black. Twenty-seven years of mourning! Unbelievable—if you don't know Stonefield.

If Miss Minerva had read Billy's letter to its brilliant finish she would have learned that "our Mr. Anderson" was shortly to visit her to present his plea in person. She didn't, however, and when old Norah that evening announced a young man calling on important business she was unprepared.

"Miss Bluebottle?" Billy Anderson grasped her hand. "And this—this is your—"

"My niece, Eloise Bluebottle," said the old lady stiffly. "You have business with me?"

"I have. I imagine you got my letter this morning."

"Good heavens, the automobile man!"

"The same."

"Then let me tell you, young—"

"Let me tell you, Miss Bluebottle. Way out in California I heard about you; how you were driving round behind a couple of antediluvian horses."

"If you refer to Romulus and Remus—"

"Romulus and Remus! Are they as old as that? As I was saying, Mr. Firkins and I talked things over."

"So Henry Firkins sent you?"

"He did. The idea was to jazz things up a bit for you; to induce you to step on the gas—hit the high spots—see the world—travel—in a Requa. Of course, to be frank, I haven't as much to sell you here as I would have out in California. I take it you have seen California?"

"I have never been west of the Hudson," replied Miss Minerva proudly.

"I'm sorry for you." He looked it. "You've never lived. Oh, what I could sell you out there!—the snow-capped peaks of the Sierras instead of a string of brown little molehills."

"Sir?"

"Beg pardon—no offense. I know the Berkshires have been in your family a long time, and you're sort of fond of them. But really—if you could see some regular mountains—"

"I have seen the Swiss Alps, and I prefer our own Greylock."

"Do you?" Billy Anderson gasped. What sort of woman was this anyhow? "Well, I—I'm not here to sell you a car tonight," he went on. "I just dropped in to get acquainted."

Miss Minerva glared at him. It was related in Stonefield how an outsider, a woman, had come to town and taken the pew opposite Miss Bluebottle in church. Six years passed, and from the Bluebottle eyes gleamed no spark of recognition. At the end of the sixth year, one morning after service, Miss Bluebottle rose and, stern with a sense of duty, approached her neighbor.

"Are you a stranger here?" she asked.

And Billy Anderson had just dropped in to get acquainted—his second night in Stonefield!

"Young man, please be good enough to let me speak," Miss Minerva said. "You are wasting your time. I will never enter an automobile, much less purchase one."

"May I ask why not?"

"Horses were made before motor-cars."

"Ah, yes—and so were fingers made before forks. I haven't had the honor of dining here—yet, but I don't imagine you eat with your fingers—now, do you?"

"That's quite beside the point."

"Not at all. Miss Bluebottle, the world is moving. Move with it. Get up on the band wagon. There are a thousand advantages attached to the ownership of a car. I'm going to slip them to you, one by one."

"I'm really sorry for you," said Miss Bluebottle. "Henry Firkins is to blame. He has sent you on a wild-goose chase."

"I'll write to you," continued Billy.

"Save your stamps."

"I'll call again."

"A waste of shoe leather."

"The next time I come I'll tell you all about California."

"I am not to be moved by threats."

"In the meantime bear me in mind," smiled Billy, rising. "I'll take a look round and see what I've got to sell you—in the way of scenery, I mean. Of course, after California, it looks a little—er—a little tame here. But I understand that in the fall your hills are at their best. All red and orange and brown."

"I forbid you," cut in Miss Minerva sourly, "to drag in my grandmother's bed."

"Not at this hour," laughed Billy. "She might be in it. Well, good night. See you soon."

Eloise went to the door to see him safely out. They stood for a moment under the gas light in the hall—no electric wiring for Miss Minerva! Here, as in the drawing-room, hung faded portraits of dead Bluebottles, grim, haughty, uncompromising. Billy looked with keen interest into the wistful eyes of the girl.

"How long have you lived with Miss Bluebottle?" he inquired.

"Ten years," she said softly.

"Ye gods!" He came closer. "I hope you won't mind my saying it, but you strike me as—kind of—er—wonderful. By gad, I'd like to see you with California for a background!"

"I—I never travel," she gasped.

"That's all right. Once I've sold your aunt a Requa, you'll travel—travel fast. Don't ask me what I mean—I'm not sure myself. But one thing I do know—we're going to meet again—mighty soon. Good night."

When Eloise returned to the drawing-room her eyes were shining.

"Of all the wild young idiots!" said Miss Minerva peevishly.

"Yes," smiled Eloise; "he—he sort of takes one's breath away."

"My breath is still intact," snapped Miss Minerva.

* * * * *

DURING the next three weeks Miss Minerva's breath grew, as the fellow said, even more intacter. She saw that she was in for a fight, and she gloried in it. Did this flippant young whipper-snapper from the West think that he could invade her stronghold and sweep her from her feet? Not likely! She'd show him a thing or two! And in showing him, she would express her contempt for the entire territory west of the Massachusetts state line.

As for Billy Anderson, before coming to Stonefield he had regarded the town as a myth of Mr. Firkins' imagination. Such a place as the Boston man described could hardly exist at this late day. Now, however, he had seen Stonefield, and knew that Mr. Firkins had not told him the half of it. He was amazed, appalled. Each day brought him some new story of the intolerance, the stubbornness of the older generation. There was, for example, Miss Minerva's friend, Miss Anna Bell Small. Anna Bell had sworn that if the city council ran the trolleys along the street before her house she would never again step out of her front door. For seventeen years she had been coming and going the back way, and still she showed no signs of weakening.

Each night Billy sat in his room reading the latest breezy books on the art of salesmanship. Good enough books in their way, but their authors had not written them with Minerva Bluebottle in mind. Billy would sigh and falter. But in the morning he would rise with renewed energy, keen to resume his attack on the immovable body. He tried letters—one a day—each setting forth a separate golden advantage attached to the ownership of a car—preferably a Requa. He telephoned. He waylaid Miss Bluebottle on the street. Water, it is understood, rolls harmlessly from a duck's back. Miss Minerva gave him frequent reason to recall the simile.

Now and then he ran across Eloise Bluebottle—on the street, once at a dance, once at a church social, whither he had gone with just such an adventure in mind. Yes, he decided, the girl was beautiful, in a vague, spiritual sort of way, so different from the hearty maidens of California. She was a new type; she appealed to him. But the poor thing was asleep—had never been anything else. What she needed was to be roused, carried away from this narrow town, given a new setting wherein she would wake and glow and live. At the end of the church social, by sort of obliterating a pale young man with eye-glasses, Billy managed to walk home with her.

"How do you like Stonefield by this time?" she asked.

"Sort of a nearsighted town," he said. "I'm introduced to people one day, and they seem cordial enough. The next day I meet them on the street, and when I speak to them they jump and look at me in terror—the frightened- fawn stuff. I'm not used to it."

"They regard you as a stranger," she told him. "After you've lived here ten years—"

"Ten years!" cried Billy. "No, thanks, not for me— and not necessary either. Why, Jacob only served seven for Rachel."

He heard her laugh softly.

"I was thinking," she explained, "of Aunt Minerva playing Rachel to your Jacob. She would be flattered! I'm sorry," she went on more seriously, "but you'll never win her in seven years. Or seventy times seven."

"Oh, I don't know. All I have to do is get her into a Requa car—just once. Then if she has any sporting blood— and I'll say she has—she's sold."

"But how are you going to get her into a car?" There was a certain eagerness in the girl's voice.

"Watch your Uncle Billy," advised Anderson mysteriously. But he said good night with a rather doubtful eye on the curtains of the stern brown house.

Billy based his request that Uncle Billy be kept under observation on the fact that he had yet to play his trump card. He was not relying entirely on the United States mail and the telephone company. No one does these days.

One evening soon after his arrival in Stonefield he had met Carleton Webster on the street and, steering him into the Requa office, had handed him another cigar and asked, "How would you like to learn to run an automobile?"

"What would Miss Minerva say?" Mr. Webster was doubtful.

"What could she say? Your evenings are your own, aren't they?"

"I reckon so."

"To do with as you please?"

"I ain't never heard no different."

"Well, I'll take you out and teach you—free gratis. What do you say?"

"I've sort of had the hankering," admitted Mr. Webster, rolling the cigar between his lips. "Had to turn out for so many devil wagons in my day I've often wished I was on one myself. Yes, sir, as I drove round behind Romulus and Remus there's been times I felt I'd like more power—more power," he added with emphasis.

"Fine!" cried Billy. "Come with me! No time like little old now."

When Mr. Webster had mastered the driving of a Requa, Billy arranged for his big experiment. Each afternoon at two-thirty it was understood that Carleton was to appear before Miss Minerva's door with his horses hitched and ready. Followed the gentle jog through the town that was Miss Bluebottle's daily taking of the air—a religious rite observed by the Brahman caste in Stonefield since the beginning of time.

On a certain sunny May afternoon Carleton drove up before the Bluebottle door. He had on his ancient silk hat, his blue coat with the brass buttons. But he flourished no whip. He had nothing to flourish it over. He was sitting behind the wheel of a bright and shining Requa.

Billy Anderson leaped from the seat at Carleton's side and ran up the walk. Norah answered his ring.

"Tell Miss Bluebottle her carriage is waiting," said Billy.

A moment later Miss Minerva stepped grandly from her door. She looked toward the curb—and gasped. Billy Anderson had sort of shivered back against the wall, his confidence oozing. Miss Minerva turned and her flashing eye met his guilty one.

"What's this?" she snapped.

"A little variation in your daily routine," said Billy. "I planned it for you. I want you to step inside and sink back amid the soft luxury of—"

"Young man, I don't believe you realize how impertinent you are. Out in the wild country where you were unfortunately born this sort of thing may be lightly regarded, but not here."

"Miss Bluebottle, you don't understand. I'm trying to brighten your life."

"You're a young idiot! When I told you I would not ride in one of those smelly things—"

"Smelly? Of roses, Miss Bluebottle. See? I filled the vase for you."

"—I was not talking to exercise my tongue. I meant it!"

"But be fair! Give it a trial!"

"No! I regard it as a rattly, death-dealing abomination."

"Rattly! Why listen to that engine! Purrs like a kitten."

"I hate cats."

"But I thought—"

"You thought all old maids liked them. I don't! Carleton, come here!"

Thoroughly frightened, Carleton extracted his person from behind the wheel.

"Carleton, what does this mean? Am I to understand that you have learned to operate that vile contraption?"

"Yes, Miss Minerva." Carleton tried the other foot. "I learned nights, my time off. And—I wish you'd try a ride, Miss Minerva. A short one. It's—it's fine. When I step on the exhilarator—"

"On the what?"

"The exhilarator," repeated Carleton, who had so christened it. "The thing that gives her the gas. When I step on that the good old Berkshire air jest sweeps over you an'—an'—it's fine."

"You poor old fool!" said Miss Minerva. "Now run to the barn and hitch up Romulus and Remus as fast as the Lord will let you. I shall be late for my drive. I'm not accustomed to being late."

"Y—yes, ma'am," said Carleton.

"I rely on you, young man"—Miss Minerva turned to the gloomy Billy—"to remove that—that thing—from before my door. And what can I say to convince you? I will not buy a car. I will not ride in a car. Can you grasp that, or is the English language unknown in the rough region that sent you forth?"

"I understand, Miss Bluebottle," said Billy. "I had no wish to be impertinent."

"Then I shudder to think what you would do if you had."

"But I'm a salesman, and I naturally want to sell. My idea was to show you how nice and comfortable you'd be, riding in a Requa. I thought that perhaps, with your own coachman driving, you might take a chance. It was only an experiment. There's nothing more to be said."

"I fancy not. Good day."

Billy Anderson went down the walk to his car. From a rear view he looked so unhappy and squelched that Eloise, at an upstairs window, pitied him. When he turned to enter the car she caught his eye and daring greatly, waved. He gravely lifted his hat and drove off. Miss Minerva's expression, as he had last seen it, reminded him that New England had furnished the inspiration for Hawthorne's story, The Great Stone Face.

* * * * *

IN his room that night Billy Anderson admitted his defeat. Out in the broad free West he had been a riot, but here in this conservative town he was a frost. His genial, handshaking, back-slapping methods frightened the good people to death. They resented his easy manner, and in Miss Bluebottle's case particularly, his campaign had been ill advised, doomed to failure from the start. But, hang it all, it was the only style of attack he knew!

Henry G. Firkins had written that he would be along in another ten days. Billy had been working on Stonefield six weeks, and what had he to show for it? A few sales to summer visitors, to factory managers; sales any one could have made. The East, thought Billy bitterly, was no place for him. He would have to confess himself beaten and hand Firkins his resignation.

During the next few days he concentrated on the other old families of the town. He sought to make his attack dignified. It seemed to him that some of them were interested, but he got no further. As for Miss Minerva Bluebottle, he let her severely alone.

On the twenty-ninth day of May, about three-thirty in the afternoon, Billy's telephone rang. The voice of Carleton Webster came over the wire.

"Say, listen!" Carleton had picked up that phrase along with the ability to run a car. "I'm out here at Cal Morton's farm, on the Eastlake pike. Miss Bluebottle's carriage has busted—rear axle just crumpled up. She's settin' in it, waitin'. Ordered me to call up Peter McQuade—he's got the only horse and carriage for rent in town. I called him, but I thought I'd tip you off too. You can beat him out here easy if you start now. Don't know as there's much use tryin' it, but—"

"Thanks, Carleton," said Billy, and hung up. A little of his old-time enthusiasm returned. Now or never, he thought.

In twenty minutes he drew up beside Miss Minerva's tipsy carriage. One side was in the ditch, and the seat slanted at an angle of about forty-five degrees. Only Miss Bluebottle could have sat with dignity under the circumstances. She managed it—with ease.

"Say, this is fortunate!" cried Billy, leaping from his car.

"I'm not surprised to see you," snapped the old lady. "Been following me, no doubt, waiting for that axle to break. Probably got into my barn last night and tampered with it!"

"Nonsense! You don't think as badly of me as that?"

"Yes, I do!"

"I meant, it was fortunate I happened along. Just step into my car and I'll whisk you home in no time."

"I have no desire to be whisked, thank you." A loud peal of thunder grumbled suddenly among the hills.

"It's going to rain," said Billy.

"Let it!" said Miss Minerva. She was in a rather bad temper.

"But I'd be delighted to give you a lift."

"I know you would. But you'll not get the chance. We have telephoned for Peter McQuade."

"He can't get here for half an hour," said Billy, "and it may be raining then. Thunder—and lightning—"

"Precisely! No time to be riding in one of those electrical contrivances."

"But the Requa isn't run by electricity. It's run by gasoline. Isn't it, Carleton?"

"Sure!" said Carleton.

"It's run by the devil, if you ask me," said Miss Minerva. "I don't know how you got here so promptly, but I have my suspicions. And it's not going to do you any good. Here I sit until Peter McQuade comes—all night if necessary."

"You stubborn, bitter, intolerant old woman," said Billy Anderson hotly—to himself. "Sit here and drown, for all I care. You should have died fifty years ago anyhow."

"I dare say," remarked Miss Minerva, "that all you are thinking about me is true. Now get into your car and hurry home before the rain comes and washes off all the nice brown paint."

This was, of course, a deadly insult, and she had hit upon it instinctively. Carleton Webster made a gesture of mute despair behind her back. Billy turned and reentered his machine.

"Ah, yes," the old lady called as he turned about, "I notice you're going back the same way you came. Carleton!"

"Y-yes, ma'am," stammered Carleton.

"Did you call Peter McQuade, or didn't you?"

"Yes, ma'am."

"I hope for your sake you did," she told him grimly.

When Billy Anderson was about a mile down the road the rain began to fall. Somehow it soothed his ruffled feelings. A little farther along he turned out for Peter McQuade, hurrying on through the storm.

That evening Billy met Eloise Bluebottle on her way home from the library. She had a pile of books under her arm.

"Let me carry them," Billy suggested.

"If you don't mind. They're rather heavy. For my aunt, you know."

"Ah, yes, your aunt. I hope she didn't get very wet this afternoon."

"Not very. I heard all about it. And I'm sorry—really I am. Do you mind if I say something?"

"I'd love it."

"You'll never sell my aunt a car. Your methods are wrong—you'll pardon my frankness, won't you?"

"Of course. As a matter of fact, I came to the same decision some time ago. But they're the only methods I know. I was thinking it all out the other night. People here are different from what they are on the Coast. When I was in Honolulu I had a chance to go to China and sell cars. If I had gone I'd have had to learn an entirely new system— and that's what I should have done when I came here. For these people are as unlike those I've been dealing with as—as Chinese. Dog-gone it, they are Chinese! Living in the past— worshiping their ancestors! How long has your aunt worn crape on her rings?"

"Twenty-seven years," said Eloise.

"That's the point. I've tried the wrong tack—and I've failed. I'm licked—through. When Mr. Firkins comes next week I intend to resign."

"Oh, I'm so sorry!" said the girl.

"Are you? Well, it helps a lot—to have you say that. By the way, to- morrow's a holiday—Decoration Day. How about taking a ride with me? We'll go somewhere for lunch—"

"Oh, I couldn't!" said Eloise timidly, wistfully even. "Aunt Minerva wouldn't like it. Besides, I must go with her in the morning—to the cemetery."

"The what?"

"The cemetery. It's a sacred rite with her. She decorates all the Bluebottle graves."

"She does, eh?" said Billy. He was silent for a moment. "I don't suppose anything could persuade her from going?"

"I should say not! A few years ago she rose from a sick bed to attend to it—and got pneumonia and nearly died. It's—well, it's one of the things she will look after herself as long as she has breath in her body. Everybody who is anybody in Stone-field will be out there in the morning. Afterward they have a little social hour amid the tombstones. You ought to see it! I suppose it's quite different from the West."

"I should say so!" smiled Billy gently. "Out West we're not much concerned with the past. It's the present—and the star-spangled future we think of. By the way, how far is it to the cemetery?"

"Oh, about four miles."

"How will your aunt get there? Her carriage is out of commission."

"She's ordered Peter McQuade to call for her at eight-thirty."

"Oh, she has, has she?" They stopped before the cheerless house. "Say—listen—I mean, can I depend on you to back me up?"

"I—I think so. What are you talking about?"

"Chinese—ancestor worshipers. I've just had a sign from heaven. I'm to be given one last chance. And—it's great of you to say you'll help me." He seized her hand. "I said that first night I saw you that you were—wonderful. After I've sold Aunt Minerva that Requa I'll have something to sell you."

"What?" Very softly.

"God's country—California! The roar of the surf below Monterey! San Juan Capistrano in the moonlight! The silent, snowy tops of the Sierras!"

She got her hand free then, and seizing the books ran quickly from him up the walk. Billy Anderson returned to his room, and before retiring made certain arrangements with his alarm clock. He set it for the hour of six on Decoration Day.

* * * * *

AT six-thirty the next morning Billy Anderson stood in Peter McQuade's back yard in solemn conference with the owner of the only horse-drawn vehicle for rent in Stonefield. Mr. McQuade was in the throes of his morning grouch; he

73

did not yield readily to arguments. A twenty-dollar bill, however, soothed his soul and brightened his whole day.

Fifteen minutes later Ma McQuade locked the front door and climbed to the side of her husband in the ancient carriage. Mr. McQuade took up the reins, then leaned forward doubtfully.

"You've give me your word," he said, "that you'll fix things with Miss Minerva."

"Don't give her another thought," smiled Billy. "So long!"

"Ge-ap!" said Mr. McQuade.

Mr. Anderson watched them drive off, to perform an entirely unnecessary errand for him in a town ten miles distant.

"It's to-day or never," he reflected grimly as he went back to his boarding- house for breakfast.

At twenty-two minutes before nine Billy Anderson drove a bright new Requa limousine up to Miss Minerva's front door. He left the car sparkling in the first warm sunshine of the spring and hurried up the walk. On the veranda he noted a collection of lilacs, snowballs, syringas, a few anemic geraniums in pots, roses and carnations from the local greenhouse. He thought of California in May and smiled a pitying smile. Eloise met him at the door.

"I'm glad you've come," she said. "Aunt Minerva is in a state! Walking the floor! I never saw her so upset before."

"What's the trouble?"

"Peter McQuade! He hasn't shown up, and no one will answer his telephone." She preceded Billy into the dim drawing-room. "Auntie, here's Mr. Anderson."

"I've trouble enough without Mr. Anderson," snapped the old lady.

"Perhaps I can help you in your trouble," said Billy gently.

"You could—if you owned a horse."

"I own sixty of them—in the form of a beautiful, smooth-running Requa. I understand you wish to go to the cemetery."

"Aha—another conspiracy!" cried Miss Bluebottle fiercely.

"Now—now!" rebuked Billy in an injured tone. "That's unworthy of you—on this lovely morning, when your only thoughts should be of these fine people on the wall." He glanced about him at the Bluebottles who had been. "I think you've hurt their feelings," he went on. "They look hurt to me."

"Eloise," said the old lady, "did you call up Mrs. Eldridge?"

"Yes, Auntie, I told you I called them all—the Eldridges, the Smalls, the Clarksons—all down the list. Everybody has started—they're somewhere on the way."

Miss Bluebottle groaned. Then silence.

"Miss Bluebottle," said Billy in a moment, "is this the proper morning to parade your foolish prejudice against automobiles? Think! You have not missed a Decoration Day morning up there for twenty years!"

"Twenty-seven!"

"For twenty-seven years! In a few minutes all your friends—all the best people—will be gathered there, doing honor to their ancestors. They will glance toward the Bluebottle plot—sad, neglected, untouched. What will people say?"

"You're right!" she cried. "Eloise, call—call me a taxi."

Eloise paused. Billy nodded and winked.

"Call her a taxi," he said. Eloise disappeared. "But I don't approve of it. Taxis are rattly, they are smelly—germs, Miss Bluebottle!"

"Germs?" sniffed Miss Bluebottle. "Not up here in our fine clean Berkshires."

"Ah, yes—even up here. For strangers will drift in, and they bring germs with them. Now my car is new, clean, with lots of room for those beautiful geraniums and what-you-may-call-'ems."

"The taxi man does not answer," announced Eloise, returning. Again Miss Minerva groaned.

"I'm not going to say a word," remarked Billy. "I'm going to let them speak for me." He waved his hand toward the Bluebottles on the wall. "A fine, intelligent-looking crowd, and good sports too. That old chap there—Uncle Ezra, I presume—"

"My father, Hezekiah Bluebottle," corrected the old lady.

"Ah, yes! Look at the twinkle in his eye! I'll bet he ran over to Albany now and then! He's watching you, Miss Bluebottle. He's wondering what you're going to do. They're all wondering. You've got a sort of a date with them this morning. Do you imagine you're justified in passing them up—disappointing them—just for the selfish satisfaction of keeping a silly vow? I don't! They won't! Stop and ask yourself, Miss Bluebottle—doesn't the end justify the means?"

He stopped. A long pause followed.

"Norah," called Miss Minerva suddenly, "bring my hat and coat!"

Billy Anderson said nothing. He ran outside and began placing flowers in the limousine. As he helped Miss Bluebottle in she gave him a withering look over her shoulder.

"Remember this!" she said. "I'll never own one of these things! Never! Never!"

"In you go," smiled Billy. "I'll have you there in a jiffy."

He started his motor, and Miss Bluebottle went to her tryst with the past—at forty miles an hour. Her arrival at the cemetery was the sensation of the decade in Stonefield. But she carried it off with her usual grand air.

Eloise helped her as she busied herself above the graves of Bluebottles, long dust. When the social hour began the girl came over and joined Billy Anderson, who was cheerfully lurking near a marble angel.

"One thing I want to ask you," he said. "How did it happen the taxi man failed to answer?"

"Perhaps"—she blushed—"perhaps it was because he never got a chance. I didn't call him."

"Hooray!" cried Billy. "You do like me then? You want me to win out?"

"Yes, I—I think I do."

"That's all I wanted to know. Now that I've practically sold your aunt—"

"But you haven't!"

"All in good time. I want to tell you—I want to say"— his usually glib tongue found the roof of his mouth and stuck there. He tried again—"It's you that's kept me here. More than once I was ready to give up—to go away. Then I thought of you—that look in your eyes—"

"Please!"

"Let me finish—if I can. I want—I want " He turned helplessly, and his eyes fell on the inscription beneath the marble angel. He pointed. "What I mean is, how would it look—carved in stone—a great many years from now, of course—Eloise, beloved wife of Billy Anderson?"

He stopped, for she was staring at him.

"Oh, dog-gone it," he cried, "I'm all wrong! I'm talking like—like they do out here—this town has got me. But you understand—you would be beloved—all through the years—if you married me. Will you?"

"Aunt Minerva would be furious. She—she couldn't hear of it!"

"Forget Aunt Minerva," began Billy, but it proved impossible, for the old lady joined them at that moment.

The social hour was over. She had found, somewhat to her consternation, that all her friends took it for granted she had purchased the glittering car. She did not point out their error. It was none of their business anyhow.

Billy Anderson helped her back into the machine. Out on the main highway he called over his shoulder, "I'm going to take you home by a roundabout route."

Miss Bluebottle uttered some protesting remark, but already they were traveling at such a rate of speed that it did not leap forward to the driver's seat.

Had she realized how roundabout the route was to be her protest would have been stronger. Billy whisked her along between newly green fields, up and down her beloved hills. For a time she raged and demanded to be allowed to walk. Then she sat back, filling her lungs with the fine, clear air she worshiped as the heathen once worshiped the sun. A faint flush came into her cheeks. Three hours passed, and Billy drew up before a country inn.

"I'm about to invite you to lunch," he announced.

"Lunch!" cried Miss Minerva. "Why, I must be home—"

"You're a hundred miles from home," he laughed.

"Kidnaper!" she cried.

But there was the ghost of a smile on her face, and as she alighted he saw that her eyes were shining. After lunch he took them back to Stonefield—again by a roundabout way. Dusk was falling when he drew up before their door.

"Home!" said Miss Minerva. "I never expected to see it again, I'm sure." She got out of the car, her cheeks still flushed, the light still in her eyes. "Won't you have supper with us?" she invited.

Delighted, Billy followed the two women inside. Waiting in the drawing-room, he bethought himself of sales talk. Miss Minerva was the first to return.

"Well," said Billy, "I guess I've shown you the difference between Romulus and Remus, and a Requa. You see now what I mean when I say that when I sell you a car I sell you more than a piece of mechanism. I sell you the western half of this great state for your playground—the farthest and the highest hills, quaint little public squares where history was made, noble Grey-lock, Jacob's Ladder, round after round of verdant beauty. I sell you romance and revel."

"I'm pretty old," sighed Miss Minerva, "for romance and revel."

"Old! You wouldn't say that if you knew how young you look after your ride. Why, you look about twenty-five, and you can always look that way if you'll only jazz things up— get out and enjoy life. Here we are," he went on solemnly, "in the presence of all these splendid Bluebottles, dead and gone. Before them you can't be anything but honest with yourself—with me. You had a mighty good time to-day— now, didn't you?"

The firelight flickered on the portraits. The aged clock ticked youthfully.

"What I want," s*aid Miss Minerva in a firm clear voice, "is a car exactly like the one we rode in to-day!"

Billy Anderson's heart stopped beating.

"You can have that one," he said softly, so as not to break the spell. "It was never off the floor until this morning." He took an order blank from his pocket. "Sign here," he said.

When she had signed and written a check she handed both to Billy. He bowed in a manner that took in most of the people on the wall.

"Ladies and gentlemen," he said, "I thank you." Eloise entered. "I've sold your aunt that car," he announced. "And oh, by the way, Miss Bluebottle—there's one thing more. Eloise and I are going to be married."

They waited for the explosion.

"It's a good idea," said the surprising old woman. "I've thought so for some time. We New Englanders intermarry altogether too much. The families peter out. We need new enthusiasm, new life." She unlocked a drawer of her desk and took out a worn old box.

Opening it, she held it before the astonished Billy. "I've been saving them for Eloise's husband. My father's cigars—just as he left them when he passed on at the time of the Civil War."

Billy took one of the cigars gingerly in his fingers. It crumbled immediately into a dry brown dust.

"War quality," he said softly. "They don't hold up."

More than a year later Miss Bluebottle was out riding in her limousine with her friend, Mrs. Eldridge.

"Yes," she said, "they've gone to California to live. I advised it. Billy was doing well in Boston, but he can get along even faster among his own people—and as for Eloise, the mild climate has made a new woman of her. I had a telegram yesterday. The baby weighed twelve pounds at bir—that is, when it arrived."

"Twelve pounds!" repeated Mrs. Eldridge.

"We don't grow them like that here, do we?" Miss Minerva tried to keep vulgar boasting from her tone. "You know, I've come to believe that California is a great state."

"But so different from Massachusetts," said her friend smugly.

"Well, a change does us all good. I've made up my mind to go out there this winter and visit them."

"Why, Minerva," protested Mrs. Eldridge, "it's a frightful trip! You'll be days in smelly germy Pullmans."

"Nonsense!" Miss Bluebottle snapped. "I may be an old woman, but I'm down off the shelf, and down to stay. I agree with Billy—it's never too late to jazz things up."

"Jazz things up? Minerva Bluebottle, what in heaven's name does that mean?"

"I'll show you," said Miss Bluebottle. She leaned forward. "Carleton," she ordered, "give her the gas. Step on the exhilarator."

Carleton stepped on it.

THE HEART OF THE LOAF

First published in The Saturday Evening Post, Aug 5, 1922

THE night had been warm in Lower Ten, and Bob Dana's mouth was dry and his head noticeably overweight as he fastened his suitcase preparatory to leaving the train. He set his bag in the aisle and dropped down again on the green plush seat. Outside the window old familiar scenes were flashing by, fields where he had played, a brook where he had gone swimming, and his heart was suddenly touched, for it often happens that the traveler is never so homesick as on coming home at last.

The train stopped and Bob followed the porter to the door and down into the bright June sunshine. Five exciting years had gone by since he last stood on this narrow platform, stared at the unwashed windows and the rotting roof of the ancient C. P. & D. station. Mayfield again, sleepy old Mayfield. The New York-Chicago express paused but briefly; already it was slipping past him as he walked along, carrying his heavy bag. When he reached the platform's end the train was no more, and he had an unobstructed view up Main Street to the green of the courthouse park beyond.

"Well, stranger, where you want to go?" said a familiar voice at his elbow.

Bob turned. There stood Clay Harkins, town hackman for thirty years and more.

"Stranger, Clay?" the young man smiled. "Where do you get that stuff?"

Clay stared for a long moment into the lean tanned face that was nearly two feet above him. "Well, I be darned," he said at last. "If it isn't little Bobby Dana."

"Little Bobby, sure enough," answered the young man. "But, Clay—I don't see the band."

"What band?"

"The band to play Hail, the Conquering Hero Comes as I ride up Main Street in an open barouche with the mayor. And say, look here—I don't see the mayor either."

"You must be joking, Bobby," responded Clay tolerantly. "Well, boy, you sure have changed. What you doin' back in Mayfield?"

"I came here to do a job of work."

"A job? Why, I heard you was a painter. Messed round with little pictures."

"Well, Clay, that's the truth."

The old man pondered. "Somebody in Mayfield want his house painted?" he asked.

"No, not his house. His father."

"His father! Well, I be darned." Clay stepped closer and seized one of the lapels of the young man's coat. "Where'd ye git the suit, Bobby?"

Bob laughed. "It was made for me by Jimmy Breen, an English tailor on the Promenade des Anglais, at Nice. Does it intrigue you, Clay?"

"Pretty good stuff," Clay admitted. "Not so good as this one I got on, though." He stepped back to permit a more comprehensive survey. "Bought her twelve years ago at the Racket Store, an' she's just as good as she ever was."

"Twelve years," repeated Bob solemnly. "Almost time to have her cleaned and pressed. Don't you think so, Clay?"

"Not much," Clay answered. "You know what they charge for that now? Seventy- five cents. Yes, sir! Well, Bobby, is they any place you'd like to go?"

The young man leaned against a telegraph post and lighted a cigarette. "Dozens of places," he announced. "The Orient, for example. China. Want to sit on the Great Wall and paint the remnants of an ancient civilization. And after that— "

Clay cut in on this nonsense. "Take you anywhere in May-field for fifty cents."

"It used to be a quarter."

"Sure it did. But they's been a war. Maybe you heard about it?"

"Heard about it? Clay, old scout, I was nearer than that. I heard it." He blew a cloud of smoke toward the blazing sky. "But you don't want the story of my adventures, do you?

Nobody ever does. Coming down to cases, I suppose the Mayfield House is still doing business at the old stand?"

A frail white-haired little man with gold-rimmed eyeglasses came hopping along the platform—Will Varney, the Mayfield Enterprise's publisher, editor and star reporter, all in one. He stopped.

"Why, it's Bobby Dana! Hello, Bob. You back again?"

"Hello, Mr. Varney. I seem to be back, that's a fact. May-field's worst penny."

"Wouldn't say that," smiled the editor. "Going up street?"

"Yes, I guess so." The young man turned and saw disappointment clouding Clay's battered face. "Think I'll walk, Clay. Do me good. But here's the half dollar, just the same." He nodded toward his bag. "You take that young trunk up to the Mayfield House and leave it there. And here's a check for his older brother. You might deliver that too."

"Sure, Bobby; sure."

The returning traveler fell into step beside the editor.

"Well, boy, you're quite a stranger," Varney remarked.

"Five years. I believe you were at the station when I went away."

Varney nodded. "Yes, I guess so. That's been my role in the drama, Bob. At the station, watching others go. Watching them—with envy."

"Like to travel yourself, eh?" said Bob. "Well, why not? Can't you get away?"

"No, I can't," answered Varney. "But it's not because I'm too busy. It's because I'm too poor. Journalism's a genteel profession, my boy. That's about all you can say for it." They walked on up Main Street in silence for a moment. "Eugene Benedict was telling me yesterday he'd sent for you," the editor continued. "Wants you to do a portrait of the old man, I understand?"

"Yes. It's kind of hack work, but I need the money. Painting is also a genteel profession."

Will Varney's eyes twinkled. "Well, I don't suppose you know it, but you're going to stir up a hornet's nest with your picture. You're certainly going to start something in this town."

"Great Scott. You don't think it will be as bad as all that."

"That's not what I meant."

"Then what did you mean?"

"Reckon I'll let 'Gene explain it to you. Where do you aim to put up?"

"Mayfield House, I suppose."

"Heaven help you! You must come up to our place for supper—often. Mother'll be happy to have you."

"That's kind of you," Bob Dana said. "I take it the Mayfield House hasn't changed."

"Nothing has changed," answered Will Varney, with just a trace of bitterness in his gentle voice. "Same old Mayfield. Eight thousand population when you went away, eight thousand or even less to-day. Sound asleep, this town is. All up and down the valley—I guess you saw 'em when you came along— steel mills, blast furnaces—"

"Smoke and grime."

"Prosperity, Bob. Life. Every town around here has grown and thrived, touched by the magic fingers of the steel industry. But slow old Mayfield—"

"You're writing an editorial," Bob laughed.

"I've written it," Varney said. "Time and again. Yes, I've blown the horn, but not a sleeper waked. A lot of old mossbacks—that's what has ailed poor Mayfield. I tell you, what this town's needed has been a few big funerals. And we're getting 'em at last. Quite a group of our leading citizens have gone this past winter—old Henry Benedict, Judge Samuel Ward. They're dropping off. You needn't look at me," he added smilingly. "I'm feeling fine."

"Hope so, I'm sure," Bob answered. "Don't feel so well myself."

"What's the trouble?"

"No breakfast yet. Silly little habit of mine."

They were now in the very heart of the town's oldest business section, and on the signs about him Bob Dana read many a name familiar to his youth. He glanced across the brick-paved street to a shabby one-story building built of wood. Gilt letters against a black background announced this as the establishment of Herman Schall, the Baker, and on the window in white letters were the words: "Schall's Bread—Fresh Every Hour." In the doorway stood a portly bespectacled old German with a white apron draped across his ponderous middle.

"Well, well," Bob cried. "There's old Herman Schall! Used to buy cookies from him—years and years ago."

"Yes, Herman's still on the job," Varney said. "Tiptoeing round the kitchen turning down the gas, just as he used to count the lumps of coal in the days before gas ranges. A penny saved is a penny earned. Leave it to Herman!"

Suddenly Bob Dana felt a glow of friendliness for the old man across the street. "I think I'll go over and ask him for some coffee and rolls," he announced. "Good place as any for breakfast, I guess. See you later." He stopped. "Say, what in the world did you mean—about this portrait I'm going to do stirring up trouble?"

Varney laughed. "Don't you worry, boy. The row won't concern you. Come in when you get a chance and tell me about your travels."

"I sure will."

"That's a promise," the little editor reminded him.

Bob crossed the street and stood before Herman Schall, impassive as a statue in his doorway. "Hello, Herman," he said.

The old man peered at him through thick lenses. "Excuse, please. The eyes ain't so good."

"Herman, you old rascal. Don't you know me? Dana. Bob Dana."

"Little Bobby Dana!" cried the old man. "Sure I know you. Sure!"

"I should hope so. How about a bite of breakfast, Herman? Just coffee and rolls."

"Coffee and rolls, hey? Come in, Bobby, and take a chair."

Bob followed him inside. The place had a run-down air, prosperity had passed, an old man was left to putter round the scene of his life's activities. Two small tables stood against the wall, their covers faded and patched, but clean.

The young man hung his hat on a rack and sat down. He watched the baker enter the kitchen at the rear, heard his instant cry: "Louie, Louie—turn down dot gas!" Heavy footsteps resounded—Herman saving the pennies. After a time the old man reappeared, carrying two rolls on a plate, and a steaming cup, muttering and protesting to himself: "Oh, dot Louie! In the poorhouse he will have me yet." He set the dishes down before his customer.

"And butter," Bob suggested. "Any butter on the program?"

"Sure. Butter—sure."

The old baker ambled off. Bob broke open one of the rolls. The crust was brown and crisp, but the inside was soggy. However, he was young and reckless—and hungry—and when Herman returned with a thin slice of butter he set to.

While he ate, Herman hovered aimlessly near by. "They tell me you was in the old country," he said presently. "Maybe you was in Germany—maybe."

"Off and on," Bob told him. "Mostly in Paris and Rome—Florence too. Studying, you know. Trying to be a painter."

"A painter? Artist, hey? Is dot so?" He pondered this for a time, standing and blinking down on Bob's brown head. "My nephew in Stuttgart—he would be an artist, too, now, maybe. Only the war " The old face clouded. He wandered uncertainly away.

His brief meal finished, Bob stood with Herman in the solemn presence of the cash register. "You had enough, hey?" the old man inquired. "Twenty cents, then."

"How's business?" Bob asked as he paid.

"Business ain't so good," sighed Herman. "Us old merchants, we get crowded out. Strangers they come and take our trade. Too much competition."

"I'm sorry," the young man answered. "But you can't complain. For years you were the only baker in Mayfield. I guess I've seen your wagon standing in front of every house in town—all the big bugs on Maple Avenue. You had things all your own way then."

"Sure, sure; but not no more." Herman shuffled from behind the counter, gathered the dishes from the table, turned toward the kitchen. "Good-by, Bobby." As Bob reached for his hat he heard the querulous old voice: "Louie—ach, would you have me in the poorhouse yet?"

The clock in the courthouse was striking nine; Main Street was astir with life. Bob Dana cut across under the elms of the park. Suddenly before him loomed the dingy outlines of the Mayfield House, a three-story building of brick with a pretentious cupola on one corner. Back in the 'eighties when it was built Will Varney's father had spoken of it in the Enterprise as "the finest hotel building in any town of comparable size between New York and Chicago. A modern hostelry in every sense of the word."

But in thirty years the most modern of hostelries may alter sadly. The marble lobby was soiled and battered, Bob noted, as he crossed it and engaged a room from the somewhat seedy stranger at the desk. His bag lay on the floor. A bell- boy seized it and led the way through swinging doors at the rear into a dark and smelly cave. Bob stumbled after him up the stairs and finally out into the light of a big room on the second floor front.

"There's a bath here, isn't there?" he inquired.

"Sure, there's a bath," the boy answered proudly. He flung open a door. "Right in here. Only room in the house that's got one. Used to belong to Mr. Cornell."

Bob remembered; old man Cornell, who sat for years before the hotel, his hands crossed on his cane, his watery eyes staring off into space. "Where's Mr. Cornell now?"

"Dead," said the boy. "Last winter."

"Who runs the hotel since he's gone?"

"Oh, I don't know. It just seems to run itself. Your trunk's down-stairs; I'll send it up."

Left alone, Bob tossed his clothes on to old man Cornell's bed and filled old man Cornell's tin tub with cold water, half of which he obtained from a faucet plainly marked "Hot." After his bath he arrayed himself in his best, and lighting a pipe sat down to read a Cleveland paper he had bought on the train. He had drawn an easy-chair into the big bay window, and after a few moments the paper fell from his hand and he sat staring out at his town.

Here he had been born and spent his youth; across the park that dozed under the elms he had gone a thousand times to and from high school; under that very tree he had stood one afternoon in 1906 and watched the old courthouse burn. Suppose God had not given him his inexplicable talent with the brush, the never- satisfied ambition that went with it. He would still be a part of Mayfield, perhaps this young mechanic driving a flivver down Market Street; or that brisk young business man hurrying to the bank for his day's cash; or even that hopeless figure out of work and lolling on a bench in the park.

But he was none of these, he was Bob Dana who wanted to be an artist and was on his way. That way had led him far from Mayfield, perhaps in the future it would lead him farther still. But this remained his town, these were his people. There was nothing but kindness in his eyes as he sat staring out through old man Cornell's window. Let others belittle the environment that had molded them. Bob Dana was one of those faithful souls who, having once given their affection, can not take it back.

A narrow, mean little town? Some people might call it that. Certainly there were narrow, mean folks in it, as in all towns; big cities too. And certainly it was, as Will Varney had said, a town that slept. All the way from Pittsburgh that morning Bob had ridden under the pall of the steel mills' smoke; up and down the valley Mayfield's neighbors prospered, but here the old order remained, the conservatives had made good their slogan, "Keep the strangers out." They had triumphed, the moss-backs. And was it such a pity, after all?

The courthouse clock was striking ten when Bob rose from his chair, brushed scattered ashes from his coat, and sought the street.

The First National Bank stood, as in former days, on the corner of Market and Park, its home a worn old business block with the figures "1888" cut in the stone at the front. On the opposite corner, Bob Dana noticed, an ambitious project was under way, a six-story office building not quite completed.

He went into the First National and asked for the president. As he entered that official's private office Eugene Benedict jumped up to greet him. A ruddy, prosperous little man, Eugene, with a flower in his buttonhole and the unlined face of a baby. He had never had a worry in his life save the presumption of the working classes and, these later years, Bolshevism.

"Hello, Bob!" he cried. "Thought it was about time for you to breeze in. How are you, anyhow?"

"Great," said Bob. He banished his smile temporarily. "Seems strange not to see your father here."

Eugene sought to be solemn too. "Yes, poor father. Passed away in April, as I wrote you. A sick man for months, but insisted on coming down here up to the day he died. Just wouldn't give up, you know."

"Ah, yes—he had that reputation." Bob Dana was sorely tempted, but he refrained from saying it.

"A great pity," Eugene went on. "If only he could have lived until we moved into our new building across the street."

"Oh—is that yours?"

"You bet. Six stories. Finest office building for a town this size anywhere between New York and Chicago."

"Pretty daring for Mayfield, isn't it?" Bob inquired.

"Oh, I don't think so. Mayfield is going to pick up. Forge ahead. 'Twenty thousand by the next census'—that's our slogan now. Got a chamber of commerce and a Rotary Club and everything. Bound to boom."

"Seems about time," said Bob. "But about our little job of work. When do I hang up my hat and begin?"

"Sooner the better. You know, it was a great surprise to me to find you could paint a portrait of father now. Really, the whole idea came from Delia—"

"Oh, yes—Delia. How is she?"

"Fine. Just came home from college last week. Graduated."

"That so? The last time I saw Dell was at the senior dance after high-school commencement. I stepped on her skirt and tore it. I believe we parted more in anger than in sorrow."

"No? Well, they're wearing 'em shorter now. But as I was saying, I was surprised to know you could paint a portrait of a man who had—er—passed on."

"Oh, sure. Of course they're not quite so satisfactory as those painted from life. But they serve. Resurrection portraits, we call them."

"Resurrection portraits! Well, that's expressive. Now, we'll help you all we can."

"You've a lot of old photographs, you wrote me."

"Well, we've several. And one crayon enlargement. And about the color of the eyes and hair and all that—I'll watch you as you go along and keep you straight. We all will."

"That will be lovely," shuddered Bob Dana. "Did Dell recommend me for this job?"

"Come to think of it, I guess she did. Now about the financial end of it. A thousand dollars, I think you said. Need any of it in advance?"

"Well, I'm just back from Europe. To be frank with you—"

"Sure, Bob—that's all right. I'll write a check. How about three hundred? Or"—he was, after all, Henry Benedict's son—"perhaps two hundred would be enough?"

"Oh, plenty," Bob told him. He took Eugene's check. "Mighty kind of you."

"Not at all. Now, Bob, I haven't told you anything of what's behind all this. In the first place I want a cracking good portrait of father—a speaking likeness. And I want it finished inside of four weeks, which is about the stretch before we open our new banking quarters across the street.

You see, I intend to hang it in a prominent place in the main banking room, and I want it there the day the doors are thrown open to the public."

"That's all right. You'll have it."

"Good! I'm going to hang it there, and underneath I'm going to put an inscription. Just a few innocent words, but they'll stir up something in this town, or I'm a liar."

"Why—what words?" asked Bob Dana, startled.

"Simply this: 'Henry Benedict; born 1858, died 1922. Banker and leading citizen, who more than any of his contemporaries influenced the life of his times and left his impress on the town.'"

"And then what?" Bob wanted to know.

"Nothing more. Just that."

"But I don't see anything explosive about that."

"No? You haven't kept up with things round here of course. Well, I want you to understand just what we're working toward. Can you spare me a few minutes?"

"Sure. All I've got."

Eugene Benedict rose and put on his hat. "Better if I let you see for yourself," he announced. He led the way outside to his car, which was parked across from the bank.

"Jump in," he ordered. "I'm taking you out to the cemetery."

"That's nice," said Bob Dana. "You've got sort of mysterious since I saw you last, Mr. Benedict."

"Oh, no," protested Benedict. "It's simple enough—or will be when I show you."

The car sped along Market Street and in a few moments turned in at the cemetery gates. "Maybe you heard," said the banker—"Judge Samuel Ward passed away last winter too."

"Somebody mentioned it. Sort of unhealthy climate you've got round here, it seems to me."

"Not at all. Three score and ten—man's usual span." Eugene stopped the car before an imposing marble obelisk. "Get out here. This is the judge's grave. I want you to read the inscription on that monument."

Bob Dana alighted and followed the banker. He stood in front of the monument and read:

SAMUEL CLARK WARD
1851-1922
Jurist—Publicist—Statesman
Who More Than Any of His Contemporaries
Influenced the Life of His Times and Left His Impress
on the Town

"Oh," said Bob Dana. "I get you now."

"I thought you would," Eugene replied. "Jump in. We'll go back." He stepped on the gas. "I want to tell you this thing has made me mad—hopping mad. It's a direct slap at father. Sam Ward was a good man in his way, but an obstructionist—an old grouch. He sat on every progressive movement that's been attempted round here. His decisions from the bench were sour and prejudiced. Of course father was a conservative too, but his conservatism was based on a sound business instinct."

"Of course," smiled Bob.

"You've been away from Mayfield a long time, but if you think back you'll realize that inscription is a lie. 'More than any of his contemporaries.' Ha! Who says so? Clarence Ward; and not another soul in town. Everybody will tell you that my father was Mayfield's leading citizen, that he financed every project that came up, that he led the way for years. Yes, sir, if anybody influenced the life of his times father was the man. And if Clarence Ward thinks he can put an inscription like that on his father's tombstone and not hear from me by return mail—well, he's got another think coming, that's all."

"I guess your come-back will give him pause," said Bob Dana.

"It ought to. Right in our main banking room. No one ever visits a cemetery if he can help it. But father's memorial will be where hundreds will see it every day—hundreds, mind you—everybody in Mayfield who counts."

"Ought to start a nice little row."

"I hope not. Unless it starts a good big row I'll be disappointed. I want this thing thrashed out now for all time. I know who will win." He brought the car to a stop before the bank. "You can see now that I've got to have the portrait on time, and that it must be good enough to be taken seriously. Where were you thinking of doing the work?"

"Why—at the hotel, I suppose."

"Nonsense! We won't hear of it. I've talked it over with Mrs. Benedict; we'll find you a place to work up at the house. Good thing to paint right there in the atmosphere where father lived. Catch his spirit better."

"All right." Bob accompanied the banker inside.

"Tell you what you do—go up to the house this afternoon. Delia and her mother will help you pick out a room. Want the right light and all that, I suppose. We'll clear it out and you can start slinging paint in the morning."

"That's a go," Bob Dana agreed. "I'll be up about three."

Eugene disappeared into his office and Bob stopped at the paying teller's window, where an old acquaintance cashed his check.

As he stepped again on to the hot sidewalk he was saying to himself: "And they're all going to help. Won't that be nice? Happy days ahead." He walked on toward the Mayfield House. "But at that, these little greenbacks sure do feel grateful to the touch."

For an hour he sat around the lobby of the hotel, hoping for a glimpse of some familiar face, but none appeared. When the dining-room doors were thrown open for lunch he went over and glanced inside. One look discouraged him—that, and the weird uncomfortable feeling in his chest. For his health didn't seem just right, his genial spirits of the morning had evaporated, he felt depressed and gloomy. He went up-stairs and lay down on the bed.

At three that afternoon he crossed the park and set out up Maple Avenue. His mood had not improved. He was conscious of a silly irritation over nothing, a sudden dissatisfaction with the world which he was accustomed to regard through cheerful, approving eyes. What, he wondered, ailed him anyhow.

Under the tallest elms in town lay Maple Avenue, unchanged. Here were the houses of the town's elite, outmoded piles of brick or stone standing in the midst of beautiful lawns. He came shortly to the Benedict mansion, the finest of all; in the old days it had represented for him wealth and the aristocracy. He smiled to himself as he entered the big gate and strolled up the front walk past a well-remembered cast-iron deer.

Delia Benedict was reading a novel on the front porch, and Bob felt a little better at sight of her. Another link with his past, and assuredly a link that had greatly improved since he last saw her. He had always liked Dell, though he remembered her as a nervous, spindling girl who moved in a constant whirlwind of energy that was decidedly wearing.

He had never thought her pretty, but time and an eastern college had changed her mightily. Her slenderness was now a rather alluring item in her favor, she had seemingly gained in repose, and you might almost call her—well, if not pretty, at least charming, and alive.

"Hello, Dell," he said.

"Hello, Bob." She gazed at him approvingly.

"Little Bobby's grown up. Not so bad, either—as far as you've gone."

"I'm not going any farther, Dell. Got to like me as I am." He dropped into a chair beside her. "You've changed, Dell. But you're still wearing it, I see."

"Wearing what?"

"Little old freckle on the end of your nose. I was wondering if it would still be there."

"What an eye for trifles," she laughed.

"Trifles," he said solemnly, "make perfection, and perfection is no trifle. Got that straight from Mike Angelo. Studied under him in Italy."

"Oh, yes—you and Angelo. Famous artist now, aren't you?"

"Who says so?"

"I read about you in a newspaper. It said you had a lot of talent."

"Did it say I had a lot of money too? You can't believe all you read in the newspapers, my child. By the way, did that article move you to recommend me for this job?"

"Did I do that?"

"Didn't you?"

"I don't know—I forget. Anyhow it isn't much of a job—not for you."

"My dear girl, it's a life saver, and I'm mighty grateful. Even the most talented of us must eat now and then. I'll give this assignment my best, to justify your recommendation. And I may add that I'm going to enjoy the row."

"Oh," she smiled. "Father told you."

"Yes. Gave me a free ride to the cemetery and everything. The old story of the Montagues and Capulets. By the way, who's playing Romeo? Clarence Ward had a precious son if I'm not mistaken."

"Herb Ward," she answered. "Just graduated from law school—Harvard."

"Oh, yes—little Herb. Pale young shrimp with curls and the air of a crown prince. Used to ride around town in a pony cart. Nearly ran over a dog of mine once, and I pulled him out of the cart and blacked his eye. Them was the happy days."

"You always did have such brutal instincts," she reminded him. "Even now you look more like a boiler maker than an artist. It's hard to believe. Are you sure you're the Bob Dana who paints?"

"Lead me to my new studio and I'll prove it to you. By the way, your father said—"

"Oh, yes. Come inside." She led him into a big cool hall. "You're the white- haired boy round here—any room in the house you want. That's orders. Anybody who happens to be established there must be dropped from the window."

"Look out or I'll take your room." He followed her up the stairs and they made the rounds of the second floor. His selection fell on a large guest-room with a good north light not too impeded by the trees. "Move everything out—rugs and all," he said. "Just a kitchen chair and maybe a little table."

"It shall be done, O Rajah," laughed Dell. They returned to the upper hall. The girl snapped on an electric light, illuminating a dark corner. "By the way, you'd better take a look at that," she said.

She pointed to a crayon portrait of a tired, dyspeptic-looking man in middle age. His lips were a thin line on a thin face, his eyes fishy, his entire aspect chill and bleak and seemingly lacking in all human feeling.

"Oh, yes—your grandfather," said Bob Dana, and his heart sank. For a long moment he and Henry Benedict stared at each other.

"I know what you're thinking," Dell said. "You're thinking, 'There's old Eight- Per-Cent. Benedict. I've got to resurrect him, and gosh, how I dread it!'"

"You wrong me," Bob smiled. "I was just wondering—how do we get from him to you? No connection that I can see."

"Thanks for the ad. Well, the least said about poor Grandfather the soonest mended. As a tyrant he made the Kaiser look weak. However, do the best you can."

"Your father says he wants a speaking likeness."

"Heaven forbid!" said Dell. She snapped off the light, and Henry Benedict receded into the shadows. "I moved him up here myself. Some battle, but I won. We've got a few other photographs—an old tintype, and one of him on his wedding day. He looked quite human then."

"Oh, I'll make out," Bob told her. "Your father has promised to keep a sharp watch on me and tell me when I'm wrong."

"You poor thing—I'm afraid he will. Pretty tough for you."

"That's all right," he assured her as he followed her downstairs. "I've got a strong constitution and a cheerful disposition. At least I always did have—up to to-day. Somehow I feel terribly depressed and mean this afternoon."

"Why's that?"

"I can't make out." He held the screen door for her and they returned to the porch. A shaft of sunlight fell across her hair. "Honey!" Bob Dana cried.

"What?" she inquired, surprised.

"Honey," he repeated enthusiastically. "The color of your hair, I mean. I've been trying ever since I saw you again to think what that shade reminded me of. I know now. It's honey—the sort of honey I used to have for breakfast at a little pension in Rome. Lots of butter, and this honey, and delicious hot rolls Oh, my lord!"

"What now? Bob, you are absurd."

"No, I'm not. I just remembered what's wrong with me. This depressed, sad feeling. This wave of bitter regret. I ate two of Herman Schall's rolls for breakfast, and the darned things weren't half baked."

"Oh," said Dell, "that's too bad. But you'll get over it. Only keep off Herman Schall's bread. Do you really like my hair?"

"Like it? It's lovely! As a matter of fact—I don't want to spoil you, Dell—but you're quite wonderful. I wish it was your portrait I was going to paint."

"Well, I'm Father's favorite child. There are no others, of course, but I'm well in the lead. Maybe after you do Grandfather you'll get an order to do me."

"No," he said, sternly shaking his head. "I couldn't consider it. Sorry—something else I just remembered. Artist, you know. Can't support myself, let alone a What I mean is, I've got to keep my mind off girls. Not so much as look at one. Dangerous. First thing I knew—"

"What are you talking about? You don't for a minute think that I—"

"No, Dell; no, I mean to say, might get to know you, like you, think better of your whole sex. Go right on from bad to worse, meet some little flapper, fall for the wedding idea—another artist gone wrong!"

"You're in no danger here, my lad," said Dell. "Shall I tell Father you'll punch the time clock in the morning?"

"Expect me at nine."

"All right. I'm afraid you'll have to put up with me around the house; I live here, you know. But I want to set your mind at rest, so I'll tell you a little secret. Keep it dark. This thing is more like the Capulets and Montagues than you imagined. I'm engaged to Herbert Ward."

"What! Little Herb Ward?"

"Yes. He's not so bad. The curls are gone and he drives a racing car now."

"Well, I'm glad," said Bob grimly.

"Thanks. I knew you would be."

"You don't understand. I mean I'm glad I blacked his eye that time. I only wish it had been permanent."

"You—an artist!" she said derisively. "With all those brutal instincts struggling inside you."

"Ain't any brutal instincts struggling inside me," he told her. "Just the little old indigestion I bought from Herman Schall."

And he went from her down the walk, as solemn as the cast-iron deer.

* * * * *

"TO-MORROW morning at ten o'clock," said the Evening Enterprise some weeks later, "the doors of the First National Bank's new home will be thrown open to the public. The citizens of Mayfield may be pardoned a keen pride in what they will behold. It is doubtful if any city of similar size between New York and Chicago can boast finer banking-rooms. Pillars, partitions and walls of marble, mahogany paneled rooms for the directors and the president, in the basement safety deposit vaults of the newest design and construction—all in all a revelation in modern banking quarters. To the strains of sweet music discoursed by the Mayfield Silver Clarinet Band the directors and officers will be happy to meet their friends and show them about. It is understood that the chef d'oeuvre of the main banking- room is to be a portrait of Henry Benedict, the late president of the institution, painted by our talented and up-and-coming young townsman, Robert Dana, son of the late Melville Dana, well and favorably known to all our people. 'Come one, come all' is the invitation extended by the bank."

At about the time Will Varney's words were being read by the citizens of Mayfield Bob Dana sat before his finished job of work in his studio on the second floor of the Benedict house. He looked at the moment neither up nor coming, but rather down and out. The feeling of hopelessness, of doubt concerning his own ability, that all true artists experience at the moment of final achievement was his, and the remarks of the small but select group of spectators gathered at his back did little to dispel it.

"Well, I don't know," Eugene Benedict was saying dubiously. "What do you think, Nellie?"

He appealed to his wife, a haughty beauty in her time, but somewhat faded now. She adjusted her glasses and stared—a stare famous in Mayfield, where she had long been the social arbiter.

"I don't know either," she admitted. "Sometimes I think it looks like Father—and sometimes I don't."

"My case exactly," said Eugene. "Around the chin—somehow. Did you make the chin fuller, Bob, as I suggested?"

"I think it's just wonderful," Dell announced.

Bob gave her a grateful look. "I've done my best," he said to Eugene. "I've changed it and changed it and changed it, day after day, as your opinions altered. Sometimes I think—you'll pardon my saying it—that the thing would have been better if I hadn't listened to you quite so much."

"But we knew Father better than you did," Mrs Benedict reminded him.

"Yes," Bob sighed wearily. "Yet you never did agree on the color of his hair. And as for the eyes—one of you said gray, and another green, and another light blue. It's what always happens on this sort of portrait. I've done my best, as I said, and if you don't like it I'll be happy to draw a knife through it now, and pay you back that advance when I can."

"No, Bob, no!" cried Benedict, alarmed. "It's not so bad as that, my boy. Perhaps we've given you a wrong impression. We were so close to Father, of course we'd be over-critical. It's not bad—not bad at all—I'll be mighty glad to hang it. Besides," he added with the usual tact of the layman discussing an artist's work, "the inscription is to be the important thing, after all."

Bob and Delia exchanged a long, understanding look. "Sure," Bob said. "That's the way to look at it. The inscription will takeoff the curse."

"Now let's get down to dinner," Eugene ordered. "I've got a busy night ahead at the bank. Will you stay, Bob?"

"Not to-night, thank you," Bob answered.

"Well, I'll take the picture down in the car to-morrow morning. Drop in about nine and help me hang it. Now, Nellie, let's get along. Delia!"

The two older people left the room. Bob picked up his coat.

"Don't you mind them," smiled Dell. "They don't know anything about art—not even what they like."

"It does resemble the old boy, Dell?"

"Bob—it's uncanny. I'm darn glad it's going to hang in the bank, and not up here. It would make me nervous."

"Then maybe that newspaper was right. I mean— perhaps I have a little talent."

"A little? Bob—what ails you?"

"Oh, I always feel like this just after I've finished a thing. Gloomy."

"Then you ought always to have some one around— some one who thinks you're—wonderful."

He stood staring into her eyes. He had been staring into them a great deal of late—in the intervals of work; at luncheon, which he had been taking daily with the Benedicts; sometimes at dinner, too; and in the evenings. There had been a period when Eugene urged him warmly to look into Dell's eyes, Eugene's feeling being that they somewhat resembled Henry Benedict's. After a thorough investigation Bob denied this.

But now the portrait was finished. Bob Dana held open the door of the guest- room studio.

"You're wanted at dinner," he smiled.

Dell followed him out on to the front porch. "I suppose you'll be going back East soon?" she inquired.

"Yes; in a few days. Got some unexpected business to look after first. Poor Father left me a little plot of land on the north side—the only thing he owned after a long hard struggle. They're thinking of a factory there, and I may sell it for fabulous wealth. All the money in the world—six thousand dollars."

"Good luck," she said. "You must come up often until you go."

"I'll come for my things," he told her. "But"—he shook his head—"that'll be about all, Dell. That had better be about all."

"Delia!" her mother called.

"Good-by," said Dell. "And the portrait, Bob—it's wonderful. I'll tell the world."

"Thanks," he smiled. "The same goes for you. You've helped me through; I'd have quit cold long ago if you hadn't been hanging around. You see, I'm sort of silly and temperamental in many ways—even if I do look like a boiler maker. Good-by, Dell."

He endured dinner at the Mayfield House, and passed a solemn evening with a magazine in the apartments of the late Mr. Cornell. Promptly at nine in the morning he appeared at the First National Bank. Entering the big front doors he found himself in a fragrant bower of roses and other blooms.

"Well, things certainly look festive," he remarked when he encountered the perspiring president. He took hold of the tag on a big basket of roses. "Compliments of the Mayfield Lumber Company," he read.

Eugene smiled. "Yes, everybody whose notes we hold has come across," he remarked. "And yet some people say there is no sentiment in business." Bob looked at him in sudden wonder. Had little Eugene a sense of humor, after all? The banker pointed to the spot where the portrait was to hang.

"Pretty good light, eh? That brass plate shows up fine. I'm glad I had it in big letters. 'More than any of his contemporaries influenced the life of his times and left his impress on the town.' That ought to hold Clarence Ward for a while. Now, boys, bring the ladder." He picked up the portrait and turned to Bob. "All the fellows have looked this over. They're delighted with it. Say it's Father to the life. Congratulations."

Bob saw the portrait hung, and collected a check for eight hundred dollars.

"Like to have you stay and meet our leading citizens," Eugene suggested. "Might interest you to hear their comments on the picture."

Bob was alarmed. "You don't insist on that?"

"Oh, no, of course not."

"Then I think I'd—I'd rather not."

"Funny fellows, these artists," thought Eugene Benedict.

Bob left the bank just as the Mayfield band began to discourse sweet music and the eager citizens were crowding in. From others later he heard of that day's happenings. The opening proved a big success, and no small part of the interest shown was accorded Henry Benedict's portrait. But the painting itself, Bob judged, figured only incidentally in the excitement. It was the sentiment on the brass plate underneath that won most comment. Every one recognized it at once for what it was, a direct challenge to the Ward family. The non-combatants were amused and warmed at once to the fray; arguments arose. The spirit seemed to be: "Is this a private fight, or can anybody get into it?"

Clarence Ward, slim, dignified, gray-haired, with the manner of the law courts, came, all unsuspecting, into the bank about noon. He was standing before the portrait of old Henry Benedict when Eugene emerged from his office on the way to lunch. There, just as the sweet music came to a sudden stop, the two met. The spectators held their breath.

"Hello, Clarence," said Eugene breezily. "What do you think of our new home?"

"Very fine," admitted Mr. Ward coldly. "I have just been reading the inscription under your father's portrait."

"Ah, yes," said Eugene, smiling sweetly.

"You ought to write fiction, Eugene," Mr. Ward advised. "Fiction, I believe, is mostly lies."

Eugene flushed. "I am not aware of any inaccuracy in that inscription," he said.

"A pinch-penny banker!" sneered Mr. Ward. "Eight-Per-Cent. Benedict, I believe they called him, though I don't recall that he was ever satisfied with that modest rate."

"That will do!" Eugene cried.

"You have insulted the memory," Mr. Ward went on, flushing, too, "of one of the finest men who ever lived, an incorruptible judge, an honored member of Congress—"

"A country lawyer with a mind as broad as a knife blade!" Eugene cut in. "A millstone round the neck of progress!"

"Enough!" shouted Mr. Ward.

"You started it," the banker said. "Boasting on your dead father's tombstone. Did you think you could get away with that fairy story? Not likely!"

"I intend," interrupted Mr. Ward, "to withdraw my personal account from this bank. I shall also withdraw all funds of which I am trustee."

"Withdraw, and be damned to you!" roared Eugene.

He turned and walked from the bank. Mr. Ward glared after him. The feud was on.

That evening, the warmest of the summer, to date, Bob Dana walked the streets of his native town. His dominant emotion was joy. Henry Benedict was finished; never again need he stare at that horrible crayon portrait, never again writhe in his chair over the problem of Henry's eyes. He had eight hundred dollars in his pocket, he was twenty-five, life stretched before him gay and wonderful.

At the corner of Park Avenue and Market Street he narrowly escaped being hit by an automobile.

He awoke in time, however, and leaped nimbly to safety. The car ran up to the curb, stopped, and a familiar voice called "Whoo-oo!"

"What's the idea?" asked Dell as he went up to her. "Trying to end it all? You gave me a turn, I'll say."

"Sorry," he apologized. "Just one of those boneheaded pedestrians. You should have run me down. World's better without my sort. Better for motorists, I mean."

"Hop in," she ordered. "I'll give you a spin. It will cool your fevered brow."

"Thanks." He climbed into the seat at her side, and seized his hat just in time as she shot the car off into the night. The cushions were soft, the breeze rushed over him pleasantly. "This is elegant," he said. "And it's an old story to you. Curse the rich!"

"Cut out the cursing," Dell answered. "We had plenty of that at dinner. Father held forth on the subject of Clarence Ward."

"That so? I heard there was quite a little grapple at the bank."

"Sure was! Father's inscription did the work. He asked for a row, and now he's got it. I hope he's satisfied."

"Well, the lad's jazzed things up. Give him credit. Say, I rather like the moon. Take a look at it."

"No, thanks. I was doing just that when I nearly ran over you. Better keep my eyes on the job."

"All right. I'll look at it for you and report. It's a grand old moon, Dell. Same moon I've seen shining on the Arno and on the roses that bloom on the long road up to Fiesole. I've seen it shining on the Colosseum and on the Seine and on lovers in the Luxembourg, and from the Embankment watched it silver the roofs of Parliament and Big Ben in his tower. I've seen it shining on the Atlantic in the wake of a ship when the band was playing an old-fashioned waltz— and now I've seen it shining on your hair."

"Still fond of honey?"

"Oh, Dell! If I could only get up in the morning and have those rolls in Rome—melt in your mouth, they would, and the golden butter, and that honey! Life, Dell, life has possibilities."

"You sound rather happy to-night," she said.

"Why not? Eight hundred hard-earned dollars in my pocket. Going to put over a big real-estate deal in a day or two. Then—there are a few places I haven't caught that old moon shining, and thank God the boats still run."

"I wish I were a man!" Dell said suddenly.

"Well, you're mighty nice as you are," he told her. "But of course—there are advantages. Now, take my own case. So many interesting things I can do. First of all, I ought to find a place to do a bit of work before I wander off again. Know what I'm planning? Little cottage out on the end of Cape Cod, in Provincetown. Exhilarating spot, air like good red licker, sea spray in your face when you go down to watch the fishing boats come in. I can get it for twenty-eight hundred cash. Going to buy it, fill it with my traps, work there when the spirit moves, pull out when the soles itch again. Good idea, eh, Dell?"

"Splendid!" she answered gayly.

"When I'm hard up," he went on, "I can eat fish. They give 'em away. Fish aren't so bad, you know."

"I know," she said softly.

"Little half acre I can call my own. Every man ought to have a place like that. Go there and paint. And when I get blue and lonely, discouraged—"

"Yes?"

"I can hit the old trail again." They drove along in silence for a time. "Say, Dell," he inquired presently, "have you told your father you're engaged to Herb Ward?"

"No, I haven't," said Dell.

Bob suddenly noticed where they were. She had swung into the Benedict drive and now she brought the car to a stop under an old-fashioned porte-cochère. Perhaps she had remembered that the front porch was in shadow, that the air was filled with the odor of syringa, and the moon so highly spoken of was tracing fantastic patterns on the close-cropped lawn. Perhaps—

The touch of her strong slender hand gave him a thrill as he helped her to alight, and as he followed her across the lawn he was saying to himself: "Be careful, you fool. Man in your position can't marry. Silly thing to do, spoils everything, travel all over, nose to the grindstone. Watch your step!"

They went side by side up on to the dark porch. A figure emerged promptly from the shadows to greet them, a rather frail figure in white flannels.

"Why—hello, Herbert," said Delia. "What are you doing here?"

"Hello, Dell. Oh, that's you, Bob. Say, Dell, if you don't mind I must see you alone—right away."

"Well, good night," Bob Dana said. "Had a fine ride, Dell."

"Don't go," Dell protested. "Herb just wants to talk about the family feud."

"None of my business," Bob answered briskly. "Must run along. See you before I leave town."

121

He walked rapidly, like a man seeking to get out from under some overhanging menace. Through the big gate, down Maple Avenue under the tallest elms in town.

"My boy, my boy," he thought, "that was a narrow one! Another minute and I'd have said something rash. She might have taken me too; women are foolish at times. Me married! Dreadful, dreadful! Herb, old boy, you saved my life. You certainly popped up in the nick of time. Often wondered what the lad was good for—now I know." He stopped for a moment under the trees. "Dell's darn sweet," he admitted. "Darn sweet. If only I had a prosperous hardware business or something of that sort. No use wishing, though. But I wonder is this Ward boy good enough for her?"

His way led him past the office of the Mayfield Enterprise. Inside, under a green shaded lamp, he saw Will Varney bending over his desk. He went in.

"I want to thank you for what you wrote about me in the paper to-night," he said. "That about the picture, you know. Did you really mean it?"

"With all my heart," Will Varney answered. His pale, kindly face lighted with enthusiasm. "You're a genius, Bob. You'll make little old Mayfield mighty proud some day."

"I hope so, I'm sure," Bob told him. "But I guess it was the inscription under my latest effort that made the big hit this morning. I hear the riot's on."

Will Varney laughed and tapped a little pile of letters at his elbow. "Here they are," he said. "The first fruits of the controversy."

"What do you mean?"

"Who did the most to influence the life of his times and leave his impress on the town? The letter writers are limbering up. This bunch came in the evening mail. It's just a beginning. Some say Ward, some Benedict, and some have other candidates. Here's a letter from poor old Mrs. Hughes. She thinks her husband, Reverend Elan Hughes—you remember, he preached at the First Church for years—should be elected. Sour old Elan—a gloomy view of the hereafter he expounded. And the Masters family wants to edge in. Their vote goes solid to Fred Masters. But these are also-rans. The main race will be between Benedict and Ward."

"Funny thing to get excited about," commented Bob.

"Isn't it?" Will Varney agreed. "Look about you. Why should any man want to see his father get the credit for sleepy old Mayfield? I can't figure it. And, thinking it over—there's my own father. You remember him, Bob. Year after year, in this paper, he chronicled the history of the town and shaped its opinions. I guess if any man can lay claim But, Great Scott, I'm afraid I'm as bad as any of them!"

"Looks that way," Bob laughed. He stood up. "I didn't mean to interrupt. Just came in to say thank you. I'm leaving in a day or two."

"No?" Varney's face clouded. "I'll be sorry, Bob. You'll never know how I've enjoyed our talks here. All those things you told me about Europe—it was almost as good as though I'd had the trip myself. And about as near as I'll ever get, I guess."

He was silent for a moment, thinking of his frustrated ambitions. "Well, I've got my job here." He turned to the pile of copy paper on his desk. "By the way, how do you spell Stuttgart? You know, that town in Germany. Two 't's' in the middle of it, or one?"

"Two, I believe," Bob told him. "But what are you doing in Stuttgart?"

"Why, that was Herman Schall's birthplace," Varney explained. "I've just been writing his obituary. You know Herman left us this afternoon."

* * * * *

"WITH regard to the controversy now disrupting Mayfield," Will Varney wrote two days later, "it must be understood that the position of this newspaper is strictly neutral. We have been accused of favoritism by both sides, which is the best proof of our disinterest. Samuel Ward was a splendid type of the old- school jurist, and Henry Benedict was well known up and down the valley as a conservative banker of the highest integrity. The question as to which exerted the largest influence on Mayfield seems to us an academic one impossible of solution, but we love excitement and we have furthered the discussion by printing all letters received, save for a few that were anonymous and abusive. Seventeen epistles written by the Ward faction have appeared in print, as have fourteen from the Benedict side. Such is the box score as we go to press. Let the battle rage."

Obligingly the battle did just that. Clarence Ward and Eugene Benedict fought the main engagement in full view of the populace, cutting each other in public, each discovering daily some new means by which to embarrass or belittle the other. Here and there minor skirmishes took place between lesser dependents of the rival houses. Nor did the women hesitate to enter the arena. Few who were present will forget the afternoon meeting of the Ladies' Guild of the First Church, when Mrs. Clarence and Mrs. Eugene encountered each other and demonstrated the possibility of fighting a war with no weapon save the human eye.

Dell Benedict and Herbert Ward alone of the two rival camps remained on friendly terms. Meeting Bob Dana on the street the morning after his abrupt departure when he found Herb Ward among those present on the porch, Dell explained the situation.

"Herb had just dropped over to discuss the great war," she said. "We decided not to let it make any difference between us."

"That's the sensible view to take," Bob approved heartily.

"I knew you'd think so," said Dell with amazing sweetness.

"Oh, absolutely. Silly row anyhow. How can you decide a thing like that? Then you and Herb are still engaged?"

"More so than ever. Herb's been awfully sweet." She held up her hand, displaying a diamond-and-platinum ring. "We told our people all about it. Sort of had to, under the circumstances."

"Must have been good news for your father."

"He nearly passed out. But he knows better than to interfere. Well, that's that. I wanted to tell you—just to make you comfortable in your mind,"

"I'm mighty glad you're happy, Dell. That is, of course— if you are happy?"

"Delirious." She smiled up at him. "Come and see me before you leave."

"I sure will."

In the bright light of the morning, with his thoughts traveling the highroad of common sense, on which no moon may shine, this seemed to him excellent news. Good old Herb! The lad was showing a surprisingly level head. But for Herb he might by now be painfully entangled, his career endangered, his wanderings ended. Herb was his insurance, his protection.

"Ought to invite Herb to lunch," he thought. "Show my appreciation somehow."

* * * * *

THE following Tuesday night, when he wandered out to the country club to the regular weekly dance, he felt the same way. His business had dragged on longer than he had expected, but it was practically settled now, and he could leave May field very soon. He sat on the club veranda, staring in at the dancers. The orchestra was playing a popular song that referred in sentimental strain to the moment "when it's moonlight in Kalua."

Kalua. Sounded like Hawaii. That was the direction in which he would travel next. The South Seas, on Gauguin's trail, and Stevenson's. He promised himself many a languorous afternoon on some white bathing beach, many a calm, breathless night with the Southern Cross flaming overhead.

Through the open window he caught sight of Dell Benedict dancing in Herb Ward's arms. Dependable old Herb! He watched them approvingly. Dell was lovely, and no mistake. Sometimes, when he was lonely and discouraged, he would think sadly of what might have been. That would, in the last analysis, be much more satisfactory than if what might have been had been. "He travels fastest who travels alone." True talk.

He was still musing gently in this strain when, ten minutes later, Dell appeared, somewhat breathless, before him.

"Bob—I want you to take me home," she said.

He jumped to his feet. "Sure. But I thought—you came with Herb Ward."

"Herb and I have just had the most frightful row," she explained. Bob saw that her eyes were flashing, her cheeks flushed. "He said you'd done a speaking likeness of Grandfather, and that several people had heard it say distinctly: 'Pay up to-morrow or I'll put you on the street.'"

"Pretty snappy for Herb."

"And I told him that his old fossil of a grandfather Oh,

I don't know what I said! I was furious! I may have my own opinion of my family, but no one else can knock it and live." She drew her cloak about her white shoulders. "Come on, Bob."

Bob started nervously. "The ring's gone!" he cried.

"You bet it's gone! For ever!"

"Well, now, Dell—you ought not to get drawn into this foolish argument. It's beneath you. If you'll take my advice—"

"All right. I can go home alone." She walked briskly away.

"Hold on! Wait a minute! Wait till I get my hat." He dashed into the club. When he reappeared Dell was far down the drive, going strong despite high- heeled dancing pumps.

128

He caught up with her. "I'm mighty sorry, Dell—I have no car. I came by trolley."

"That's the way I'm going home."

"May I—er—come along?"

Dell hadn't a penny with her, and his company was rather essential. But all she said was, "If you think you can choke off your fatherly advice."

Conversation sort of languished in the moonlight. He helped her on to the trolley and climbed up beside her. "Not so soft as the seat of Herb's car," he suggested.

"If you can't talk about anything but Herb, don't talk."

He subsided, hurt. Oh, well, women were like this, of course. All sorts of moods and whims and fancies. Sunshine and shadow. Keep a lad stirred up all the time. Better hang on to that precious freedom of his. "When it's moonlight in Kalua"—couldn't get the insidious thing out of his head. "Because you are—not there." Just as well too.

He glanced sidewise at Dell's haughty countenance. In spite of himself he could not smother his approval. "Your profile's pure Greek," he said admiringly.

"Grandfather didn't start with a fruit-stand, if that's what you mean," said Dell.

Well, if she wanted to be cross, let her be cross. He'd keep his future thoughts to himself.

In silence they alighted from the street car and crossed the park; still with no word spoken they passed on up the avenue and through the big gate. The porch lay calm in shadow, syringa bloomed on the lawn. Dell held out her hand.

"Thanks for bringing me home. Good-by—if I don't see you again."

"But, Dell—look here—of course you'll see me. I'll come round."

"Oh—don't trouble."

She was gone inside the door—hadn't even asked him to stop a minute. Treated him like a rather tiresome stranger. Women, inexplicable women!

He strolled along down the avenue. Certainly did act haughty, that girl. He pictured her now in her room, head held high, eyes flashing.

Which was all he knew about it. In her room Dell had flung herself across the bed and was weeping bitterly. For Herb, and all the lost glories of romance? Herb, of course.

Will Varney's light was burning. Looking through the window, Bob saw the little editor bending above his pile of exchanges. He went inside.

"See here, Mr. Varney—something's got to be done."

"What do you mean, Bob?"

"This silly feud between the Montagues and Capulets. It's gone far enough. Hearts are being broken, young lovers wrenched apart."

"I suppose so. Such is life in the feud country."

"You know," Bob told him, "before I leave town I'd like to settle this foolish argument once for all. Just naturally kill it."

"Easier said than done. Unless you have an idea."

"Well—something flashed through my mind the other day. I don't know—it seems reasonable. I'll sit down if you don't mind."

"Sure, Bob; sure. Push those papers off the chair—that's right."

Bob Dana sat and crossed his long legs. "You know, when I'm away from Mayfield and think about the town I always remember the amazing amount of sickness here. My mother was never very well, and I used to go to the doctor for her—in the evenings mostly. And I can still picture Doc Cunningham's office, every chair taken, people standing along the walls—dreary, discouraged-looking people."

"Yes." Will Varney nodded. "Always been a surprising lot of doctoring here. Doctoring for this and that. You've noticed Cunningham's big house on Maple Avenue. Doctoring built that."

"Precisely. Now, Mr. Varney, tell me—what sort of men were the leading citizens here—the ones who ran the town?"

Will Varney smiled.

"You mean Ward and Benedict and that crowd? Take a look at Mayfield for your answer. Twenty years behind the times, this town is; you've heard me say so before. Lying here sound asleep through the biggest boom this valley has ever known. Benedict and Ward and their gang did that—conservative, suspicious of everything new, shouting their selfish slogan 'Keep the strangers out.'"

"I thought so," Bob Dana said. "Sour old parties, as I remember them. Looked at life through jaundiced eyes. Depressed and irritable and grouchy."

"You've said it," Varney agreed. "And their dispositions molded this town. I could give you a thousand examples, and Benedict would figure in a lot of them. We might have been on the main line of the railroad, but Benedict got a stubborn spell over some land he owned that was necessary to the scheme. Oh, he was a lovely old chap. I can still see him sitting in that little office of his, looking at prospective borrowers through those cold fishy eyes. Heaven help the man who had to go to Benedict for a loan! It didn't take long for the word to spread that the banking interests here were unfriendly, so new business gave this town a wide berth." The little editor leaned back in his chair; it creaked faintly beneath him. "And Ward! The Turner steel mills might have located here, but Judge Ward blocked the move. Said it would bring in a lot of dirty foreigners. I think of him as he sat on the bench—never dishonest, I don't mean that—but severe. Too blamed severe. Mercy wasn't in his vocabulary. He wrecked a great many lives that a little sympathy and understanding would have carried along to happiness. I tell you, Bob, this town owes a lot to Ward and Benedict and their gang," Will Varney finished. "A lot they're not boasting about now, wherever they may be."

"Rather mean old men," Bob Dana said. "That's how I picture them. Mean and dissatisfied and bitter." He leaned forward suddenly. "I'll bet both Ward and Benedict suffered tortures from dyspepsia," he added.

"Most people do—most middle-aged people," Varney replied. "In Mayfield, at any rate. For years we've had a lot of trouble with hired girls here—eating has been a rather catch-as-catch-can affair. Now you mention it, Ward and Benedict did have dyspepsia. Yes, both of 'em had it mighty bad,"

Bob Dana laughed, and stood up. "That's all I want to know."

Will Varney gave him a long look. "By gad," he cried, "I begin to get you!" He leaped enthusiastically to his feet. "And you're right, boy, you're dead right!"

"I'm going to hop on a train and run up to Cleveland in the morning," Bob told him. "I can get what I need up there. A modest supply of modeling clay."

"Modeling clay," Varney chuckled. "Yes, that's what you want."

"You'll help me with this?" Bob asked.

"Will I?" The little editor's eyes twinkled. "You bet your life I will!"

For three days Bob Dana was not much in evidence on the streets of Mayfield. The hotel help reported that he seemed to be extremely busy in his room.

On Saturday morning Eugene Benedict drove down to the bank about eight- thirty, as was his custom. The sun lay blazing hot on the brick pavement of Maple Avenue, and Eugene sped over it savagely, for he was feeling hot himself.

He had just seen Clarence and Herbert Ward strolling down to their law office, and the sight of them nowadays tended to infuriate him.

As Eugene approached the corner of the park at Main and Market Streets he was surprised to see a crowd gathered on the lawn in open violation of the notice, posted everywhere: "Keep Off the Grass!" He slowed down his car. An old friend caught sight of him and waved.

"Come here, 'Gene," he shouted. "This will interest you."

His curiosity suddenly aroused, Eugene parked his car at the curb and pushed his way through the crowd. It parted to give him gangway, a favor he accepted as due to the president of the First National Bank. In another moment he came upon the center of Mayfield's interest.

On a cheap oak pedestal that suggested the Mayfield Furniture Store he beheld a figure about three feet high. It was modeled in clay and took the form of a short, heavy man in middle age. The face was flat and on a pudgy little nose spectacles rested. The generous stomach was covered by what appeared to be an apron; a cap rested on the head. It was a tribute to Bob Dana's skill that Eugene, like all the other spectators, recognized the figure at first glance. As the banker stood there staring he could almost hear the querulous, cracked voice: "Louie—Louie—turn down dot gas!"

Hanging about the feet of the figure was a placard that might have been printed in the job department of the Mayfield Evening Enterprise. Eugene read:

ERECTED IN MEMORY OF HERMAN SCHALL
THE BAKER
Who Gave All His Contemporaries Indigestion and
Thus More Than Any Other Man Influenced the Life
of His Times and Left His Impress on the Town
We Asked for Bread and He Gave Us a Stone

While the citizens of Mayfield grinned and nudged one another Eugene Benedict read the placard a second time.

* * * * *

AT six o'clock that evening Bob Dana sat in old man Cornell's easy-chair with the last edition of the Enterprise before him. In his leading editorial, entitled Herman Schall, Will Varney ably seconded Bob's efforts of the morning. He began with the Herman of fifty years before, a young man newly arrived from Germany, who came to Mayfield and started the town's first bakeshop. He carried him along until the time, years later, when Herman's delivery wagon stood before the houses of both high and low, and Herman's bread was the daily diet of all May-field.

"Such bread!" Will Varney wrote. "Herman had the habit of thrift. To the outward view his product was O.K., but the heart of the loaf was only partially baked, still fermenting, indigestible. Those who ate it experienced very shortly a deep and dark depression, their outlook on life turned gloomy.

"Herman never figured as a leading citizen of Mayfield. Other men were in the limelight, directing the destinies of the town. But back of these men were a number of vital influences, and not the least of these, moving on tiptoe through his dim kitchen, doling out the coal or turning down the gas, was Herman Schall the baker. It is not at all improbable that to Herman's bread may be traced a thousand heartaches and tragedies—divorces, business failures, meannesses and wrongs.

"The editor of this newspaper has thought things over, and he has no hesitation in announcing that, in so far as his columns are concerned, the controversy that has been raging hereabouts for some days is settled for all time.

"Settled by the election of Herman Schall to the post of honor that stood as the ultimate prize."

Bob dropped the paper and sat staring out across the park. His telephone rang.

"Hello," he said. "Hello, Dell. What's the good word?"

"Seems to be Schall," she answered. "Started a lot of excitement, didn't you?"

"Think so? How is your father feeling?"

"Oh, he'll recover. As a matter of fact the old dear seems to have a sense of humor, after all. His dignity was outraged for a while, but he's come round. He's just talked with Clarence Ward over the telephone."

"No! An armistice?"

"Permanent peace, I fancy. They agreed that maybe you're right. Father is going to take down that inscription and replace it with a simple plate—just grandfather's name and the dates. Clarence Ward is wondering how you edit a tombstone. You see, that famous sentiment won't sound anything but ridiculous round here for a long time to come."

"Well, Dell, I'm certainly glad to hear all this. It's what I was trying to do, you know. Put an end to the feud."

"I gathered that."

Silence over the wire.

"Er—have you called up Herb and waved the white flag?"

"Me? Say, Bob, you certainly know all about girls. An open book to you."

137

"Well, has he called you up?"

"I don't know. I've been out. Mighty kind of you to take such an interest."

"Not at all. Want the young people to be happy."

"Old Grandpa Fixit. Leaving soon?"

"Been packing all afternoon. Pull out to-morrow."

"Well, good-by—if I don't see you again."

"Dell—where do you get that stuff? I'll be up this evening to say good- by."

"Sweet of you to trouble. I'll try to have Herb on hand."

"Oh, never mind Herb."

"I'll have him here. Want you to be happy, too, old lad. See you later."

Bob ate one final dinner at the Mayfield House. His pockets bulged with money, life was beckoning, rumor had it that the boats still ran. But somehow he wasn't feeling so elated after all.

At eight o'clock he came abreast of the cast-iron deer on the Benedict lawn, and three seconds later Dell gave him her hand at the top of the steps. An amazingly lovely Dell, starry-eyed in the dusk, gentle and calm and restful.

Bob looked anxiously about. "I don't see young Herb." "No," said Dell. "Herb hasn't called up. Pity, isn't it?" "Oh, don't worry. He'll come round. Herb's no fool." "I'm not worrying. Have you time to sit down?" "Sure." Bob dropped into a chair. Life was certainly mighty peaceful, there in the shadow on the porch. He leaned back and heaved a sigh of deep content. The syringa was still in blossom, lilies nodded in the distance, roses climbed a trellis. Roses with the moon on them, recalling the fragrant walls on the long road up to Fiesole.

"Are you really leaving to-morrow?" Dell asked. "I'd begun to think you were never going."

"That's true hospitality. But don't fret—I'm off this time." "Provincetown, I believe you said."

"Yes—Provincetown," he answered. "I've wired a friend to get me an option on that cottage. Going to be just the place for me."

"Sounds like it, I'm sure." Her tone was brisk and cheerful. "I love the roar of the surf. Some people find it disturbing. Restful, I call it."

"That's good. You'll get a lot of work done, I hope." "I'll certainly have a try at it. And afterward—well, look to the East for me. The South Seas. China. Pick up all in a minute some bright morning. Just lock the door and go."

"It must be wonderful," Dell said. "I mean—to have no ties. Nothing to hold you. Just yourself." Somewhere in the house a telephone rang.

"Yes—pretty good feeling," Bob assured her. A maid appeared. "It's that Mr. Ward again, miss." "I'll go," said

Dell. "If you'll excuse me, Bob." She was away some time. When she reappeared, Bob Dana was anxious.

"Young Herb, eh? Fix everything up?"

"Count on me. It's all fixed. Nothing to worry about."

"Sensible thing to do, of course," said Bob.

"Of course," Dell agreed.

He tipped back his chair, leaned his head against the cool bricks of the house. After a long silence he spoke: "That cottage only has three rooms."

"Three ought to be plenty for you," said Dell.

"For me—yes. But I've been thinking—times when I've just finished a picture—sort of depressed—need somebody round who thinks I'm wonderful."

"How about a dog?"

"Dog, nothing."

"Some people prefer cats," Dell said.

Another silence. "Dell," he said, "I don't know what ails me.

"Something ail you?" she inquired politely.

"Seems to. My head's all wrong. Mind's affected. Keep thinking to myself how almighty sweet you are."

"Better stop it," Dell advised. "Spoil all your fun, a girl would."

"Oh, I don't know. Depend a lot on the girl. If she happened to be a good scout—ready to pick up and go at a minute's notice—"

"Ain't no such animal," said Dell.

"How'd you like fish, Dell? As a steady diet, I mean?"

"I'd hate 'em."

He pondered. "Sorry to hear that. There's one room in that cottage—you'd love it. Looks right over at Spain."

"Spain—where the boats run? You'll travel faster alone. For your own sake, Bob—try to be sensible."

Again the telephone rang. The two on the porch waited in silence. In a moment the maid reappeared, and Dell rose. Bob stood beside her.

"It was only Mr. Ward, miss. I hung up the receiver—just the way you did."

The girl vanished into the dim hall. Bob turned slowly toward Dell. He seized her hand.

"Look here, Dell—you never intended to take him!"

"Who says so?"

"I do. Well, this settles it." He held her close. "And maybe it won't be so bad. You didn't really mean that—about hating fish?"

"I—I guess not, Bob."

"Dell! And that bright morning—just before we lock the door. It won't take you long to pack?"

"Five minutes. Only an overnight bag."

"That's the talk!"

He kissed her. He was a little breathless. "Hard luck for you, Dell. I mean—marrying me."

141

"Oh, I don't know," Dell whispered. "I believe I'm going to like it."

POSSESSIONS

First published in The Saturday Evening Post, Feb 3, 1923

THERE are many scenes at which the high gods must laugh; but surely none which elicits from them heartier guffaws than this: A moonlit night, a shadowy veranda. On the veranda a young man; one of those carefree, casual lads who has sworn never to marry. Not for him the ties and cares of wedded life; his soul, an artistic one, craves constant excitement, perpetual change, freedom to travel unhampered. Roses are blooming on a trellis; roses with the moon on them. The young man is not alone. A girl is close by—in his arms in fact, her head upon his shoulder. He has just asked her to marry him.

When Bob Dana came back to Mayfield, his home town, to paint a resurrection portrait of the late Henry Benedict, there wasn't a girl on his horizon. Eugene Benedict, now president of the First National, had written that he desired a portrait of his father to hang in the new quarters of the bank, and Bob had welcomed the opportunity. He was just back from Europe, where he had been studying art; and five years of wandering had depleted his purse, but had not satisfied him. His immediate plan was to earn a little money, after which, he told himself, he would fare forth once more, and every port where a ship touched was on his itinerary.

Even after he had seen Delia Benedict again his purpose did not consciously alter. The grown-up Dell was sweet and clever and desirable, and if he had been settled in a good business—but he wasn't; he was an artist, and he knew well that artists should not marry. The very idea frightened him. His wanderings over, his career endangered, stagnation, worry, responsibilities. Oh, no, he was too agile to be caught like that! And all the while the high gods were laughing: "We heard different. What do your little pictures matter? The urge, young man, is as old as the race. Here is the girl, your future wife. Get on with it!"

He was pretty far on with it this July night, standing there in the shadow on Eugene Benedict's porch, dazed, a little breathless, with Delia in his arms. Give the girl credit. She had not led him on; rather she had discouraged him from the first. And none save the most hardened cynic would intimate that she knew only too well the provocative nature of discouragement.

"What's it all about, Dell?" the boy said. "Something's happened—something wonderful. Are you really fond of me?" She nodded, lifted her head.

"I'm fond of you, Bob; fonder than I ever expected to be of any one. And you—you haven't said it, you know—"

"I can't find words, Dell. I can usually talk, but now

You know, something has been wrong, something lacking, for a long time. I didn't understand. I was just—kind of lonesome, lonesome for you—and I didn't suspect. I had to come back to Mayfield to find it out."

"To find what out, Bob?" she prompted.

"That I loved you. Oh, Dell, the words seem weak. But I do—I love you, and from now on I'm going to prove it in other ways; not words alone."

Somehow they were sitting together in the hammock.

"Isn't life funny, Bob?" Dell said. "Only a few weeks ago I was here on this porch and you came wandering up the front walk. The same old Bob—and different too. And you said—do you remember what you said?"

"I only remember what I thought—about how almighty sweet you were."

"But I remember what you said," Dell told him. "You said that girls weren't for you; that you had to keep away from them. Otherwise you might marry one, and you intimated that would be terrible."

"I was crazy," he cut in. "Foolish! Why shouldn't an artist get married the same as anybody else?"

"Well, why shouldn't he, Bob? You tell me. You seemed to have a lot of reasons—when you first came here. Money, I believe, was one of them."

"Silly reason, Dell. Why I'll work as I never have before! Marrying you—it will give me new inspiration, a new thrill, new excitement."

"And after the thrill wears off?" she suggested.

"It never will, with you. Why, Dell, you're a thousand girls! And every one a wonder."

She smiled at him.

"I like to hear you say it," she admitted. "And yet, how about that talk—the travel business? Simply had to keep going, you said. 'Dell, there are a few places I haven't caught that old moon shining, and thank God the boats still run.' All that about having no one to bother with, no responsibilities, just locking the door some bright morning and hitting the old trail again."

"But you'll go with me. You said so. Not five minutes to pack—you promised; an overnight bag."

"Yes, I know." She was silent for a moment. "Oh, Bob, I'm frightfully fond of you, and yet—I suppose it's the Benedict in me—practical people always. I wonder—" She stood up. "Look," she said, "out there in the moonlight; the front walk. It isn't just Maple Avenue at the end of it. It's the Orient you've been talking about, the South Seas, China. It's Europe and the whole glittering world. Just wandering as you please, no responsibilities, no girl tagging along. Think hard, Bob." He seized her hand, but she drew it away. "It's not too late. In less than a minute you could be out on that walk, on your way. I wouldn't blame you, dear boy. I wouldn't even ask you to kiss me before you go. Bob, it's your chance."

The idea appalled him.

"Do you want me to go?"

"That isn't the point."

"Do you want me to? Because if you do you're going to be disappointed. Not a step! Not a step again, Dell, without you—tagging along!" He seized her in his arms.

"Oh, Bob, that's what I wanted you to say! We'll make a go of it, won't we? I'll be the kind of wife you need."

"You couldn't be any other kind, dear, have I told you the news? I love you."

"Go on saying it," Dell urged. "Get the habit, Bob. I've heard it now and then from other men, and it always bored me. But you, Bob—you certainly do make it sound interesting."

He continued his interesting talk for three hours, with suitable interruptions from Dell. When he walked down Maple Avenue on his way back to the hotel he was a happy man. Only a few weeks before he had traveled this same thoroughfare, saying to himself, "Me married! Terrible, terrible! Watch your step, old son!" Yet here he was, abroad in the midnight calm, engaged and exulting. Life was a funny proposition. Big ambitions stirred within him.

"Got to get busy now—do something fine, make Dell proud of me; and when the work's done we'll look about a bit. She'll be game. She's that kind. Five minutes to pack? She said so. And why not?"

He was roused the next morning by the ringing of his telephone. Leaping to his feet, he crossed the room, bright with hot July sunlight. His spirits rose with every step. Pretty good old world, now that he remembered. Dell's voice came pleasantly to his ear:

"Bob, what's happened to you?"

"Wha-what's that? Hello, Dell."

"You don't mean to say I woke you! Why, I've been up hours! I couldn't sleep."

"Well, I—I've been gathering strength, Dell. That's me from now on; gathering strength to work for you."

"Bob, I had to know. Do you still feel as you did last night?"

"I surely do, honey! Why not?"

"Well, I couldn't be sure. The moon's no longer shining."

"But the sun is. And look here—how about you, my girl?"

"Me? Well, I called up. Shows I'm still interested."

"Glad to hear that." A bright idea recurred to him. "Say, Dell, on the way home last night I got to thinking—why can't we be married to-day and go East?"

"To-day! Why, Bob, what a notion!"

"Well, why not? It's very simple. Just call round at the city hall or something like that."

"Bob! Mother would be horrified! And I—well, every girl expects a wedding. I know I do."

"A wedding?" His heart sank. "You mean one of those big affairs?"

"Oh, no! Just a little wedding here at home. Do you mind? It's probably the only chance I'll ever have."

"Why, that's all right, Dell. Anything you say. When? About Saturday?"

"You silly old thing! It would take a month at least."

"Dell! I couldn't wait that long. I'll give you two weeks."

Silence.

"We-ell, perhaps I could make it if I rushed. Of course, there are a million things—clothes—"

"Yeah, clothes. Well, I'm all ready now. I've got a new suit. Give me a gardenia and I'm practically married."

"Have you evening clothes, Bob?"

"Sorry—no. I had an outfit, but I couldn't get it into my trunk when I went abroad, so I gave it to the janitor. You see, it's always been my rule, Dell—never own more stuff than you can crowd into a steamer trunk."

"Oh!" She was silent for a moment. "I haven't told a soul, Bob. The trains are running. You can still escape."

"Dell, I won't listen to you. I'm going to be a married man or know the reason why."

"Then you'll order evening clothes, won't you?"

"And a red vest, if you tell me to. Oh, by the way, I don't suppose I could rent a suit."

"Bob!" He heard her laughing.

"Well, I may never need it again."

"Oh, yes, you will!"

"You know best. I'll get measured this morning. It will mean another trunk."

"Get a good big one. I can fill it if you can't."

"All right, Dell."

"And come up to lunch. If I'm to be a bride in two weeks I may as well get going. I'll break the sad news to the family before you come. Then you'll be in for it."

"I suppose so. However, I'll go through. I'll be up about one. And, Dell— "

"Yes, Bob?"

"What was I going to say? Something of no importance— oh, yes, I love you."

"Stick to it," said Dell. "And heaven help you!"

He had need of heaven's help at lunch. Dell had evidently spread the news, and the atmosphere in the big house on Maple Avenue was mostly gloom. Mrs. Benedict, that haughty beauty of the 'nineties, was red about the eyes, and she greeted Bob as though he were a bailiff come to dispossess her. Eugene, having rushed home from the bank for his usual luncheon and met unusual tidings, was fussy and pompous and disturbed.

They sat in the drawing-room, talking about nothing. All about were the tokens of material prosperity and success—wide chairs, soft carpets, expensive hangings; a stronghold of convention and respectability; the sort of home that had been only a memory to Bob Dana these past five years. Yet here Dell had been born and grown up; it was all she had ever known; and now he was planning to link his life with Dell's with this sort of household. For the first time he had misgivings. But they vanished when he looked at Dell—Dell, who was smiling and competent and clever, and who would see him safely through the most difficult luncheon of his life.

They went into the dining-room—gleaming silver, costly linen and an old colored butler who moved as silently as time. When the man had gone and they were alone Eugene seemed to feel that it was incumbent on him to begin.

"Er—well, Bob, what's all this?"

"You mean about Dell and me?" Bob tried to smile. "I—¦ I suppose she told you?"

"She certainly did. It's come as a great deal of a shock."

"Well, I—I suppose I ought to have spoken to you first."

"Heavens, Bob!" said Dell. "That went out with Victoria!"

"Oh, did it?" He hoped the perspiration on his forehead was invisible. "You see, it—it happened so suddenly. All at once we discovered we loved each other. A shock to us, too, but a pleasant one." He waited hopefully. No one seemed disposed to help him along. "Of course, I suppose I'm not just the sort of son- in-law you would have picked—"

"Hardly," said Mrs. Benedict; but that was no help.

"I—I mean, I'm not in the Rotary Club, and I haven't got a business, and—and—"

Well, this sort of thing wasn't doing any good. He stopped.

"Of course, all we want," said Eugene, "is Dell's happiness."

"Then, Father dear," Dell suggested, "there's nothing more to be said."

"Oh, yes, there is!" Eugene insisted. "Happiness depends on many things—money, among others. Can you support a wife? That seems to me to be the question."

"Precisely," said Mrs. Benedict. She never appeared to need more than one word. That was plenty.

"You haven't, I take it, found the art game very profitable," went on the president of the First National.

"Not as yet. I'm just getting started. For a while Dell and I will have to live very simply. She understands that."

"Of course I do!" said Dell.

"However, we'd be sure of a roof anyhow. I've already wired about a cottage at Provincetown. I intended to buy it even before I—I thought of getting married. You know, I just sold some land that belonged to my father—got six thousand for it—and I've nearly eight hundred left from what you paid me for the portrait. I can get this place for twenty-eight hundred."

He paused. Was he buying Dell, or what was all this?

"Is it—er—a large cottage?" asked Eugene.

"Cottages aren't, as a rule," Bob reminded him. "This one has three rooms."

"Three rooms!" repeated Eugene.

"Three rooms!" said Mrs. Eugene, and wailed it.

"It's really quite a charming place," Bob said. "Stands back of the town and you get a fine view across the roofs to the harbor."

But Eugene was not interested in views. "Were you planning to pay for it outright?" he inquired.

"Why not? I've got the money."

"Well, it might be better to leave a thousand on mortgage."

"Oh, no!" Bob shuddered. "I couldn't get mixed up with that sort of thing; I'm too innocent. All I know about mortgages is that somebody always forecloses them in the dead of winter. I'd hate to see Dell put out in a Provincetown snowstorm; they're pretty fierce."

Mrs. Benedict glared at him.

"It seems to me," she said, "an odd subject to joke about."

"I'm not joking. I mean it. I'd be afraid of a mortgage. Never could remember the interest."

"Still, it would be an advantage," Eugene persisted, "when you came to sell."

"But why should I want to sell?"

"Why—when you need a larger house."

"But I don't—I didn't think—" He looked helplessly at Dell.

"Father," said Dell, "aren't you ashamed? Talking business to poor old Bob; he doesn't know what it's all about. It's true that he doesn't make much money, and that we'll have very little; but don't expect him to enlighten you on his plans. I'm to be secretary-treasurer of the corporation; if you want information about the prospects of dividends come to me. I guess you can trust the granddaughter of Eight-Per-Cent. Benedict to steer clear of the rocks."

"Dell!" cried her mother.

"Well, what I mean is, with one of our family managing finances, it seems to me the subject is closed," Dell said gayly.

"It isn't just the money," Mrs. Benedict began. "Going way off to Massachusetts to live! I've always hoped Dell would settle down right here in Mayfield. And what's all this about travel? Travel isn't for married people; at least not when they're young. I didn't even get to New York until Dell was eighteen. It seems to me—"

It seemed to Dell that the discussion should end.

"Mother dear," she broke in, "you and Father have been wonderful and I hate to leave you—I honestly do. But Bob's told you the whole story—we love each other and we're on our way. What happens from now on is our worry, not yours. You two dears deserve a rest. Besides, just now you've got your hands pretty full, what with a wedding in your house in two weeks' time—"

"That's another thing," protested Mrs. Benedict.

"I think we'd better go to Cleveland in the morning and begin our shopping. Have you any ideas, Mother—"

Of course, she had behind her long years of experience in managing them, but her technique was admirable none the less. When the luncheon ended, Eugene and his wife seemed reconciled if not enthusiastic, and preparations for a wedding were well under way.

After lunch Bob found himself alone in the library with Eugene. The banker offered him a cigar, lighted one himself.

"Well, Bob, when I got you out here to paint that portrait of Father I never dreamed of this." He puffed away for a moment. "I hope I haven't seemed lacking in cordiality. As a matter of fact, I like you—like you enormously. And as far as your getting engaged to Dell is concerned—well, she's always had her own way in everything, and if she wanted you I don't suppose, when we come right down to it, you had an awful lot to say about it."

Somehow this idea didn't appeal to Bob.

"I proposed, if that's what you mean," he said. "You don't think for a minute that I went into this against my will."

"No, no; that's not what I meant. You don't quite understand. As I was saying, Dell's always had her own way—the only child; a bit spoiled perhaps. I'm mighty fond of her; but you'll have your hands full—"

"Oh, I'll manage."

"I hope so. I'm looking at it from your angle now. Always try to see the other fellow's side. You're an artist. I don't know much about artists. I'm a small- town banker myself; but even I—all men—I guess there are times—well—" He looked anxiously over his shoulder, lowered his voice. "You know—times where all this paraphernalia of marriage gets on your nerves; when you wish you could chuck the whole business and have your freedom back again. And what I'm getting at is, if I've had spells like that it seems to me that a boy like you, with a temperament—it seems to me he'd have 'em pretty often."

Bob stared at him. He was beginning to like Eugene. The little banker was human after all.

"Maybe I shall," the boy admitted. "But if I do—Dell's mighty clever and sensible too. She'll see me through. We'll get along."

"Well, of course, there's a lot in that. Dell's a bright girl." Eugene stood up. He appeared a bit embarrassed by his confession. "Going down street with me?"

"No, thanks. I'll see Dell a minute before I go."

"Of course." They went into the hall. Eugene picked up his straw hat. He held out his hand. "I just want to say, Bob, I wish you all the luck in the world."

His handclasp was friendly, his look sympathetic. Somehow Bob got the idea Eugene felt he was saying good-by to a man who was starting out on a long and hazardous journey.

During the next two weeks Bob called daily at the house on Maple Avenue. Dell had little time for him, however; she was busy shopping, busy with modistes and caterers. Up there round Eugene's back door it appeared that something was going on, something that was news to Bob. Wedding presents were pouring in—crates, barrels, boxes. At first Dell insisted that they must open these together; he struggled with nail pullers, hammers, wallowed in excelsior. Steadily the loot increased.

Bob found the sight of it a bit disturbing, but Dell was thrilled.

"Oh, Bob, look! Isn't that sweet of her? Aunt Helen. She's sent that Italian silver she picked up in Genoa. I never dreamed she'd part with it. Isn't it wonderful? It's as old as Columbus—all hand-made—oh, you don't care! Mother! Mother, where are you? Look what Aunt Helen—"

As each gift was unwrapped Dell and her mother would croon over it, pat it, behave toward it as though it were a child. Even a bonbon dish seemed of international interest.

"Bob, see what came to-day! I couldn't wait. I had it opened. A Georgian chair! And this mirror—Chippendale. Isn't it lovely?"

"Yeah. Going to be hard to pack."

"Oh, you don't appreciate anything!"

"But it's different with men, Dell. I guess just—er— things don't mean so much to them. Say, Dell, give a thought to the bridegroom."

"Not now—later."

The big evening came. Bob checked out from the Mayfield House and went with his luggage up to Maple Avenue. Eugene met him at the door.

"Hello, Bob! How are you?"

"I'm—I'm all right."

"I guess you'll be glad when the ceremony's over." Eugene always referred to it as the ceremony, in a solemn way that sent the cold chills down Bob's back. "Your best man is upstairs. My room, you know. Say, just step in here!"

He led the way into the library at the rear, an enormous room. Bob gasped.

"Presents look pretty well, eh?" said Eugene.

He waved his hand. It was like a combination furniture and jewelry store. Sheffield plate, a great chest of table silver, French, Italian and old English chairs, pottery, tall, fragile-looking vases, mirrors, linen, an antique sideboard, a highboy. A large, red-faced person with flat feet plumped anxiously about.

"What's that?" Bob whispered.

"Plain-clothes man," Eugene explained under his breath. "I thought it best to have him here."

"Great Scott!" Bob cried. "They're not worth all that!"

"My boy, some of this stuff is priceless."

Bob stood there. Into his mind flashed something he had said to Dell—why, it was only two weeks ago—"I've always made it a rule not to own any more than I can crowd into a steamer trunk."

He began to laugh. Eugene looked at him anxiously.

"See here, my boy, what's the trouble? You're hysterical."

"Yes, I guess I must be."

"You go right up-stairs. Better lie down on the bed until the ceremony. Don't get too excited. People have been married before."

Bob went up to the room where he was to cower until the summons came. The succeeding two hours were never very clear as he looked back on them. Dazed, just dazed, that was all. He found himself standing with Dell before a little man in black. "I do—I will—all my worldly goods." It was over. Dell did look wonderful. He began to be conscious, to breathe again. People were crowding in upon them.

It was, Eugene whispered, time for them to go. The man was invaluable. Dell poised on the stair, her bouquet in her hand. Bob would never forget the picture she made— must paint it some day from memory. Then he was back in his up- stairs haven, clad again in his regular suit, beginning to feel his regular self. Eugene bustled in.

"Well, Bob, all over now. Got your tickets—everything? The car's in the drive. You'll have to make a dash for it. Dell's ready—take good care of her—all we've got—naturally anxious. By the way, I meant to tell you—I had the packer up to- day to look over the presents. He figures on twenty barrels and twelve crates."

"Twenty—twelve—"

"I'll get them off to you by express right away. It's quicker than freight. Have to put a pretty stiff value on them—five thousand—"

Some one knocked on the door—Dell was waiting. Bob seized her arm at the top of the stairs and they dashed down through the crowd and out into the moonlight. He helped her into the car and sank down beside her.

"Well, we made it!" he cried.

He was mighty happy now. The car sped toward the station. Thank heaven that was over. Married! He was married—that was what had happened. Well, why not? Pretty good idea. He felt in his pockets—tickets all right. What was Eugene fussing about? Oh, yes, the presents. Twenty crates, twelve barrels! Good lord!

Suddenly there flashed through his mind a picture out of the past.

He was standing on a curb somewhere, waiting for a trolley. A truck went by, an enormous truck. On it was painted in great gilt letters: The Acme Fireproof Storage Warehouse, Inc.

Ah, yes. So that was all right too.

"Bob dear, what are you thinking about?" asked Dell.

"About life, Dell. Life's looking up. The future never seemed so bright. It's filled with you."

"Happy?"

"Happy!" He held her close. "Words, Dell, words! I'm stumped again—clean stumped. But wait till I get back to my easel. I'll say it with paint."

* * * * *

THEY were settled in the cottage at Provincetown. It was bought and paid for, the deed reposing in the bottom of the grandfather's clock that had been one of the wedding presents. It seemed to Bob Dana that for ages he had been pulling nails, wallowing in excelsior; but now the twenty barrels and twelve crates were unpacked. As each precious item emerged again into the light of day Dell had gone into ecstasies. It really was remarkable how she could delight in things.

On their way to Provincetown they had stopped for a week in New York, and Dell had done a bit of shopping. Eugene had been represented amid the wedding gifts by a generous and easily carried draft on a New York bank. In the midst of the honeymoon Bob had discovered that Dell had lists—long, appalling lists of things that were needed. For it seemed that this prodigious array of presents would not serve; there were other things vital to housekeeping—beds, tables, more chairs, prosaic kitchen ware. As soon as they reached the cottage Dell's purchases began pouring in.

"Where are we going to put all this stuff, Dell?"

"Oh, we must make room somehow. Not a thing we don't actually need. I'll find a place."

She found it.

"Bob, I don't believe you half appreciate how kind people were to us. All these lovely things!"

"Oh, Dell, sure I appreciate it. But after all, they're just things. They don't live and breathe. And what I'm thinking is—if we should want to travel—"

"Oh, but we don't—not yet. Let's not cross that bridge till we get to it."

He began to paint, a little disturbed by the things heaped up around him. Dell was learning to cook, and proving efficient, as always. Almost daily, it seemed, there was something more she simply had to have. He took to joking her about it.

"Another package for you, Victoria."

"Oh, it's that copper wash boiler. That's good. But why Victoria?"

"Seems to me the late queen was your only known rival, Dell. You know, she had so much stuff that in her last years she wasn't able to get round and pat it. So she had it all photographed and put into albums, and she'd sit by the hour turning the pages.

"That'll be you, Dell. I'll have albums made for you, and when you're old you can sit and gloat over the things you own. 'Oh, that darling highboy! Ah, what a kettle that was!'"

"Bob, don't be silly! I believe you're beginning to be sorry—"

"Nonsense, Dell! I'll never be that."

Late in August she said casually, "Bob, I meant to tell you—Father is sending on my car."

"Your car! Great Scott, Dell! Where shall we put it?" He looked anxiously about the studio living-room.

"We'll have to build a garage, of course. I've got figures on one—only five hundred dollars."

"But—but"—his spirits sank; a car—oil, gas, tires, repairs—"but, Dell, we don't really need a car."

"Of course we do! We can take an occasional trip along the Cape. It will do you good—the change, the fresh air."

"But the air—the air's pretty fresh right here."

"All right, if you don't want me to have it," a little note of martyrdom creeping in. "It's already started, but I can send it back."

"No, Dell, don't do that."

"I'll call the carpenter in the morning. Bob, it will be fine for you. We've been sticking here too closely. Every evening we can take a spin." She stopped. "Only we must have a stronger lock on the back door, and new locks on the windows. I'll speak to the carpenter about that too."

For days thereafter he worked with the noisy evidences of a five-hundred- dollar project drifting through his windows. Then the hammering came closer, new locks all round—new locks to protect this vast collection of things that had come along with Dell and were so precious—to Dell.

One evening a few weeks later she came home with a dog, a quaint specimen she had bought from a man downtown.

"Oh, Bob, look!"

"What? Say, Dell, who does he belong to?"

"He belongs to us. Company for me when you're working. Isn't he too cute?"

Bob was annoyed.

"But, Dell, look here—just another thing to care for."

"You don't mean you begrudge me—why, Bob!" He sensed impending tears. "You'd turn this poor little thing out?"

She held the dog in her lap, fondling it. Further objections, Bob knew, would be futile. He went outside. The car was standing before the cottage, its engine running merrily. Dell, excited over her newest acquisition, had forgotten it. Running along, using up gasoline—gasoline that cost money. But Dell never thought of such things. He reached in and savagely snapped off the power.

A dog! He sat down on the running board of the car. A dog, of all things! What did you do with a dog if you wanted to set out and see the world? Things, things, things! Piling up, barricading the road! He wasn't joking about them any more. They seemed in his thoughts constantly. Each article was a separate millstone about his neck, pulling him down, down into domesticity.

The dog came out and sniffed at his feet. A cunning little chap. Bob smiled, leaned down and patted him.

"Nothing personal in all this," he said. "No offense intended." He picked him up and carried him inside. "It's all right, Dell," he said. "The dog tells me he's fond of travel. What shall we call him?"

In October Bob finished what he was doing—a portrait of Dell ordered by Eugene. It was shipped to Mayfield, acknowledged by a letter of kindly praise and a check. He would have preferred the latter from some one else. Still, he had earned it; it was no gift from the First National.

The days grew increasingly cold; an icy wind began to sweep in from the sea. They couldn't remain in Provincetown through the winter. The knowledge cheered him, buoyed up his spirits. He became the gay lad of old, a bit of sunshine round the house. For he was studying the newspapers— certain pages of the newspapers, that is; the pages headed, "Steamships and Tours." What magic words!

"Reduced Fares to Europe."
"It's Summer on the Mediterranean."
"Have You Ever Heard the Beat of Desert Drums?"

One Sunday afternoon late in October, as they sat together in the studio before the fire, he decided it was high time to speak.

"Look here, Dell, I've been thinking—"

"Yes, Bob?"

"How about winter? We don't want to spend it here."

"No, of course not."

"Have you—er—noticed the newspapers lately?"

"Not particularly. Why?"

"There's a great deal of talk about ships, Dell. Summer seas and strange, interesting ports."

"Is there, Bob?" She smiled a little sadly.

"Look here, I've got nearly three thousand in the bank. Why can't we just lock up and beat it? I'd like to show you round the Mediterranean. It's my old-home ocean; I know it well. Gibraltar, Algiers—a few months in Sicily and Naples. You'd love it."

"And how about your work, Bob?"

"Oh, I could get a little done. Not much, perhaps; but I'd pick up a lot of color. Then when we came back in the spring—"

"We'd be broke," said Dell. "And we can't be broke next summer, Bob, you know that."

His heart sank.

"I suppose you're right," he said, remembering.

"I'm sorry, dear," Dell went on gently. "Some time later, but not now. Now—if you stop work for an instant we're lost. You've got to go on making money. I'm afraid it's like that, Bob. Being married, I mean." He said nothing. "I've been thinking, too," Dell continued. "My plan is, let's go up to Boston and take a studio apartment. It's cheaper than New York, and I've got a lot of college friends there; people who would help us. I'll arrange an exhibit of your work and we'll sell something, I'm sure. Then, too, there's Myra Tell. They've loads of money, and they want a portrait of the grandmother. I've practically arranged it. It's a big chance. You don't know; it might lead to great things for us."

He stared at her in wonder.

"You've arranged it!"

"Yes; and I've got on the trail of an apartment for the winter. We can get it, furnished, beginning next month. They want to know right away."

The dog rose from beside the fire, stretched lazily.

"What would you do with him?" Bob asked.

"Mrs. Goodrich, down in the town, will take him; and her husband will keep an eye on the house for us."

"You—you've arranged that too?"

"I've spoken to her. What do you say, Bob? Don't you think it's the thing— "

"What does it matter what I say? It's all arranged, I guess." His tone was bitter.

"Why, Bob, it's a grand scheme! A change for you, and no interruption in your work. We'd have to take only a few things—I think it would be nice to have the car. We could keep it in a public garage. And then just silver and china, bed and table linen—"

He got up from his chair. His face was terrible.

"Bob, Bob, where are you going?"

"For a walk. Let me alone. I want to—think."

He strode blindly from the house, took unconsciously the path toward the town. What was all this that had happened to him? Had he nothing to say about his own life any more? Only a few things! Things, things! Linen and china and silver! The confounded car! So this was to be his winter!

He went out upon the pier, sat down on a pile of rope and stared across the harbor. He used to be so glib; why couldn't he find words to assert himself? Why couldn't he explain to Dell, win her over? The water was cold and rough, little white-caps on it. In the Mediterranean it was warm, unbelievably brilliant; this same water, washing far shores. Algiers, the desert drums, the Bay of Naples, with the green hill of Posilipo, smoking Vesuvius beyond. He wanted them again—wanted them; not later—now. Later? How many years? Old, maybe, all the joy of life gone. Married, indubitably married.

For a long time he sat there. Well, he had let himself in for this. Dell had warned him, given him his chance to escape; he had refused to go. Poor Dell! If only she had married somebody in Mayfield—somebody who would be content to dedicate his winters to a furnace. He mustn't be unkind to Dell. He was fond of her. He must try to be like other people for Dell's sake. Dell was right too. Her plan was sensible. Boston wouldn't be so bad. Painting an old woman's portrait. Not Capri, not Sorrento. But he was married now.

He went back to the cottage. Dell was sitting as he had left her, on the sofa before the fire. As he drew nearer he saw she had been crying. He hated himself.

"It's all right, Dell." He dropped down beside her, put his arms about her. "It's a good idea. Write and tell 'em we'll take that apartment."

She looked up at him.

"Poor Bob," she said.

"Oh, no," he objected. "Don't pity me. I won't have that. I'm going to try to be a solid citizen. Help me, Dell."

"You were so innocent," she said. "Some other girl would have got you if I hadn't."

"I'm glad it was you," he smiled. "I love you, Dell; now more than ever."

"Stick to it," Dell whispered.

He glanced about the room.

"I'll do the packing myself," he told her. "I'm getting good. How long will it take us to get ready?"

"Not more than a week," said Dell.

A busy week; barrels, crates and nails again. Dell flew about wildly but efficiently, wrapping, packing, storing. On a dull, foggy morning early in November Bob sat on a packing case, his work done. Just inside the door reposed a huge pile of luggage ready for the car. He lighted a cigarette.

His mind went back to that night when he had stood with Dell on Eugene's porch—only last July, but it seemed longer ago somehow; that calm night when he had discovered that he was, after all, a marrying man. What was it he had said? "And that bright morning—just before we lock the door. It won't take you long to pack?" And Dell had answered, "Five minutes. Only an overnight bag."

It wasn't that she had meant to deceive. She just didn't know how things would be.

He had been at it a full week. Hammering for a week, and they were going only as far as Boston. And the bright morning was glum with fog. He smiled, glanced round the dismantled room, at the clutter of barrels and boxes all about him.

"I know what marriage means," he thought. "It means possessions."

The expressman was knocking at the door.

* * * * *

IN the Boston apartment was sunny and cheerful, and Bob settled himself for a happy winter. Then along came the question of the afternoon clothes. An invitation had arrived, suggesting that they drop in for tea some Sunday at the Tell home in Brookline, and immediately Dell had begun. It seemed he must array himself in a cutaway, a silk hat.

"But see here, Dell, I don't want any more clothes. I've got too many now. And why pose as a tea hound? I'm only a poor boy trying to get along."

"I won't have you looking like a tramp."

"Like a tramp? When was this?"

"There are certain things required by convention, Bob, especially in Boston. Besides, this is a very important call. If you're to get the commission for that portrait—"

"But surely they won't think I'm a better artist because I'm all dolled up. If I had my way I'd go out there in a soft shirt and my oldest hat."

"I know you would. But you're not going to have your way, Bob dear."

He held out for two days, then went to a tailor. When they finally made the call he announced that he felt like a clothing-store dummy. He acted more or less that way, too, but it didn't matter. By the time the call was over Dell had landed the job.

Grandmother Tell was too frail to come to the studio, so Bob began making daily visits to the Tell house. Dell's car came in mighty handy. "You see, I knew it would," she said. The old lady was a famous character in her set, a brilliant talker; the days slipped pleasantly by. Also, she offered possibilities for a striking portrait, and Bob worked hard.

Life was empty of annoyance, his old enthusiasms returned. The furniture in the apartment didn't trouble him; it didn't belong to him; any morning he could walk out and leave it. A comfortable feeling; he could have stayed on for ever.

By midwinter the portrait was finished and loaned by the Tells to play a leading part in an exhibit of Bob's work Dell had arranged with a Boylston Street dealer. The Tell family was well connected in Boston; the old lady had many friends and the exhibit attracted attention. Bob sold a number of his paintings—things he had done abroad. That is, Dell sold them. Not for nothing was she the granddaughter of Eight-Per-Cent. Benedict. She asked prices that took Bob's breath away, and got them too.

"Some little business manager," he said admiringly.

"You'd never have done it," she reminded him quite truthfully. "You see, Bob, you needed me. Marriage wasn't a mistake, after all."

"Not with you, it wasn't," he said. He meant it with all his heart.

And then rumors of spring began to get abroad, and depression like a great black cloud settled down on Bob Dana's soul. For Dell was chattering gayly of the cottage at Provincetown, and through Bob's mind were floating thoughts of rugs and highboys and taxes and repairs, and the old round of locking up at night.

Particularly unwelcome thoughts in April, when the soles itched and the far corners called insistently again. About this time—Italy! He pictured a village on the shores of Lake Como, a village he had been meaning to go back to long before this. And Paris—Paris with the moon on it—the boulevards in spring!

On May first, said Dell; on May first—back to Provincetown, back to all those possessions. There was no escape; she had spoken. It seemed to Bob that time had never gone so swiftly. Already he felt the nail puller in his hand.

The morning came when he actually had it there. He sat on a crate in the middle of the dismantled studio. Outside, the sun was sparkling on the harbor, the town was coming to life.

Dell had gone down to the village for groceries, and he was left alone amidst their goods and chattels. He paused in his work of unpacking and stared about him. He hated everything he saw. Things, things! Never had he felt so hopeless in his life, and yet he must clear away a little space and go to work; go to work—full of inspiration and good cheer.

It occurred to him that there was no real reason why they must unpack—not just yet, at any rate. If he could only put it off for just a little while. Why not? They had plenty of money now. Why not get aboard a ship

"See here, Dell," he began, rehearsing, "let's take a short run to Europe. Land at Genoa; little town on the shores of Como I want to show you. Buried in roses now—lovely. Then down the Riviera; season's over, we'll have it to ourselves. Then up, just to make sure Paris is still there—and home. We could be back here in plenty of time for work, and—and all that. It's nearly a year, Dell, and that morning hasn't come; that bright morning when we lock the door and go. And you know you said—"

The door opened and Dell came in, radiant, very much alive, enthusiastic. She tossed an armful of groceries on a chair.

"Bob, listen to me! I've just called at the real-estate office. What do you think? The Minturn house is for sale!"

The old, familiar sensation—that sinking feeling. His heart in his boots.

"The Minturn house!" he repeated faintly.

"Eight rooms, Bob—and only nine thousand dollars! I talked it over with the real-estate man. He said he could sell this place in a minute for twenty-seven hundred."

"Twenty-seven? Wait a minute. I paid twenty-eight, and we built a garage."

"Yes, but you paid too much. I wasn't managing things then. Twenty-seven hundred would do for a first payment on the Minturn house, and the balance on mortgage—

you know, first and second, with the second to be paid off semiannually."

He rose to his feet. The nail puller dropped from his hand, making a great clatter on the floor.

"It's the chance of a lifetime, Bob," Dell went on. "We've got to have a larger house; you know that. The Minturn place has a wonderful furnace, if we have to stay there a winter or two. And we won't need many more things—a few rugs, a regular dining-room set—a thousand dollars would cover it."

He stared at her, his face stricken. Things, things! More things! Oh, lord, was there to be no end? Mortgages—two of them—assorted mortgages. And to-night the little lake steamer would put into that town he had been dreaming of, and the people would clatter down the long flight of stone steps, and there would be the tinkle of guitars and the sound of happy voices singing, and the scent of roses in the air. Mortgages!

"I told the real-estate man I'd talk it over with you and let him know this afternoon," said Dell.

He turned toward her.

"Bob, Bob, what's the matter?"

"The matter!" he repeated. He stood looking down at her. "Do I have to tell you, Dell? Are you blind? I'm supposed to go to work—isn't that the idea? Clear a space and go to work. Well, I can't do it. I'm stifling." His voice rose. "I'm stifling under the weight of all these damned possessions you're heaping up about me. I hate them. I can't stand it any longer— I can't stand it. I never dreamed it would be like this. Just you and I and a trunk, I thought, traveling through the world, and then you began to acquire things. Things! And now a bigger house, more rugs, mortgages!"

"Oh, Bob, I didn't know " It was Dell's turn to look stricken.

"No, I suppose not. I haven't said anything. But I've been heartsick, Dell. I wasn't ready for all this—to settle down. If I'd been middle- aged, if I'd seen everything—but I was just starting out."

"You should have thought of that before you asked me to marry you."

"Did I ask you? Oh, forgive me, Dell! But I don't know yet just what happened last spring—back home. I went to May-field to paint a picture, and I never intended to get married, and the first thing I knew—"

"Bob! How can you?"

But he couldn't stop. Everything was coming out now—things he had never intended to say. Mean things, too, and unkind.

"You didn't play fair, Dell. All that talk about five minutes to pack—an overnight bag—was that on the level? Or did you know what I didn't know—how things would pile up? Possessions! I'm sick of it all, I tell you!"

Dell was standing, too, facing him now; proud, high-spirited Dell, who would endure very little talk like this.

"All right," she said in a low voice. "If that's how you feel, Bob." Her face was very pale.

"That's how I feel," he answered. He had hurt her, he knew, but he mustn't weaken now. "Listen to me, Dell. I'm going to do a bit of managing myself. Forget that house! There's nothing doing! I'm going over to Paris for a month or so. I'd like to have you come along, but that's up to you. Think it over. But whether you go or stay, I'm taking the evening train."

He walked past her, picked up his hat, went on out into the sunlight, never even looked back. He moved along, his heels sinking deep into the sandy path. At last he had asserted himself, said all the things he never meant to say. Oh, well, it was better so; better that she should understand how he felt. Eight rooms—a thousand dollars more for things! She'd think twice before she brought that up again.

If only he didn't feel so much like a little boy who had been naughty! Confound it, was he a grown man, or wasn't he? Was he captain of his soul, or was Dell? He walked on and on, labored through the heavy sand to the other side of the Cape.

Late in the afternoon he returned to the cottage. He had made up his mind he would not surrender. He had been a little harsh; he would admit it; he would assure Dell he was fond of her. But pleadings would not move him, nor tears. He must get away. They were going to Paris, if only to turn about and come home.

The door of the cottage was unfastened, the key still in the lock. As he entered the studio Dell's dog, brought back that morning from his winter home, barked joyously, leaped against him. He strode to the middle of the room.

"Oh, Dell!" he called.

No answer. A sheet of note-paper was lying on a packing case, held down by the nail puller. He picked it up.

"I'm sorry, Bob. We haven't made a go of it, I guess. But there's no sense hanging round to cry over spilled milk, so I've gone—with my trunks. You know what that means. You're free. Take a good long trip, and when you come back we'll decide what's best—divorce, separation, anything you say. But that's for the future. Just now I want you to do three things—lock the door on all these damned possessions, get aboard the first ship you come to and forget me as completely as though I'd never happened. Good-by and good luck!"

He read it over twice. Why, what—what—was the girl crazy? Just like her though. Precipitate! One word and she was off like a whirlwind.

What should he do? He sat down on the packing case and thought, while the dog whimpered at his feet. Go after her—that was one course. To Mayfield, probably. Humble himself, beg her to return. Well, hardly. She didn't appear to be brokenhearted, come to think of it. Pretty cold calm letter in the circumstances. Maybe she was fed up herself. Maybe she hadn't possessions enough.

"You know what that means. You're free." Well, that was what he had been longing for; to get shut of all these things; to be out on the highroad again. He had sworn to go abroad, alone or with Dell. Alone, said Dell. O. K., my lady.

He rose and switched on the light. His things were not yet unpacked—a suitcase, two trunks. However, he'd need only the steamer trunk; the other held nothing of importance—evening clothes, that silly cutaway. There was a train to New York in an hour; he telephoned the expressman. His most intimate acquaintance, that expressman.

The groceries were still lying on the chair where Dell had thrown them. He carried them to the kitchen—Dell's spotless kitchen, where he had helped with the dishes each evening. He went into the bedroom. There in the window they had stood every morning, scanning the harbor to see if their ship was in.

He wandered about, taking one last look at all these things that Dell had loved. The highboy—how she did fuss over that stiff old thing! The Georgian chair. The sewing table. He encountered the packing cases again—look here! Full of silver—valuable—how about it? An idea came, even without Dell there to suggest it. He piled them all in the one closet that had a lock, fastened the door securely. Dell'd be glad of that!

The expressman appeared.

"Third trip here to-day," he announced. "Best customers I got, you people." He took the trunk and suitcase.

Bob called the dog; it frisked about his feet.

"Come on, Pat," he said. "Big moment's here. Just lock the door and go. No cares; no responsibilities; nothing to hold us back."

The lock clicked. He stood for a moment. Where was the thrill, the elation? He'd been cheated. A heavy weight still rested on his heart.

"Get rid of that," he assured the dog. "Only natural. Wear off in time."

He stopped at the Goodrich house, was admitted to the parlor. The odor of steak frying for supper filled the world. He explained his errand. The old lady peered at him through her glasses.

"But good land, you just come home," she cried.

"I know; but Mrs. Dana has been called West. We'll try to make some arrangement soon."

"Well, I'd do anything fer Mis' Dana. But Pat's full of mischief. An' he wasn't so well last winter. I was real worried. Then there was that burglar scare; we fretted over that. They might have broke into your house."

"Don't you fret. Just keep an eye open and report."

He handed her the key. She followed him to the door, stood a gaunt shadow against the yellow lamplight.

"Come back soon," she said. "Folks that's got possessions should stay round an' look after 'em."

Bob walked slowly to the station, bought a ticket for New York, checked his trunk. Not a year ago Dell and he had stood together on this platform, Dell all excitement. "Bob, we're home!" He could picture her now in the spring dusk. The train backed in laboriously, he climbed aboard, dropped into a seat.

A ten-minute wait, then the bell rang, there was a scampering along the platform and the little train pulled out. Free—he was free! Off again on the big adventure. The key was turned on his possessions; he must forget them, that was the idea. Forget every last one of them. Nothing easier. Only—only—

"She never happened!" he said fiercely under his breath.

The high gods, who hadn't noticed him for a long time, were smiling at him again.

"She never happened!" repeated the boy on the train.

The high gods looked at one another and laughed outright.

"We heard different," they said.

* * * * *

HE was on a steamer outward bound for Naples; they were passing Sandy Hook. Again the old odor of rubber in the passageways, the old throb of engines beneath his feet. But where was the old joyous thrill of freedom, the sense of dazzling adventure waiting somewhere ahead? Well, perhaps in time

He went up and stood by the rail. The last dull vestige of land had melted away, dissolved in a sparkling sea.

"Off again, my lad," he said. Going to be gay or know the reason why. He took hold of the rail, set his teeth and determined to be carefree.

A moment later he was thinking about that key—the key to the closet where the silver was stored. He had a dim memory of hiding it somewhere, but had he? Perhaps in his excitement he had left it lying right beside the nail puller— left it where any sneak thief could find it. And Dell fairly worshiped that Italian stuff.

With a start, he came to. Fine way to be setting out, worrying about a key! Dell hadn't worried; just calmly took her trunks and went. Wasn't up to him, then. Lots of interesting-looking people aboard. Get talking with them— that was the idea—forget.

Naples again. He was back in the narrow streets he loved, under a sun already uncomfortably hot; back at his old pension. Chocolate and rolls and honey for breakfast— honey that was just the color of Dell's hair.

He was a grown man. Why did he feel like a schoolboy playing hooky? Was this what marriage did to one?

Yet that was how he felt, all the ten days in Naples; and then in Rome, in his old haunts in Florence, and even when he sat in the window of that little hotel on Lake Como, listening to snatches of grand opera drifting up from the cobbled street. Unhappy, somehow. Like a truant determined to enjoy the fishing but for ever seeing the teacher's face in the calm surface of the pool.

Restless, unsatisfied, he moved steadily northward. By mid-June he had reached Paris. There, one radiant afternoon, he lolled on a window seat in the studio of his old friend Harry Osborne, lazily smoking a cigarette and observing Osborne at his labors. Fragrant and warm through the open window came the breath of the most beloved of all cities. Under the trees in the Luxembourg Gardens a military band was playing, and now and then above the steady beat of the music arose the joyous shrieks of children at play.

"I hope I don't annoy you, loafing round here like this," Bob said.

Osborne did not turn. He was middle-aged, bearded, a man who had picked up many bits of wisdom along the way.

"You annoy me very much," he answered.

"Why, I—I'm sorry."

"Oh, not because you're in my way, Bob. But because you are—loafing. What's the idea, my boy? Work—work's the great medicine."

"I know; I ought to get busy; I meant to." Bob's face clouded. "But it's like I told you. I don't feel right somehow. I can't explain, but I keep thinking about Dell all the time— more even than when I was with her; wondering what she's doing. Oh, it's silly! But I saw from the first how it would be. I knew it even before I left New York."

"Then why did you leave?" Osborne asked.

"Well, I—I don't know exactly. I couldn't creep back to May-field, you know. I had to show my independence."

Osborne smiled, still turned toward his canvas.

"Ah, yes, your independence," he repeated. "Yet you've been pretty busy, as I see it, carrying out orders. What was it she told you to do? Lock the door—get on a ship—"

"And forget her just as though she'd never happened," Bob finished. "That was once I disobeyed anyhow."

The older man put aside his brush, rose, stretched wearily.

"Yes; but that was once she wanted you to disobey." He came over and stood looking down at the boy with a kindly glow in his brown eyes. "She was sure you could never manage it, Bob, because she understood you so well. She knew you're not all artist. If you were you could be utterly selfish, forget her in twenty-four hours. There's another strain in you—in

185

all us temperamental people from the Middle West—the heritage left us by a long line of solid, respectable citizens to whom marriage was always marriage. She was depending on that to bring you back—and she's a clever girl."

"You bet she is," said Bob.

Osborne was hunting round on a paint-stained table for a cigarette. He found it, applied a match. Over in the Gardens the band launched into an English music-hall song of ancient vintage, Hold Your Hand Out, Naughty Boy!

The older man smiled.

"Poor old Bob," he said. "You had a devil of a year, didn't you. You wanted to be married, you wanted to be free—you didn't know which. You loved your wife, and you hated your surroundings. Youth slipping away, responsibilities creeping up—ah, you didn't like that. It was war—war inside you. But that sort of thing doesn't go on. There comes a moment—resignation. After that, life straightens out. You do your job. You're at peace."

Bob stared at him.

"You always were the wise old bird, Harry."

"Do you think so? Then take my advice: I'd go home now, if I were you."

Bob Dana stood up. "Why not? I've been on the verge of it for weeks. Why not?"

"Good boy! I may see you in the fall," Osborne said. "I'm coming over."

"Oh, you are? And how about this apartment?"

"I intend to rent it for the winter."

"Say, that's an idea. We might take it—Dell and I."

Osborne smiled.

"Talk it over with your wife and let me know," he suggested. "Drop in again before you sail."

Down the narrow rickety stairs Bob Dana sped, and out into the sunlight of the Boul' Mich'. His plans were made, his course set. He was going back to Dell. He'd tell her how he'd missed her, longed for her—but it was not abject surrender he intended. Oh, no, indeed! "Dell, here's the scheme: Harry Osborne's apartment—a winter in Paris. That's the schedule." Just like that. Kindly, loving, but firm.

He hurried on through the Luxembourg Gardens, threading his way among happy children, past the bent white-haired bird tamer, past the carousel with its chipped, weather-beaten wooden horses, past corpulent old senators at rest on benches after a drowsy session in the Upper Chamber. Then through narrow streets down to the quays of the Seine, and across the Pont Royal to the right bank. Along his route lay a number of post offices, from any one of- which he might have sent his message; but somehow he wanted to put it into American hands. In the office of the cable company itself on the Rue Scribe he wrote at last what was in his mind, three words—"I'm coming home."

He returned to the street. Nearly six o'clock in Paris, but his message should reach Mayfield in the early afternoon. He pictured a blue-coated boy going up Maple Avenue on a bicycle, turning in at the Benedict drive; Dell on the steps, waiting, holdout her hand; then standing there reading his message, the sun on her honey-colored hair.

For the first time since that May evening in Provincetown Bob Dana was really happy. A great burden seemed lifted from his heart.

The next morning he arranged the earliest possible booking, then went shopping for Dell; bought her things— things she would love and look at again and again. On board the ship the only matter that interested him was the noontime posting in the smoking-room of the day's run. Three hundred and forty miles, three hundred and forty-eight—they couldn't go fast enough for him.

He paused for a few hours at his club in New York. There was no word from Dell; his heart sank. What was happening to her? He arranged to leave that evening for Mayfield.

There was a letter from Mrs. Goodrich, an incoherent, worried letter. The dog had not been well, the veterinary had seen him. A storm had blown the door from the garage, and before they could get it repaired the car had disappeared. There was a rumor of one found in Harwich, but it must be identified. Some one had broken a kitchen window. Mrs. Goodrich did wish they'd come home soon.

There was also a brisk snappy note from the real-estate man. He had a purchaser for the cottage. The Minturn house was still on the market. Mrs. Dana had spoken of buying it; would suggest immediate action both cases. Please advise.

Bob put the letters away in his pocket; must talk these things over with Dell. If they were going to Paris—still, his ideas on that point were not so clear. Maybe—but just now the important thing was to see Dell again, hear her voice, her laugh, look into her eyes. Strange she had sent no word of greeting— she knew his ship. Perhaps—no, hardly. But what had happened?

Night came, and he boarded a train for the West. An hour after he left New York a telegram from Mayfield arrived for him at his club.

On the following afternoon his train pulled up beside the ancient C. B. & D. station in his old home town. Instantly he was out on the platform, looking eagerly for Dell. No sign of her. And then Eugene came toward him, a solemn, dignified Eugene at sight of whom he felt that old sinking of the heart.

"Hello, Bob," said Eugene. "The car's right here. Jump in."

He climbed meekly to Eugene's side. The train slipped by, Main Street stretched ahead.

"I figured you'd be on Number Four," Eugene remarked, starting his engine. "It was the first train you could get after my telegram."

"What—what telegram?" asked the prodigal.

"You mean to say you didn't get it?" Eugene demanded. The car started.

"Not a word! What—what's happened? Is Dell all right? You—you don't mean—"

Eugene, still solemn, nodded. "Yesterday," he said.

"But—but I thought—not for three weeks yet. I intended to be home, of course."

Bob was solemn too.

"You never can tell about these things," said Eugene wisely.

"But Dell—poor Dell—is she—"

Eugene, ever ready with the ancient, hackneyed phrase, answered promptly.

"Mother and child," he said, "are doing well."

They were on Maple Avenue now, speeding along. A calm, sleepy old street, under its arch of elms, seemingly an uneventful street. Yet on Maple Avenue big things had happened to Bob Dana—were happening now; complete surrender, the end of a war. For he knew that the debate was over, and he wasn't sorry. "You do your job. You're at peace."

He thought of the Minturn house—eight rooms. He'd take it by wire. He could go on and move the stuff himself—the nail puller, the hammer again. Into his mind flashed a picture of himself opening the door of the grandfather's clock, tossing a key inside; the key to the closet that held the silver. He remembered at last.

Eugene was losing a bit of his solemnity.

"I'm glad to see you, Bob," he said. He brought the car to a stop by the side door. "Dell's mother and I don't know what this was all about, but we hope it's fixed now."

"It's fixed," Bob said. He ran inside, on into the front hall, up the stairs two at a time.

"Dell!" he cried. He paused for a moment in the doorway, then went to the side of the bed, took her hands. She was looking surprisingly well, her eyes shone. "Dell, dear"—he kissed her gently—"I'll never forgive myself—not being here—"

"Why, that's all right, Bob," she said. "I sent you away." There was something in the clasp of her hand that was different—not so strong, not so confident as it had been. "Did you enjoy your freedom, Bob dear?"

"It didn't seem the same old freedom, Dell."

"Oh, Bob, I'm sorry."

"No, you needn't be. I'm not. And it was a pretty good thing for me to find it out. I wonder if that's why you sent me off. You're such a clever one."

"I wonder," she smiled.

"I won't leave you again, Dell. I couldn't. It wasn't just words in the drawing-room; it wasn't the license over at the city hall; it was getting married—you and I. Together—from now on!"

"And you won't mind the things that come along with me, Bob?"

"I'll love 'em."

She waved a white hand toward the other bed. He had almost forgotten, but he turned now with sudden interest. A small, still bundle lay there, wrapped in a fluffy blanket. Bob stared at it in awe, and as he stared it moved.

"Another thing that's come along with me," Dell said.

The bundle moved again. And Bob Dana knew what he had known under the elms on the avenue—his days of revolt were over. Houses might be sold, furniture stored, automobiles stolen, a dog left with the neighbors; but this— this was different.

"It's his turn next," Dell said. "His turn to be young and free and see the world—before some girl gets hold of him."

"That's true," Bob answered. He rose, walked to the bed. "I guess we'd better start right in—gathering things— for him. So he'll have passage money when his time comes to sail."

He tiptoed closer to the bed. Dell's vision of him blurred a little, for she saw in him the pathos of all the gay, casual lads caught and domesticated since the world began.

But Bob was not unhappy. He was humble, awed; then amazed, for the bundle stirred again and a thin voice emerged. He leaned over, lifted a corner of the blanket. A roving gaze was suddenly fixed on his face. He was looking into the blue eyes of his latest possession.

THE DOLLAR CHASERS

First published in The Saturday Evening Post, Feb 16 &
23, 1924

IT was a lovely, calm evening in San Francisco, and the sun was going down on Simon Porter's wrath. An old habit of the sun's—often it rose to find Simon in an equally turbulent mood, for twenty years of daily newspaper editing had jangled Simon's nerves and wrath sprang eternal in his human breast.

He crossed the city room in his quest of the youngest— and, as it happened, the ablest—of his reporters. The boy he sought was seated before one of the copy-desk telephones, gazing fondly into the transmitter and speaking honeyed words.

"Say, that's mighty kind of you, Sally.... No, haven't heard about it yet, but I probably will.... To-morrow night at six. Pier 99. I'll be there. And I may add that in the interval, time will go by on lagging feet. No, I said lagging. It's poetry. See you to-morrow, Sally. Good-by."

He turned to meet the chill eye of his managing editor.

"Ah," Simon Porter said, "so you call her Sally."

"Yes, sir," Bill Hammond answered respectfully. "It saves time."

"Does old Jim Batchelor know how you address his only child?"

"Probably not. He's a busy man."

"He'll be a lot busier when he hears about you. He'll have you boiled in oil. A newspaper reporter at fifty a week!"

"A mere pittance," Bill Hammond agreed, and would have pursued that topic further.

"All you're worth," added the editor hastily. "I suppose the girl told you. I begin to see now. The whole idea came from her."

"She mentioned a delightful possibility," said the boy. "However, I take my orders from you."

Simon Porter relapsed into wrath.

"Gives me about enough reporters to get out a good high-school magazine," he cried. "And then sends one of them off on a picnic to please a girl!"

"Yes, sir," put in Bill Hammond brightly.

"I'm speaking of our respected owner. He's just called up—you're to go aboard Jim Batchelor's yacht for a week-end cruise to Monterey. Golf at Del Monte and Pebble Beach; and if there's anything else you want, ask for it. The launch will be at Pier 99 to-morrow evening at six. But you appear to know all this."

"It sounds more authentic when you say it, sir."

"Bah! It's an assignment. I don't suppose she told you that."

"No, sir. She didn't mention sordid things."

"There's been an Englishman named Mikklesen afflicting this town for the past week. He's just back from ten years in the Orient and he isn't fond of the Japs. Neither is Jim Batchelor. Neither is our beloved owner. You're to listen to Mikklesen talk and write up his opinions."

"Sounds easy," commented Bill Hammond.

"It's a cinch. Listening to Mikklesen talk is what those who hang round with him don't do nothing else but. All rot though. With real news breaking every minute—and me short of men!"

He started to move away.

"Er—I presume I don't come in to-morrow," suggested the reporter.

His chief glared at him.

"Who says you don't? That line you got off about time going by on lagging feet—you spoke too soon. It won't lag. I'll attend to that—personally. You report to-morrow as usual."

"Yes, sir," answered Bill Hammond meekly. A hard man, he reflected.

"And listen to me." The managing editor retraced his steps. "About this Sally Batchelor—I suppose she's easy to look at?"

"No trouble at all."

"Well, you keep your mind on your work." His expression softened. "Not a chance in the world, my lad. Old Jim Batchelor couldn't see you with the telescope over at Lick Observatory. It's money, money, money with him."

"So I've heard."

"He's still got the first dollar he ever earned. He'll show it to you. Where is the first dollar you earned?"

"Somebody," said Bill Hammond, "got it away from me."

"Precisely. That's where you and old Jim are different. I'm telling you. I don't want to see a good reporter go wrong."

"A good reporter, sir?"

"That's what I said."

Bill Hammond smiled. It brightened the corner where he was.

"To-morrow," he ventured, "is Friday—the day before the pay check."

"I'll give you an order on the cashier," said Simon. He wrote on a slip of paper and handed it over.

"Twenty-five dollars!" Bill Hammond read. "And I was thinking of a yachting suit!"

Simon Porter smiled grimly.

"You take your other shirt and go aboard. Your role is not to dazzle. I've just got through telling you."

And he strode away to the cubby-hole where he did his editing.

His departure left Bill Hammond alone in the city room, for this was an evening paper and the last edition was on the street. Jim Batchelor's prospective guest remained seated by the copy desk. He was, to judge from his expression, doing a bit of thinking. Some of his thoughts appeared to be pleasant ones, while others were not so much so. The grave mingled with the gay, and this had been true of his reveries ever since that exciting day when he first met Sally Batchelor.

Sent by his paper to cover a charity fete for the benefit of some orphanage, he had caught his first glimpse of Sally's trim figure while she was yet afar off. Instantly, something had happened to his heart. It had been, up to that moment, a heart that had lain singularly dormant in the presence of the opposite sex. But now it leaped up, threw off its lethargy and prepared to get into action. It urged him to fight his way at once to this young woman's side.

Arrived in that pleasant neighborhood, he realized that his initial impression, startling and vivid as it had been, had not done the poor girl justice. She smiled upon him, and his heart seemed to say that this was the smile it had been waiting for. She was selling flowers, her prices were exorbitant; but the soft, lovely voice in which she named them made them sound absurdly reasonable. The somewhat unsteady Bill Hammond became her steady customer. Gladly he handed her all the money he had; and in other ways, too, it would have been evident to an onlooker that he was ready and willing to take her as his life's companion. If not, why not?

The answer was not slow in coming. Some busybody insisted on introducing them, and at mention of her name Bill Hammond knew that this girl was, alas, not one of the orphans. True, she had at the moment only one parent—but what a parent!

Jim Batchelor, president of the Batchelor Construction Company, was the sort of man who never let an obstacle stand in his way; but as an obstacle he himself had, off and on, stood firmly in the way of a good many other people. And he would certainly make the stand of his life in the path of any practically penniless young man who had the audacity to admire his daughter.

This bitter thought clouded the remaining moments Bill Hammond spent in the girl's company, and presently he left the charity fete, resolved never to speak to her again. But as time went on it began to appear that the afternoon had been more eventful for him than for any one else, the orphans included. He had fallen in love.

Love comes to many as a blessed annoyance, and so it came to Bill Hammond. Up to that moment he had been happy and carefree; which is to say, he had been young in San Francisco, no more appropriate city in which to spend one's youth having as yet been built by man. Now he had a great deal on his mind. Should he give up all thought of the girl and go his way a broken man? Or should he get busy and acquire such wealth that his own paper would speak of the subsequent marriage as the union of two great fortunes? Generally, he favored the latter course, though the means to wealth did not appear to be at hand, as any one who has worked on a newspaper will appreciate.

Meanwhile he was accepting dinner and dance invitations of the sort he had previously eluded. If his plan was to avoid Sally Batchelor, it did not work. She was frequently among those present, and, seemingly unaware of the vast difference in their stations, she continued to smile upon him. A sort of friendship—nothing more, of course—grew up between them. She accepted his escort occasionally, had tea with him at the St. Francis. And now she had arranged for him to go on this yachting trip and meet her famous father. He was to beard the mighty lion in his palatial floating den.

He was, there in the dusk of the city room, a bit appalled at the idea. Ridiculous, of course. Why should he fear Jim Batchelor? As far as family went, he had all the better of it. His ancestors had been professional men and scholars, while Jim Batchelor's were neatly placing one brick in close juxtaposition to another. But money—ah, money. Those few bonds his father had left him, the paltry additional bunch that would be his when Aunt Ella died—chicken feed in the eyes of Batchelor, no doubt. In this cold world only cash counted.

Cynical thoughts, these; he put them from him. The spirit of adventure began to stir in his broad chest. Sally had been kind enough to arrange this party; she would find he was no quitter. He would go and meet this demon father face to face. He would discover what it was all about—the awe with which men spoke of the money king. Probably a human being, like anybody else. Yes, as Simon had suggested, he would take his other shirt Suddenly his thoughts took a new and more practical turn. He pictured himself arrayed for dinner on the Batchelor yacht. In what? There was, he recalled, not a single clean dress shirt in his room, and his laundry would not be returned until Saturday. As for buying new linen, the dent in that twenty-five dollars would be serious. What to do?

He pondered. Beyond, in the cubby-hole known—secretly—among the reporters as the kennel, he saw Simon Porter frowning savagely over a rival paper's last edition. Should he ask more money from Simon? The profile was not encouraging. Then into his mind flashed the picture of a Chinese laundry on Kearny Street he had passed many times. It was, according to the sign, the establishment of Honolulu Sam, and a crudely lettered placard in the window bore this promise:

LAUNDRY LEFT BEFORE EIGHT A.M. BACK SAME DAY

What could be fairer than that? Honolulu Sam solved the problem.

Bill Hammond rose, called a good night to the man in the cubby-hole and was on his way. It was his plan to go somewhere for a brief and lonely dinner, then hurry to his apartment, gather up his laundry and place it in the hands of the speedy Honolulu Sam at once. After which he would return home and get a good night's sleep. It had been a long time since he'd had one, and he felt the need of it—

But such resolutions are rarely kept in San Francisco. Men hurry to their work in the morning, promising themselves that it will be early to bed that night for them. And then, late in the afternoon, the fog comes rolling in, and vim and vigor take the place of that cold-gray-dawn sensation. As a consequence, another pleasant evening is had by all.

Bill Hammond met some friends at dinner, and when he finally returned to his apartment it was too late to disturb the Chinese from Hawaii. He made a neat bundle of his proposed laundry, set his alarm clock for six and turned in.

"Get lots of sleep on the yacht," he promised himself.

At seven-thirty next morning he stood at the counter of Honolulu Sam.

"Back five-thirty this afternoon," he ordered loudly.

"Back same day. Maybe seven, maybe eight."

"Five-thirty," repeated Bill Hammond firmly.

Sam stared at him with a glassy eye and slowly shook his head.

"Dollar extra for you if you do it," added Bill, and laid the currency on the counter.

Sam appropriated it.

"Can do," he admitted.

"All right," said Bill. "I'll depend on you." He had meant the dollar only as an evidence of good faith, to be paid later. But no matter. A Chinese always kept his word.

He went out into what was practically the dawn, feeling confident of the future. With five clean shirts and other apparel in proportion, let them bring on their yacht. Easy, nonchalant, debonair, he would make himself the pride of the deep—and of Sally. Ah, Sally! At the corner of Post and Kearny, the flower venders were setting out their wares. Bill took a deep breath. Life was a garden of blossoms.

When he reached the office, Simon Porter robbed the garden of its fragrance by sending him on a difficult assignment. All day he was kept hustling, with no time for lunch. It was exactly five-thirty when he grabbed his suitcase and set out for the bounding wave. Simon met him at the door and bowed low.

"Bon voyage, little brother of the rich," he said. "By the way, I've just heard you're to have a very distinguished fellow passenger."

"Of course. The Prince of Wales."

"Nobody so jolly—Henry T. Frost."

"What? Old Henry Frost?"

"Our beloved owner, our dear employer, the good master who has it in his power to sell us all down the river—and would do it without batting an eye. Here's your chance. Make the most of it, win his love and respect, and when I die of overwork, as I certainly shall inside a week, maybe he'll give you my job."

"I can't say I'm yearning to meet him," admitted Bill Hammond.

"You're talking sense. I've met him at least three hundred times, and I've always had cause to regret it. You know, something tells me you'd better stay at home. You could develop whooping cough, and I could send one of the other boys."

"Nonsense!"

"To-day is Friday."

"What of it?"

"Friday the thirteenth. Does that mean nothing to you?"

"Not a thing, sir. See you later."

"Well, fools rush in " began Simon, but Bill Hammond had disappeared.

* * * * *

YOUNG Mr. Hammond felt not at all foolish as he hurried down Market Street, bound first for the establishment of Honolulu Sam and later for Pier 99. The going was slow, for the street was crowded with commuters on their way to the ferries. This little cruise, he thought, might very well prove the turning point in his life. The next few days were as bright with glittering possibilities as a Christmas tree decked for the great occasion.

He turned down Kearny Street, that thoroughfare of adventures, and at Post an adventure befell him. The traffic was held up, and he was hurrying to cross in front of a very wealthy-looking automobile, when a familiar voice called, "Whoo-hoo, Bill!" He looked, and from the window of the car he beheld protruding the head of Sally Batchelor. It was a lovely sight, but one he would gladly have dispensed with at the moment. However, he had gazed straight into her bright eyes, and to pretend not to see her was now out of the question. He circled a plebeian taxi and reached her side. She was holding open the door of the car.

"This is luck," she cried gayly. "We're on our way to the pier. Jump in."

Jump in! Without his laundry! A cold shiver ran down his spine. Luck, she called this meeting, but he was not so sure. He noted that there were three other people in the car—an elderly woman and two men. One of the latter was undoubtedly Jim Batchelor, and—yes, the other was Henry Frost. Millions sitting there!

"I—I'm sorry," Bill stammered. "I've got a very important errand first. I'll see you later."

"What sort of errand?" inquired Sally.

"It's—it's just round the corner—"

"Get in. We'll take you there."

He shuddered at the thought of this fifteen-thousand-dollar car, with two Japanese servants on the driver's seat, pulling up before the headquarters of Honolulu Sam, laundry left before eight a.m. back same day.

"Oh, no, no, really—you go along, Sally. I'll follow in a taxi."

The traffic cop had signaled for an advance and a presumptuous flivver was honking indignantly just behind Jim Batchelor's magnificence.

"Go along, Sally," urged Bill Hammond nervously. A passing car flipped his coat tail.

"We'll draw up at the curb in the next block and wait for you," she answered, smiling sweetly. Obedience wasn't in her, evidently. "Here, give me your suitcase. I'll keep it for you."

"Ah—er—no—no." He hugged it tight. "I'll keep it. I need it."

Another picture anguished him—the vision of himself rushing back into Jim Bachelor's presence with a large package all too obviously laundry. The clamor in the rear increased; the traffic cop was approaching.

"What's the idea here?" he wanted to know.

"Go along, Sally," Bill pleaded again.

Now that he had the law on his side, she obeyed. Sinking back into the car, she closed the door in the policeman's face.

"Don't be long, will you?" she smiled.

The car began to move, and Bill dodged between it and the flivver, holding the precious suitcase close. Leaping for his life, he made the opposite curb, while angry chauffeurs inquired as to his sanity. He hurried on, groaning. Of all the inopportune meetings—

A bell clanged loudly behind him as he entered the steamy precincts of Honolulu Sam. He tossed a red check on the counter, and plumping his suitcase down beside it, began to unfasten the clasps.

"Come on," he called. "Little speed here. Give me that wash."

The figure that emerged from the rear was not that of Honolulu Sam, but of a bent and aged Chinese wearing a pair of badly steamed spectacles. Sam, having business over on Grant Avenue, had left the place in charge of his uncle, down from Sacramento on a visit.

"Hurry, man, hurry!" cried Bill Hammond, waiting impatiently above his open suitcase.

But speed was not one of uncle's inborn traits. He deliberately wiped his spectacles on the tail of a handy shirt, took up the red check, and stood helplessly in front of the finished work.

"Please, please!" cried Bill. "It's done—I know it's done. I paid a dollar extra to make sure. Where's Sam? Say, listen, we're keeping all the money in San Francisco waiting. Let me help you—oh, I can't read that stuff. But please get a move on."

The old man made a gesture as of one requesting peace. He turned reproving spectacles upon the customer. They were steaming up again. Once more he studied the rack, while Bill Hammond chattered wildly at his elbow. Finally the Chinese reached up and captured a fat package. Bill snatched it from him, tossed it into his suitcase and began to strap the latter up. The Chinese was holding the two pieces of the check close to his eyes.

"One dolla," he announced.

"And very cheap too," said Bill.

He paid with a five-dollar bill, receiving in change four of those heavy silver dollars still in circulation on the coast. As he dashed out the door the bell rang again like an alarm. The old Chinese was once more applying the tail of the shirt to his spectacles.

Making admirable speed, Bill Hammond returned to Post Street and located the splendid equipage that awaited him. One of the Japs stood ready to take his bag and open the door. A bit breathless, he climbed in and established himself on one of the little collapsible chairs in front, the other of which was occupied by Sally. He sat sidewise and Sally sat sidewise, and the introductions began.

"Aunt Dora, this is Mr. Hammond." Bill bowed. The large, commanding woman on the rear seat, who was mainly responsible for the congestion there, bowed also—sternly. "And do you know Mr. Frost?" Sally continued. "You ought to—you work for him."

Bill looked into the cold, fishy eyes of his employer. Henry Frost had the appearance of a deacon, though such was not by any means his reputation.

"How do you do, sir?" said Bill, uncomfortably. "Mr. Frost can't possibly know all those who labor in his cause," he added.

"And Father. Father, this is Mr. Hammond."

Father held out a thin small hand. He was, indeed, a thin small man, quite unlike the accepted figure of the great financier. His face was ascetic, his eyes rather dreamy; there seemed, at first glance, nothing about his personality that would strike terror to an opponent. The aunt, towering like Mont Blanc at his side, was far more impressive, and knew it.

209

"I'm glad to meet you, Mr. Hammond," said the millionaire. "Sally has spoken of you, I believe."

"It's mighty kind of you, sir, to take me along like this—"

"An office assignment, I understand," put in Henry Frost in a high, unlovely voice.

"Oh, that's merely incidental," said Batchelor. "You'll find Mikklesen very interesting, Mr. Hammond. Ought to get a good story. But you're not to let work interfere with your outing, even if Henry—Mr. Frost—does happen to be with us."

He smiled.

"I'll try not to, sir," Bill answered, smiling too. He felt much better. A human being, after all.

"I'm afraid my party's going to be rather a stag affair," Jim Batchelor said, as the car swung into the broad expanse of Market Street.

"Well, we're used to that," said Sally. "Aren't we, Aunt Dora?"

"We ought to be by this time," sniffed that lady.

"There'll be Mrs. Keith, however," Batchelor went on.

"Mrs. Keith!" Henry Frost raised his bushy eyebrows.

"A very charming woman, Henry," said Jim Batchelor. "Lived in China a great deal, I believe. I want to have a talk with her about conditions over there. You see, this isn't only a pleasure cruise for me. There are two rather important questions I have to decide before I get back. There's that contract with the Chinese Government for bridging the Yang-tse-Kiang. I guess I mentioned it to you. I haven't made up my mind whether to make a bid for the job or not. Talking with Mrs. Keith and Mikklesen may decide me."

"I understand that Blake has already put in hi9 figures," said Frost. "He'll probably underbid you."

"Very likely. But everybody knows Blake is a crook. I imagine I can get the contract away from him if I go after it. They tell me he's waiting anxiously to know what move I'll make. I'll spoil his game if I go in." Batchelor smiled, and it was no dreamer smiling then. "However, I've got several days. The bids don't close until next Thursday."

"And the other question, Jim?" asked Frost.

"Oh, the senatorship. I'm still thinking of entering the primaries."

"Nonsense!" growled his friend. "Why get mixed up in that sort of thing?"

"Just what I tell him," said Aunt Dora. "Still, Washington would be interesting."

"Well, I don't know," mused Batchelor. "Every man has ambitions that way, I guess. At any rate, I'm taking O'Meara, the lawyer, along on this cruise to talk over the situation. When it comes to politics, he's one of the wisest."

"O'Meara!" Mr. Frost spoke rather sourly.

"It's a very mixed crowd, I'm sure," said Aunt Dora, and Bill Hammond felt that the glance she cast at him was a bit personal.

"A lot more interesting than a bunch of society folderols," Batchelor told her. "And when it comes to elegance, that end's taken care of too. I've invited Julian Hill."

"Good news for Sally, I'm sure," remarked Aunt Dora, and again the look she gave Bill Hammond had a meaning all its own.

Bill knew that they were speaking of the third vice-president of the Batchelor concern, a young man of good family and social position whose engagement to Sally Batchelor had more than once been rumored. He glanced at the girl, but she was staring straight ahead, and her charming profile told him nothing.

The car was gliding along the Embarcadero now, that romantic threshold to the Orient. Ships that were destined for far ports waited motionless but ready, and on the piers was abundant evidence of the great business done upon the waters. Suddenly Henry Frost spoke.

"It's a wonder to me you could get any one to go with you today," he said.

"Why, what do you mean?" asked Batchelor.

"Friday, the thirteenth," explained the newspaper owner.

"The thirteenth! Say, I didn't realize that!" Batchelor's tone was serious, and glancing back, Bill Hammond was amazed at the gravity of his face.

"I didn't think you did," smiled Frost, "knowing your weakness as I do."

"What do you mean—weakness? I'm not superstitious." And Jim Batchelor smiled, as though he had just remembered something pleasant. "Besides, no bad luck can happen to us—not while I've got my little lucky piece in my pocket."

His lucky piece? Bill Hammond looked at Sally.

"For goodness' sake," she laughed, "don't ask him to show it to you! That calamity will befall you soon enough, and at a time when I'm elsewhere, I trust."

The car came to a halt before Pier 99, the property of a steamship company in which Jim Batchelor was a heavy stockholder. At the end of the pier, close to where a smart launch was waiting, they found the remaining four guests who had been invited on Jim Batchelor's week-end cruise.

An oddly assorted quartet, Bill Hammond thought, as Sally hastily introduced him. Mike O'Meara he already knew, having more than once sought to pry an interview out of him. A huge, bluff, ruddy man, the lawyer was decidedly out of his element and seemed to know it, but he had a gift of gab to see him through. Julian Hill proved a suave, polished man in his thirties, garbed in just the right apparel; he had no interest whatever in meeting Bill Hammond and didn't pretend any. Mrs. Keith was at that age where a woman knows that youth is going despite her gallant struggle. She had been, Bill sensed, a clinging vine in her day; but now she was a bit too plump and no doubt found the sturdy oaks elusive.

As for Mikklesen, he delighted the eye; he made the senses reel; he was magnificent. Tall, languid, with china-blue eyes and yellow hair, his slim figure clothed in tweeds, the Englishman added an artistic touch to any scene he chose to adorn. Save when he looked at Sally Batchelor, boredom afflicted him, and the indifference he showed in meeting Mr.—er—Hammond made the attitude of Julian Hill seem a bit too eager by comparison.

When the Japanese had got all the luggage aboard the launch, the guests followed. Bill Hammond had intended to sit beside Sally, but Mikklesen and Hill beat him to it, and he reflected that competition was going to be keen in the near future. He sank down beside Mrs. Keith. The launch sputtered and was on its way to where the seagoing yacht Francesca waited haughty and aloof, lording it over the more plebeian craft that lay about her.

"Isn't this thrilling!" gushed Mrs. Keith. "You know I haven't been on a yacht for ages."

"Same here," said Bill. "Grand to be rich, don't you think?"

"It must be," sighed the woman. "I never could manage it. You must tell me all about it."

"Me?" Bill Hammond laughed. "You've got the wrong number—excuse it, please. I happen to be one of the humble poor—only a newspaper reporter."

"Oh, indeed!" Her smile faded. "How exciting—a reporter! You have the most wonderful experiences of course. You must tell me all about it."

Evidently one of the you-must-tell-me-all-about-it sisterhood, a species that dated back a bit.

"Well," said Bill Hammond cautiously, "if I'm not too busy with my work, I'll be delighted."

"Work—on the yacht?"

"I'm supposed to interview Mr. Mikklesen on conditions in the Orient."

She laughed.

"Oh, really? Mr. Mikklesen is an old acquaintance of mine. I knew him in China. I'm sure he'll tell you the most interesting things—only you mustn't believe all you hear.

"He's a dear boy, but—imaginative. Oh, so very imaginative." She glanced across to where Mikklesen was bending close to Sally Batchelor. The look in her eyes was not friendly.

On the deck of the Francesca her captain waited to greet his owner. Japanese in white coats appeared to receive the baggage.

"Dinner's at seven-thirty," Jim Batchelor announced. "After the boys have shown you to your quarters, I suggest that you gentlemen join me in the smoking- room."

"'Stag party' is right," smiled his daughter.

"Oh, well, the ladies too, of course," amended the owner of the Francesca. "I thought they'd be too busy—"

As a matter of fact, he had forgotten all about the ladies. It was his habit; he was a man's man.

One of the Japs, burdened with luggage, politely requested Bill Hammond to follow, and led the way to the deck below. Mikkleson also was in the procession, and Bill wondered if they were to share a stateroom. It was not a happy prospect, for he knew the Englishman would coolly take seven-eighths of any room assigned them. They entered a passageway off which the cabins evidently opened, and at the third door the Jap dropped Bill's modest suitcase and, staggering under the load of the Englishman's traps, led Mikklesen inside.

"This is your cabin," Bill heard him say.

"Thank heaven," Bill thought. The Jap emerged, took up the solitary bag and led the way to the next door.

"So this is mine, eh?" Bill said. "Fine! Got it all to myself, I suppose."

"Yes-s," hissed the Jap. "Francesca sleep fifteen guests."

"Good for the Francesca."

"Bath here," the servant said. He nodded toward an open door, beyond which gleamed spotless plumbing. Even as Bill looked, Mikklesen appeared in the doorway, gave him a haughty glare, shut the door and locked it.

"Bath for two cabins," the Jap said. "Yours too." He seemed distressed.

"Well, you'd better explain that to him," suggested Bill. "Otherwise I'll never see the inside of that room again," he added.

The servant disappeared. There was the sound of voices in the next cabin. Then the lock clicked in the bathroom door and the Jap was again in Bill's room.

"All right now," he smiled.

"Maybe," said Bill. "What's your name?"

"Tatu."

"Well, Tatu,—"

He handed him a bill. The smile broadened.

"He leave door locked, you go through his room, unlock," said Tatu.

"Some judge of character, Tatu. You got his number, boy. Don't worry about me, I'll bathe all right."

The Jap disappeared, and Bill stood for a moment staring through the port- hole at San Francisco's interesting sky-line. This was the life, he reflected, sailing gayly off into the unknown. His heart sank. Had he remembered to bring his shirt studs? Feverishly he opened his suitcase—thank heaven, there they were.

He went out in search of the smoking-room. On the upper deck he encountered Jim Batchelor.

"Ah, my boy, come along," said the millionaire. "Maybe we can scare up a cocktail."

They found Henry Frost already in the smoking-room.

"When do we get to Monterey?" he wanted to know.

"Early to-morrow," said Batchelor. "There'll be plenty of time for me to trim you a round of golf before lunch."

"You hate yourself, don't you?" answered Frost. "Ten dollars a hole is my answer to that."

"Piker!" chided Batchelor. "Play golf, Hammond?"

"In a fashion," Bill said. "Not so expensively as that, however."

"Oh, it wouldn't cost you anything to take him on," Batchelor replied. "He always pays. Henry's golf's a joke to everybody but Henry himself."

O'Meara came in. "Some boat you got here, Mr. Batchelor," he said, "I'll tell the world."

"Yes, it's quite a neat little craft."

"Little! It's the Leviathan of the west coast."

"Say, look here, O'Meara," Frost put in, "Jim here's got a crazy idea he's going to enter the senatorial primaries. Now you know the game—I'm relying on you to tell him he hasn't got a chance."

"I can't do that, and speak true," O'Meara replied. "He's got as good a chance as any of them. You put up your name, Mr. Batchelor," he added, "and leave the rest to us."

"Well, I haven't decided," the millionaire answered. "We'll talk it over later. Ah, Mr. Mikklesen, come in. Are you comfortably settled?"

"Oh, quite," said the Englishman. "It was most frightfully good of you to invite me."

"Well, my reasons weren't wholly unselfish," Batchelor admitted. "I've sort of lost track of things in China lately—thought you could set me straight."

"Any information I have, my dear sir, is yours. I believe you're thinking of that bridge contract."

"I am—seriously."

Mikklesen nodded.

"Of course, it's a bit risky," he said. "The government isn't any too stable, to put it mildly. There are other difficulties—I'll speak of them later. Yes, it's decidedly risky."

"You bet it is," remarked Julian Hill, who had just come in.

"But I like risks," smiled Batchelor.

"I know, Governor, but this is the limit." Mr. Hill seemed very much in earnest. "I'm bitterly opposed."

"You were opposed to that lighthouse job in South America too," Batchelor reminded him.

"I happened to be wrong that time. But something tells me I'm not wrong now. Let's keep out. Don't you say so, Mr. Mikklesen?"

"I will say this"—the Englishman studied the end of his cigarette—"if you do go in, it will be a matter of what you call the breaks. They may be for you; they may be against you. You'll need all the luck in the world."

"Ah, luck," smiled Batchelor. "That's where the Batchelor Construction Company shines. For more than thirty-five years the breaks have been our way. And I've still got my lucky piece." He took from his waistcoat pocket a silver dollar.

Frost and Hill smiled at each other and turned away, but the three other men regarded the coin with interest.

"Gentlemen," said Jim Batchelor softly, "there it is. The first dollar I ever earned. I was a kid of eleven at the time. My father was a mason and he was working on an apartment building they were putting up on Russian Hill. He heard they wanted a water boy and he got me the job. I had to fetch the water from a well that was a block away—a block down the hill. I carried an empty pail the easy route, but coming back it was filled, and I puffed and sweat and staggered up the grade. It was my first lesson in how hard money comes. On the first Saturday night I got my pay—this dollar—and I walked home with my father past shop windows that were one long temptation. 'What you going to spend it for, Jim?'

my father asked. 'I'm not going to spend it,' I told him. 'I'm going to keep it—always.' And I have. For thirty-seven years it's been my lucky piece and it's made good on the job. I've felt it in my pocket at the big moments of my life, and it's given me confidence and courage. A little silver dollar coined in 1884." He appeared to be holding it out to Mikklesen, and the Englishman reached forth his hand to take it. But Jim Batchelor restored it to his pocket.

"And it's still working for me, gentlemen," he added.

"Poppycock!" said Henry Frost.

"Maybe," smiled Batchelor. "But I hear there is a standing offer of one thousand dollars in the office of Blake & Co. for that little lucky piece. Poppycock, eh?"

"Oh, well, Blake & Co. know what a fool you are," said Frost. "They realize the psychological effect on your mind if you lost that thing. They're willing to pay for that."

"They'll never get the chance," answered Batchelor, and his eyes flashed. "I think I will go into that China thing. In fact I know I will. Gentlemen, here are the cocktails."

They stood about a table, each with a glass in his hand. As Bill Hammond looked around him, he saw that the eyes of each man present were on the pocket that held the little silver dollar. Mikklesen lifted his glass.

"Here's to your good luck, sir," he said. "May it continue."

"Thank you," answered Jim Batchelor, and they drank.

At seven o'clock Bill Hammond set out for his stateroom to dress for dinner. At the top of the main companionway he met Sally—Sally in a breath- taking gown and looking her loveliest.

"Hurry up," she said. "I'm eager for some one to help me enjoy the sunset."

"Keep the place open," he begged. "I'm really the best man for the job. Sally, I know who it is I have to thank for this little outing. You're always doing something for the orphans, aren't you?"

"Were you glad to come?"

"Glad? What weak words you use!"

"I thought you would be. The yacht's a lot of fun, really."

"It's not the yacht I'm thinking of. If you'd invited me out in a rowboat my joy would have been the same. You know—

Henry Frost and Hill came up behind them.

"Dear me," said Sally, "what a long cocktail hour! I'm afraid Dad's been telling you the story of the dollar."

"He did mention it," said Hill.

"And I'm glad he did," Bill Hammond said. "It made him seem mighty human to me. The picture of him struggling up Russian Hill with that water pail—"

"Dear Dad!" Sally smiled. "There is something rather appealing about the story. The first time you hear it, I mean.

But when you've had it pop up constantly for twenty years, as I have, you're bound to get a little fed up on it. I've been very wicked. There've been times when I wished to heaven he'd lose that dollar."

"Here too," said Julian Hill. "Particularly when it leads Mr. Batchelor into some wild adventure like this China bridge contract."

"Lose it!" cried Henry Frost. His little eyes glittered. "Why, it would ruin him!"

"Yes, I rather think it would," said Hill; and it wasn't so much what he said, Bill Hammond reflected as he hurried off to his cabin. It was the way he said it.

* * * * *

MIKKLESEN had left the smoking-room some time before, and as Bill Hammond passed the door of the Englishman's cabin he was glad to hear a voice lifted in song inside. But when he reached his own room and tried to enter the bath, he found himself locked out. As he savagely rattled the knob he was happy to recall that George Washington won his war. Confound this Mikklesen—had he no consideration for anybody?

The answer was that he hadn't; one look at him told that.

As Bill turned angrily back into his room, Tatu entered from the passageway.

"Very late, very busy," said the Jap. "Now I lay you out." And he lifted a dinner coat from Bill's suitcase.

"Never mind, I'll attend to that," Bill told him. "You go in and lay that Englishman out. Lay him out cold, and then unlock this bath for me."

Tatu hastened away, and again there was the sound of voices in the next cabin. Again the lock in the door leading to the bath clicked, and Tatu emerged. Bill dashed by him and turned the key in Mikklesen's door. He was sorry that the gentle click resulting didn't begin to express his feelings.

"You run along, Tatu," he said. "I'm in too much of a hurry to learn how to be valeted to-night. Some time when we're both free you can give me a lesson."

"You want me, ring bell," suggested Tatu, going.

Bill was hastily peeling off his clothes. If he was to have a few moments alone with Sally and the sunset, speed was the watchword. But he had been known to rise in the morning, bathe, shave, dress and reach the office in less than twenty minutes, and he was out now to smash the record.

As he was putting the finishing touches on an elaborate shave, Mikklesen began to rattle the door-knob. He rattled long and earnestly, and it was music to the reporter's ears.

"Oh, I say, old chap, you're not annoyed, are you?" Bill murmured. "Not really? How beastly!"

"Damn!" said a voice, and the clatter ceased.

Bill hurried from the bathroom, leaving the lock in statu quo. By way of preparation, he laid out his diamond shirt studs—rich-looking, if old- fashioned—the property of poor Uncle George, handed to Bill by Aunt Ella the day after the funeral.

Humming happily to himself, he lifted the great fat package of laundry into the open. Good old Honolulu Sam, he had certainly come across as promised. That back-same-day thing was on the level. Must have hurried some. Great little people, the Chinese; you could bank on them. If they said they'd do a thing, they did it. He snapped the string with his fingers and gently laid back the wrapping-paper. A bright pink shirt stared up at him.

It is astonishing sometimes, in the crises of our lives, how slow we can be in comprehending. Bill's first reaction was to wonder how this sartorial atrocity had got in with his things. He tossed it aside and was confronted by the purplest shirt he had ever met. Next in the line of march came a green shirt that would have made excellent adornment on St. Patrick's Day. Then some rather shabby underwear and eloquent socks. A few collars. But no more shirts!

Bill Hammond sat down weakly on the berth.

"Good lord," he cried. "It's not my laundry!"

And if comprehension had been slow in coming, it came now with a rush. Alone, alone, all, all alone on a restless ocean, and without a dress shirt to his name. Dinner in fifteen minutes. At least two rivals for Sally's favor present, and each an elegant dresser on and off.

And this was the cruise on which he had hoped to make a dashing impression, to win Sally's family, to say nothing of the girl herself, by his charm. How did one do that without a shirt?

Anger overcame him. Nor did he have any trouble locating the object of his wrath. That half-blind old Chinese with the steaming spectacles—there was the guilty party.

The old idiot! In one careless moment he had destroyed the priceless reputation of his race for accuracy, built up laboriously through many years of giving back the right shirt to the right customer—destroyed it utterly, doomed his race to extinction. For Bill Hammond would attend to that personally, and he would begin in the establishment of Honolulu Sam.

But time was passing; he mustn't waste any more of it planning the massacre of an aged Chinese. The problem was here and now. What to do? The weather was calm enough, but the Francesca was tossing about a bit. He might retire to his birth and plead seasickness. And leave Sally to the company of Mikklesen and Julian Hill? Not likely! No, he must have a shirt—must have one—robbery—a killing or two, maybe—but he had to have a shirt.

Was there any one aboard who would help him? O'Meara, perhaps; but no, O'Meara's shirt would go round him at least twice. As for the other men, there was not one to whom he would consider revealing his plight. Sally—if he could bring himself to tell her—would be sympathetic, but Sally had no dress shirts to distribute. That left—hold on— that left Tatu. Thank heaven he had given Tatu five dollars.

He rang the bell, and while he waited put on his underclothes. Tatu appeared. Frankness, it seemed to Bill, was the only course.

"Terrible thing's happened, Tatu," he said. "See"— he indicated the frightful pink shirt—"Chinese laundry returned the wrong wash. I haven't any dress shirt."

"Chinese not reliable people," commented Tatu.

"You've said it, my boy. Sometime you and I'll have a long talk about that. But now, Tatu, now—dinner coming on like this. What to do?" An idea flashed into his mind. "You haven't an extra shirt, have you?" he inquired hopefully.

Tatu opened his coat and revealed a fine white bosom— but no shirt went with it.

"Have extra bosom," he said. "Maybe you would like—"

Bill recoiled in horror.

"No, no, I couldn't take a chance. Must have an entire shirt. There's five more dollars waiting for you if you can dig one up."

Tatu considered.

"Maybe," he said. "I find out."

He went on his momentous errand. Bill, left alone, put on stockings and a pair of pumps. Slowly but surely the structure was approaching completion. But the shirt! Would that necessary, that vital bit of facade come to hand? Or must he sit shirtless in his cabin while the gay diners made merry round the festal board?

Something in Tatu's eye had made Bill feel that this was a moment for caution. He turned off his light and opened the door leading into the dim passageway. No one in sight. Where was that Jap anyhow? The door of the cabin at the end of the corridor began to open slowly, and a man emerged. He looked warily about him, and then, walking on tiptoe, started down the passageway. Tatu? No, it wasn't Tatu. Bill Hammond, peering from the darkness as the man passed his stateroom, saw clearly who it was. He watched him open the door of a stateroom farther down and disappear.

Nervously Bill sat down on his berth. Would Tatu never come? Why, he'd had time enough to scare up a whole outfit—Tatu appeared in the doorway. Bill leaped up, closed the door behind him and snapped on the light.

Rapture! There was a gleaming dress shirt in the Jap's hand. Like a drowning man going after the well-known straw, Bill pounced upon it.

Tatu hung on to it.

"Maybe too big," he said. "I put in studs."

He took up one of Uncle George's diamonds and began to struggle with the shirt. "Very stiff bosom," he announced. "Oh, very stiff."

"What size is it?" demanded Bill, feverishly investigating the collars bequeathed him by the owner of the pink shirt. He had a vision of sending the Jap out again for a collar.

"Doesn't tell size," whispered Tatu. "No name of maker, also. That very good."

Bill experienced a momentary qualm.

"Where'd you get this shirt, Tatu?" he demanded sternly.

"I get him," replied Tatu. "Here, try on."

"A little large," said Bill. "But it's a shirt. And say, look—this collar fits. Luck, Tatu, luck. Wow, the bosom is stiff! Got to be proud and unbending to-night." He was silent, working on his tie.

"Everything fine," Tatu hinted.

"Oh, yes, the five dollars. Here you are. Say, listen, Tatu, I'm not sure that we ought to have—er—borrowed this. We'll have to return it."

"I return it," Tatu agreed.

"That's right; of course we'll give it back, along with a dollar to cover depreciation and washing. Honesty, Tatu— the best policy. Ask anybody."

"Yes-s, thank you."

"Always be honest and you'll fear no man." The Jap was at the door. "Say, Tatu, I really ought to know where you got it."

"I got him," smiled the Jap, and went out.

Well, a desperate situation required a desperate remedy. Bill leaped into his trousers and was slipping on his waistcoat and coat when the first notes of The Roast Beef of Old England, played falteringly on a bugle by a pantry boy with ambitions, floated down to him. Mikklesen was once more rattling at the bathroom door, and first extinguishing all lights, Bill noiselessly unlocked it, then hurried up-stairs to the after deck to find Sally. Her eyes reproached him.

"The sun went down," she said, "and you never came up."

"I know," he answered; "forgive me." He straightened his collar nervously. "I was detained."

"That's not much of an explanation," she told him.

"Thank you," he said absently. He was thinking that the owner of the pink shirt certainly needed some new collars. This one had a razor edge and seemed to have been recently honed.

"You're perfectly welcome," smiled Sally, "whatever it is you're thanking me for. Pardon me for mentioning it, but are you in your right mind?"

"Of course not," he said. "I knew you were lovely, but somehow to- night—well, as the fellow said, my senses reel."

Sally rose. "We'd better have the next reel in the dining saloon," she suggested. "Dad hates people to be late."

Bill found he was to sit on Sally's right, and the discovery cheered him, particularly as Henry Frost was on the other side of her—an arrangement that couldn't be improved upon. His spirits rose rapidly. A moment before plunged in the depths of despair, he had emerged triumphant and all was right with the world. What a lot of difference somebody's shirt had made!

During the first course Jim Batchelor suggested that Mikklesen tell something of his experiences in the Orient, and from that point on the dinner was a monologue. But like most Englishmen of his class, Mikklesen was a charming talker and well worth attention. He spoke of his adventures as subeditor of an English newspaper in Shanghai, of the time he had typhoid in the General Hospital in Yokohama, of the fight he got into one gory night at the old Danish hotel where the beach-combers hold forth in that lovely port. He took his hearers into the interior of China on a scientific expedition, thrilled them with a hold-up by bandits, and brought them back in time for an audience with an ambassador or two in Peking. Life as he had known it had been glamourous.

It was not until the coffee that he appeared to run down and the conversation became general. Suddenly there was one of those inexplicable lulls in the gentle buzz of talk, and the voice of Jim Batchelor rang out in converse with Mrs. Keith at his right.

"And I have kept it—all these years. In the big moments of my life I've felt it in my pocket, and it has given me courage to go on. A little silver dollar coined in the year—"

"Oh, dear," Sally laughed, "he's telling her about his lucky piece."

"Thrilling!" Mrs. Keith said. She smiled encouragingly on the millionaire. "You've got it with you still?"

"I certainly have." He removed something from his pocket. "My little lucky piece." He stared at it, his face paled slightly. "This—is not—my dollar," he said slowly.

A tense silence fell. Sally finally spoke:

"Not your dollar, Dad? What do you mean?"

"Just what I say. This is a dollar coined in 1903." He threw it down on the table and began a search of his pockets. Again the silence. His search was evidently fruitless. "I—I'm very-sorry this has happened," said Batchelor. "It may seem rather trivial to you, but to me it's almighty important. If— if it's a joke of some sort, I—I don't appreciate it. However, I'll overlook it if the joker will speak at once. In heaven's name"—his voice trembled—"is it a joke?"

He looked eagerly into each face about the table. No one spoke. Batchelor's eyes hardened.

"Then there's some more sinister motive back of it," he said.

"Nonsense, Jim!" said Aunt Dora. "You're making a mountain out of nothing."

"I'm the judge of that," the millionaire told her, and his voice was like chilled steel. "However"—with an effort he managed to smile—"you're right, in a way. I mustn't spoil the party."

The tension lessened somewhat, and Mrs. Keith took that moment to show sympathy.

"What a pity!" she said. "Perhaps one of your crew—"

"No, Mrs. Keith," Jim Batchelor said; "my crew has been with me for years. The servants—I'm not so sure. They will all be examined before leaving the yacht. And before we drop the subject, has any one else missed anything?"

Bill Hammond's heart stood still. The shirt! Somebody would speak up regarding the mysterious disappearance of a shirt, and where would that lead? Little beads of perspiration stood on his forehead. But no one said anything. Evidently the owner of the shirt was still ignorant of his loss. Bill breathed again.

"Well, that's that," said Batchelor. "We'll let the matter drop."

"One minute!" O'Meara was on his feet. "Before we do that I've got a suggestion to make. Mr. Batchelor here has lost something of value, and until it's found we're all under a cloud. I for one want to be searched, and I guess every honest man here feels the same way."

"Nonsense!" Batchelor cried. "I won't hear of it!"

"But Mr. O'Meara is right," said Mikklesen. "I recall a dinner at the British Embassy in Peking two years ago, when the hostess lost a diamond necklace. It was a most distinguished party, but we were taken one by one into an anteroom and gone over with amazing thoroughness." He, too, stood up. "I also insist," he said.

"Rot! I wouldn't insult my guests," Batchelor was still protesting.

"You'll have nothing to do with it, Governor," Julian Hill told him. "We're going through with this for our own satisfaction. If the ladies will wait for us in the saloon—"

Reluctantly Aunt Dora, Mrs. Keith and Sally left the room. O'Meara promptly removed his coat and waistcoat.

"Now one of you go over me," he said, "and I'll do the job for the rest of you."

Julian Hill stepped forward to oblige. With a none too easy conscience, Bill Hammond also removed coat and waistcoat. That shirt was a none too successful fit—suppose some one recognized it. O'Meara, having been pronounced innocent, went at his work with enthusiasm. Evidently he had been in similar situations before. But the search had no results. Through it Jim Batchelor sat staring at the table as though the matter held no interest for him. O'Meara finished, red- faced and empty-handed.

"Well, if you boys have done with your nonsense," remarked Batchelor, "we'll join the ladies. And as a favor to me, we won't speak of this again—to- night."

Aunt Dora was superintending the placing of two tables for bridge in the main saloon. It appeared there was just the right number—with one left over. After she had disposed of the usual impassioned pleas from those desiring to be the one left out, Julian Hill was elected to that position, and shortly disappeared from the room. They cut for partners, and to his horror Bill found himself seated opposite Aunt Dora. She had the air of being the person who invented bridge, and so she had, practically.

Bill dealt. Majestically Aunt Dora took up her hand and glanced through it.

"Count your cards," she ordered. "That's the first rule. What rules do you play by, Mr. Hammond?"

"Rules?" repeated Bill wanly. "I don't know. I just play."

"We'll pivot," said Aunt Dora promptly.

"I'm afraid I don't understand," said Bill meekly.

"I mean to say, we'll change partners frequently."

"Oh," said Bill heartily, "I'm for it."

The glare she turned on him moved him to look the other way, and his eyes met those of the man he had seen creeping along the corridor just before dinner. He became suddenly thoughtful, so that Aunt Dora's voice suggesting that he bid seemed miles away. However, it came rapidly nearer.

* * * * *

AUNT DORA found, as the play progressed, that she alone seemed to be giving the matter her best thought. She was a woman of superb endurance, but after a distressing rubber with O'Meara as partner, she called it an evening and rang the gong. The ship's clock had recently struck six bells, and after a careful calculation and a look at his watch, Bill Hammond knew that to mean that it was now just after eleven.

Mikklesen and Julian Hill both seemed determined on a bedtime chat with Sally, but after a meaning look at Bill Hammond the girl dissuaded them.

"Wait till I get a wrap," she whispered to Bill. "I want to tell you about that sunset."

He had nothing in particular to do, and maybe he would have waited anyhow. When she returned she led the way to a couple of chairs that stood close together in a secluded spot on the after deck.

"Wonderful night," Bill murmured. He had sized it up about right too. The Pacific was calm—for the Pacific—the water was liquid silver in the moonlight, the breeze was not too chill. A great night to be young, and they both were.

"Glad you like it," said Sally. "It's just what I ordered."

They sat silent for a moment.

"How was the sunset anyhow?" Bill inquired.

"Not bad at all," said Sally, "for the sun. I think I prefer the moon myself." A long, long silence. "Bill, say something," the girl protested at length. "What are you thinking?"

"I'm just wishing. I'm wishing your name was Sally Jones and your father was principal of a high school—and paid accordingly. It's what I've been wishing ever since that day at the charity bazaar."

She laughed.

"Dad never wasted any time on high schools," she said. "Still, it does no harm to wish."

A cooler breeze arrived from the Pacific. Bill rose, took up a rug from a near- by chair and tucked it about her. His hand touched hers, and contrary to his intention, he seized and held it.

"Sally!" he said ecstatically.

"Bill!" she answered.

He gave up the idea and sat down. Another silence.

"How—how do you like my father?" she asked presently.

"Oh, he's all right. But it doesn't matter what I think of him. He'd be just as interested to get the opinion of one of those goldfish in the main saloon."

"Well, I don't know," said Sally. "Dad's pretty human. You must remember, he hasn't always traveled on yachts. At one time he was a stonemason, earning a hundred a month."

"How long ago was that?"

"About the time he was—married."

The way she said it, somehow; the night, the moon, the bracing effect of ocean air—whatever the cause

"Sally," Bill heard himself saying, "I'm in love. With you, I mean. But I guess that isn't news, is it?"

"Not precisely," she answered slowly. "However, I'm glad you said it. We couldn't have got anywhere if you hadn't."

"Sally!" The moon was under a cloud. It was just as well.

"It's no use, Sally," said Bill, coming to. "Your father would never hear of it."

"He'd be bound to."

"You know what I mean. He'd have me—boiled in oil."

"He'd have to boil me too."

"Sally, you're wonderful! Will you—will you take a chance with me?"

"I don't like the way you put it. I'll marry you, if that's what you mean."

"On our own—that's what I'm getting at. I've seen so many men marry rich girls and degenerate into lap dogs. I wouldn't take a cent from your father—nor a job either."

"Don't worry, you wouldn't get either."

"Sally, I never intended to tell you this. I was just going to eat my heart out in silence, like the great strong man that I am."

"Well, that would have been romantic. But I think I like it better this way. My role is a bit more active."

"Darling! Wha—what do you think I'd better do? Should I speak to your father the next time I see him?"

"Of course. Say good night or good morning, as the case may be, and that's all."

"Well, I suppose he would hit the ceiling."

"He wouldn't stamp round and forbid it, if that's what you think. It's not his way—he's too subtle. He'd just quietly queer it; nobody would ever be sure how it was done either. He's fathoms down, Dad is."

"Certainly sounds too deep for a frank, wholesome lad like me.

"I think we'd better—just drift along," Sally said. "Give him a chance to take a fancy to you."

"You believe in long engagements, then?"

"Nonsense! I'm fond of you. And Father and I are much alike." She pondered. "If you could only make a hit with him somehow. I'd never be quite happy about marrying anybody—not even you—if he was opposed. He's really wild about me."

"Naturally."

"Poor Dad. He's broken-hearted. That silly little dollar meant so much to him."

It was Bill's turn to ponder.

"You know, Sally," he said, "I've done considerable police reporting, and on more than one occasion a hard-boiled detective has complimented me. I've dug up some rather important evidence."

"Oh, Bill, that's an idea!"

"If I found that dollar for him, do you think he'd give me you as a reward?"

"He wouldn't stop there. He'd throw in Aunt Dora and the yacht."

"You give me pause. I mean—I couldn't afford the yacht."

"Bill!" Her eyes were shining. "Let's work on the case together. What's the first move? We talk over the suspects, don't we?"

"That might be a good idea. We'll start with you. You said yourself there were times when you hoped he'd lose it."

"Yes, I know. I'm sorry I said it now. Do be serious, Bill. Aunt Dora—she wouldn't take it."

"But you can't eliminate anybody that way."

"Yes, you can. A woman's intuition. Mr. Mikklesen—no motive. Mr. O'Meara—how about him?"

"He's a politician. Their ways are deep and dark."

"I feel that; and he was so insistent on being searched. That's always suspicious."

"I thought it was rather fine of your father"—said Bill—"his courtesy to his guests. He was against the search."

Sally laughed.

"Don't be fooled by Dad's courtesy," she warned. "He knew darn well nobody would be fool enough to steal his dollar and then walk in to dinner with the thing in his pocket. Dad's the soul of hospitality and all that, but he wants that dollar back, and before he gives up he'll put all his guests through the third degree, if necessary. Let's see, there's Julian Hill. He seems awfully keen to keep Dad out of that China job."

"Yes, Hill's a possibility. And how about Mrs. Keith? Know anything about her?"

"Not a thing."

"Well, she's poor," said Bill. "She told me so. But then, so am I. By the way, don't let's overlook me."

"Nonsense! You wouldn't take anything that didn't belong to you."

"You think not?" Certainly a stiff bosom on that shirt.

"Oh, Bill, it's all so hopeless," she sighed. "If we only had a shred of evidence to go on!"

"Maybe we have."

"Bill—not really?"

"You've forgotten one guest. What motive would Henry Frost have in stealing that dollar?"

"None whatever, so far as I know."

"That's the way I feel," Bill went on. "Yet as I understand it, your father's cabin is the one at the end of the corridor off which our rooms open." She nodded. "And just before dinner I certainly saw Henry Frost come out of that room, acting very queerly. He tiptoed along the corridor and slipped into his own room very unostentatiously."

"Bill! It seems ridiculous!"

"I know it does. My saintly employer! He'll be awfully pleased with me if I can fasten this thing on him."

"What are you going to do?"

"I don't know. It's a delicate situation. If I go to your father with my story, Frost will probably have some simple explanation that will make me look like a fool. It seems to me it wouldn't be a bad scheme if I put the matter up to Frost and let him explain to me—if he can."

"Good-by job."

"Probably; but in the interests of justice—and there are other newspapers."

"Well, if you really think it's the best plan—"

"Maybe not, but I'm going to try it. I can't treat old Frost as a criminal, and shadow him. I don't really think he took the dollar anyhow. But I should like to know what he was doing in that room. I'd better see if I can find him."

They rose.

"How thrilling!" Sally said. "We're in this together, remember. Sherlock Holmes and Doctor Watson. Do you think I'll do for Watson?"

"No, you're altogether too intelligent," Bill told her.

"Oh, Bill, do you think I've got brains? I love brains."

"And I love you. You—you really meant all that—about marrying me? It doesn't seem possible."

"It's more than that; it's probable. Good night—and good luck."

"This is my lucky night," he told her. And it was, for she was in his arms.

His luck held even after he left her, for he found Henry Frost sitting alone over a highball in the smoking-room. His employer evinced no joy at seeing him, but Bill casually lighted a cigar and seated himself.

"Unusually smooth passage," he remarked.

"Smooth enough," said Mr. Frost.

"Awfully jolly cruise, it seems to me. Nothing to mar it—except, of course, the disappearance of that dollar. Too bad about that."

"A great pity."

The old man drained his glass and seemed about to rise.

"Just a moment, Mr. Frost," Bill said. "You're an older man than I am, and I'd like to ask your advice."

"Yes?"

"If any one of us has any evidence that might prove useful in tracing the—er—thief, it should be passed on to our host. Don't you agree?"

"No question about it."

"I'm in a rather difficult position, sir. I happened to be standing at my door just before dinner—the light was off at my back—¦ and I saw a man come out of Mr. Batchelor's cabin and go down the corridor to his own. His actions were rather—peculiar."

"Really?"

"Now what would you do in my position, sir?"

"I'd certainly tell Jim Batchelor all about it."

"But, Mr. Frost—you were the man."

Business rivals sometimes referred to Mr. Frost's countenance as a great stone face. Not without reason, thought Bill as his employer sat grimly regarding him.

"How much," said Frost, "do they pay you at the office?"

Bill drew himself up.

"This is not a case of blackmail, sir," he said.

The old man's eyes flashed dangerously.

"Who said anything about blackmail? I was just going to add that whatever you get you're overpaid, for you're the stupidest whippersnapper I've ever met. Why should I take Jim Batchelor's dollar?"

"I don't know, sir."

"No, nor does anybody else. I did go to his room, and I filched something from him; but it was nothing of importance. I'll explain it to you, though I don't know that I'm under any necessity to do so. For years Jim and I have had an argument about valets. He claims I need one, and I claim I'm still competent to dress myself. When I opened my bag to-night I discovered that I had foolishly come aboard without any collars."

"No collars?" repeated Bill. Then millionaires had their troubles too.

"Precisely. I wasn't going to tell him—I never would have heard the last of it. I knew we wore the same size shirts, so when he was in his bath I slipped in and annexed one of his collars. That explains what you saw, and you're at liberty to go to him with your story any time you like."

"You sound fishy, old boy," Bill thought. But then, so would his tale about the shirt. "I'm not going to say anything to Mr. Batchelor," he announced. "Not for the present, at least."

"Just as you please." Frost stood up. "I'll bid you good night."

"One moment, sir. Should I go on with that interview with Mikklesen? I mean—am I still working for you?"

For a long moment they stared into each other's eyes. It was the employer who first looked away.

"Ah, yes, the Mikklesen story. Go on with it by all means."

Bill smiled knowingly as he watched Henry Frost leave the room.

"Who said anything about blackmail?" he murmured to himself.

The decks of the Francesca were deserted as Bill hurried to his stateroom. The little old berth looked good. Hastily he removed his coat, his collar, and then the ill-fitting shirt. Glad to get that off. Still, it had been better than none. He laid it down on the narrow settee that would have been requisitioned as a berth had the Francesca been sleeping her maximum fifteen. Uncle George's studs seemed to flash up at him reprovingly. A Hammond in a borrowed shirt!

"Get Tatu to return it in the morning," he thought. "I can buy another in Monterey."

Once in the berth, he lay for a time reflecting on the great event of the evening. Sally loved him. It had seemed a dream too remote to consider, yet here it was, coming true.

Life was certainly kind to him—all this happiness—obstacles in the way, of course

Ho-hum. Must find that dollar. Who had it? Funny about old Frost. Explanation didn't sound right somehow. Yet it might be true. He himself had, at a vital moment, been minus a shirt. Old boy might be absolutely on the level. How about the others—Hill, O'Meara, Mrs. Keith? So many possibilities. Confusing—sure was confusing—possibilities He slept.

He awoke with a start. It was still dark; he could see nothing; but he knew instinctively there was some one in the room.

"Whoosh there?" he muttered, still half asleep.

A noise—the opening of a door. Bill leaped from the berth, snapped on the light and looked out into the corridor. At the far end of that dim passage he saw a dark figure mounting, two at a time, the stairs to the upper deck. He grabbed his dressing gown, shuffled into his slippers and followed.

His pause to add a finishing touch to his attire was fatal to the pursuit, for when he reached the saloon deck he appeared to be alone in the world. He was fully awake now, but completely at a loss as to his course. He walked along the rail, uncertainly, toward the stern of the boat. Suddenly he stopped.

The sight that arrested him was not on the yacht, but on the calm surface of the moonlit waters. There, floating rapidly away from the Francesca on the wet Pacific, was a white shirt—a dress shirt. The thing was unbelievable, yet there it was; and—did he imagine it?—were not those Uncle George's precious diamond studs sparkling in the bosom that lay on the broader bosom of a very large ocean?

Farther and farther away drifted the shirt with Uncle George's legacy aboard, and, fascinated, Bill moved along the rail, his eyes glued upon it in fond farewell. A voice spoke suddenly and his heart stood still.

"Hello! Out for a stroll?"

He turned. A dark figure was sitting in the lee of the dining saloon, and the red light of a cigar burned steadily.

"That you, O'Meara?" Bill asked.

"Sure is. Lovely night, ain't it?"

"Have you been here long?"

"About an hour and a half. Seemed a pity to turn in a night like—"

"Never mind the night. Who was it ran up here just before I did?"

"Who was what?"

"Somebody was in my cabin—I followed him up here."

"Say, Kid, you'd better take something for your nerves. You're the first human being I've seen for an hour and a half."

"Been here all that time, eh?" said Bill. "Yet that cigar's just been lighted."

"It happens to be my third," said O'Meara. "And if I was you, I wouldn't try the detective business. It ain't for kids. There's something doing on this boat—we all know that. But I'm not in on it. I'm just on a little cruise for my health—see?

Just out to get a little peace and quiet after a busy week in the city. And that's what I was gettin' until you dashed up like a wild man and made a nasty crack about my cigar."

"Oh, no offense," said Bill. "Only—"

"Only what?"

"I suppose you were so taken with the peace and quiet you missed that other fellow completely."

"You go back to bed and rest them nerves."

"That's what I'm going to do," Bill answered, and left him.

He was, indeed, in a great hurry to return. He dashed into his stateroom and looked anxiously about. It was as he feared—the shirt was gone! And Uncle George's studs! What would Aunt Ella say?

He sat down on the edge of his berth, trying to grasp this weird turn of events. Somebody had taken a violent dislike to his having that shirt. Who? The owner probably. That was it, the owner had recognized his property at the time of the search, and now But who was the owner? Well, he could find that out in the morning from Tatu.

He yawned. It was all very confusing. Why should this mysterious stranger come to claim his property in the silent night? Why, having regained it, should he toss it on the chill Pacific's bosom? Had all this any connection with Jim Batchelor's dollar? Questions—questions. All very confusing. One thing was certain—O'Meara had been lying. Bill yawned again; his berth looked warm and inviting. He rose, turned out the light, left dressing gown and slippers in the middle of the floor, and was soon deep in slumber.

* * * * *

BILL HAMMOND was awakened next morning by the noise of Mikklesen singing in his bath. The Englishman had a pretty fair voice, through which at the moment rang a note of triumph natural to one who was securely locked in and had the plumbing all to himself.

The splash of water served as a merry accompaniment.

"The same old story," Bill muttered, "Britannia rules the waves." He looked at his watch—eight-thirty—high time to be up and doing.

If he knew Mikklesen, however, it would do him no good to hurry. He lay where he was, watching the fresh salt breeze flutter the curtain at his port-hole. Outside was a clean blue world, an empty world. Restful, this cruising on one's yacht.

Something pleasant had happened—ah, yes, Sally. She loved him. Other things had happened, not so pleasant. That silly little dollar he had sworn to find. Might be more of a job than it had looked last night in the moonlight with Sally by his side. Somebody had it; somebody who knew only too well its value and was guarding it close against the time when it could be traded in for a goodly supply of its little playmates. Somebody—but who?

He thought of Henry Frost, with his foolish story of a collar shortage. He thought of O'Meara, falsifying with the ease that comes from long practise, on the quiet deck at half-past one in the morning. He thought of the man who had invaded his stateroom, fleeing with that dress shirt in his arms. But that was too absurd—he must have dreamed it.

He rose hastily and searched his cabin. No dress shirt there—only the violent pink, purple and green. He had not dreamed it then. Uncle George's studs were floating far, journeying to some romantic port. A South Sea Islander, no doubt, would wear them next—in his ears, or maybe through his nose. What would Aunt Ella say?

Aunt Ella's reactions, however, were unimportant just now. He had agreed to assume the role of detective and his course was clear. He must discover the owner of that disappearing shirt.

He rang for Tatu and, while he waited, rattled at the door leading to the bath. Not that he expected to gain anything by it, but it relieved his feelings.

Tatu entered, minus his accustomed smile. The boy was worried; there could be no mistake about that.

"Very much trouble to-day," he announced. "Dollar gone. All Japanese boys catch hell. You want something, please?"

"How about taking back that shirt?" asked Bill, looking at him keenly.

"Yes-s," said Tatu. All expression left his face.

"Are you ready to take it back?"

"Yes-s," said Tatu.

"Well, you can't. It was stolen from me in the night."

"Yes-s," said Tatu.

No surprise; no interest even. Did Tatu know all about the shirt, or was this just his Oriental stoicism going full tilt? Bill stared at him, and Tatu stared back. And the white man felt suddenly hopeless, as though he had just sighted a stone wall dead ahead.

"Look here, Tatu," he said, "this is very important. I want to know where you got that shirt."

Tatu looked at the berth, at the bathroom door, through the port-hole, at the ceiling, then back to Bill. "Forget," he said.

"What? Say, don't try that on me!" Bill was annoyed. "Now we'll start all over again. W T here did you get the shirt?"

"Forget," said Tatu.

A wonderful little people, the Japanese. Bill Hammond managed to control himself.

"You told me a minute ago you were ready to return it. How could you return it if you don't know where you got it?"

"Forget," said Tatu.

East is East, and West is West. They stood facing each other, the white man glaring, the Jap merely staring. Bill Hammond turned away. Never get anywhere by losing his temper. Patience, amiability might do the trick. Try them in a minute.

"Morning very nice," said Tatu. "Bathroom door lock? Too bad."

"All right, Tatu," said Bill. "You and I won't quarrel. You helped me out of a tight place last night and I appreciate it."

"Most welcome," Tatu assured him, busily brushing Bill's dinner coat.

An idea flashed into Bill's mind.

"I tell you, that fix I was in was no joke. And I understand I wasn't the only one in trouble. I hear that Mr. Frost came aboard with no extra collars." He paused. Tatu brushed industriously. "Yes, sir, I hear that when he came to dress he didn't have any more collars than a bathing suit."

Tatu laid down the coat.

"Mr. Frost have plenty collar," he said.

"Oh, he did?" Bill sought to appear casual. "I guess I didn't get it straight then. Well supplied with collars, was he?"

"Very big box. Maybe ten. Maybe twelve. Plenty."

"You don't tell me!"

"I lay him out. I know."

Bill turned away lest his face betray him. Here was news! Henry Frost's story disproved already. It certainly began to look as though this Hammond boy was a born detective.

The ownership of the shirt was of no importance now.

"The morning is O.K., Tatu," he remarked, staring out the port-hole. "I'll back up all you said about it. When do we get to Monterey?"

"Maybe not go to Monterey," said Tatu. "Anything else, please?"

"Not go to Monterey? What are you talking about?"

"Things very bad this nice morning," answered Tatu. "Hear bell ringing. Yes- s. Thank you." And he bowed out.

Bill turned again to the bathroom, silent now. He rattled the knob, called, but there was no answer. Donning dressing-gown and slippers he stepped out into the corridor, warm with honest anger. He knocked at Mikklesen's door.

The Englishman opened it, smiling sweetly.

"Ah, good morning," he said. "What can I do for you?"

Bill was proud of himself. A grand thing, self-control.

"I believe," he said, "that you and I are supposed to share that bathroom fifty-fifty."

"Certainly, old chap," agreed Mikklesen. "Any time you feel inclined."

The struggle this time was a bit more difficult, but again Bill won.

"Then will you please unlock the door?" he said through his teeth.

"Oh, I'm so sorry. Frightfully careless of me. Just a moment." And Mikklesen closed his door in Bill's face.

The reporter reentered his cabin and managed to spring into the bath before Mikklesen had regained his own quarters.

"I'd like to see you to-day sometime," he said to the Englishman.

"Really? I fancy we'll run into each other. Bound to on a yacht. I mean to say, rather close quarters."

"You never spoke a truer word. You know, I'm supposed to get an interview from you—for my paper."

"Fancy! You're a pressman then?"

"I work on a newspaper, if that's what you mean."

"Not really? It wouldn't be done in England, you know."

"What wouldn't be done?"

"I mean to say, inviting a pressman as a guest. How extraordinarily—confusing!"

"Well, I'll give you time to get a grip on yourself before we start the interview," Bill answered. "And now, if you don't mind, even a pressman prefers to bathe in private."

"Oh, I'm going," said Mikklesen haughtily.

"It's a great idea," said Bill, and turned the lock on him.

"Lovely lad," he muttered; "so frank and open."

But his resentment was short-lived, and by the time he had finished shaving he had decided that maybe he wouldn't exterminate Mikklesen, after all. Perhaps the fellow served some useful purpose. Who could say? He whistled cheerfully as he dressed, though yesterday's shirt was nothing to whistle about. However, he had it on good authority that clothes don't make the man, and he sincerely trusted that all aboard had heard that one.

In the dining saloon he found Mrs. Keith and O'Meara breakfasting together. They appeared to be on excellent terms, and not particularly pleased at sight of Mr. Hammond's shining morning face.

"Good morning," said the reporter. "We seem to be rather late."

"Frightfully," admitted Mrs. Keith.

"Natural result of staying up half the night," went on Bill. "Late hours make late breakfasts, eh, O'Meara?"

"Was Mr. O'Meara up late?" asked the woman.

"I ran into him on deck at one-thirty this morning," smiled Bill.

"Yes, and it's lucky you did," growled the lawyer. He turned to Mrs. Keith. "This kid had a funny dream about seeing somebody in his stateroom," he explained. "I had a terrible time quieting him and getting him back to bed."

Mrs. Keith smiled sweetly on Bill.

"So you have queer dreams," she cooed. "How thrilling! You must tell me all about them. By the way, I hope you play golf. I'm looking for some one to take me round the Del Monte links this morning."

"Look no further," Bill said. He was face to face with the Californian's big ordeal—the eating of a California grapefruit.

"Oh, that's awfully good of you," Mrs. Keith smiled.

"I mean," Bill added hastily, "you're not going to Monterey."

"What's that?" O'Meara cried. "Where are we going?"

"Don't ask me," Bill answered. "All I know is, we'd have been at Monterey long ago if that had been our destination."

"But—I thought it was all settled," O'Meara objected.

Julian Hill came in. He was fresh as the morning in linen so spotless Bill Hammond began to wonder where his stateroom was. O'Meara at once applied to him for information.

"It's quite true," said Hill. "We're not bound for Monterey—or any other port. We're just cruising."

"Just cruising?" O'Meara repeated.

"Just wandering about the ocean," Hill went on, "playing for time."

"I don't get you," the politician said.

Hill smiled.

"You know Jim Batchelor as well as I do. He's lost something—something of great importance—to him. And he's not the sort of man to land his servants and crew—and his guests—until he's been over each and every one with a vacuum cleaner. Yes," added Mr. Hill, looking hard at O'Meara, "I'd advise the man who has that dollar to hand it over. Otherwise we may not get back to town this year."

O'Meara stood up.

"It's an outrage!" he cried. "Oh, of course I know how Batchelor feels. But this isn't fair to those of us who happen not to be—thieves." And he in turn looked hard at Julian Hill. "I've got to be back in town by Monday morning," he added, and turned away.

"It's all very exciting, at any rate," purred Mrs. Keith. She, too, rose, and they went out together.

"It begins to look as though there might be an opening here for a first-class detective," Bill Hammond ventured.

"Not at all," Hill answered coldly. "Mr. Batchelor is quite competent to manage his own affairs." The rest was silence.

His breakfast over, Bill went in search of Sally. He found her in the dazzling sunlight on the after deck, and not minding it, hers being that sort of complexion.

"Hello," he said. "This is a surprise!"

"What are you talking about?" she wanted to know.

"When I'm away from you, I keep thinking how lovely you are. Then I see you, and you're even lovelier than I thought. That's why I say—"

"Yes, but Bill, where in the world have you been?"

"Eating breakfast. Did you miss me?"

"I certainly did."

"Fine!"

"Are we in this detective business together, or are we not? I'm dying to know what you've found out."

"Oh! Well, I'm here to save your life."

He told her of his interview with Henry Frost and of his more recent discovery regarding the collars. A puzzled little frown wrinkled her otherwise perfect brow.

"I can't understand it," she protested. "Henry Frost is father's dearest friend."

"Always dangerous—dearest friends," Bill told her. "How is your father, by the way?"

"Worried to death. He claims he didn't sleep a wink, and I believe him. The first night without his lucky piece in thirty-seven years. I told him you were on the job, and all about the wonderful evidence you've run down in the course of newspaper work. I was quite eloquent, really."

"Good! I hope you'll always be eloquent when discussing me."

"I always shall, I'm sure."

"You darling! Go on, expand that idea, please."

She seemed about to obey, but at that moment Jim Batchelor joined them. He appeared nervous and upset.

"Good morning, Hammond," he said. "Sally's told me that you're willing to help in this unfortunate affair."

"Well, if it's not presumptuous of me—"

"Nonsense! You've had more experience in this sort of thing than I have, and I'll be glad of your assistance. Besides"—he glanced about him—"it's rather a hard thing to say about one's guests; but—well, I trust you, my boy." The emphasis on the "you" was marked.

"That's very kind of you, sir. May I ask what steps you have taken in the matter?"

"The servants and the crew have all been questioned. They've been carefully searched, and their quarters too. I may say that I don't suspect any of them. Some time during the day the guests' cabins and luggage will be—er—examined. I'm hospitality itself, but this is a vital business for me and I'll stop at nothing. I've also given orders to the captain not to put in anywhere. There are supplies and coal enough aboard to carry us for five days, and I'll stay out that long if I have to."

"It's a good idea, sir," Bill agreed.

"I've also just posted a notice on the board offering a reward of three thousand dollars for the immediate return of my lucky piece, and no questions asked. 'Immediate' is the important word there. The money's yours if you run down the thief."

"Oh, but I wouldn't take your—money, sir," Bill said. The emphasis on the "money" was not so marked as he had intended.

"Rot! Why not? I'd be getting off cheaply at that. Three thousand is a small price to pay for the peace of mind the return of that dollar would bring me. My boy, I'll never know a happy moment until I get it back."

"Bill, why don't you tell him?" Sally suggested.

"Tell me what?" Jim Batchelor asked quickly.

"Bill's unearthed the most amazing things, Dad. You'll never believe—"

"Good lord, why keep me in the dark?" He was all excitement. "What's up?"

"If you don't mind, sir," Bill said, "I'd like just a moment more before I let you in on it. You see—"

"A moment? Well, well—if you say so. But only a moment. My boy, don't keep me waiting."

"I'll make it snappy, sir," said Bill, and hurried off.

Tatu, making up the berth in Henry Frost's cabin, informed him that the millionaire had slept late and was now at breakfast.

Bill looked round inquiringly.

"How about the collars, Tatu?" he said.

"Him lock collars in suitcase," Tatu explained. "Put key in pocket."

Smiling to himself, Bill went to the dining saloon, where his employer sat alone at his breakfast.

"Good morning, sir," said Bill.

"Good morning. You breakfast late." Frost's tone implied that it was a bad sign.

"I've had my breakfast, Mr. Frost. I want to speak to you, if you don't mind."

"And if I do mind?"

"I'd have to speak anyhow," said Bill firmly. Henry Frost looked up sourly from his grapefruit.

"I'll say this for you: You're the most offensive man on my pay-roll."

"I'm sorry, sir. I'm only trying to do the right thing."

"People who are only trying to do the right thing generally make fools of themselves. What is it now?"

"Last night I told you I didn't intend to go to Mr. Batchelor with certain information I had picked up. I've been forced to change my mind."

"Really? What forced you?"

"That story of yours about the collars. I've found out it wasn't true."

"Indeed?"

"Yes, sir. You say you went to Jim Batchelor's room for a collar. I say that's a typographical error. You went there for a dollar."

Henry Frost rose and tossed down his napkin.

"Will you come with me?" he said.

"Certainly, sir." Bill followed his employer on deck. "This is all very painful for me, Mr. Frost."

"Yes, more so than you think. Do you happen to know where Jim Batchelor is?"

"He's on the after deck."

Henry Frost turned in that direction.

"Regarding that interview with Mikklesen, you needn't trouble. You're not on the paper any more."

"Just as you say, sir," Bill replied smilingly.

But his heart sank. In love and out of work—a great combination.

Jim Batchelor was waiting with Sally on the spot where Bill had left them. He looked up eagerly as the two men approached.

"Jim, I've got something to say to you," began Frost.

"All right. What is it?"

"This young idiot thinks I took your dollar."

"Oh, nonsense!" said Batchelor, disappointed in Bill. "I know you wouldn't take it."

"Well," continued Mr. Frost, "I—I " His face turned scarlet. "As a matter of fact, Jim—I did."

Jim Batchelor leaped from his chair.

"What's that? Say that again!"

"Now, Jim, don't get excited. I give you my word, it was all a joke."

"A joke! You old simpleton! Getting funny at your age! Well, hand it over!"

"I want you to understand how it was," Frost continued.

"I was determined to take you out and trim you at golf today. Last night somebody happened to say something about your losing that dollar, and it came over me all at once that if you did you'd be so upset you'd be easy picking on the links. So just for fun, Jim—that was all—I slipped into your room and substituted that other dollar."

"You're a criminal at heart, Henry. I always knew it. But where in Sam Hill- -"

"Of course I never dreamed you'd take it so seriously. And I want to talk to you about that. Really, Jim, that dollar's become an obsession with you. No man ought to build his whole life on a thing like that. It's wrong—all wrong. Let this be a lesson to you."

"Will you cut out the sermon and produce my dollar?"

"I'll get it. It's in my room. There's no hard feelings, Jim—"

"There will be if you don't shut up and get that dollar."

Frost departed. Jim Batchelor stalked the deck. He was mad and he showed it, for no one had told him repression was the fashion.

"The old idiot!" he stormed. "What's got into him? Second childhood, I call it. A joke! You heard him—he said it was a joke!"

"Never mind, Dad, it's all right now," said Sally soothingly. "And you must remember, it was Bill here solved the mystery."

"Mighty clever of him too. I'll write him a check in a minute."

"Oh, I couldn't allow that, sir," Bill protested. "Not under the circumstances."

"Rot! Just as serious as a real theft. And for that matter— who knows? The old fox! I never did trust him."

"Dad! Your best friend!" Sally was shocked.

"Well, how do I know what he's up to?"

At that moment Mr. Frost reappeared. For once his famous poker face failed him. It registered emotion.

"Jim," he said, "I feel like a fool."

"You're certainly acting like one. Where's my dollar?"

Frost slowly extended his bony hand. Eagerly Jim Batchelor reached out a hand to receive. Into it Henry Frost dropped a bit of paper, a greenback, the promise of the United States Government to pay one dollar on demand.

"What the devil's this?" roared Batchelor.

"I found it in the place where I'd hidden your dollar, Jim," said Henry Frost humbly.

Jim Batchelor did not speak. He cast the paper dollar to the deck. His face purpled, so that Bill Hammond wondered what one did first in case of apoplexy.

"What can I say, Jim?" Frost pleaded. "I wouldn't have had this happen for a cool million."

"Apologies!" gurgled Batchelor. "Regrets! What do I care for them? I want my dollar!"

"It was all a joke," said Frost—an unfortunate remark.

"Yeah, a joke! Ha-ha! Fine joke! Somebody else thought so too. Somebody decided to steal your stuff. And now where are we? Just where we started!"

"With this difference," said Frost. "I'm in on this now. You and I will run the thief down together. I've something at stake, too, and my first move will be to add another couple of thousand to that reward you offered."

"A lot of good that will do," shrugged Batchelor. "If three thousand wouldn't bring it, five won't either. I tell you, we're up against it." tie turned suddenly to Bill. "You—you haven't any other clue, have you?" he asked. The trustful note in his voice was pathetic. It made two young people very happy.

"Well, I have one," Bill admitted.

"You have?" Batchelor brightened at once.

"Yes; it may not be very important. But I'll work on it. I'd like your permission to do whatever I think necessary— to invade other people's staterooms if I think best."

"You go as far as you like." Batchelor turned to Frost. "This boy's promised to help me."

"Oh, he's a wonder!" sneered Frost.

"You bet he is," Batchelor answered. "He ran you down in record time, and I'll back him to get the other thief."

"Dad!" Sally reproved.

"All right, Jim," said Frost. "I've got it coming to me."

"I'll say you have!"

Bill bent over and picked up the greenback from the deck.

"I'll take charge of this, if you don't mind. And by the way, Mr. Frost, did anybody else aboard know you took that dollar?"

267

"Yes—come to think of it," said Frost. "It seemed best, in case my motives should be misunderstood, to let a second party in on the—er—the joke. So I told Julian Hill."

"When did you tell him?"

"Last evening—before I took it. And afterward I mentioned to him that I had it in my stateroom."

In the silence that followed, Bill had a vision of the night before—two tables of bridge, with Julian Hill wandering alone somewhere outside.

"By the way," said Batchelor, "this may not mean anything; but I heard this morning that Mrs. Keith lunched last Wednesday at the Palace with Norman Blake. The Blakes are old rivals of mine," he explained to Bill, "and they've never made any secret of their interest in that dollar."

"And who told you about Mrs. Keith, sir?"

"Julian Hill."

"Ah, yes," Bill smiled. "Well, I'll do my best."

"I'm sure you will, my boy," said Batchelor. "Don't forget, there's five thousand in it for you now."

"I hope there's more than that," thought Bill. "Yes, sir," was what he said. He smiled at Sally and moved away. Frost called after him.

"By the way, Hammond," he said, "if you get the time you'd better do that Mikklesen story. Simon Porter will be expecting it."

"Thank you, sir," Bill answered. Sally joined him and they went forward along the rail.

"What did he mean, Bill?" she asked.

"Oh, he was just handing me back my job. You see, he fired me a little while ago. Now he loves me again. And speaking of that, where do you stand this morning?"

"Just where I stood last night," she told him.

"The day of miracles arrived last night," he said. "You can sit down now, my dear—if you'll tell me all about it."

"All about what?" They found a couple of deck chairs.

"All about how you—like me pretty well."

"Never mind that. You tell me. You love me, don't you, Bill?"

"Sally, words can't put it over! I gave 'em a chance last night, and they fell down on the job."

"When did you start, Bill—being fond, I mean?"

"That day when you were helping the orphans. The moment I saw you—honest, Sally, I loved you on the spot. And for ten minutes I madly worshiped you. Then somebody told me your name. So I went away and never loved you again."

"Bill!"

"Well, that was the idea. Only it didn't work out very well."

"I'm glad it didn't. But business before pleasure, Bill. What's your other clue?"

His bright look faded.

"It isn't any good," he said. "I thought for a minute there might be something in it. I see now I was wrong."

"But what is it, Bill?"

"It's a shirt."

"A shirt?"

"Yes, we've run the collars to earth, and now we'll get busy on the shirt. I tell you, Sally, this is beginning to look to me like the annual outing of the Laundrymen's Benevolent Society."

"You interest me strangely. What's it all about?"

He told her. The misadventure in the steamy laundry of Honolulu Sam, his agony when he found himself shirtless, Tatu's prompt rescue, the theft in the night, the Jap's reticence on the morning after—all these he detailed at length.

"The trouble with the detective game," said Sally, when he had finished, "is that it's so full of mystery. Whose shirt do you imagine that was?"

"Well, there's Julian Hill. He appears to have an extensive wardrobe."

"Bill, you don't think that Julian—"

"I don't know—just a guess. My job now is to get hold of Tatu and pry the information out of him."

"Japs are difficult," said Sally.

"You bet they are, and this boy is Gibraltar's little brother. But I'll make him come across."

"I'm sure you will."

"I'll get the facts out of him if I have to strangle him," Bill told her, "just to prove to you how tenderly I love you."

* * * * *

BUT Bill Hammond's optimistic prediction failed to come true. He did not get the facts from Tatu. After fifteen minutes of the third degree, the little Jap still stood as firm as Gibraltar—or maybe firmer. Bill cajoled, pleaded, threatened. Tatu looked at him with all the calm mystery of the Orient in his eyes, and suavely protested that he had forgotten just where he acquired that shirt. The luncheon bugle came as a merciful interruption.

"All right, go along," said Bill. His efforts had wilted him. "But I'm not through with you, my lad."

"Yes-s, thank you," answered Tatu, and had the audacity to smile as he went out.

Near the door of the dining saloon Sally was eagerly waiting.

"Well?" she asked.

"Salute your hero," said Bill. "He's just been licked by a Jap."

"Tatu wouldn't tell you?"

"Adamant, that boy. He's never heard the word, but he can act it out."

"Why not set Father on him?"

"No," protested Bill, "let's keep Father out of it. I've got to pull this off alone. You know why."

"But what are you going to do?"

"Just what a regular detective would do," he told her. "Wait for a lucky break."

"Is that the way they work?" she asked, unbelieving. She was all for action—her father's daughter.

"It certainly is," said Bill. "I read an interview once with a great French detective. I didn't pay much attention to it at the time, as I didn't know then that I was going into the business. But I remember one thing—he said that the detective's chief ally was luck."

"But suppose you're not lucky?"

"Something that happened last night," smiled Bill, "proved I'm the luckiest man in the world."

Jim Batchelor came up.

"What's doing?" he whispered hoarsely.

"I'm working." Bill tried to make it sound businesslike.

"Results—that's what we want," Batchelor reminded him.

"You bet we do," said Bill, and they went in to lunch.

At the table there was little of the cheery animation of the night before. The guests ate in preoccupied silence, and Jim Batchelor's intimation that they might wander about the Pacific for several days added nothing to the general gayety.

After lunch, Bill Hammond saw Mikklesen enter the smoking-room, and followed. He sat down opposite the Englishman and offered him a cigar.

Mikklesen took it suspiciously and lighted it in the same spirit. Although it was a perfectly good cigar, his subsequent expression seemed to indicate that his worst fears were realized.

"If you've no objection," Bill said, "we might as well get that interview over with."

"As you wish," Mikklesen agreed. "Where's your notebook?"

"My what? Say, listen, it's only in plays that reporters carry those things."

"But I shouldn't care to be misquoted," the Englishman objected.

"Not a chance. I've got a mind like a phonograph record."

"Ah—er—what shall I talk about?" Mikklesen asked.

"Give me something snappy," Bill suggested. "Something they can hang a headline on."

"Oh, but that's hardly my style. Very bad taste, sensationalism. We have practically none of it at home. If you don't mind, I'd like to talk about the Chinese. A really admirable people, old chap."

"You think so?" asked Bill Hammond, without enthusiasm.

"I know it. I had charge of a copper mine in one of the northern provinces, and I found the Chinese absolutely reliable. If they promised a thing, they did it."

"I heard different," Bill said. "But go on, this is your story."

Mikklesen told his story. Beyond question he had the gift of speech, and Bill Hammond reflected as he listened that he was getting something. By an adroit question now and then, he led the talker on. Some ten minutes had passed, when suddenly the second officer of the France sea, who had charge of the yacht's wireless, entered.

"Mr. Hammond," he said, "a message for you."

"Oh, thanks," said Bill. The officer handed it over and departed. "Pardon me just a second."

"Certainly," agreed Mikklesen.

Bill opened the folded paper and read what the second officer had set down. As he read, he smiled happily to himself. The message was from Simon Porter.

"Never mind interview," Simon wirelessed. "Have investigated by cable. A little black sheep who's gone astray. Kicked out of the English colony in Yokohama because they didn't like his shirts."

His shirts! Oh, lady luck!

"Anything important?" inquired Mikklesen.

"Not at all," said Bill. "Go on, please. You were saying—"

Mikklesen went on, but Bill no longer listened. The interview was cold, but the quest of the dollar was warming up. His shirts! They didn't like his shirts. Well, that might mean much or little; but Mikklesen's shirts certainly must be looked into.

"I fancy that's about all I can give you," said the Englishman finally.

"That's plenty," Bill answered heartily. He stood up. "You know, considering how fond you are of the Orient, I'm surprised you came away."

Mikklesen regarded him with a sudden interest.

"Pater's getting old," he explained. "Cabled me to come home. Couldn't very well refuse—family ties and all that. But sooner or later I shall return to the East."

"I'm sure you will," said Bill. "Thanks ever so much."

Eagerly he hurried below. Things were certainly looking brighter. Midway down the passageway he encountered Tatu.

"I want you," he cried, and seizing the Jap by the arm escorted him energetically into the cabin.

"What now, please?" inquired Tatu.

Bill pointed an accusing finger.

"That was Mikklesen's shirt," he announced.

"Somebody tell," said Tatu, with obvious relief.

"Yes, somebody's told. That lets you out. Now come across with the whole story."

"Nothing to say," Tatu replied. "I see he have two shirt. You have no shirt. I hear him talk unkind remarks about Japanese people. I take a shirt. Why not?"

"It was a noble impulse. But why the dickens wouldn't you tell me this before?"

"Last night, maybe twelve o'clock, Mr. Mikklesen ring," Tatu explained. "Tell me I take shirt, give to you. I say no, indeed. He say very well, but will give me fifty dollar I not tell to you whose shirt you have. I accept with pleasure." His face clouded. "Japanese boy lose fifty dollar," he added.

"Has he given it to you?"

"Give one dollar for a beginning. Very small beginning."

Bill's eyes narrowed.

"Let me see the dollar," he demanded. Tatu handed over a crisp new greenback. "You're sure this is the one?"

"Yes-s. Only dollar in pocket," said the Jap.

Bill took out a silver dollar, glanced at it and handed it to Tatu.

"I'll trade with you, if you don't mind. Now listen, my lad! From now on you and I are friends."

"Yes-s. Very nice," agreed Tatu.

"You stick to me. I'm helping Mr. Batchelor—he's asked me to. No more secrets with Mikklesen. Otherwise trouble for you—much trouble."

"I know."

276

"The first thing in order is an examination of Mikklesen's one remaining shirt."

"Can't do," Tatu said. "Shirt locked up."

"I suppose so," Bill replied. "However, I'm going to take a look. Go and see if there's any one in Mikklesen's cabin."

Tatu departed through the bath. In a second he was back.

"Empty," he announced.

"Fine," said Bill. He stationed Tatu in the corridor with orders to signal if the Englishman appeared. Then, with the bath offering a way of escape, he examined the room with care. But Mikklesen had left no dress shirt where eager hands could find it. Undoubtedly it was in the one piece of luggage that was securely locked—a huge, battered bag that had a London lock.

"Nothing doing," said Bill finally. He returned to his own cabin, followed by Tatu.

"You want bag open?" inquired Tatu.

"It would be a good idea," Bill admitted.

"Maybe dollar inside," suggested the boy.

"I don't know. It might be."

"Pretty strong lock," mused Tatu.

"Oh, so you noticed that?" Bill stared at the impassive face. "Well," he continued, thinking aloud, "my chance will come. It's bound to. Mikklesen's got to wear that shirt tonight, and perhaps Oh, good lord!"

"Yes-s," said Tatu.

"Look here, my boy, what do I wear to-night? I'm worse off than I was last night. I haven't even got any studs."

"Excuse, please. Hear bell ringing," lied Tatu, and departed in great haste.

Bill Hammond sat down on his berth to consider developments. So it was Mikklesen's shirt he had worn so jauntily the evening before. Then it must have been Mikklesen who came in the night to reclaim his property. Knowing himself closely pursued, he had not dared turn into his own cabin, once he reached the corridor, and for the same reason he had thrown the shirt overboard. But why all this fuss about a dress shirt? And how, Bill asked himself, was it connected with Jim Batchelor's dollar, as he was sure now it must be. Well, detectives certainly earned their pay.

Bill left the cabin and returned to the upper deck. The Francesca appeared to be deserted.

He dropped into a chair that stood invitingly in a shady spot and began to consider his problem. Must get into that bag of Mikklesen's. But how?

Heavy footsteps sounded on the deck and O'Meara passed by. He did not speak or turn his head. He appeared worried. Bill Hammond began to worry too. Was he wasting time on a false trail? O'Meara, Julian Hill, Mrs. Keith—all possibilities. Ought to be looking them up a bit too.

But no. For the present he would follow that shirt—see where it led. He'd get into Mikklesen's bag. How would a regular detective go about it? Break open the lock perhaps? No, too crude. Find out where Mikklesen kept his keys? Much better. Find out—how?

It was a rather drowsy afternoon, and a full twenty minutes passed before Bill had an idea. He rose at once to try it out. When he reached the door of the smoking-room Mikklesen was just leaving.

"Hello," Bill said. "I've been thinking about that story of ours. We really need a few photographs to dress it up."

"Oh, no, old chap," said Mikklesen hastily. "I shouldn't care for that at all."

"I don't mean pictures of you," Bill explained. "Just some snapshots taken in the Orient. You surely have some of those."

"Well, as a matter of fact, I have," admitted Mikklesen. "I'll give them to you later."

"But if you don't mind"—Bill summoned his most winning smile—"I'm at work on the story now."

For a moment Mikklesen stood regarding him.

"Oh, very well," he said, "come along."

He led the way below and Bill followed close, determined to miss nothing now. When they reached the Englishman's cabin Mikklesen took a bunch of keys from his pocket. Bill Hammond tried not to look too interested.

"I keep my bag locked," Mikklesen explained. "Things disappearing right and left, you know."

"It's the only safe thing to do," Bill agreed.

The Englishman bent over his bag.

"Look there!" he cried.

Bill looked. The lock on Mikklesen's bag had been smashed to bits.

"How beastly annoying!" The Englishman's face was crimson with anger. "This is too much, really it is. I understood I was to go on a cruise with gentlefolk, not with a band of thieves." He was hurriedly investigating the contents of the bag.

"Anything missing?" Bill asked.

"There doesn't appear to be," said Mikklesen, cooling off a bit. "But whether there is or not, I shall certainly complain to our host." He took out an envelope and glanced into it. "The photos, old chap. Pick out what you want and return me the rest, if you will."

"Surely," Bill agreed. He waited hopefully. "If you'd like me to stay here and keep an eye on things while you look up Mr. Batchelor—"

Mikklesen stared at him. Did he imagine it, or was that the ghost of a smile about the Englishman's lips?

"Thank you so much," he said. "But I shall ask Mr. Batchelor to come to me here. I shan't leave my cabin again this afternoon—if you're interested."

If you're interested! Now what did he mean by that? Did he know that Bill was on to him, or was it a shot in the dark?

"Oh—er—of course " said Bill lamely, and departed.

Back in his own room, Bill tried to think things out. What did "if you're interested" mean? And who had broken the lock on that bag? Evidently Mikklesen wasn't the only shady character aboard.

He took out a book and settled down in his berth to read, his ear attuned to eventualities in the next cabin. Would Mikklesen keep his word and remain on guard by his mysterious shirt? An hour passed, and it began to appear that such was the Englishman's intention.

It was, as has been noted, a drowsy afternoon. Bill dropped his book and lay back on the pillow. Ah, this was the life! No harsh call from his city editor or from Simon Porter sending him forth for a bit of leg work on the hard pavements. No feverish hurry to make the last edition. Nothing but the soft swish of water, the thump of the engines—sounds that suggested slumber. Bill accepted the suggestion.

He was awakened some time later by a sharp knock on his door. Leaping up, he opened it. A servant stood outside.

"Mr. Hammond, you're wanted above, sir."

Wanted! What now? Some new development in the matter of the dollar, no doubt. He hastily brushed his hair and went to the upper deck. At the top of the companionway he encountered Aunt Dora, looking extremely competent.

"Ah, Mr. Hammond," she said, "I hope I haven't disturbed you. We've a table for bridge and we lack a fourth."

Trapped! Bill looked wildly to the right and left.

"I—I thought it was something important," he stammered.

"I beg your pardon?"

"I mean—you don't want me. I'm a terrible player. You have reason to know."

"Practise makes perfect. I'll give you a few pointers."

"It's awfully good of you, but—I'm very busy and—my eyes aren't in very good shape."

"I noticed your failing eyesight," she answered, "last night when you trumped my ace of spades. However, we'll put the table in a strong light. Come along."

"I—I'll be very happy to," said Bill, surrendering.

Aunt Dora didn't care whether he was happy or not. She had him. He wasn't her ideal bridge player, but he was all she could get. And as Bill followed her into the main saloon he prayed to see Sally there.

But he didn't. Julian Hill and Henry Frost sat glumly at a table, their manner that of captive slaves on Caesar's chariot wheels. Aunt Dora sat down and the big game was on. It proved a long and painful session. At the close of each hand Aunt Dora halted the proceedings while she delved into the immediate past, pointing out to one and all the error of their ways. Bill got a lot of undesirable publicity out of these little talks.

The dinner hour was not far away when Sally came in and released him. When they left the saloon Aunt Dora was going strong. Mr. William Hammond, it seemed, had done something for which he should have been drawn and quartered.

"She'll never forgive me," said Bill. "I got her signals mixed."

"I'm afraid she's rather tiresome at times," Sally smiled.

"Well, she will insist on crossing her bridge after she's got well over it. There are people like that."

"You were good to play, Bill," Sally said.

"Yes, but I didn't play so good, and I wasted a lot of time when I should have been sleuthing."

"Has anything happened?" she inquired.

"I should say it has. It was a big afternoon up to the moment I met your aunt." He told her of Simon's message and the accident to Mikklesen's bag. "Things are moving," he added.

"They seem to be," she admitted. "What are you going to do now?"

"Ah—er—something very bright, you may be sure. I'm keen eyed and alert. My brain is hitting on all twelve."

"Yes, but what are you going to do?"

"My dear, don't be so literal. Can it be you don't trust me?"

"Oh, I know you're simply wonderful. Only—"

"Never mind the only. We're on the verge of big things. Watch and wait!"

His manner was confident, but by the time he had reached his cabin his confidence had begun to wane. He stood for a moment wondering just what his preparations for dinner were to be. No evening clothes to-night, that was certain. He would have to make some sort of apology to Jim Batchelor and let it go at that. At any rate, he had appeared properly clad the night before, and the other guests could draw their own conclusions regarding his appearance to-night.

He tried the door into the bath—locked of course. He rattled and called—there was no sound within. Have to go and open the door again. As he paused outside Mikklesen's cabin something told him not to knock. He entered very quietly.

The cabin was empty and in semi-darkness. He moved farther into the room—and his heart stood still. A white blur in the dusk—Mikklesen's dress shirt! It was lying on the settee under the port-hole, within easy reach. He put his hand down and touched it, and as he did so a faint sound in the bath startled him. He drew his hand back from the shirt, but in that brief second he had made an interesting discovery. Mikklesen appeared in the bathroom door.

"Good lord!" he cried. "You gave me a shock! What are you doing here? Confound it all, is there no privacy aboard this yacht?"

"I'm sorry," said Bill. "I didn't know you were in the bath, and I was coming through to unlock it. I thought you'd gone off and left it that way—it wouldn't be the first time, you know."

"Well, I happen to be using it," said Mikklesen testily, and the fact that half his face was lathered and he carried a razor seemed to bear him out. "In the future, I'll thank you to knock before entering my cabin."

Bill considered. He had Mikklesen where he wanted him, but his sense of the dramatic told him to bide his time. Better an unmasking in Jim Batchelor's presence than a scene with only two people in a half-dark cabin.

"I beg your pardon," he said. "Sorry I disturbed you."

"It's rather upsetting," complained Mikklesen. "First my bag broken into, and then you popping up like a ghost." He followed Bill to the door and shut it after him in a manner suggesting extreme annoyance.

Out in the corridor, Bill gave himself up to a moment of unalloyed joy. It was almost too good to be true. Too easy.

A bright lad, this Mikklesen; but not too bright for young Mr. Hammond, the peerless detective. For Bill knew where the dollar was now!

He must have a word with Jim Batchelor before he staged his big scene. He tiptoed down the passage and knocked at the millionaire's door. Batchelor called an invitation to enter, and when he did so he was glad to find that Sally also was in the room. She was tying Batchelor's dress tie, for she was a faithful daughter and didn't like Tatu's work as a valet. Her father broke from her ministrations at sight of Bill.

"Something doing?" he inquired, with pathetic eagerness.

"I'll say there is," replied Mr. Hammond cheerily.

"You've got it?"

"I've got it located—same thing."

"Not quite." Batchelor's happy look faded. "However, where is it?"

"That'll be revealed at the proper moment," Bill told him. "I just dropped in to lay my wires for a little scene after dinner to-night. Sally, I'm glad you're here. After the coffee you're to take your aunt and Mrs. Keith from the dining saloon and leave us men alone."

"What—and miss the excitement? Not much!"

"Sally, you heard what Mr. Hammond said," reproved her father. "Obey."

"But, Dad—"

"Sally!"

"Oh, well, if you think Mr. Hammond knows best," smiled Sally.

"I'm sure he does."

"I'm sorry, Sally," Bill said. "But the subsequent events will be such that I don't think it the place for the so-called weaker sex. Mr. Batchelor, I want you to back me up from that point on. Anything I say—and anything I propose to do."

"Of course. But you might give me a little hint—"

"I will, sir." He handed over Simon Porter's wireless message. "Read that, please."

Batchelor read.

"Who's he talking about? Not—Mikklesen!"

"Yes, sir, Mikklesen."

"Good lord! I never thought of him. What about his shirts?"

"You wouldn't believe if I told you, sir. I'll show you after dinner."

"Fine!" Batchelor's spirits rose. "I'll be mighty glad to get this thing solved to-night. The captain's just told me there's something wrong with the engines, and we're circling back to Monterey." He submitted while Sally put the finishing touch on his tie. "By the way, Mikklesen called me into his stateroom this afternoon and put up a terrible howl because his bag had been broken into. I was very sympathetic, I didn't tell him the captain was the guilty party."

"Oh, the captain broke that lock."

"Yes; pretty crude work. He swore he could pick it open with a jack-knife, but his hand slipped and he ended by smashing it. I didn't approve of his going quite that far."

"Did he find anything?" asked Bill.

"Nothing. He went over the thing carefully—so he claims."

"He didn't have the combination," smiled Bill. "By the way, sir, I shan't be able to dress for dinner to-night. I'll come as a plain-clothes man, if you don't mind."

"Come in your pajamas if you want to," said Batchelor. "Only get me that dollar."

"I'll get it," Bill assured him. As he left the cabin he smiled triumphantly at Sally and Sally smiled back.

The conquering hero—that was how he felt.

* * * * *

A TENSE air hung about the dinner table that evening, as though all present knew that some important development in the dollar chase was close at hand. Only one guest was entirely at ease—Mikklesen. He resumed his tale of far corners and strange adventures, and once more Bill Hammond had to admit that the boy was good.

When the women had left the saloon a pointed silence fell. Jim Batchelor sat for a moment staring at the end of his cigar.

"Gentlemen," he said, "I know you'll pardon my mentioning again the matter of the missing dollar, for I'm sure you're all as interested as I am to see the property recovered. Mr. Hammond has been making an investigation, at my request, and I understand he has something to report."

They turned with interest to Mr. Hammond. Bill smiled cheerily about the circle.

"We've made several discoveries," he began. "For instance, we know that the dollar was taken from Mr. Batchelor in the first place as a rather ill-advised joke." Frost squirmed in his chair, but Bill mentioned no names. He told how the unfortunate jokester, on seeking to return the dollar to its owner, had found in the hiding place a greenback of equal value. He took the bank-note from his pocket.

"This is a brand-new note," he said, "and its serial number is 2B7654328B. Some of you may have noticed that when you are paid money by a bank, and receive new bills, the serial numbers follow in perfect sequence." He removed another bill from his pocket. "I have here," he added, "another new dollar note, and the serial number is 2B7654329B. Is it too much to suppose that the two notes came from the same pocket?"

"Good work!" remarked Batchelor, beaming. "Where'd you get that other one?"

"The second note," Bill explained, "was given to Tatu, the valet, in return for some trifling service. It was given to him by one of you gentlemen here present." He paused. No one spoke. "It was given him by Mr. Mikklesen," Bill added.

They all turned and looked at the Englishman. His nonchalance was admirable.

"That may be true," he smiled. "I may have given the Jap that note—I don't recall. What of it?"

"Pretty flimsy, if you ask me," said O'Meara. "I'm a lawyer and I want to tell you, young man—"

"Just a moment, Mr. O'Meara," Bill smiled. "We don't need a lawyer just yet. I recognize that this evidence is rather inconclusive. I mentioned it merely because it makes a good prelude to what will follow. The close relationship of these notes points to Mikklesen. Other things point to Mikklesen. I point to Mikklesen. I ask him to stand up and be searched—that is, of course, if Mr. Batchelor has no objection."

Batchelor nodded. "Go to it," he said heartily.

"Fine!" Bill said. "Now, Mr. Mikklesen, if you'll be so good—"

Mikklesen flushed.

"This is an insult," he protested. "Mr. Batchelor, I appeal to you. The simplest laws of hospitality—"

"You've abused my hospitality, sir," said Batchelor. "I know all about you. Stand up!"

Slowly the Englishman got to his feet.

"The coat and waistcoat, please," Bill Hammond ordered. "Thanks. Now the collar and the tie. I'll help you, if you don't mind." He rapidly unfastened the studs in Mikklesen's gleaming bosom. "Our friend here," he explained, "has made a close study of his profession. He has perfected the Mikklesen shirt, for which he was famous in the Orient. The bosom is unusually stiff; it holds its shape well. And at the bottom, on the left side, an extra strip of linen makes a convenient pocket. You wouldn't notice it if the shirt were freshly laundered—I didn't"—he smiled at Mikklesen—"but after prying it open you have a handy receptacle for carrying slender booty—bank- notes, or even a silver dollar. And the loot doesn't show, particularly if you are built concavely, as is young Raffles here." Bill removed from the bosom of the shirt a silver dollar and tossed it down before Jim Batchelor. His heart was thumping; this was his big hour. "Your lucky piece, I believe, sir," he said.

Batchelor's eyes shone.

"My boy, how can I ever thank you " he began. With trembling hand he picked up the dollar. A hoarse cry of rage escaped him. He threw the dollar back on to the table and got to his feet. "Damn it," he cried, "how long is this thing going to keep up?"

"Wha-what thing, sir?" asked Bill, his triumph fading.

"That," roared Batchelor, "is not my dollar! It was coined in the year 1899."

"Good lord!" cried Bill; and glancing at Mikklesen, he saw on that gentleman's face a look of undisguised surprise.

The saloon was in an uproar, everybody talking at once. But above the clamor Batchelor's voice rang out. He was facing Bill, and he was talking to Bill.

"You a detective! You're a defective, that's what ails you! You get my hopes way up, and then you—you—you—"

"Well, I'm sorry, sir," said poor Bill. He was a bit dazed.

"Sorry! What kind of talk is that? Sorry! I could—I'd like to—I tell you this, you unearth any more dollars for me, and I'll skin you alive!" He turned to Mikklesen, who was tying his necktie as best he could without a mirror. "And you, sir! What have you to say? What explanation have you to offer? Honest men don't go about with trick shirts. I know your reputation in the Orient. How came that dollar where it was?"

"I'm afraid I've been done, sir," said Mikklesen suavely, putting on his coat.

"Done? How so?"

"Under the circumstances, I can't do better than tell you the truth. If you will pause to consider, there has been no real theft. In each case, nothing but substitution—one dollar for another. The value of your lucky piece is purely sentimental. Remember that, if you will."

"Go on," said Batchelor.

"I went to your cabin last night to get that dollar. I'm a bit of a jokester myself. I heard Mr. Frost at the door and had just time to reach the closet. From there I watched him make the substitution. I followed him, and when he left his cabin to go to dinner, I slipped in. After locating your dollar, I made a little substitution of my own. I had your dollar last night, I had it this morning—right where our young friend here found this other one. I put the shirt with the dollar in it in my bag and securely fastened the lock. Mr. Hammond here will bear me out when I say that some time in the early afternoon the lock of my bag was broken. That must have been when the dollars were exchanged."

"Nonsense!" answered Batchelor. "You mean to say you haven't made sure of that dollar since?"

"I saw that there was still a dollar in the bosom of the shirt and naturally supposed it was the—er—lucky piece."

Jim Batchelor slowly shook his head.

"I don't get you," he said. "You're too deep for me. However, I know one thing—you're not the sort of guest I care to have around. Something has happened to the engines and we're turning back to Monterey. In the morning you will greatly oblige me by taking your luggage and going ashore."

"Oh, naturally," calmly agreed Mikklesen.

"After you've been searched," Batchelor added. "Shall we join the ladies?"

As they left the dining saloon, Bill Hammond saw O'Meara seize Mikklesen's arm and hold him back. The politician's ruddy face was a study in various emotions, none pleasant.

Entering the main saloon last, Bill encountered Sally just inside the door. Her eyes were shining with excitement as she maneuvered him outside.

"Oh, Bill, I felt dreadfully," she said. "I mean, to miss your big scene of triumph."

"Ha-ha," he remarked mirthlessly.

"Why, what's the matter?"

"Some triumph, Sally! A dud! A raspberry! As a detective I'm a great reporter." And he told her what had happened.

"What did Father say?" she inquired when he had finished.

"Ah," he answered, "you go right to the heart of the matter. Father said plenty, and if a look ever meant poison in the coffee, his look meant that to me. I tell you, Sally, it's all over now. As far as Father goes, I'm out."

"Don't give up," she urged. "Haven't you any more clues?"

"Well," he replied slowly, "a little one."

"I knew it!" she cried. "What is it, Bill?"

"Oh, nothing much. But I happened to pick up that dollar we found on Mikklesen, and—"

Jim Batchelor and Henry Frost emerged from the main saloon and came up.

"Ah," said Frost sarcastically, "the young detective."

"Don't kid him, Henry," said Batchelor. "The boy's got a future. He can dig up more dollars than John D. Rockefeller."

"Mr. Batchelor, I certainly regret—" Bill began.

"Never mind that. Where are we now? Things are more confused than ever."

"If you'll take a suggestion from me," Frost began, "how about your captain? He opened Mikklesen's bag. Was he alone at the time?"

"Nonsense!" Batchelor answered. "You're wrong as usual, Henry."

"Well, I don't know. What's all this about the engines, and turning back?"

"Rot, I say! The captain's been with me for more than ten years." Batchelor shook his head. "I tell you, I'm up a tree. A lot of things I don't understand. Very strange, for example, that Mikklesen should have made that confession. He could have denied everything and let it go at that."

"Dad," said Sally, "Bill's got another clue."

"I suppose so," her father replied. "He certainly is a marvel for clues. I shouldn't be surprised if he conjured a dollar out of somebody's ear next. But it won't be my dollar, I'm sure of that."

"If you'll give me a chance, sir," suggested Bill.

"Well, you're a broken reed, but you're all I've got to lean on. What is it now?"

"Mikklesen's luggage was broken into about two-thirty. He didn't discover it until after three. The captain couldn't have been in there more than ten or fifteen minutes. What happened in the interval between the time the captain went out and Mikklesen came in?"

"Tell me that and I'll say you're good."

"I can only surmise, sir. But that 1899 dollar we found on Mikklesen—I know who had it last."

"What? You do?" ^

"Yes. That's the dollar I gave Tatu this morning in exchange for the greenback he got from Mikklesen."

"Tatu! That's an idea! Come into the smoking-room and we'll have Tatu on the carpet."

The owner of the Francesca led the way, and Frost, Hammond and Sally followed. Tatu, summoned, appeared a bit lacking in his accustomed calm. He feared his employer, and showed it.

"You've seen this dollar before, Tatu," said Bill, holding it out. "I gave it to you this morning. What did you do with it after that?"

Tatu stared at the silver dollar.

"Give him back," he said.

"Back to whom?"

"Mr. Mikklesen."

"The truth, Tatu," Batchelor demanded.

"So help," answered the Jap. "Mr. Mikklesen say I do not keep promise. That not true. Make me give dollar back, anyhow."

That was Tatu's story, and he stuck to it. After a few moments of further questioning, Batchelor let him go.

"Well, where does that get us?" the millionaire wanted to know.

"The Jap's lying," declared Frost.

"I don't think so," Bill objected. "No, something tells me he speaks true. Mr. Batchelor, that big confession scene of Mikklesen's was staged with a purpose."

"What purpose?"

"I can't say. But I've a hunch he's still got your dollar."

"Where?"

"That's for me to find out, sir." Bill was again the man of action. "Sally, I wish you'd go in and lure Mikklesen into a bridge game, if you will, please. After that's under way, I'll act."

"You sound good," admitted Batchelor. "But then you always do. I wish I could be sure you'd get the right dollar this time."

"I'll get it," said Bill. His heart sank. He'd said that before—with what result? But this time he must make good—he must! However, he wasn't so sure.

When he saw the Englishman uncomfortably settled as Aunt Dora's partner in a game, he hurried below. Without hesitation he turned on the light in Mikklesen's cabin and began to search. He did a thorough job—under the carpet, in the closet, everywhere. But he found no dollar. Nothing at all of interest, in fact, save a little coil of flat wire which lay on the floor almost under the berth. It seemed of no importance, but he put it in his pocketbook. His heart was heavy as he turned out the light and started to leave via the bath. He had one foot in the bathroom and the other in Mikklesen's cabin when the door into the corridor opened.

"Hello," said a voice—O'Meara's—very softly.

Bill fled. He silently took the key out of the door leading from the bath into his room, and, safe in his cabin, fastened the lock from that side. He laid his hand gently on the knob of the door and waited. Footsteps sounded faintly in the bath, and then the knob began to turn slowly in his hand. He let it turn. A gentle shake of the knob, and then the footsteps receded. As soon as he dared, Bill unlocked the door and opened it an inch or two. He made out the occasional glimmer of a flashlight in Mikklesen's cabin.

For a time O'Meara searched industriously. Suddenly the flash went dark. Some one else had entered Mikklesen's cabin. Who? In a moment the politician enlightened him.

"Mrs. Keith!" he said in a low voice.

"Mr. O'Meara!" came the woman's answer.

"What can I do for you?" O'Meara inquired sarcastically.

"Is this your cabin, Mr. O'Meara?" she asked, equally sarcastic.

"It is not."

"Then what are you doing here?"

"Just what you're doing. Looking for that dollar."

"Why, Mr. O'Meara—"

"Come across. I made you early in the game. See here, our interests are the same. Let's work together."

"I don't know what you mean."

"Oh, yes, you do. You're here to get that lucky piece for the Blakes; and I—well, I represent other interests; interests that want to keep Jim Batchelor out of the primaries. Let me have that dollar until next Wednesday at six p.m. and you can have it after that."

"But I haven't got it, Mr. O'Meara."

"I know you haven't. I mean, in case we can get hold of it."

"You think it's in this room?"

"I think Mikklesen's got it somewhere. You know, I had my deal all fixed with him. I caught him last night throwing a shirt overboard, and after a little talk he admitted he had the lucky piece and agreed to deliver it to me in Monterey for twelve hundred cash."

"I thought of making him an offer myself," said the woman. "I knew his talents of old, and I was sure he had it."

"It's just as well you didn't. This morning, when Batchelor offered that whale of a reward, the dirty crook began to hedge. He'd have double-crossed me then and there, only I threatened to have him framed before he could get out of the state. He knew I could do it, so he held off."

"Then that performance to-night was all staged?"

"It sure was," O'Meara said. "I could see it in his eye. It was all for my benefit. I wouldn't be surprised if he led that young fool of a Hammond right into it. He wanted me to think he'd lost the dollar. Probably he's figuring on getting ashore with it, and then sending it to Batchelor by a messenger. But only over my dead body. Let's get busy."

"Where does this door lead?" asked Mrs. Keith.

"Into a bath. There's a door into another cabin, but it's locked."

And it was, for Bill Hammond took the hint just in time. He went to the upper deck and left them to their search, confident that it would have no results.

300

The bridge game was just breaking up, with the enthusiastic cooperation of every one save Aunt Dora. Bill took Sally aside in a corner of the saloon, but before he could say anything her father joined them.

"Anything doing?" he inquired.

Bill told them of the conversation in Mikklesen's cabin. Jim Batchelor was indignant.

"Fine business I" he said. "O'Meara, and the woman too! I knew blamed well I couldn't trust anybody on this boat. Well, they'll go ashore, bag and baggage, with Mikklesen in the morning. But not until I've been over all three of them personally."

"Father."

"Yes, I mean it. Well, Hammond, where are we now? Mikklesen's still got the dollar, you think? But where's he got it?"

"Well " began Bill.

"You've got a clue, of course," said Batchelor. '

"Not one," Bill answered sadly.

"What?" Batchelor stood up. "Well, if you've run out of clues, then the skies are dark indeed. Something tells me I'll never see my dollar again. You may be a good newspaper man, my boy, but as a detective—well—oh, what's the use? I'm going to bed. Good night."

Sally and Bill followed him outside. In a shadowy spot on the deck they paused.

"Oh, Bill, what are we going to do now?" the girl sighed.

"Well, I have one—one little clue. But it's so silly I didn't have the nerve to tell him about it. Just a little coil of wire I found in Mikklesen's cabin."

"What would that mean, Bill?"

"I don't know. But I'm going to think to-night as I never thought before. I can't lose you, Sally. I won't—that's all."

"Not if I have anything to say about it, Bill, you won't," she answered, and the wisdom of stopping in a shadow became at once apparent.

In his berth Bill settled down to do the promised thinking. He began to go over in his mind, carefully, every point in the equipment of a man like Mikklesen. But somewhere in the neighborhood of the military brushes he fell asleep.

* * * * *

THERE is a subconscious self that never sleeps, but applies itself to any problem in hand. Which probably explains why Bill awoke the next morning with the hunch of his life. It was very late; and struck by an unaccustomed quiet, he looked out the port-hole. The little town of Monterey and the green forest of Del Monte met his gaze, and he knew the Francesca had reached port.

The bathroom door was unlocked, and the door leading into Mikklesen's cabin stood open. There was no trace of the

302

Englishman, nor of his many pieces of luggage. Alarmed, Bill rang for Tatu; but from the Jap he learned that no one had yet gone ashore.

"Hurry," Bill ordered, "and tell Mr. Batchelor not to land any one until he hears from me." And he prepared himself for a busy morning.

Jim Batchelor arrived just as Bill was tying his necktie.

"Any news?" inquired the young man.

"Not a glimmer," answered Batchelor. He sat down on the berth, his gloomy face in striking contrast to the sunny morning. "The second officer was in Mikklesen's cabin while he dressed, and examined everything he put on. We've been through his luggage again too. But there was nothing doing. Either he hasn't got that dollar or he's too smart for us."

"Where is he now?" Bill asked.

"He's on deck, waiting to go ashore. The launch is ready. O'Meara and Mrs. Keith are there too."

"Did you search them?"

"Well, no. There are limits. Besides, I'm sure they're just as much in the dark as I am. Both of them came to me this morning and said both wanted to leave the cruise here, so I simply told them to go. There seemed no occasion for a row."

"You were quite right, sir," Bill agreed.

"You—you sent me word not to let anybody land until you came up," said Batchelor.

"I did," Bill smiled.

"Are you—are you on a new trail?"

"I think so."

"My boy! No, no, I mustn't let you get my hopes up again."

"You're very wise, sir," Bill admitted. "This isn't much—a fighting chance, that's all."

"Well, let's fight it," said Batchelor as they left the cabin. "I tell you again, you get that dollar back and there'll be nothing too good for you."

"Careful!" said Bill under his breath, and they went on deck.

Sally joined them, as lovely as the California morning, but with a worried look in her eyes. Bill smiled his reassurance. They moved along the deck and came upon Mikklesen, O'Meara and Mrs. Keith sitting amid their luggage.

"We're losing some of our guests," said Batchelor.

"So I see," Bill answered. "I'd steeled myself to part with Mikklesen, but these others—I'm awfully sorry—"

O'Meara glared at him. Henry Frost, alert for news, came up.

"Mr. Batchelor," Bill went on, "before Mikklesen goes out of our lives for ever, I'd like to ask him one question."

"Certainly. Go to it."

"Mr. Mikklesen"—the Englishman stood up, and he and Bill faced each other—"Mr. Mikklesen," Bill repeated, "what time is it?"

The Englishman's eyes narrowed.

"I don't understand."

"The time—by that watch of yours. I've seen you consult it before. Why not now?"

"My dear fellow"—Mikklesen was quite at ease—"it's a frightfully old thing, really. Belonged to my grandfather. Something has happened to it. It's not running."

"Not running? That's too bad." Bill held out his hand. "Let me have a look at it. I might be able to fix it."

Mikklesen's eyes turned quickly to right and left. He appeared to be measuring the distance between the Francesca and the shore.

"Come on," said Bill. "There's no way out. Hand it over."

"Why not?" said Mikklesen. He took from his pocket a large ancient timepiece and unfastened it from the chain. He was smiling. Bill's heart sank—was he wrong, after all?

His strong fingers closed eagerly on Mikklesen's watch. Anxiously he opened the back. The thing was packed with tissue-paper. He lifted out the paper—and smiled, for underneath lay a silver dollar.

"I hope it's the right one this time," he said, and handed it to Batchelor.

"By the Lord Harry!" cried Batchelor. "My lucky piece! The first dollar I ever earned. Little secret mark and all. My boy—my boy, I take back all I said."

Bill glanced at Sally; her eyes were shining. He handed the watch case back to Mikklesen.

"When you took out the works," he said, "you shouldn't have let the mainspring get away from you. Lively little things, mainsprings. Elusive, what?"

"I fancy so." Mikklesen, still smiling, still nonchalant, restored the watch to his pocket. "Mr. Batchelor, I'll toddle along. There's been no actual theft."

"Who says there hasn't?"

O'Meara, purple with rage, was on his feet. "Batchelor, you turn this crook over to me. I'll put him behind the bars, where he belongs."

Jim Batchelor shook his head. "Your passion for justice is splendid, O'Meara," he said, "but I prefer it otherwise. Publicity never did appeal to me. Mr. Mikklesen, I congratulate you. You must have been a wonder at hide and seek when you were a kid. You may as well—go along."

"Thanks, awfully," said Mikklesen. "It's been a frightfully jolly cruise, and all that." He glanced at O'Meara, and his smile faded. "I'm going to ask one last favor, if I may."

"Well, you've got your nerve," Batchelor said. "What is it?"

"Will you be so good as to send me ashore alone, and let the launch return for—these others?"

The owner of the Francesca was in high good humor. He laughed.

"Of course I will," he replied. "I can't say I blame you either. It isn't always safe for birds of a feather to flock together. Get into the launch. And you, O'Meara"—he put himself in the angry politician's path—"you stay where you are."

Mikkleson indicated his luggage to a sailor and hastily descended the ladder. The launch putt-putted away. O'Meara moved to the rail and shook a heavy fist.

"I'll get you," he cried, "you low-down crook!"

Mikklesen stood in the stern of the launch and waved a jaunty farewell. He was off in search of new fields and better luck.

"Oh, Mr. Batchelor," purred Mrs. Keith, "it's a woman's privilege to change her mind, you know. If you have no objection I'll stay with the party."

"Oh, no, you won't!" said Batchelor. "I've got my dollar back and I intend to hang on to it."

"Why, what do you mean?" she said, staring at him with wide, innocent eyes.

"I'm on to you—and O'Meara too. I'm sorry you've forced me to say it. Go back to your friends the Blakes, Mrs. Keith, and tell them they've got me to lick on that China contract—if they can. As for you, O'Meara, my name will be entered in the primaries next week. And I'm glad to know where you stand."

"What's it all about?" O'Meara inquired blandly.

"You know very well what it's about. The second officer has some errands in the town, but he'll be back with the launch in an hour or so. When he comes I'll ask you both to leave the Francesca." Batchelor turned and his eyes lighted on Bill Hammond. Smiling, he put his arm about Bill's shoulder. "Some detective, if you ask me. Come into the saloon, Son. There's a little matter of business between us. Henry, you're in on this. Got your check-book?"

"I've got it," said Frost, and he and Sally followed the pair into the main saloon.

"Two thousand from you, Henry," Batchelor reminded him.

"I know it." Mr. Frost reluctantly sat down at a desk and prepared to write.

"Wait a minute," Bill interposed. "I don't want any money, Mr. Frost."

"What do you want?" asked Frost.

"A better job."

"And he deserves it too," said Batchelor.

"Well," began Frost, whose first instinct was always to hedge,

"I don't like to interfere at the office " Still, his expression seemed to say two thousand is two thousand.

"The Sunday editor quit last week," Bill went on. "A word from you and the job's mine. It pays a hundred, I believe."

Frost stood up.

"All right," he agreed. "We'll consider the matter settled." He patted his check-book lovingly and departed.

"Now that was sensible," beamed Jim Batchelor. "A job—a chance to make good. Better than money."

"It looks better to me," smiled Bill. "You see, I'm thinking of getting married."

Batchelor got up and seized his hand.

"Fine! Fine!" he cried. "My boy, I wish you all the luck in the world."

"Then you approve of it?"

"The best thing that could happen to any young man. A balance wheel—an incentive."

"That's the way I feel, sir," said Bill heartily.

"And it does you credit." Batchelor sat at the desk. "My little check will come in the way of a wedding present." He stopped. "I hope you're getting the right sort of girl?"

"I'm sure of that, sir."

"Of course you feel that way. But these modern girls— not the kind I used to know. Flighty, extravagant—they don't know the value of a dollar."

"This one," said Bill, "knows the value of one dollar. At least, she ought to."

"What's that?" cried Batchelor.

"Put away your check-book, sir," said Bill. "It isn't your money I want."

Batchelor threw down his pen. "I—I didn't dream— Sally, what about this?"

She came and sat on his knee.

"Dad, you've never refused me anything yet. You're not going to haggle over a little thing like Bill."

"But—but I don't—this young man—why, he hasn't anything!"

"What did you have when you were married?" she asked.

"I had my brains and a strong right arm."

"So has Bill," she told him.

He turned slowly and looked at Bill.

"I'm thinking of you too," he said. "I like you, my boy—I won't deny it. But this—this—could you get away with it? A girl like Sally—it isn't so much the initial expense—it's the upkeep. Could you manage it?"

"With your permission," said Bill, "I'd like to try."

Batchelor kissed his daughter and stood up.

"You'll have to give me time on this," he said. "All so sudden. I'll think it over."

"Yes, sir," Bill answered. "And in the meantime—"

"In the meantime " Batchelor stopped at the door. He looked at Bill Hammond long and wistfully. "You know," he said, "I'd give a million dollars to be where you are now." And he went out.

"Poor Dad," said Sally. "Isn't he a darling?"

"It runs in your family," Bill told her. "I've noticed that."

"Bill, you'll always love me, won't you?"

"Love you—and keep you close," said Bill. "In the big moments of my life you'll give me courage to go on. The first wife I ever earned."

"Bill, be careful!" she said. "Somebody might come in."

IDLE HANDS

*First published in The Saturday Evening Post, Jun 11,
1921*

ON the stroke of eight, as was his custom, Jim Alden
opened his eyes and sat up in bed. With a brisk movement
of his arm he threw back the covers. His mind was racing
smoothly, efficiently, ready to tackle any problem no matter
how hard or intricate. As his feet touched the rich rug beside
his bed he suddenly remembered. A sense of bafflement,
of despair, swept over him. His head sank forward on his
breast.

Every morning was like this. Every morning he sat up
in bed, craving an exciting active day as of old, only to recall
a moment later that he was sixty and out of it, that he had
retired, that he was dying by inches in a beautiful house in
Southern California.

He walked slowly to his window and looked out.
Pasadena is a city of leisure. There was no one in sight. He
sighed and turned to his bath. The empty day that loomed
ahead appalled him. It would be like all the other days
through which he had wandered like a lost soul ever since
he came out here three months before. Nothing to do, no
place to go, no one to talk to. Torture, finished off by a dull
dinner and then more torture—a long quiet evening while

he waited for bedtime. Bed, sleep, leading to another day, exactly the same.

"Better dead!" he muttered.

In the bath his despair turned to bitter anger at the doctors who had condemned him to this. Why had he allowed himself to be frightened by their silly twaddle about high blood-pressure, neuralgic heart, hardening arteries? Why had he listened to his wife and daughters when they urged him to sell his automobile interests in the East, to desert the famous Alden engine, the engine he had designed, the engine that was his baby? What would have happened if he had been firm, stuck to business? Death, perhaps—death in the harness. Well, that was where most men died; that was the place to die, the happy place.

To some men, he reflected as he dressed, this life of idleness might appeal. Arthur, Edie's husband, showed no inclination to work. But Arthur was a lazy young pup who had been born into the leisure class. And Carter Andrews, the bright young butterfly who was hovering about Angie, had apparently no other interests than polo and golf. All right, all right, Jim Alden thought, heartily disliking them both. It was not surprising they were fond of that sort of thing. They had never known anything else. That was where they had started.

But his own start had been so different. He thought back over his forty years in the harness. Twelve years a mechanic in the Pontiac shops, with soiled hands and vast ambitions. Then the birth of the Alden engine, the modest beginnings of the Alden car. The gradual increase in business—life working up to a big climax like a well-written play. Finally the office, electric with the thrills of trading, big decisions to be made amid the clicking of a hundred typewriters, the stream of telegrams and cables, big stacks of mail. And then to be suddenly pushed off into nothingness, to have all these things disappear as though they had never been. It was, he thought bitterly, too late. In forty years he had gone too far to stop.

He went gloomily down the stairs, grumbling a good morning to his Japanese butler in the hall. In the drawing-room beyond he heard Angie singing a foolish little song. His face brightened as he went in to her. She came toward him, fresh and beautiful as the California morning, the best beloved of all his possessions.

"How are you feeling, Dad?" she asked as she kissed him.

"Me? Oh, I'm all right." The question annoyed him even when it was Angie who asked it. "Do I look like an invalid to you?"

She glanced at him, then quickly turned away. He did look like an invalid, whether he knew it or not. The change that was to do so much for him had proved a ghastly failure.

His hands were old and veined, his face pale, great dark pouches were under his eyes. Angie sighed unhappily.

"What you got there?" He pointed to a slip of paper in her hand.

"It's a cable from Carter Andrews. He's living up to his promise—a cable a day."

"Huh! He must be crazy about you."

"He claims to be," she smiled.

"Funny thing to me he'd leave you to go round the world."

"Oh, but he went on business! Business connected with his estate."

"Every one knows why he went," Alden said. "His private stock gave out and he went abroad for a drink. He's drinking his way around the globe."

"Now, Dad, that's not kind."

"It's the truth. I suppose he wants to marry you."

"He does, but don't worry. I'm not getting married just yet. Of course, Carter is amusing."

"So's a monkey, but you wouldn't marry one, would you?"

"Cross old Dad! Come on in to breakfast."

They went into the breakfast-room. Mrs. Alden, Edie and Arthur were already at the table. Dutifully Jim Alden went round and kissed his wife, a stern unbending woman of fifty. On his way to his seat he pecked fearfully at Edie's calcimined cheek. Arthur greeted him warmly, said how well he was looking. All the world looked well to Arthur. Jim Alden picked up his newspaper.

"Put that down, Jim," ordered his wife. "You've got all day to read it."

"So I have," he said humbly, obeying. "I forgot."

"What's your program for the day?" she asked.

"Me? Oh, I'll just run into Los Angeles to my office."

"Your office!" she said. "You came out here to get away from offices. Yet the first thing you do is go and rent one. What you need of it I can't see."

"Oh, we old fellows who've retired like to keep an office," he smiled. "It gives us an objective in the mornings—a place to answer our mail."

"Your mail!" Her tone was scornful. "All the mail you get you could answer here in the library in twenty minutes." He winced. This was true. "If you'd only go out and play golf," she complained.

"That's the ticket, Dad!" cried Arthur with forced enthusiasm. "Edie and I are going to the club. Come along."

"No, no, thanks. Not to-day. Some other time."

"Glad to have you," lied Arthur, concealing his relief. He and Edie were skilful players, and were looking forward to a sporty foursome at ten dollars a hole.

"You ought to go," Mary Alden said. "Doctor Tillson told

"Yes, yes," agreed Alden. "I'll get worked round to it. I'm not opposed to golf. It's all right—as a recreation after a hard day's work. But to make it the chief business of life, as some people do—"

"Edie," said Arthur, "he's looking at me!"

"Dad, you let Arthur alone," ordered Edie.

"Jim, you worry me," said his wife sharply. "You're not happy out here."

"Me? Of course I am!"

"You ought to be happy." She glared at him. "Be happy or I'll brain you," was her tone. "But you're not. The change isn't doing you a bit of good, and it's all your fault."

"Yes, I suppose it is," he admitted.

"You won't relax—won't let yourself go. I should think you might make the effort, if not for your own sake, why then for mine and that of the children."

"Speaking as one of the little darlings," put in Angie, "I say give the poor soul a chance. You've knocked all the props out from under him, and just now he's floating about in space. He'll settle down in time—become a nice old duffer kicking a ball around the links all day like the rest."

"Angie's said it!" cried Jim Alden gratefully. "I'll adjust myself in the end. Just now I don't quite know where I am."

"Well, you'd better find out," his wife told him. "I'm sure that in the past, when I've had to adapt myself to new conditions, I've always- -"

She went on to tell what she had always done. Nobody listened—still, it passed the time.

After breakfast Jim Alden went out on the veranda. Edie and Arthur, brilliant figures in golf togs, followed. The latter had telephoned the chauffeur's room at the garage. A smart little runabout was waiting in the drive. Alden took out a cigar and defiantly lighted it.

"Better not let Mother see you with that," admonished Edie. The policewoman to whom she referred appeared, evidently ready for a busy day.

"What's this, Jim?" she cried. "Smoking again!"

"The first to-day, Mary."

"But Doctor Tillson said—"

"He said to go slow on 'em, and I am, my dear—trust me."

"Not out of my sight, where smoking is concerned." She turned to her elder daughter. "You and Arthur can drop me at the Book Club. There's a big luncheon and I'm on the committee. Now, Jim, do take things easy to-day—relax."

"Me? I'll relax all over the place."

He stood staring after the little car as it glided away down the sunny street. Angie came down-stairs, a light and pretty wrap about her shoulders.

"Dad, I'll ride into town with you—if you don't mind. Got some shopping to do—and lunch with a girl from home."

"Delighted," he said, and went for his hat and coat. When he returned his limousine, with a stolid Jap at the wheel, was waiting. He helped Angie into it. "Let's go, Haku," he said.

They rolled along through the bright morning in the direction of Los Angeles. Angie put her hand on one of his, which lay idly in his lap.

"Dad, Mother was right—you're not happy."

"Oh, now, Angie, I'm all right. Only something has happened—something I don't like. I mean—I'm an old man."

"Nonsense! Sixty isn't old."

"It didn't use to be, but nowadays it seems to be the finish. And it came on me—so sudden. In the past when something I didn't want was about to happen—I prevented it. But this time there was nothing I could do." She squeezed his hand. "I suppose all us old fellows feel like this—rebellious. We want to turn back the clock. You know, I'd give every penny I have if I could go back—back to the start—with the fun all ahead of me."

"And where would I be?" asked Angie.

"You? You'd be lying in your cradle in the old house down on Third Street—a lovely fluffy baby. That was a mighty happy year—that year you came—twenty-four years ago. I was just getting started. We were poor as the devil. I had a terrible time paying the doctor who brought you into the world, but it was the best investment I ever made."

Tears came into Angie's blue eyes. She looked away at a misty string of billboards, part of the famous scenery.

"Dad, it's just as Mother said. You must brace up. If you'll only be contented you can live for ever out in this country. Promise to try—for my sake."

"I promise, Angie," he said.

"If you could find something to take up your time," she went on, thinking aloud. "Something to turn your mind to—"

Angie lapsed into silence. When the car came to a stop before the tall building where he maintained his absurd office she bent over and kissed him. He looked so forlorn and lonesome.

"Be here at five, as usual, Haku," said Alden as he left the car.

"At five!" Angie cried. "What in the world " She stopped. What in the world would he do with himself until five? But after all it was his problem. "Good-by, old dear," she called, smiling brightly.

Three minutes later he pushed open the door of his little office on the tenth floor. The room was hot and stuffy. He hastened to open a window, letting in the widely advertised fresh air. Coming back, he saw a single envelope lying on the carpet. He picked it up, opened it:

JAMES M. ALDEN.

Dear Sir: We beg to acknowledge the receipt of ten cents in stamps, in return for which we are sending you under separate cover, as per your request, a catalogue of the electrical appliances manufactured by our firm.

"Under separate cover?"

He looked about. The catalogue had not arrived. He was disappointed. It had occurred to him that by studying it he might hit on some idea that would occupy his time. Rotten mail service!

He sat down before his flat-topped desk, clear save for an empty mail basket, a blotter and inkwell. With a key from his chain he unlocked the drawers, opening the top pair a few inches. Next he spread out his newspaper and began the morning's careful perusal. After the news columns, stock market and editorials—his daily routine—he turned to the obituary column.

"Died at his home here, Edward Mackay, former president of the Mackay Supply Company, retired from active business a year ago.

"Died at his home, Peter Faxton, retired.

"Henry Downs, gave up active business six months ago—"

First they retired—then the obituary column. What a short step it was for most of them!

He tried to cheer up on the sporting page. Presently the moment arrived when there was nothing more to be found in the paper. He put it down regretfully and looked at his watch. Ten o'clock. Seven hours before the arrival of Haku and the car.

Seven hours! The movies—yes, but not until afternoon. He hated the movies, but went regularly. He knew he would go to-day. He took up the paper again, and after a careful study of the advertisements selected his afternoon's picture. But how about the morning? He might go for a long walk. Tillson had urged walking. Or he might sit in the park with other idlers. Or there was the public library, on the sixth floor of an office building, because Los Angeles, home of million-dollar picture theaters, had no better place to house it. There he could sit and read among his fellow derelicts, some of them smelly and unbathed.

He stood at the window in that quiet little room. Outside sounded the roar and bustle of the world that had thrust him aside. Far down below, in the crowded street, men hurried about their business—their business!

Jim Alden went back to his desk, sat down limply and stared at the blotter Angie had helped him select. It was pink—a cheerful color, Angie had said. The door opened and a brisk young man stepped inside. He stood staring about him for a moment as though trying to decide just where he was.

"Ah—er—good morning," he said. "To whom am I speaking?"

"Alden's the name. Jim Alden."

"Ah, yes, Mr. Alden. Your name's not on the door, and I didn't notice it on the directory down-stairs."

"No, my business doesn't require it. What can I do for you?"

"Mr. Alden, I want to ask a favor. I want you to pause in the midst of life's busy whirl—to pause a moment and think."

"Of what?"

"Of the future."

"Ah, yes," smiled Jim Alden. "As a matter of fact, my boy, I was doing just that when you opened the door."

"You were? Fine for me! Then you must realize how uncertain the future is. In case anything happened to you, what would become of your family?"

"I've got you, Son. You're selling insurance."

"I am. Life and accident. I don't imagine the company would care to write you a life policy at your age, but what about accident? Los Angeles is a mighty accidental city. Out of every thousand people walking these streets to-day five will be killed by automobiles before the year ends."

"Yes, but I'm careful. I lead a quiet life."

"That's just what Mr. Jamieson used to say. Poor Mr. Jamieson!

"He used to have an office in this very building—on this floor, I think it was. He used to sit leaning back in his chair, just as you're sitting now, when I called on him and tell me nothing was likely to happen to him. Do you know what happened?"

"No. What?"

"Well, one day his chair slipped out from under him." Jim Alden came forward quickly. "He hit his head on a radiator. I don't know what his last thoughts were, but at the end I'll bet he was wishing he'd listened to me."

"You're a cheerful visitor, Son," Alden laughed. "I don't want any insurance to-day, but any time you're passing, drop in."

The young man stood up.

"Mr. Alden, I'm going to ask you a rather peculiar question. Are you inviting me to call again because there's a chance we might do business, or do you want me around to talk to?"

"Why, I—er—"

"You're retired, aren't you?"

"Yes, three months ago."

"And you feel like a fish out of water? Just plain bored stiff?"

"You've said it!"

"I thought so. You see, I run into a lot of men in your position. There are hundreds of them in Los Angeles. They keep little offices like this, and sit in 'em day after day doing nothing. When I show up they greet me with open arms. They give me a cigar—"

"Pardon me. Have a smoke."

"Thanks. And then they talk their heads of T—politics, stock market, even religion. Now I'm sociable by nature, and I'd like nothing better than to hang around and chat, but I've got a family to support. You get me?"

"I do. So there are lots of men like me? I never thought of that."

"There's a dozen of them in this very building. I'm sorry for all of them, poor devils. I've offered some of them, free gratis, a little idea of mine, but up to now not one has been sport enough to act on it."

"An idea?" Jim Alden asked.

"This is a mighty good cigar," smiled the young man, resuming his seat. "I'll give you ten minutes more on the strength of it. You read your newspaper pretty carefully, I guess. But have you ever looked in the classified columns under Business Chances?"

"I can't say I have."

"Pass me the paper, please. Here we are—three columns of it: 'For Sale—Best Paying Barber Shop in San Diego—two chairs, three baths, steady trade.' No? Look! 'Butcher—Go in Business for Yourself ... Partnership, Auto Top Trimming Shop, $650 ... Half Interest in Busy Beauty Parlor.' No, keep away from the busy beauties. 'Wanted—Party with $1000 and Self, Half Interest Factory Manufacturing Pure California Fruit Juices ... Investigate This! Half Interest Old Established Insurance Business.' Keep out of that, it's done to death. 'Transfer and Express ... Man and Wife Can Purchase Good Restaurant ... Partner Wanted, Auto Garage and Service Station.'"

"Ah, a garage," said Jim Alden thoughtfully.

"I haven't time to read them all," the young man said. "But you get my idea: If I was one of you retired millionaires I wouldn't sit down and wait for the undertaker. If they'd shooed me out of my regular business I'd get me an interest in one of these little places and I'd run it—just as a toy, of course. I'd have something to take my time and thought; I'd be happy and contented; I'd fool the doctors and live for ever. Does it sound reasonable?"

"It certainly does," Jim Alden smiled.

"I'm glad you think so. I must run along now. If you decide to take my advice, and it works out O.K.—well, you'll owe me a little policy. How about it?"

"If, my boy, if. At any rate, drop in later on."

"Count on me. Kurtz is my name. I'll leave a card. So long, and don't get mixed up with the beauty parlor. Outside of that anything's worth a chance."

He breezed out, leaving Jim Alden with the paper in his hand. For a long time the designer of the famous Alden engine sat deep in thought. "Why not?" he asked himself. Why not a little garage somewhere, a place where he could go and meet people, gossip with them, discuss engines with men like those he had known and been fond of in the Pontiac shops? A splendid idea!

But what would Mary say—and her stern ally, Doctor Tillson? No more business—he had sworn it! No more big business, that meant. And Mary wanted him to be contented—to stop fussing. Besides, she needn't know!

He sat there chuckling over this last thought. His was far from a deceitful nature, but it seemed that he was justified in following the trail to happiness wherever it led, without interference. Why not a bit of a double life? Only Angie need be told. Angie would understand, sympathize. Not two hours ago Angie had been wishing he had something to turn his mind to.

He read those three columns through carefully. There were many auto repair shops in the market, but one advertisement in particular appealed to him. He cut it out and read it a number of times:

PARTNER WANTED—Auto Repair Shop and Gas
Station on busy road, outskirts of San Marco—$2500
buys half interest, tools, equipment, tow car, building
and lease on lot. Books open to prospective buyer.
Grab this—big bargain. Call San Marco 5376, ask for
Petersen.

Jim Alden hesitated but a moment, then took up his
seldom-used telephone and asked for the number. Petersen
himself answered.

"I saw your ad," said the millionaire, "and I don't know—
maybe we might do business. What's that—my name?" He
paused for a moment. It would never do to mention Jim
Alden, famous in the automobile trade. His secret would not
last an hour. "Oh, this is John Grant talking," he went on,
speaking the name of an old pal in the Pontiac shops. "I'd
like to have a look at your establishment. You needn't do that.
Well, if you insist. What time can you come? All right—at
two. You'll find me in room 1018, the Surrey Building, Los
Angeles. Know where it is? Fine! I'll be here."

He hung up the receiver and walked briskly to the
window. His eyes were sparkling. At two that afternoon! He
had an engagement—a business engagement!

"Better than the movies!" he thought exultantly.

* * * * *

MR. PETERSEN appeared promptly at the appointed hour. Jim Alden was ready to like him, but his first glance discouraged him. Petersen was an undersized man with mean, shifty eyes; not at all the jolly mechanic. Alden resolved at once to do no business with him. It seemed hardly polite, however, to break off relations at mere sight of the man, so he agreed to run out for a look at the property.

In a battered old flivver the garage man whisked Jim Alden out to San Marco by what seemed a rather round-about route. When the designer of the Alden engine alighted before Petersen's garage he began to weaken. It stood amid beautiful surroundings at the meeting of two roads, one of which appeared to be much traveled. Across the street was an orange grove, and back of the little frame building, seeming much closer than they really were, the friendly snow-capped mountains stood on guard.

Petersen showed him over the place. He saw at once that the equipment was complete and in good condition. When they returned to the office three cars waited in line for gasoline.

"It's like that all day long," Petersen said, waving a hand. "I can prove it to you by the books. I want you to look 'em over."

For an hour Jim Alden studied the records. They extended over a period of three years and showed a steadily mounting trade, especially big during the last six months. Petersen returned.

"How does it look to you?" he inquired.

"Not bad," said Alden. "You own the building, eh? How about the ground?"

"Got it on lease," replied Petersen. "Pay eight hundred a year—you saw that in the books. Rent's cheap, everything considered."

"Seems so," agreed Alden. He didn't like Petersen, but the thing looked good. Probably he could get used to the man. And there was a bright cheerful boy named Al working about the place. "Make terms?" he asked.

"No," said Petersen sharply, "I got to have cash."

"U'm!" Jim Alden thought of the eleven million dollars for which he had sold his eastern holdings, and smiled. "Well, I guess maybe I could raise the money."

"You'll buy in then?"

"Yes. I'll meet you to-morrow at " He stopped. He was about to say "at my lawyer's." But that wouldn't do. "Anywhere you say. I'll bring the cash with me."

"Good for you." Petersen managed a faint smile. "Have a cigar." He passed over a good ten-center.

"You'll come out by street car, I suppose. Get off at the corner of First and California, in San Marco—ten o'clock tomorrow morning. I know a lawyer. We'll go to his office and clinch the deal."

Jim Alden returned to his own office by trolley. He had just time to lock his desk and meet Haku and the limousine at the appointed hour. It hustled him a bit. He loved to be hustled. He was a happy man.

The next morning at the lawyer's it was decided that he was to assume his partnership on the first of the month, which happened to be the following Monday. This was Thursday. After the papers had been signed and the twenty-five hundred in cash reached a haven in Petersen's grimy hands the latter made a suggestion.

"Look here, Grant," he said. "I've had a lot of answers to my ad. I know it says in the agreement neither of us is to sell without the other's consent; but I been wondering— if I could dig you up a willing, good- natured guy, would you mind if I sold my interest to him? I'd like to clear out completely and go back to Dakota. What say?"

Alden smiled. Petersen was the one flaw in his happiness, and he would be glad to shake him.

"All right with me," he said. "Of course you'd get somebody who knew the business—a good mechanic." He realized for the first time that Petersen had made no such stipulation in his own case.

"Sure!" said the garage man. He asked for and received a memorandum giving him permission to sell. "Much obliged, Grant. Well, see you at the garage on Monday."

"With bells on," laughed Alden. Mr. Petersen must have caught the contagion of that laugh. He seemed in almost a gay mood when they parted.

Sunday night Angie and her father happened to be alone in the library. He was puffing contentedly on a forbidden cigar.

"Mighty nice night, ain't it?" he said. "You know, Angie, I'm beginning to like California."

"I've noticed," she smiled. "You've been a new man the past few days. How do you account for it?"

"Oh, I'm just settling down, I guess. Getting used to idleness."

"Nonsense! You're up to some mischief. You can't fool me!"

He laughed, got up with mock caution and tiptoed to the door. Coming back, he solemnly faced her.

"My dear," he said, "this is deep and dark. Never reveal what I am about to tell you."

"I swear it," she answered. "What's the secret?" "Angie, I'm half owner in Petersen's garage, which stands in the shadow of the mountains just abaft San Marco. A nifty little business, believe me." She gasped.

"Honey," he went on, "I've turned back the clock. If you come out there to- morrow you'll find me in overalls right at the start of my career, and I may say the prospects for success look very bright."

"But—but, Dad, what will Mother say?" "Plenty—if she knew. But that's the beauty of it. Mother isn't going to know. Poor old broken-down Dad toddles off to his office early in the morning, does a quick change, nabs a street car and beats it for his business. Comes back at night tired but happy. If you breathe a word of this you're no child of mine."

She leaned back in her chair, laughing.

"A double life at your age," she said. "Dad, it's too funny!"

"But you approve, don't you? You know you said—"

"Of course I approve. It's just the thing. Why, the very idea has done wonders for you! But if Mother finds out—"

"I know." His tone was apprehensive. "But San Marco's ten miles from here—I'm fairly safe. If you need anything in my line look me up. I'm just a poor young man trying to get along."

"I'll drop in to-morrow. Tell me again where it is." He drew a map for her on the back of an envelope. "Remember," he said, "my name out there is John Grant." "Oh, Dad!" she cried. "An assumed name! How thrilling!" In the morning he hunted round in his closet until he found an old blue suit. It was a bit shiny in spots. His wife had informed him he was not to wear it again. Defiantly he put it on and went down-stairs. There ensued a brief argument about it, but his wife did not seem up to her usual form, and he won.

At nine o'clock Haku deposited him before his office building. The building stood on a corner and could be entered from either of two streets. Jim Alden passed through the lobby and out the side door. At a clothing store he supplied himself with dark-blue overalls and jumper, then walked another block, hopped on a car and rode to San Marco. When he reached his new property there seemed to be an air of aimless leisure about the place. Al was sitting on the running board of a car reading the morning paper. Petersen was nowhere in sight. Jim Alden went into the office. A long lean young man with humorous gray eyes untangled himself from a chair and rose to greet him.

"Where's Petersen?" asked Alden.

"Is this Mr. Grant—Mr. John Grant?" inquired the stranger.

"What? Oh—er—yes, I'm Grant."

"Merrick's my name—Bill Merrick. Shake hands with your new partner, Mr. Grant. I bought Petersen out last Friday."

"What? Well—er—glad to meet you. Petersen didn't lose any time."

"I hope you don't object. He showed me a memorandum you wrote—"

"Oh, no, that's all right. I was a bit surprised, that's all. I don't mind a change of partners—rather like it in fact. I guess we've got hold of a live business."

"Seemed so from the books. I must say, though, I've been sitting here an hour and a half, and not a nibble."

"Oh, well, it's early yet. Monday morning, too. I'll just get into my outfit so as to be ready." The millionaire undid his bundle and spread out his suit of armor. He removed his coat. "I suppose you understand all about automobiles?" he inquired.

"Oh, yes, I know it's the gasoline seeping through the what-you-may-call-it that sort of encourages 'em to continue. Further than that, I'm a little in the dark. Petersen said you were an excellent mechanic and would be glad to teach me."

"He did, eh?"

Jim Alden buckled on the overalls thoughtfully. Mr. Petersen grew even less attractive as his character developed.

"You see," the young man went on, and his manner was winning, "I came darn near being a lawyer. I was studying law in my father's office in Duluth when the war broke. After I got back from France I was like a lot of the boys—the soles of my feet itched. An aunt died and left me three thousand dollars; and I'd swallowed a bit of gas in the Argonne, which supplied me with a mighty convenient little cough, so it was me for California. I've been here two months looking for work. Have you tried to find work out here?"

"You bet I have!"

"Supply seems a bit short of the demand, doesn't it? My money was sort of dribbling away in the cafeterias, so I plunged with Petersen. Two thousand dollars—the balance of Aunt Elvira's wad."

"Two thousand!" repeated Jim Alden, again thinking hard.

"Yes, sir. All little Rollo's available cash. We've got to make good."

"Oh, we'll make good all right," said Alden. But he wasn't so sure. Petersen was taking on new aspects every minute.

They spent a couple of hours looking over their stock and once more studying the books, which Petersen had accommodatingly left. By noon just two cars had halted at their establishment—one to buy five gallons of gasoline, the other to inquire the way. A suspicion was growing in Jim Alden's mind. He went to the door of the little office and summoned Al. The boy came in looking rather sheepish.

"See here, Al," said Alden. "This place does a pretty good business, doesn't it?"

"Well," said Al, "it did—up to last Saturday."

"Eh? What happened on Saturday?"

"Don't you know?" Al seemed genuinely surprised. "Last Saturday they opened up the new state highway two miles east of here. The road over there has been torn up for six months."

"I see," Alden said, "You mean we're sort of off the main line from now on?"

"You sure are," admitted Al. "This road is about as necessary as a fifth wheel. You won't see much traffic here except the folks that live up the line." He stopped. There ensued a poignant silence. "I thought Petersen let you in on it," the boy went on. "He claimed he had. Told me he was sellin' out at a sacrifice."

"He didn't tell us, Al," said Alden slowly. "Go back to your— er—work." The boy went out.

"Well, that's cheery news," cried Bill Merrick bitterly. "Swindled! Every cent that Aunt Elvira and I had in the world!" He paused and looked at his partner. On Jim Alden's face was an expression of deep chagrin, which Bill Merrick conveniently took to be distress. "How about you?" the young man asked. "All your savings gone blooey, eh?" Alden did not reply. "It's a darn shame," the other went on. "It doesn't matter so much about me, but you—you're an old—that is, you're not so young as you were. Well, leave it to me. I'll find this crook Petersen wherever he is, and when I do—oh, boy!"

"Wait a minute," Alden cut in. "Finding Petersen won't help. Perhaps we can pull through yet."

"How?" asked Bill Merrick. "Come out here." He led the way outside. "Nice, quiet, pastoral scene, eh what? Not a car in sight—not one!"

"Oh, yes, there's one," said Jim Alden.

He pointed. Coming down the otherwise deserted highway, driving the newest and gayest of the Alden roadsters at sixty miles an hour, was Angie. She dashed in at the drive that cut the corner and deftly brought her car to a stop between the gas tank and the garage door. Then for the first time her eyes fell on Jim Alden, standing there looking rather foolish in his painfully new mechanic's uniform. A peal of laughter was her instant tribute.

"Dad!" she cried. "You old rascal! I hardly knew you!"

At once an expression of contrition crossed her lovely face. Regret, chagrin, an appeal for forgiveness, all were in her eyes. Coming down the road she had been saying to herself, "John Grant, John Grant," over and over. And now she had blurted out the truth instantly—ruined everything. How like her!

Jim Alden was watching his partner. That young man at sight of Angie had stood as one who beholds an angel descend from heaven. As the import of the angel's first words dawned slowly on his dazed brain he turned to Alden.

"Dad?" he cried. "She called you Dad!"

"So she did," said Alden. He raised his voice so that Angie might hear: "This young lady and I are old friends. Her father and I once worked together in the Pontiac shops— that was before he made his money. When her dad—her real dad, I mean—bought his first car I was the family chauffeur.

I used to drive this little lady about Pontiac, and she'd fall asleep on my lap and her hair'd get all mixed up with the wheel. She started to call me Dad in those days, and I'm proud to say she's never stopped." He paused, and saw that Angie's eyes were on him, fascinated. "Come over here, Bill. Miss Angie, I want you to meet my partner, Bill Merrick. Bill—Miss Angie Alden."

Mr. Bill Merrick seemed devoid of speech as his hand touched that of Angie Alden.

"How's your father?" Jim Alden asked.

"Better, much better," replied Angie, still looking her admiration. "Dad, I think this is a darling place for a garage." She stared about her. "And then—having a partner—such a nice partner—"

"Yes, it's lucky I've got Bill. We'll be company for each other. Otherwise it would be mighty lonesome here. You see, we've just discovered they've opened a new road east of us, and we're left high and dry."

"Oh, I'm sorry to hear that!" cried Angie.

"I knew you would be. I told you the other day—when I happened to run across you in Pasadena—that things looked pretty good for me, but I'm afraid I spoke too soon. However, while there's life there's hope. We'll put it over yet, eh, Bill? Bill ain't more than twenty-five, and I feel younger every minute. Now what can we do for you, Miss—er—Miss Angie?"

"You can sell me ten gallons of gas—if you will, please."

They leaped to do her bidding. Alden assumed charge of the pump and Bill Merrick presided at the car. He leaned close to its fair driver.

"I must have seemed stupid when we were introduced," he said. "You see, I was overcome. It was too good to be true. I mean—meeting you again."

"Again?"

"Yes, we met once before. I guess you don't remember."

"I'm so sorry."

"You wouldn't, of course. There were hundreds of us. We were on a train—in 1917—on our way to camp. It was at the station in Detroit. I was leaning out the window, very greedy, and you came along the platform and gave me a sandwich."

"Ah, yes! Ham or cheese?"

"I don't know to this day."

"Was it as bad as that?"

"It was—wonderful. I wanted to put it in my memory book—only I didn't have a memory book, so I ate it. I was hungry. Afterward I wished I hadn't. I wished I'd saved it— always. Wow! Say, hold on a minute! Stop pumping!"

The tank was overflowing.

"I'm so sorry," said Angie. "I remember now—I had it filled yesterday."

"That's only three gallons," Jim Alden said, disappointed. "Do you need any oil?"

"Always need oil," answered Angie. "Never can think of it."

Bill Merrick recalled that he was a partner in the enterprise. He went for the oil, while Alden lifted the hood of the car. Angie watched them. She reflected that Bill Merrick was a very agreeable young man. Just the pal for her father. How nice!

"Need any tires, chains—anything like that?" asked Alden. "No? Well, you owe us two dollars and twelve cents."

She handed him a five-dollar bill.

"Keep the change, Dad," she said grandly.

"Oh, no, Miss Angie, I couldn't, really!"

"But I insist." She turned to Bill Merrick. "Don't get discouraged," she smiled. "You can count on one steady customer."

"You'll come again? Say, that's great!"

"For Dad's sake," she said. "He's the best ever. Be good to him." She stepped on the gas and was gone.

Slowly Bill Merrick walked over and set down his burden of oil.

"Say, Dad," he began, "I'm going to call you Dad, too, if you don't mind. I believe you said something about—before her father made his money. Who is she, anyhow?"

"Why, she's old Jim Alden's daughter."

"Alden! James M. Alden, the automobile man!" An expression of acute despair spread over Bill Merrick's face. He sank down upon a bench. "Of all the rotten luck!" he moaned.

"Oh, I don't know," said his partner. "Alden's not so bad. Pretty good father, I imagine."

"Rotten luck for me, I mean."

"How's that?"

"I guess you heard me tell her how I'd seen her before—in Detroit. I've never got over it—never been able to see any other girl since. She's—she's wonderful. I've thought of her, dreamed of her—"

He sat staring gloomily in front of him. Jim Alden regarded him with new interest. He liked this boy, liked the look in his eyes, the smile which was for the moment submerged.

Yes, there was something appealing about Bill Merrick. The older man thought of Carter Andrews, who had cabled that morning from Yokohama.

"But why all this gloom?" Alden inquired.

"Why? You know who I am. You know what I've got. And now to find out that she's Alden's daughter—a man worth millions—"

"Nonsense! Jim Alden's no better than you or me. I knew him when he was a mechanic in Pontiac. We worked at the same bench. Why, I can remember—"

"Yes, you can remember. But can he? I'll bet you couldn't prove to him that he ever worked for his living, not with the aid of a diagram. They get like that. I can see him—pompous, blustering, important. Can you imagine my going to him and saying, 'Mr. Alden, I have come to ask for your daughter'? 'And who are you?' 'Oh, I'm the Napoleon of finance who bought a garage on a road nobody ever travels. And in addition to your daughter, Mr. Alden, I'd like to ask you for ten cents car fare back to town.'"

Jim Alden laughed.

"It seems to me you're a bit previous," he said. "As far as I could see, Miss Angie is still heart-whole and fancy-free. And I tell you right now, Son, we're up against it here.

"We've got a problem on our hands. Are you going to face it with me or must I get a new partner?"

Bill Merrick got to his feet.

"You're right, Dad," he answered. "It sort of upset me, seeing her again. But the moment of weakness has passed. Let Alden take his daughter and his millions and go his way.

I'm poor but proud. I'm darn poor, come to think of it. What do you suggest?"

"One thing's clear," his partner told him: "We've got to get over on that main road. This shack isn't worth moving. We'll have to rent ground over there, put up a new building and vamoose."

"But the lease here has two years to go."

"Yes. Too bad. That's eight hundred a year we must set down on the wrong side of the ledger—no help for it. We can thank Petersen for that. But he hasn't put me down and out. I was stunned for a minute, but now I've just begun to fight. We'll be mighty careful picking our new location."

"But see here, Dad, that's all a rosy dream. How about funds? I'm nearly broke."

"Don't worry about funds. I told you Jim Alden was an old friend of mine. I'm sure he'll stake us to the limit. I'll go out to his Pasadena house to-night and have a long talk—"

"Jim Alden!" Bill repeated. "Somehow I don't like the idea of borrowing money from him—her father."

"Rot! It will interest him in you. If you make good he'll respect you."

"Think so? Maybe I'd better go with you to-night."

"No, no, that's all right. I can handle him better alone. Now let's leave Al in charge here while we run over to that new highway and take a squint around. Then when we get this money—"

"You seem mighty sure we're going to get it."

"Of course I'm sure. Jim Alden would do anything on earth for me."

"Gosh," said Bill Merrick as they climbed into the car, "I wish I could say the same!"

* * * * *

THAT evening Angie left the family group in the drawing- room, where Arthur was seated at the piano singing a ballad—he had an excellent tenor voice; he would have— and hunted up her father in the library. She found him at his desk thinking hard.

"Hello," she said, "it's the old Alden retainer. Our first chauffeur. We treat him just like one of the family."

"Hush, Angie, hush!"

"So I used to fall asleep in your lap, did I? Really, Dad, I didn't care for that. It made me seem such a dopy child."

"Every word I said was the plain truth. I think I did mighty well under the circumstances. A fine fix you put me in."

"Oh, Dad, I was frightfully sorry—"

"After I'd prepared you—to rush up and bawl out 'Dad' the first crack out of the box."

"It was stupid of me. But you looked so funny. Ha, ha!"

"Hush, I tell you! See here, Angie, what did you think of him?"

"Of whom?"

"You know who I mean. My partner, Bill Merrick."

"Why, he seemed a worthy young mechanic. Of course I scarcely looked at him."

"Oh, no, of course not! Well, give him a glance next time. He thinks very highly of you—for some unknown reason. That sandwich you gave him must have been poisoned. He's never recovered."

"You don't say! Well, that's nice. We aim to please. But how do you know?"

"Oh, he told me all about it afterward."

"Now, Dad, that isn't fair—to let him run on to you, not knowing who you are."

"Nonsense! It's a great chance for me. I guess a father never had a better opportunity to study a possible son-in-law."

"Dad! What rot!" Angie stared at him, amazed. "I'm willing to let you run off and play with these rough boys, but you mustn't drag your grimy little pals into your private life. It won't do."

"Oh, you'll wake up later," her father said. "This boy has a better education than I have—he's a gentleman. More than that, he's got a way with him."

"A dog-gone dangerous man, eh? Thanks for the warning. But dear old Dad, the family friend, will always be on hand as a chaperon."

"I will—and I want you to drop in often. A girl like you can buck a young man up—keep him on the job. Our friend needs cheering. Every cent he had went into that garage—and it looks as though we'd been stung." He told her of Petersen's duplicity. "I acted too hastily," he admitted. "It's one on me. But of course it doesn't matter in my case. It's the boy I'm worried about."

"What are you going to do?" Angie asked.

"Well, we've got to raise some money and move. As I explained to Bill, I know Jim Alden pretty well. Just as you came in I put it up to the old man. I asked him to lend us ten thousand dollars, and I think he's going to do it. We were arguing about the rate of interest when you interrupted."

"But Alden's fond of you. He won't charge you any interest."

"Alden's a business man. Besides, the deal has got to look like the real thing. I've got it—four per cent! I beat Jim down from six for old sake's sake. Should auld acquaintance be forgot?"

"Fine! Now that's settled come out and join the family. I hear echoes of a bridge game, which means that Arthur's song is stilled."

"All right, but remember what I said. Drop in frequently. I've taken a shine to Bill."

"I suspect," said Angie, "it's not that you love Merrick more, but Carter Andrews less. However, I don't mind acting clubby. I noticed myself that Bill has—rather nice eyes."

The next morning at eight, as was his custom, Jim Alden sat up in bed. His mind was racing as smoothly, as efficiently as the famous Alden engine. He was ready for whatever business problems the day might bring. As his feet touched the floor he remembered that those problems were likely to be many and serious. His heart leaped for joy.

"'Maxwelton braes are bonnie, where early fa's the dew,'" he bellowed.

His wife, in the room adjoining, couldn't decide whether to be glad or suspicious.

When Jim Alden reached the garage his partner was waiting eagerly in the doorway.

"I'm a little late," puffed the millionaire. "Have to get up earlier, I guess."

"Never mind that," said Merrick. "Nothing stirring here. Did you go out to Pasadena last night?"

"You bet I did!"

"And did you—did you see—her?"

"Her? Now look here, my boy, this is business! I didn't go out there to call on Miss Angie. I went to see her father—and I did. It's all fixed. Ten thousand dollars at four per cent. If we need any more we're to let him know."

"Say, he must be a good old scout!"

"I think so, but maybe I'm prejudiced."

"Well," said Bill, "it's up to us now. We've got to hustle our heads off. I'm not going to lose her father's money—you can understand why. I wish I knew more about automobiles."

"That's all right. I know a lot, and I'm going to teach you."

"You're mighty kind," Bill Merrick replied. "I was busy, too, last night. After I left here I had dinner at a little place in San Marco. Then I hunted up the best boarding-house in the town, got a room there and moved in. I figure it's like this: We ought to get a location somewhere close to town, and then mull round and mix with people. Get acquainted, I mean, with the leading citizens. It wouldn't be a bad idea for you to move out here. I haven't asked—are you a married man?"

"Er—yes, I'm married," smiled Alden.

"Well, why not bring the family out to San Marco?"

"I'm sorry; I can't very well at present. You see, I've got a lease where I am."

"Too bad. Well, I'll start the ball rolling. This morning at breakfast I met the leading real-estate man of the town. I made a date with him for ten-thirty. He's going to show us round."

"Fine! Now you're moving!"

"I lay awake half the night thinking," Bill went on. His partner stared at him. He wished he could lie awake half the night and look so fresh and fit in the morning. "There are a million garages here in Southern California. We've got to do something distinctive, something that will make us stand out from the crowd. The human touch—I'm strong for it."

"Me too," said the millionaire heartily.

"Let's just talk to folks—in the San Marco paper—on signs along the highway. 'A service station with the accent on the service.' How's that for a catch line?"

"I like it."

"You know what motorists usually get when they're in trouble and stop at a garage. Some grouchy incompetent picks their pocket and gives 'em a swift kick on their way. No sympathy, no friendliness. Let's you and me get clubby with our customers. Let's chat things over and make friends, so they'll come back.

Let's live in a house by the side of the road"—Bill Merrick lapsed into poetry—"and be a friend to man. Let that be the motto of the Mission Garage."

"The Mission Garage?"

"Oh, I forgot to tell you! Most of these garages are just ugly shacks. They all look alike. So why not a distinctive building? With Jim Alden back of us we can swing it. Let's put up a neat little stucco affair, a reproduction of one of the old missions. That will be our trade-mark. The mission latchstrings were always out—hospitality was the word—our motto too. What do you say?"

"My boy, you're putting new heart in me. Some partner!"

"I knew you'd approve. Why, man, they can't stop us! In time we'll have a string of Mission Garages all up and down California. We'll patent the idea. We'll get the agency for some good car—by gad—"

"What is it?"

"There's an idea! Your friend, Jim Alden! We'll go after the agency for his car!"

"But he's retired."

"Sure, but he's still got influence! Of course I'm getting a little ahead of myself, as usual. We've got to put the first one over—the rest will be easy. You and me—the garage kings of Southern California." Bill Merrick laughed. "And to think I studied law! We'd better start for that real-estate office."

Half an hour later they stood with the real-estate man on a corner about ten blocks from the center of San Marco, where the new state highway was crossed by another road, frequently traveled.

"Believe me," warbled the agent, "if this road wasn't brand new you'd never get a shot at a location like this. You're close enough to get a lot of town business, as well as transients. If you say the word we'll hang round here an hour and count the passing cars."

It seemed a good idea. The count ran remarkably high.

"Just a normal week-day morning," the agent said. "I leave you to imagine Sundays and holidays. No funny business this time. Here's all the traffic Petersen drew from, and twice as much more. If you want to build a shack to do business in while your building's going up I can arrange a temporary lease on the ground next door. Your gas tank and pump can go in at once."

They succumbed, returned to his office and signed a five-year lease. That being settled, the real-estate man led them into the office of a young architect in the same building. That gentleman took his feet off his desk, laid down a volume of zippy stories and entered whole-heartedly into the spirit of the occasion.

"Gentlemen," he said, "I'll be frank. You fall on me like manna from heaven. Building is at a standstill and I'm bored stiff. Even a garage sets my heart leaping."

"Where do you get that even-a-garage stuff?" Bill Merrick said. "We don't propose to desecrate the landscape with the ordinary shack," and he explained what they wanted.

"Glory be!" the architect cried. "Just turn me loose! I'll give you a building that will cause tourists, at first glance, to reach for their guide-books, and it will be practical too."

He promised to sit up all night and finish the job. Many men, he said, were out of work. He could promise them a temporary home in a week and their main building in a month.

"Let's go!" was his war cry.

"I think," said Jim Alden, when the partners returned to the street, "I'd better jump on a trolley and run in town. I'll get that money from Alden and deposit it to our joint account. Then we can release the check we just gave on the lease. And I'd better see the gasoline people and arrange about the pump."

"Go to it!" replied Bill Merrick. "We're on our way, partner! Looks like happy days."

"Happy days for me," smiled the millionaire.

When Jim Alden returned that afternoon from his business in the city Bill Merrick was filling the gasoline tank of a handsome car of Alden's own manufacture in which sat a lean, pleasant man of sixty or more. The hands that rested on the wheel were brown and gnarled.

"Hello, stranger!" Jim Alden said. "What do you hear from Iowa?"

"Things are pretty quiet," smiled the man. "But how did you know—"

"Tell an Iowa man anywhere," laughed Alden.

The other was evidently delighted. Jim Alden leaned over the car door and began a discussion of politics. They thought alike. It was the start of a beautiful friendship.

"I see you've got an Alden," said the automobile man presently. "How's your engine?"

"Rotten," said the other. "Acts like it had the heaves. Nobody seems able to tell me what's wrong."

"Best engine made," answered Alden, his pride touched. "Ought not to go back on you."

He lifted the hood of the car. The Iowa man climbed out and joined him.

"Never would have gone back on me of its own free will," he said. "There was a little carbon in it and I left it at a garage. You know—one of those places where there's one thing wrong with your car when it goes in and twenty when it comes out. I'd give a hundred dollars for the name and address of a competent mechanic in this neighborhood."

"U'm!" Jim Alden studied his beloved but rather soiled child. "Look here! Look at this!"

With expert eye and hand he ran over the mechanism. He pointed out several things that were wrong, and corrected them as he pointed. The Iowa man stared at him open-mouthed.

"By George," he said, "you know more about this engine than old Jim Alden himself!"

"Not more," replied Alden, laughing. "But just about as much. Now get in and start your motor."

The stranger returned to his seat, connected his battery and stepped on the gas. A soft purring sound like a cat in clover rewarded him.

"Great!" he cried. "Say, you're a wonder! It's too bad you're way over here—sort of off the main thoroughfare."

Alden told him of their proposed move.

"You won't be far from my house," the Iowa man said. "You get all my business from now on. A competent mechanic—I'll spread the good word among my friends. I'm one of the town commissioners, and I reckon I know everybody in San Marco."

"Send 'em around," said Alden. "We aim to please."

The Iowa man paid his modest bill and went happily on his way.

Bill Merrick rushed up and seized the older man by the hand. "Dad," he cried, "the Lord sure was good to me when he sent me a partner like you!"

"Come inside for ten minutes," said Alden, "and I'll tell you all I know about this game." But he was mightily pleased with himself.

At half past four Angie appeared on the scene.

"I don't need anything for the car," she explained. "Just happened to be passing. If you're going into Los Angeles, Dad, I'll be glad to give you a lift."

"Say, Miss Angie, that's mighty good of you."

"In heaven's name, go and scrub your hands!" she whispered.

For the first time he remembered that tinkering an engine was a soiling task. He had not been conscious of those grimy hands—they had seemed so natural, so like old times.

He hurried into the office.

Angie and Bill Merrick were left alone. The girl studied her father's partner—without his knowing it—keenly, appraisingly. A conquest is a conquest, even in overalls, especially when it is young and handsome.

"Is business picking up?" she asked.

"Not much," he told her. "But that's all right. We're going to pick up the business," and before he knew it he found himself relating all that had happened during the day.

"I'm so glad," Angie smiled. "You're on the road to success already, aren't you?"

"So it seems. But I'd be on the road to the poorhouse if it wasn't for Dad."

"Dad!"

"Yes, I call him that too. He's the finest partner a man ever had."

"You like him?"

"I'll tell the world he's a prince! Do you like me—for liking him?"

"Naturally. He's an old and dear friend."

Mr. Bill Merrick leaned closer. "I'd better warn you—I'm going to do more than like him. He's so gentle and kindly and capable—before I'm through I fancy I'm going to—to love him."

"Oh!" said Angie.

A brief speech for her, but all she could think of, with Bill Merrick's gray eyes so close, and all.

Fortunately Jim Alden reappeared at that moment, after a somewhat unsuccessful washing up. He got into the roadster.

"This is a bit of luck for me, Miss Angie," he said, sinking back wearily.

"Me too," smiled Angie sweetly. "By the way, Mr. Merrick, any friend of Dad's must consider himself a friend of—er—my family too. Won't you come and call some evening—soon?"

"I should say I will!"

"Dad will tell you where we live. Good-by."

The little car shot down the road.

"I told Haku not to stop for you to-night," she added to her father. "Thought I'd save you the trolley ride."

"It was kind of you, Angie—but don't do it often. Our young friend might grow suspicious."

She turned and looked at him, then laughed.

"If you could see yourself you wouldn't say that. Nobody will ever connect you with James M. Alden—you look too tired and happy. I think I'd better slip you in the back way."

"Maybe you had." The car sped on. "I notice," said Alden, "you didn't lose any time inviting Bill to the house."

"That's all right with you, isn't it?"

"Yes—in a way. But what's to become of me? Where do I hide?"

"Well, there's the garage," laughed Angie. "Or, on rainy nights, under the bed."

That evening Jim Alden sat with his wife in the drawing-room in front of an open fire. The young people had gone to a dance at one of the hotels.

"Jim," she said suddenly, "what's happened to your hands?"

"My—er—my hands?"

"They're not clean. I noticed them at dinner."

"Well—er—I got to monkeying with one of our engines at—at the garage. That fool Haku doesn't know the first thing about an engine. And it isn't so easy to get your hands clean after you've been fooling round a car. You ought to remember that."

She made no reply. Jim Alden smiled.

"Lord, Mary," he said, "how you used to fuss about my hands—in the old days! Those—those were great days, weren't they? Don't you sometimes wish we could travel back—be young together again?"

It seemed to him that her face softened.

"Don't be an old fool, Jim," she said gently. "What's the good of wishing for the impossible?"

* * * * *

BUT it was not so impossible as Mary Alden thought— at least not for her husband. For him the hands of the clock were whirling back. He stood again at the beginning of his career, facing a dozen obstacles daily, overcoming them one by one. All his energies were bent on making good.

Inside of a week he and Bill Merrick had moved most of their equipment to a temporary shed on the lot next to the one they had leased. Their gasoline pump was already installed and their new building well under way. Their first day in the new location was brightened by the appearance of the man from Iowa, who stopped for gasoline and to renew his promise of trade from friends. This promise he kept. Business increased daily.

Jim Alden found himself in far deeper than he had intended. When he had first acted on the insurance man's suggestion he had pictured himself hovering over the little business like a rich benignant uncle, lending a hand with the work only when he happened to feel like it. As the situation stood, however, much more was required of him, and he gave his time gladly. Every week day found him on the job. The light evening business was entrusted to Al. The old man explained in various ways his inability to serve Sundays and insisted that his partner should draw down a slightly larger salary because of it.

Two evenings after Angie extended her invitation, Bill Merrick made his first appearance at the Alden house. Jim Alden was in the drawing-room when he heard his partner's voice in the hall, and was forced to make use of the servants' stairway at the rear in order to escape. For a time he stalked about his room rather peevishly. His masquerade had its drawbacks. He ended by going early to bed.

The next morning at the garage Bill Merrick was gloom personified.

"What ails you, anyhow?" his partner asked.

"I called at the Aldens' last night," Bill explained. "It's worse than I thought. I mean—I didn't know there was so much money in the world. A royal palace. I'll never make the grade. Might as well give up."

"Nonsense! Did you see the old man?"

"Oh, no! He was off somewhere—sitting on his golden throne, I suppose. Couldn't be troubled with trifles like me. But I did meet Mrs. Alden. Ugh! Wished I'd worn my woolens. The icy shoulder, Dad—"

"But, Angie—Angie was friendly?" said Jim Alden hastily.

"She's a darling," Bill Merrick admitted. "Gosh, how I wish she didn't have a penny! Oh, for a break in the stock market and the old man dead broke!"

"In which case he'd call in our ten thousand," Alden reminded him. "Come in here. It's time for your morning lesson, and please keep your mind on the job."

Bill was proving an apt pupil—had always been interested in mechanics, he said. In a month he knew enough to qualify as a fair mechanic. The middle of February found their new building complete. It was a reproduction of the mission at Carmel, a really beautiful thing. The Women's Club of San Marco passed resolutions thanking Grant & Merrick for the taste they had displayed. The whole town was friendly.

Jim Alden grew younger daily. If at first his muscles had ached horribly and his step faltered when he returned home of an evening, that passed, and he returned merely tired and ready for his bed. He delighted in puttering round cars. More than that, he enjoyed the daily contact with all sorts of people, the exchange of views on many topics. The ease with which he played two parts in the world amazed him. When he reached the garage in the morning and donned his uniform he was no longer James M. Alden, but John Grant. He could stand off and regard his old pal the millionaire with an air of utter detachment. There were some traits in Jim Alden, he found, that were admirable; others he did not like, and he resolved to speak to his friend about them.

His wife, always breathlessly busy with social affairs, seemed to have no suspicions—at least she gave no sign. Occasionally she mentioned having called him up at his office without success. He had a variety of alibis—the movies, the club, long walks. One evening late in February she spoke to him about another matter.

"That young fellow, Merrick"—she began.

"What about him? Who is he?" Alden asked, startled.

"He's nobody apparently, and he's coming to see Angie altogether too often. You ought to look into it. He's nothing but a mechanic—owns a little garage somewhere. In partnership with a man named Grant, who claims to be an old friend of yours."

"Oh, yes, John Grant."

"You know him then? I tried to recall the name, but it was all so long ago. Well, I wish you'd meet this boy and squelch him. It seems that whenever he appears you're somewhere else."

"Oh, I'll meet him sooner or later."

"But, Jim, this is serious. I believe Angie likes him. Please do something at once, otherwise we may find ourselves in a rather awkward position."

He put her off with vague promises. So Angie liked Bill Merrick.

"Well, what's awkward about that?" he said fiercely—to himself.

The fifteenth of March Grant & Merrick were able to pay Jim Alden two thousand dollars of his principal. The younger partner was elated.

"Slowly but surely," he said. "You know, Dad, I've taken an oath. I've made up my mind to tell Angie I love her—some day. Then if she pushes me out of her life for ever—well, that's that. But one thing I've sworn—I'll never tell her while we owe her father money!"

"A mighty sensible idea," Alden admitted.

"If I can only hang to it," Bill Merrick sighed. "You know, Dad, she's almighty sweet—and spring is on the way! Sometimes I'm afraid I'll lose my head—and her—all in one glorious tragic night."

"Ignore the spring," advised Jim Alden.

He knew, however, that he asked the impossible. Even his own aging heart could not remain insensible to the wonders of the changing seasons. April came, perfuming the universe, and on Jim Alden's lawn the landscape architect at last began to earn his fee.

Walking up his driveway in an aisle of blooming beauty one evening early in the month, he found an old friend on the veranda. Doctor Tillson, from Detroit, was waiting, keenly anxious to view the effect of his prescription.

"Well, Jim Alden," said the doctor, after the greetings, "you always thought you knew more than I did."

"Oh, I wouldn't say that."

"Maybe not, but you'd think it. Now you'll pardon me if I gloat a bit. When I ordered you to cut loose from everything, to come out here and take a complete rest, what did you say? You said it was a death sentence."

"I know I did."

"And now look at you! Why, man, you're ten years younger than when I last saw you! It's a miracle! Excuse me if I press my point. Was I right—or were you?"

Alden hesitated. He wanted to gloat a little himself, but the moment was not propitious.

"You were right, as always, Doc," he laughed.

The doctor bowed. He admitted it.

"What do you do with yourself all day?" he asked. "Your wife says you have an office. I don't quite approve of that."

"Oh, just a place to loaf, Doc. I go in every morning and moon round. Then the club, the movies, long walks."

"Fine! Not a stroke of work, eh?"

"Nothing I'd call work." Alden thrust his hands deep into his pockets. "You're going to stop with us while you're out here?"

"Mrs. Alden has very kindly invited me."

"Good!" Alden reflected that his moment of triumph might yet come. "Make yourself at home. I'll be down shortly." He went up to his room.

That evening as he sat with the doctor in the library his wife entered.

"Jim," she said, "that young Merrick is here. He's taking Angie for a ride. Will you come and meet him now—or must I drag you out?"

"No, no, not to-night," he protested. "Later."

She stood eying him. He thanked heaven for the presence of the doctor. Otherwise he felt there would have ensued an argument likely to be a losing one for him.

"Very well," said Mary Alden. "We'll discuss it later."

She went out. Jim Alden rose uneasily and walked to a window. He felt that his masquerade could not be maintained much longer—things were approaching a crisis. He saw Angie and Bill Merrick going down the drive. The perfume of a night beautiful beyond words swept in on him. A moon made for lovers rode high amid the stars. Could Bill Merrick keep that promise to himself? Jim Alden rather hoped he couldn't.

He got his wish. His partner appeared at the garage next morning apparently a stricken man.

"Well, I'm done for, Dad," he announced. "It was just the way I was afraid it would be—spring and the moon and the perfume of her hair. I knew as well as I know anything that we still owe her father eight thousand dollars. And yet— "

"Tell me all about it."

"We were loafing along a country road out San Gabriel way. I'd been so excited at the thought of seeing her I'd forgot to fill the gas tank. The car stopped dead—in the shadow under a tree. It seemed the hand of Providence. She was mighty close—the seat in that old bus of ours is pretty narrow. The next thing I knew she was in my arms and I was telling her—pouring it all out."

"And she refused you," finished Jim Alden sympathetically.

"Refused me? Hell, no! She loves me, Dad. She said," continued Bill Merrick out of his vast gloom, "it was the happiest moment of her life."

"Judging by your looks, you can't say the same."

"I could only—dog-gone it, before she'd finished speaking I realized what I'd done. Jim Alden's daughter! It's preposterous!"

"Well, it's happened. What's your next move?"

"I don't know. I was a little mad last night. I urged her to run away with me—without a word to her family. I didn't know what I was saying."

"What was her answer to that?"

"She told me to ask your advice. Said she'd be guided by you."

"Wise girl," smiled Alden.

"I want to tell you, however, that I've changed my mind overnight. I couldn't run away with her. I'm not such a coward as that."

"Of course you're not!"

"But what am I to do?" moaned Bill Merrick. "She loves me. She's willing to marry me. I can't just let the whole matter drop."

The older man rose and put his hand on the boy's shoulder.

"There's only one thing to do," he said.

"I know what you mean."

"Go up to Jim Alden's house to-night. Demand to see him. Take a search warrant with you and drag him out from under the bed, or wherever it is he hides. Tell him you're a clean, decent young man with all your faculties and you want to marry Angie."

"It's got to be done," admitted Bill Merrick, "and I'll do it. But I'm scared to death. You know what he'll think I am—a fortune hunter." He got to his feet and glared fiercely at his partner. "Damn Jim Alden's money!" he cried.

"His money!" repeated John Grant, the middle-aged mechanic, glaring back. "Don't you let him mention his money to you! He won't, anyway—not if he's the Jim Alden I used to work with in Pontiac. But if he does—if he does—"

"Yes, Dad."

"Back him into a corner and jam a question down his throat. Just one question! Ask him how much he was getting at your age. If he's honest with you he'll tell you—twenty-six dollars a week, and darned glad to get it!"

He stopped, perspiring. He was vastly indignant with this arrogant millionaire.

"Dad, you're a peach," Bill Merrick said. "To-night's the night! I'll beard him in his den. But, gosh, I hope this is a long day!"

At three that afternoon Jim Alden was standing in front of his garage enjoying a moment of leisure. Al was busy inside. Bill Merrick had motored into town to obtain a new part for a car they were repairing. Suddenly Alden noticed his own limousine coming down the boulevard with Haku at the wheel. In the back seat were Mary Alden and Doctor Tillson.

Once or twice before Mary had driven by the place. On those occasions her husband had invented urgent business inside. But now he stood his ground. His heart beat a little faster, however, when Haku swung in the drive before the garage door and paused beside the gas pump. Alden pulled his old hat low over his eyes and stepped forward.

"Ten gallons of gasoline," ordered Mary Alden. She did not add "my good man," but it was in her tone.

"Yes'm." Jim Alden filled the tank. When he had finished he went to the door of the car. "Two-eighty, please," he muttered.

It was a point of pride with his wife never to notice a menial. She handed him a ten-dollar bill. He went inside and returned with the change. As he put it into her hand a spirit of deviltry seized him. He pushed his old hat far back on his head and looked her full in the eye.

"All right, Mary," he said. "That fixes you. Drive on."

An expression of—er—well, decidedly an expression appeared on Mary Alden's face—and froze there.

"Jim Alden!" cried the doctor. "What does this mean?"

"It means," said Alden, "that you were wrong, after all. I tried your prescription for a while. I got worse—worse every day. If I'd stuck to it I'd have been under the daisies by this time. I had sense enough to get down off the shelf—to unfold my hands. I bought a half-interest in this business. For the past five months I've been here every day, tinkering cars, talking politics, having a darn good time. You told me last night I look ten years younger. Well, I feel that way."

"Ah, yes," cried his wife, finding her voice. "Satan finds mischief for idle hands to do."

"If this is mischief, give me more of it," said Alden. "And as for Satan, he has saved my life." Over his shoulder he saw Bill Merrick approaching. "We'll talk it all over to-night. Just now I repeat my suggestion—please drive on!"

No one moved. Alden saw Haku staring at him. It is a general belief that the Japanese face can not express deep emotion. A mistaken one.

"Drive on, Haku," ordered Alden. Haku did not stir. This was a big thing and he wanted to get it straight. "Will you take my orders, or not?" roared the millionaire.

Haku came to life and stepped on the gas. The big car shot into the road, carrying Mary Alden's stricken face from her husband's sight.

"Well," said Bill Merrick at five o'clock, "all good things must end, including the condemned man's last day. Shot at sunset! I think I would have preferred the morning."

"Cheer up," smiled Alden. "If it helps any, I'm going to be at old Jim's house to-night myself. I've been invited."

"Good!" replied Bill, smiling wanly. "You can take charge of the remains."

In spite of his bravado at the garage Jim Alden crossed his veranda that evening feeling rather sheepish. He was like a small boy who had gone swimming without permission and been found out. He was surprised to find Mary in his room. She was sitting in a chair by the window, her hands idly folded in her lap. He went over and sat down beside her.

"Well, Mary," he said, "I guess I've been a pretty bad boy."

"I guess you have, Jim."

"What are you going to do to me?"

"Angie has told me the whole story. There's only one thing I don't like—why did you keep it a secret from me?"

"You'd have been against it, Mary."

"Probably I would at first. I'd have talked a lot, but you'd have had your own way in the end. You always do. And afterward, when I saw how much better you were— how happy—"

"You want me to be happy, Mary?"

"Yes, Jim," she answered gently. "That's all that matters now—keeping happy the rest of the way."

"There's one thing more," he said. "My partner at the garage—Bill Merrick—a fine boy, Mary. I know him inside out. He's coming up to- night to ask for Angie. He doesn't know I'm Jim Alden. It will be a shock to him. All I'm going to say is—that it's all right with me."

"A mechanic!"

"Just as I was—when you married me. He's got a future too. This business of ours is going to grow. I'll attend to that, once I've told him my real name." He leaned closer. "They'll be standing just where you and I stood thirty years ago. We can't have our own youth back, but we can live it over again—with our children."

She went over to a table and picked up a package.

"What's this?" he asked as she handed it to him.

371

"I hunted all over Los Angeles, but I finally found it," she said. "It's that soap, Jim—the kind I used to get for you in Pontiac. You remember? It's so good for your hands."

He stood up and put his arm about her.

"There was just one fly in the ointment, Mary," he said—"your not knowing. I didn't like it. It seemed to be driving us so far apart. But that's all over now."

"All over now," she repeated, smiling at him. He kissed her. It was like coming home in Pontiac.

When he came down-stairs dressed for dinner he demanded immediate audience with Doctor Tillson.

"I forgot to tell you, Jim," his wife said. "The doctor went into town this afternoon. He's going East in the morning."

She laughed. "He left a message for you. He said he'd resigned in favor of Satan."

After dinner Arthur and Edie sought intellectual nourishment at the movies. Jim Alden, his wife and Angie sat together in the drawing-room. When he heard the bell ring Alden stood up.

"It's poor Bill," he said. "I'll go into the library. Hustle him right in, Angie. Don't prolong his agony."

He had scarcely seated himself behind his massive desk when the door opened and Angie smilingly entered, followed by Bill Merrick. The younger partner in the San

Marco garage wore evening clothes, and his face was as white as his hard-boiled front.

"Dad," said Angie, "here's Bill Merrick. He wants to marry me."

"I know he does," said Alden. "He's told me so from time to time."

Bill Merrick opened his mouth, but no sound that could possibly be regarded as speech issued forth. He stood there staring at the distinguished-looking man who seemed so like the soiled partner he had parted from not three hours before.

"Bill," said Alden gently, "we've treated you rather shabbily, but we didn't go for to do it. Angie will explain it all to you later on. For the moment all I need say is that they'd put me up on the shelf with the rest of the dust, and I didn't like it, so I climbed down and bought a half-interest in Petersen's garage."

"Good lord!" cried Bill Merrick. "You—you are James M. Alden?"

The old man came from behind the desk and put his arm round the boy's shoulders.

"Where do you get that James M. stuff?" he said. "You might as well go right on calling me Dad."

And since that seemed to sum up all he had to say, he left the room, closing the door softly behind him.

THE GIRL WHO PAID DIVIDENDS

First published in The Saturday Evening Post, Apr 23, 1921

MR. HERMAN WINKLE, the eminent producer of film masterpieces, sat in his office staring at the director he had but recently lured away from a rival concern. California's special brand of early morning sunshine poured through a window at Mr. Winkle's back, bathing in golden splendor his vast expanse of bald head.

"Well, Kenyon," he inquired, "did you go over that new script for Malone?"

"I did," said the director. "It looks like an A-l story to me."

"Yeah, it's a good piece of property," replied Mr. Winkle, making use of his favorite phrase.

The director smiled.

"Now that shot where Malone appears on the fire escape in her nightgown— "

"Wasn't in the property when I bought it," Mr. Winkle informed him. "I wrote it in." He paused a moment, his chest swelling with the pride of authorship. "Well, I guess you're ready to begin shooting as soon as Malone shows up. I hope you two get along O. K."

"Oh, we'll hit it off," smiled Kenyon. "I understand that Peggy Malone is a regular fellow."

"She's a mighty fine kid," said Mr. Winkle. "Five years we been working together, and never a word between us that wasn't as pleasant as a good week's gross. Yes, sir, five years ago I found her in the Follies chorus, getting her measly little fifty a week. Just for an evening of pleasure I go to the theater, and the minute this girl walks on I know I'm there for business. Right away I went back stage and signed her up. It was one of my big strokes."

"One of many," flattered Kenyon.

"Yeah, you said it," Mr. Winkle admitted. "Well, get busy. All I got to say is, treat her right. I never knew her to be peevish yet, but I ain't taking no chances. I wouldn't lose her for Rockefeller's millions. She's the best bit of property I got." He rose and waved an emphatic finger at his new director. "Believe me when I say it, she's the best bit of property in the films."

Up at the other end of Hollywood, in a boudoir done, to quote Peggy herself, "in a Los Angeles imitation of Louis the Quince," the film star sat before her dressing-table. She was running a tortoise-shell comb through her hair, which she wore bobbed that season. On top it was a tangled glory of gold, but it stopped abruptly just below her ears, as though it would think twice before concealing those charming shoulders.

In the mirror Peggy Malone could see, at her back, the trim figure of her maid moving silently about the room, straightening it up. She found the sight of so much calm efficiency, so early in the morning, rather wearing. Again she lowered her eyes, under the famous long lashes, to her dressing-table, where amid the toilet things lay an opened letter. At sight of the letter Peggy smiled.

"Good old Nell!" she said.

"Beg pardon, miss?" said the maid.

"It's a letter from an old pal of mine," explained Peggy Malone. "A girl I used to know in the Follies—Nell Morrison. She went over to London, and turned out a riot. She's all pep, all ginger, Nell is. And the English are so taken with that sort of thing, poor dears, having so little themselves!"

"Yes, miss," said the maid stiffly. She was English and proud of it.

Peggy yawned.

"To hear Nell tell it, she's grabbed off a duke. She wants me to come over and go shopping. Says the titles are all lined up on the shelves, and you just go in and serve yourself— like a cafeteria."

"Why don't you go, miss? The rest would do you good."

"If I only could!" sighed Peggy, and smiled again—that twisted, wistful little smile that held her public enthralled.

She could do with a rest, she told herself. She was rather tired. She lowered her hand with the comb to the edge of the table and yawned again. This getting up at eight in the morning was no joke. Not like the old days in the chorus, days that began when the noon whistles were blowing. Happy days; not much money, but excitement—thrills. Sometimes she wished

How foolish, she reflected. With all her luck! Her thoughts flew back beyond the chorus, back to the smoke of Pittsburgh, out of which her beauty had so unexpectedly emerged. It was six-thirty when she rose in the mornings then. She smelled again the steamy little kitchen; saw her mother wearily hovering between stove and table; her father, the motorman, drinking his coffee from a saucer, then rushing off to the barn to take out his car; and Joey, her brother, whimpering under foot, cross in the mornings even at that age. She remembered her own hurried breakfast, her race to the big hotel where, as telephone operator, she was one day to meet the Broadway manager who was so keen a judge of beauty wherever found. Lucky—yes, she was lucky. She looked round the luxurious room her beauty had paid for.

"Nearly nine o'clock," suggested the maid.

Peggy Malone stood up, slim and straight and boyish in her lacy negligee. It was one of her chief assets, that figure of hers. Whenever a film story faltered, whenever the author's invention failed him, they rushed Peggy into a negligee, a bathing suit, anything that was nothing much. And right there the picture went over—scored a big success. Her face was lovely—innocent, appealing, a necessary part of her equipment, of course—but it was not her face Herman Winkle was thinking of when he fixed her salary at eight hundred a week.

When she was ready to go down-stairs her maid spoke.

"We're all out of the face cream, miss."

"So we are." Peggy opened her purse and took out a bill. "How much is it a jar?"

"I—I don't recall, miss." The eyes of the maid, fixed on that greenback, were cold, grasping. "The price keeps going up. Two dollars, I fancy, the last I bought."

Peggy tossed the ten-dollar bill down on her dressing-table.

"Get me a couple of jars," she said.

The maid seized the bill and tucked it away in her bosom. She looked keenly at her mistress. She wondered if Peggy suspected that the cream was only fifty cents a jar. Probably not. Anyhow, Peggy Malone should worry—with her salary! The woman smiled and patted her bodice above the bill. Nine dollars clear, and the day yet young. She must tell Henry, the chauffeur, about this. Not that Henry would be impressed; he wouldn't stoop for such chicken feed. His arrangement with the garage brought him, he boasted, more than a hundred a month.

Peggy went down to the breakfast-room. Her father, Peter Malone, was already at the table. A powerful-looking man you would have said, and, indeed, strength had been his boast in the days when he piloted a trolley car about Pittsburgh. But he was not so strong now. His back, he said, hurt him. Three years before, when his wife died, he had come out to sample the climate of California. The idea had been that he was to obtain a job, but he had found the air of the Coast strangely enervating. Now and again he had come into dangerous proximity to work, but when he had asked the salary and compared it to the money Peg was getting— well, it was precisely at that moment that he was likely to experience a twinge of warning from his back.

"Hello, Peg," he said cheerfully.

"Good morning, Dad. What are you up to?"

"Waiting for you," he said. "You know, Peg, I was just settin' here watching the sunshine on the silver, an' it come to me—how your poor mother would have enjoyed all this."

"Would she?" asked Peggy. She sat down and attacked her grapefruit. "Somehow I don't believe she would have been contented just to loll round and enjoy. She was always a worker, Mother was. I imagine I'm like her."

"What do you mean by that?" asked her father.

379

"Nothing," smiled Peggy. And it was true, she had intended no rebuke. "Where's Joey?"

"Ain't down yet," scowled Peter Malone. "I heard him come in last night. Past three it was. I looked at that watch you gave me. If you ask me, he was probably over at Hunt's room at the hotel playin' poker."

"Think so?"

"Sure! An' they cleaned him out again, I'll bet you. He ain't got no sense, that kid. You ought to speak to him, Peg."

"Oh, no!"

"But, Peg, it's your money he loses."

"What if it is? Let's not have any row."

"Well, it's up to you, of course. An' speakin' of money, my dear—"

"Uh-huh."

"I bought a bunch of silk shirts yesterday. There was a sale on. I got 'em at rock-bottom prices. But it took every penny I had."

"More silk shirts? Dad, you've got a thousand already."

"Well, what if I have?" He poured rich, heavy cream on his oatmeal. "The father of Peggy Malone's got to look snappy, hasn't he? You don't want me goin' round shabby?"

"Of course not, you old dear. How much do you want?" She rose and went to the table where her pocketbook lay. His eager eyes followed her.

"Oh, not much, honey. Just car fare, that's all—and a few little extras."

She threw a bill down beside him.

"Will twenty do?" she asked.

"Plenty, plenty!" he answered cheerfully. He tucked the bill away in his vest with a sigh of relief. It assured him the pleasant little adjuncts of his aimless day—a bunch of expensive cigars, a good lunch, the cheap vaudeville or movie that was his solace of an afternoon. "You're a good girl, Peg," he assured her.

"Never been a word against me," she laughed, resuming her seat.

Joey came into the room, sour-faced, the corners of his mouth drooping. A sporty youth of twenty, pulpy faced, dressed like a clothing advertisement, and with mean little eyes. His greeting to his father was short and sharp, but he made an effort to be more genial in his manner toward Peg. Joey was, as usual, at liberty. He had graced numerous jobs round motion- picture lots, but none for long. He sat down and took up his spoon with fingers that bore the stain of many cigarettes.

"Where was you last night, young man?" his father asked.

"That's my affair," snapped Joey. His eye fell on a letter beside his plate. He snatched it up and read. "The devil!"

"What's the trouble?" Peggy inquired.

"That money you gave me to invest in oil stocks," replied Joey sadly. "The market's all shot to pieces, and the broker's hollering his head off for more margin."

"Oh, dear," said Peg. "I thought you were going to get rich!"

"Maybe I will—some day. But the market's in the cellar, digging itself in."

"How much does the broker want?" she asked.

"He—he says he's got to have three hundred. If he don't get it we're wiped out." Peggy had finished her brief breakfast. She rose and went toward her desk in the next room. Joey got up and followed. "Might make it a little more," he suggested. "I'm stripped. Not a drop of gas for my car."

Back at the table Peter Malone had picked up the broker's notice.

"Three hundred, you say?" he called. "It looks more like two hundred to me."

Joey swung on him, his little eyes flashing.

"Keep out of this, will you?" he cried. "You've made your touch, I'll gamble on that. Now you're trying to queer me! You—you dog in the manger!"

"Hush!" cried the girl. "Please—you know how I hate a row." Joey muttered something about being sorry. She took up her rather worn check-book and wrote. "Here you are, Joey. Four hundred—will that do?"

"Fine—fine!" cried the boy, elated. "You're an ace, Peg."

"Am I?" She smiled at him. "Joey, I wish you'd keep away from Hunt and that crowd at the hotel. They're too clever for you—you're only a kid."

"Sure I will if you say so!" He went back to the table, his hot fingers clasping the check. "You're the boss round here, Peg," he added, with a contemptuous glance at his father.

Peggy stood pulling on her gloves.

"By the way, Dad," she said, "I had a telegram from Martin Fox. He's on his way to Los—gets in to-day. If he calls the house tell him to look for me at the studio."

An expression of alarm crossed her father's face.

"Martin Fox! Coming all the way from New York again—to see you!"

"Well, I guess that's the idea."

"He's crazy about you."

"Wouldn't it be nice if he was—and him worth millions?"

"Now don't you go and get married, honey. You're doing mighty well as it is. I don't care what Fox is worth; it wouldn't be your money—like this is. Remember that!"

"Married?" She snapped the catch on her glove. "I may as well tell you what I told Martin the last time I saw him. I'd marry him to-morrow—if I was free."

Malone remembered then, and a look of relief came into his eyes.

"But you ain't free, Peg," he said. "You got one husband already. You ain't forgot Jimmy, have you?"

"No"—her voice softened somewhat—"I haven't forgot Jimmy. He can never say that I did—not once in two years have I missed. The first of every month—regular—like rent day—he's got his check from me."

"But Jimmy's a sick man," her father protested.

"Sure! Don't forget what I said. Send Martin round to the studio. If you go out leave word with the Jap. Ta-ta!"

She waved good-by from the hall and disappeared into the bright outdoors. Malone turned worried eyes on his son.

"You heard what she said? She'd marry Fox to-morrow if—"

"Yes—if. They got to get rid of Jimmy first. And believe me, Jimmy will take some getting rid of! He's a wise old bird, sick or well." Joey got up from the table.

"Here," said his father, "you better take this notice from the broker."

"To hell with the broker! Four hundred cash—I ain't had so much money in a month."

"You listen to me—"

"Let the oil stock slide. You may not see me for a day or two. I'm going down to Tia Juana to play the ponies. I'll come back with a wad."

Peter Malone got to his feet.

"I forbid it!"

"You? Don't make me laugh!"

"How dare you speak to your father—"

"Oh, fade away! Fade away!" And the front door slammed behind him, while Peter Malone stood raging, helpless.

In a few moments the older man's anger had cooled. He sat down in Peggy's chair, in Peggy's house, looking out over Peggy's lawn. He took out a cigar she had paid for, and spread on his knees the newspaper for which she subscribed. Slothful content filled his soul. She was a good girl, was Peggy. She would look out for him, whatever happened. Other men set aside stocks and bonds as a protection against old age, but he had that which was far, far better—a loving, indulgent daughter.

His daughter was riding in her open limousine down Hollywood Boulevard. Spring comes to California as to other places, though there, of course, it merely gilds the lily. Peggy was conscious of a feeling of spring in the air. She saw, on the lawns bordering the pavement, new blossoms that had sprung into being overnight. On a corner an old, bent, ragged man was selling violets.

Peggy Malone's thoughts drifted lazily back over seven years.

It was spring in Atlantic City too. In front of the theater, on the Boardwalk, an old, bent, ragged man sold violets. They were down there to open a new musical show—just another of those things. It never had a chance in the world. Its backers were broke before they rung up the curtain. The only clever thing about the production was Jimmy Parsons, its press agent, then at the beginning of his brief but brilliant career as the white-haired boy of Broadway—its pet, its darling. Quaint, whimsical, given to quixotic adventures, to know him was to love him; not to know him was to argue oneself unknown on the Great White Way.

On a warm, lovely Monday night, when the Atlantic whispered softly just outside the walk, their show opened and bade the public come and see. The girls worked hard that night. They danced like demons, smiled eternally, and at the finish wondered whether the piece went over. When the next morning at ten, sleepy-eyed and weary, they reported for rehearsal, their question was answered by a notice on the call board. The show would close that evening! Five weeks of rehearsal and two nights of work!

When Peggy Malone returned to the Boardwalk the morning had lost its savor and life its thrill. She was dimly conscious of the flower man, who stood directly in her path.

"Violets, lady! Violets!"

"No—no!" she cried, and stopped. Something in that voice

"Violets, lady, from the hand of one who loves you!"

She looked again. Jimmy Parsons, in the coat and hat of the flower man, was proffering the purple blossoms. How like him!

"Jimmy!" she cried. Her voice broke.

"Thirty-two bunches of violets—all for you," he said gayly. "With my undying love."

"Jimmy, you silly old thing! The show's busted."

"Sure it has! I knew that last night. Good idea too. Gives us plenty of time to get married. I dare you!"

She was not one to take a dare. Besides, she loved him then. Jimmy and the flower man once more traded costumes, and there was a quick wedding, with violets for all the girls, though many of them would have preferred roast beef.

"What do we care if the show's a bloomer?" Jimmy had cried. "Our love is a big success."

So it had been—for a time. But Jimmy Parsons' career as the most popular man's man on Broadway left him little leisure for a wife. Wherever he went his pals were waiting. They would drag him in somewhere for a drink. Each night at the club they surrounded him, urging him on to that flow of brilliant talk for which he was famous up and down the big street. He would grow more witty as the day approached, which was probably why they seldom let him off till dawn. Very soon the love that had seemed so wonderful in Atlantic City was dead and forgotten, like the show that ran two nights. Peggy went back to the chorus.

Now, as her car turned off the Boulevard into a side street, Peggy smiled softly to herself.

"Violets, lady, violets! From the hand of one who loves you!" He had been a dear in those days. But when she had seen him last—two years ago!

She shuddered. Broadway had got him—too many highballs, too many four- o'clock breakfasts. When she met him at the Los Angeles hotel he was coughing with a cold that somehow he could not shake off, and there were red splotches high on his thin cheeks.

"The doctors say I'm all in, Peg," he told her.

She shrank from him.

"You can't believe all you hear, Jimmy," she said. There was something in his eyes she did not like, a beaten look, a terrible fear of death. "Listen! There's a place down on the edge of the desert—it's called Palm Springs. They say the air is fine for—for sick people. You go down there and get a house—"

"I'm broke, Peg."

"I'll stake you. You can pay it back when you get well."

He shook his head.

"You'd be throwing your money away," he told her.

He was very sure he would not go, but there was little fight left in him. She persuaded him, she made all arrangements, rented the house, instituted the custom of the monthly check. It was characteristic of her that she set the figure at two hundred and fifty dollars, twice the sum that he needed.

Jimmy went off to Palm Springs, and not once since then had she seen him or heard from him, save through her canceled checks that came back from the bank.

"Crawling off to the desert to die," he had told a friend on leaving. But he still lived; he lived this beautiful April morning, the only obstacle between Peggy and Martin Fox, who loved her and wanted to take care of her.

Peggy alighted from her car before the studio and went quickly to her dressing- room.

As she seated herself to make up there came a knock on her door and one of her sister actresses entered, carrying a weekly theatrical newspaper.

"Something in here about you, Peg," she said, and held it out. Peggy took it and read:

"Jimmy Parsons, who went out to California two years ago to recover from an illness, writes to a friend that he's a riot with the cactus plants. It is understood that Jimmy has been approached by the lawyer of a certain Wall Street man and offered a cool fifty thousand to allow his wife to divorce him. The rumor goes on to say that Jimmy is holding out for a bigger split on the gross."

Peggy Malone flushed and handed back the paper. "That's all news to me," she said.

"Oh, sure it is, dearie!" remarked the actress with open sarcasm.

"You heard me!" Peggy's eyes flashed.

"Well, don't get sore," said the girl, and went out.

Peggy sat for a moment staring at her glass.

So Jimmy was holding out for more money! How he had changed since Atlantic City seven years ago! And Martin Fox was on his way—would arrive this very afternoon.

"I'm coming to settle things once for all," he had wired.

She was conscious of the imminence of a crisis in her affairs.

Another knock at her door, and Kenyon, the new director, looked in.

"Whenever you're ready, Miss Malone," he smiled.

"Just a second," she smiled back, and with flying fingers she prepared herself for a day's hard labor.

* * * * *

WHEN Martin Fox met her at the Los Angeles hotel for dinner that evening he had another man with him whom he introduced as Mr. Greenwood. The stranger was a mild, genial little chap, with eyes that beamed behind thick spectacles.

Peggy was surprised. It was not Fox's custom to welcome a third party to their meetings.

Fox himself was looking more efficient, more prosperous than ever. He was a big, silky-smooth man, blond and handsome; the sort who, in a play, remarks at intervals: "Remember, I always get what I go after."

In real life he was not so crude as to say it—he just looked it. At the moment two devastating passions engrossed him—Peg and money. The former was recent, the latter of long standing.

They went in to their table in a quiet, partially hidden corner.

"Don't order for me, please," Greenwood said. "My wife is expecting me at the apartment. I'll just report and then I'll run along."

Peggy looked at him wonderingly.

"Greenwood is my lawyer," Fox explained.

"Oh!" she said. She understood now. "Martin, I heard what you've done, and I can't say I like it."

"Why not?" He seemed surprised. "I'd do anything to get you, Peg. It means my very happiness—and yours too. Isn't that so?"

"Yes, of course. But money never counted with Jimmy."

391

"It didn't, eh?" sneered Fox. "Well, I never met the man yet who hadn't his price. Dear old Jimmy's seems to be a bit higher than we expected, but let Mr. Greenwood tell it."

"Well, I went down to Palm Springs," began Greenwood. "There are a few sanitariums, some simple little houses—and the air was wonderful."

"You didn't go down to take the air," Fox suggested.

"No, of course not." The lawyer's tone was sharp and held no apology. "I had Mr. Parsons' house pointed out to me—a neat little bungalow set amid orange trees. When I came along he was lying in a hammock in the dooryard. He got up and met me."

Peggy Malone leaned eagerly across the table.

"How was he looking?" she asked.

"He was looking mighty well," said Greenwood. "In fact, I was greatly surprised.

"'You don't look much like a sick man to me,' I told him.

"He laughed. T can't imagine how that rumor started/ he said. 'I'm as strong as a horse.'"

"You see?" Martin Fox's tone was triumphant. "He doesn't deserve any sympathy. He's all right; just lazy—lying up there in a hammock waiting for your two fifty a month— grafting off you like all the rest."

"Go on," Peggy said to the lawyer.

"Well, he made it difficult for me, I'll have to admit that," Greenwood continued. "He was so darn glad to see me. Said I was the first visitor he'd had in two years. He called his Chinese boy and ordered lunch, and he talked. It was pathetic, somehow, the way he talked. Just ran on and on—couldn't stop. And such talk! It was as good as a show."

"But you hadn't come there to hear him talk," Fox put in. "You made that clear?"

"Oh, yes—naturally—after lunch. I told him my mission was sort of delicate. I explained how things stood. I said his wife wanted to marry. 'Did she send you?' he asked sort of sharp. I said no, that I represented the gentleman in the case. 'Ah, yes,' he said, 'I know his sort. I've never seen him, never heard of him until to-day; but I can describe him.' And he went on to tell me all about you. It was— uncanny."

"Go ahead," growled Fox. "Repeat it."

"Oh, no—no matter," said the lawyer hastily. "I got to the point at once. I told him I was authorized to offer him twenty-five thousand to—to step aside."

"What did he say?" asked Peggy Malone.

"He said he was sorry I hadn't come a month earlier. 'The desert is at its best in March,' he told me. I went to thirty thousand. 'Though it's no slouch of a desert even now,' he says, 'what with the cactus blooms and the palo verde.'

393

'Thirty-five thousand,' I said. 'The Spaniards.' says he, never cracking a smile, 'called this spot where Palm Springs stands the Coachella Desert, which means the desert of the little shells.'"

"Kidded you, eh?" said Fox.

"Well, at that I stood up. 'I'm authorized to go to forty thousand, and not a cent higher,' I said. 'Oh, must you go?' says he. 'That's too bad, really it is. I was hoping you'd stay overnight. The desert air is wonderful at night. Man, I'm telling you, it's the very breath of heaven!'"

Peggy Malone was smiling gently to herself.

"He was kidding me, as you say," the lawyer went on. "But I didn't mind. I sort of liked it. When I was about to leave I told him I'd be absolutely frank with him—that I could pay fifty thousand, but no more. 'What shall I tell my client?' I asked. 'Tell him,' says this boy, 'that we've had a lovely season up here, but we sure need rain.' So I came away."

The three sat for a moment in silence. Then Martin Fox spoke with decision.

"He wants more money," said Fox. "I recognize the symptoms. The figures you named didn't happen to touch him. I've changed my mind—I'll pay a hundred thousand. Now you go up there to- morrow—"

The lawyer got quickly to his feet.

"I'm sorry," he said, "but I'm through. You'll have to get somebody else."

"What?"

"I never liked this job, anyhow. However, we were under obligation to you, so I took it. But now—I've seen Jimmy Parsons. I've seen him just once, for a couple of hours—and he's a friend of mine. I—I like him. I withdraw completely. Good night, sir. Miss Malone, a great pleasure to meet you. I wish you all the happiness in the world. Good night."

"Sentimental old fool," said Fox peevishly. "I'll get some one else—some one who's not so easy."

"Let's drop it, Martin," Peggy said.

"Drop it? Not I! I came out here to settle this, and I will. I'm crazy about you, Peg. And you said last time you'd be willing to marry me if—see here, you aren't still in love with that husband of yours?"

"Oh, no! That was over and done with years ago!"

"That's all I want to know. Now you leave things to me. I won't annoy you with details. I'm out here to get you your freedom, and after that I'll win you if it's the last act of my life. I—I can't get along without you, Peg. You're such a good pal. You do like me a bit, eh?"

"I like you a lot. You—you'd take care of me, wouldn't you?"

"Give me the chance!"

"So that I wouldn't have to work. I'm—I'm tired. Somehow that's what I want most—somebody to take care of me, and of Dad and Joey."

"The whole blame family. Marry me and all the burdens shift from those little shoulders over here." He tapped his own. "Nothing to do but look pretty and spend money. How does it sound?"

"Why, it sounds fine!" she smiled. But for some reason she was thinking of Palm Springs. "Let's go to a show, Martin."

It was close on midnight when he dropped her at her door and took the kiss he had been looking forward to all evening. She went softly up the stairs to her room. As she hastily prepared for bed she found herself thinking again of Jimmy, Atlantic City, violets. She sighed. Marrying Martin Fox would be so different. Well, she had been twenty in Atlantic City—twenty and breathlessly in love. The sort of thing that could happen but once in a lifetime. And Martin was a good fellow at heart. He would take care of her, protect her, pay the bills.

When she crept into bed her thoughts had swung round to Jimmy again. Jimmy better, cured by the air that was like a breath of heaven. But lazy, shiftless, content to wait for her checks. Was that true? Perhaps not. Perhaps he was not so well as he pretended to be. And he was lonesome—one visitor in two years. It was sort of pathetic, that lawyer said, the way he talked. Peggy closed her eyes, tired with a day's hard work. There was a harder one awaiting her to-morrow. Jimmy—in a hammock—she mustn't forget—the first of the month was close at hand—she'd write a check in the morning. "Tell him we've had a lovely season up here, but we sure need rain." She was smiling when she fell asleep.

She overslept the next morning, and rushed down to breakfast in an apologetic mood. Her father was alone at the table.

"Hello!" he said. "Martin Fox called up yesterday. Did he find you all right?"

"Yes; I had dinner with him."

"Any—anything new?" he ventured.

"Nothing new," she smiled.

"Joey didn't come home last night," he told her. "He took that money you gave him and went down to Tia Juana to play the races. Probably cleaned out and hungry by this time." She looked her distress. "He doesn't amount to a rap, Peg. Going to the dogs. You ought to do something—"

"What can I do?" she asked wearily. "When he was a baby I remember I used to follow him about, saying 'No, no, Joey! Joey mustn't touch!' I can't do that out here in Hollywood. He's grown up—and I'm too busy, anyhow."

"Shut down on him. Don't give him any more money."

"That's easy to say, Dad; but I haven't the heart."

"You've got too much heart. You're too good to Joey—and me, too, for that matter. I got to thinking about it last night."

"Why shouldn't I be good to you? My own father and brother. I'll have a talk with Joey when he gets home. Now I've got to rush along. Got a tough day ahead—out on location."

It proved a tough day indeed. In her newest picture Peggy Malone played, as usual, the beautiful daughter of a multimillionaire. In this instance she must fall in love with a simple country boy, late of the A. E. F. The manner of their meeting was romantic. Driving her smart racing car up a mountain, she was to round a curve and meet, head-on, the cheap little car of the simple lad who—played by an ennuied Broadway actor—was growing less simple every minute. By doing it very slowly and carefully there was no real danger, and the film could be speeded up to reveal a rather thrilling collision.

It had been raining, but when they reached the hill just outside Hollywood, where this bit of script was to be filmed, the sun was out again. They found exactly what they wanted, a sharp curve with both approaches hidden. Pickets were sent a hundred yards in each direction to warn off the cars of outsiders, and Peg drove her little racer down the road and turned it carefully about on the wet asphalt.

She heard the sound of the director's whistle and started up the hill. Small things alter human destinies. The picket who was guarding the upper approach turned his back a moment to light a cigarette, and as he did so a heavy limousine filled with tourists shot silently by him.

Peg was thinking of Jimmy as she came on up the hill. The little bungalow amid the orange trees, the cactus blooms, the nights when the air was so wonderful. She bore down rather heavily on the gas—saw that the curve was surprisingly near.

"Put on your brakes!" shouted Kenyon, directing.

She seized the brake handle; the light car quivered a moment, then began to skid. She brought it to a stop just before the curve, but at right angles to the road. At that instant the big limousine shot round the corner and hit Peg's car amidships.

The little racer turned over with Peggy Malone underneath.

On their way to the office of a near-by doctor, Kenyon, sitting in the back seat of a car, white-faced and grim, with the unconscious Peggy in his arms, kept thinking, "Winkle will never forgive me for this. His best bit of property—practically ruined."

When she was conscious again, and all her injuries were dressed, Peggy pleaded so hard to be taken home rather than to a hospital that the doctor finally consented. At five o'clock that afternoon old Peter Malone returned from the vaudeville theater where he had been killing time. As he came up the front walk he was humming a new song that had taken his fancy. He opened the door of the house. At once to his nostrils came the odor of hospitals; at the top of the stairs he saw the fleeting figure of a trained nurse. He went up two steps at a time, and into his daughter's room.

"Peg!" he cried.

He saw her slim figure under the sheets in the darkened room, caught a glimpse of her bandaged face, a whiff of iodoform that sickened him.

"Don't be scared, Dad," he heard her say faintly. "I got banged up a little doing a picture. I'll be all right tomorrow."

"Peg!" he cried again. The nurse came and led him out.

"You mustn't excite her."

"What—what happened?" he wanted to know.

"Some one else will tell you. I'm busy," snapped the woman, and he found himself in the hall.

He went down-stairs, dazed. The front door opened, admitting Joey. Joey was dusty, sleepy, seedy and, to one who knew him, broke.

"Dad, what's up?" he cried.

"Peg," said Malone. "Hurt doing a picture."

"Hurt? Not bad?"

"I don't know. Her face—her face is all bandaged."

"Her face!"

For a long moment they stood staring at each other.

Neither spoke, but each knew what the other was thinking. Joey went over and with trembling fingers took a cigarette from a silver box and lighted it. He went back to the foot of the stairs and listened. He heard Peg's voice.

"Turn up the light and give me a mirror—please, please!"

Joey sat down weakly on the stairs.

* * * * *

PETER MALONE did not sleep well that night. A final spark of manhood had flared up in his breast to trouble him. He was ashamed of himself; he made brave resolutions in the dark. He would find some sort of employment, earn his own money. Something easy that would not encourage the pain in his back. And Joey—Joey, too, by heaven, must go to work!

In the bright sunshine of the morning after, his good resolutions, so far as they concerned himself, began to waver. Everything looked so much more cheerful. Joey and he waited in the drawing-room for the doctor's verdict. After what seemed a very long time the latter came down-stairs and joined them.

"Well," he announced, "she's not hurt so seriously as I feared. No internal trouble. Just badly bruised and shocked.

401

She mustn't think of working again, for, say, six or eight weeks."

"Oh, then there's nothing to interfere with her working?" said Malone. He saw Joey's face lighting up like a Christmas tree.

"Of course not," the doctor answered.

"You see," Joey explained, "we was sort of afraid—her face—"

"Ah, yes!" The doctor looked at them keenly.

"She seems to have had the same fear. But I have assured her there will be no permanent scars—at least not where they will matter. But it's my opinion she's been working too hard of late. She ought to have a long rest."

"Sure I" cried Malone, beaming. "That's easy fixed."

When the doctor had gone he sat down in his favorite chair, sinking back with a great sigh of relief. He lighted a twenty-five-cent cigar. His quixotic plans, born in the dark of a restless night, vanished with the smoke. After all, he was along in years. He had worked hard once; he deserved a bit of comfort, a bit of his daughter's charity. But Joey! He looked Joey over coldly. Joey was young—nothing wrong with his back. He intended to tell Joey where he got off—a little later. Just at the moment it was pleasant merely to sit and enjoy his renewed sense of security.

Joey was walking the floor, elated.

"Her salary will go on whether she works or not," he was saying, "and I'm not sure she couldn't hold Winkle up for damages. Somebody must have been darned careless. Anyhow, she can use the accident to get a boost in pay."

"Perhaps," Malone agreed. "Here—what are you doing?" For Joey had gone over and was rummaging about in Peg's desk.

"I wonder what became of her pocketbook," said Joey. "I had a run of hard luck down at the border. Had to borrow ten to get home, and I need a shave. I don't suppose you got anything."

"No!"

"No, of course not."

They heard the door-bell ring; heard the Jap go to answer it, and then a strong voice in the hall, a voice they did not recognize.

"Tell Miss Malone I'd like to see her if she's well enough. What? Oh, nobody in particular—only her husband, that's all. Beat it, Baron!" And Jimmy Parsons walked into the drawing-room.

"Hello, boys," he smiled. "Busy as usual, I observe. Before you do another stroke—may I see your union cards?"

"Came on the run, didn't you?" Joey sneered. "Sort of afraid the checks might stop."

"Must have been it," said Parsons. His face grew serious. "Is Peg badly hurt?"

"Don't worry," Joey answered. "She'll be back on the job in a few weeks."

A look of relief appeared in the eyes of Jimmy Parsons. The Japanese servant entered with the word that Peg would see him. He walked to the center table and picked up the morning newspaper.

"Have you boys read this?" he inquired innocently.

"What do you mean—about Peg's accident?" asked Malone.

"No, not exactly. Have you read it line for line—I mean, the way you should? No, something tells me you haven't"

"I don't get you," said Joey.

"Ought to go over it pretty carefully, both of you," went on Parsons. He put the sheet into Joey's hand. "Word for word—line for line. Just a suggestion on my part. Afterward I'll have a little talk with you."

He went into the hall. Joey stared at the paper.

"What's he talking about?" he wanted to know.

"Don't ask me," Malone replied. "I never could follow him half the time. Give me that paper. I've been all over it once, but I'll look again."

In the hallway beside his hat and coat Jimmy Parsons found a small package wrapped in tissue-paper. He picked it up, and as he entered Peg's room left it on a table just inside the door.

He went over to the bed. "Well, Peg," he said.

"Hello, Jimmy." Her voice came faintly from out the bandages. "I'm sorry about your check—this is the first of the month—I never missed before—"

"Good lord, Peg," he cried, "is that all you have to say to me?" His voice broke.

"No, that isn't all. Put up the curtain, please. The doctor said I could have more light. I want to look at you. You're better, Jimmy?"

"I'm well," he said. He lifted the curtain and stood for inspection. "There wasn't anything wrong, Peg, except too much Broadway. I got rid of that cough the second month down there by the desert. I've been all right—for a long time. I'll sit down if you don't mind."

"Sure, Jimmy."

He drew up a chair.

"I was on my way here before I heard about your smash-up, Peg. I read about it this morning in Los Angeles. It—it sort of knocked me all in a heap."

"Nonsense, I'm all right!" she said. "And you—you're all right, too, Jimmy. It does me good to look at you. So different from that—that last time I saw you. What have you been doing these last two years?"

He smiled.

"Peg," he said, "you'd be surprised!"

"Surprised?"

"Yes, when I tell you what I've been doing. I've been thinking—down there by the desert, with only a Chink and the cactus plants for company. Great place to think. Otherwise not a darned thing stirring."

"What did you think, Jimmy?"

"Mostly I thought about you—what a corker you are. Up here working your pretty little head off, while we vultures hovered around, waiting for your pay day."

"Jimmy, please—"

"Well, one thought sort of led on to another." He reached into his pocket and took out a little slip of pink paper. He put it into her hand. "This is a big moment in my life, Peg," he said softly.

"What—what is it, Jimmy?"

"It's a check. My check for six thousand five hundred dollars made out to you. It represents twenty-six checks from you for two-fifty each. Every cent you ever gave me, Peg—back in your hands—where it belongs."

She swallowed the lump that came into her throat.

"I—I can't take it."

"Yes, you can—for my sake. That's my self-respect you're holding there. Keep it, and thank heaven there's one man in your family who can take care of himself."

"But how did you manage it, Jimmy? In a place like Palm Springs!"

"Well, a lot of it is your money that I never touched. And the rest"—he drew his chair closer—"I wasted three months wondering how I could swing it. And nights, when I lay on my cot out under the stars, they kept marching by me—the people I used to know—trying to show me the way. And me too blind to see—at first. But one night it came to me, and the next day I sent down to Banning for a typewriter." He smiled reminiscently. "I could hardly wait till it arrived. I wrote that first story in two days. It was about Nell Morrison and Billy Archer. I changed everything, of course. No one could possibly have recognized them— except you, perhaps. You—you didn't happen to see it?"

"I'm sorry, Jimmy, I didn't."

"No time to read, of course. Well, I wrote some more stories. Great bunch of people I had to draw on, and that's what counts, Peg—real, live human beings. The first year I made seven hundred dollars—not much, but a start. And this year I cleaned up nearly eight thousand. I could have made more, but I've been fooling with a play I've had in my mind a long time. I sent the scheme of it to Georgie Cohan, and he wrote me a wonderful letter. Said he liked my idea. You know what that means."

"Oh, Jimmy! But I always knew you were clever."

"It's been a great satisfaction to me, Peg. And this big moment—this large third-act curtain—I've been looking forward to it so long. Of course, it's not so wonderful as I'd hoped it might be—"

"What do you mean?"

"Well, down there in the shadow of old San Jacinto I'm afraid I got to thinking—pretty silly things."

"What?"

"I got to thinking that maybe when I brought you this check I could tell you that one man in your family was ready to take care of you at last; that maybe I could carry you away—look after you—that is, if you could be fond of me, as you were once. Wasn't I the fool, Peg? That fussy little lawyer dropped in the other day, and then I knew what a fool I'd been." His voice softened. "I want to tell you—it's all right, Peg. If it means your happiness you don't have to pay me to get out of the way. You must have known that. I'll do all I can to help—and I'll wish you luck."

The nurse entered suddenly.

"Mr. Martin Fox is calling," she announced.

"I'd like to see him," Peg said.

"He makes a good entrance," smiled Jimmy, and Fox came in.

Peg introduced them. Fox started at sound of Jimmy's name, gave him a cool nod and passed him by.

"I was here last night, Peg," said the millionaire. "They wouldn't let me see you. By gad, you are banged up! Poor little kid!"

"Only a few scratches," she told him.

Jimmy came over and tapped Fox on the shoulder.

"Just a moment," he said.

The big man turned and stared at him.

"Well?" he said sharply.

"Well," drawled Jimmy. He looked down at Peggy Malone. "It's no use, Peg," he said. "I can't stage the grand renunciation scene, after all."

"What are you talking about?" asked Martin Fox.

"It's like this," smiled Jimmy graciously. "I thought I'd come up from Palm Springs to hand you my wife—take her, old man, God bless you both, and all that stuff—but I'm damned if I do. A fellow doesn't draw a wife like Peg more than once in a lifetime. I've been looking you over. I cut out a dozen like you seven years ago—some of them wanted to marry her too—and what I did once I can do again."

He went to the table just inside the door and took up his package, unwrapping the tissue-paper covering. He carried the object over and laid it on the pillow close by his wife's face.

"Jimmy!" she cried.

"Violets, lady, violets! From the hand of one who loves you." He turned again to Fox.

"I suppose you do a lot of motoring out here in California?"

"What the devil—"

"Maybe you can tell us about a house that's for sale—or for rent," Jimmy went on. "A little house—we won't have much money at first. We'll want something with snow-capped mountains at the back door, and if it's not asking too much, a glimpse of the sea down in front—yes, I rather want the sea—and it ought to face the west, so that the sun can pour in on us all day long. Have you run across anything like that in your travels?"

"I guess Peg will have something to say about this!" growled Fox.

They waited.

"I want you two boys to shake hands," she said. "You're regular fellows, both of you, and there's no reason why you shouldn't be friends. And after that—if you know any such house, Martin, you might tell us; but if not—just wish us luck—before you go."

Martin Fox stood for a long moment; then he held out his hand. Jimmy took it.

"All the luck in the world to both of you," said Fox. He walked unsteadily to the door and turned. "You—you want to hurry up and get well, Peg," he said, and went out.

Jimmy leaned over and dropped a kiss among the bandages. Then he followed Fox down-stairs and politely helped him find his hat and stick.

"She's the greatest little girl in the world," Fox said. "You don't blame me if—if I tried—"

"To grab her? Man, it does you credit!" Jimmy held open the door. "A pleasant journey East," he said.

He returned to the drawing-room. Joey and Peter Malone were sitting there, the latter with the morning paper still in his hand.

"Well, boys," said Jimmy genially, "I've got important news for you. Peg isn't going to work again."

"Wha—what's the trouble?" Joey cried.

"No trouble at all," Jimmy told him. "Everything's lovely. She's just picked up a husband she mislaid, and strangely enough he's able and willing to take care of her."

He paused for a moment to enjoy their faces, then stepped over and removed the newspaper from Malone's limp hand. "Now in regard to the morning paper—"

"What did you mean about the paper?" asked Malone. "I been all through it and so has Joey—"

"Ah, yes! But I'm afraid you sort of skimmed through the page that ought to interest you most. Just a minute— here we are! There's more than a page; there's a page and a half. What luck!" He folded the paper carefully, thrust it into Joey's reluctant hands and pointed. "Study it well, both of you," he said.—" 'Help Wanted—Male'—that is, if you think you still come under that classification."

He stood for a moment, smiling at them. Then he turned and went up-stairs to his wife.

A LETTER TO AUSTRALIA

First published in The Saturday Evening Post, Feb 11,
1922

TOM MEADE was walking home under the bare
branches of the trees on Center Avenue. High in the heavens
shone a chill October moon, tracing a weird network of
shadows along his pathway. His step sounded briskly on the
wooden sidewalks, his head was thrown back, the events of
the evening had set him dreaming of great things.

Over Center Avenue, over all Mayfield, hovered a
somnolent calm. The hour was late, well past nine, and
Mayfield was always a nine-o'clock town. At that hour came
regularly the sound of the imperfectly stifled yawn, the click
of the back door following closely on the exit of the cat,
the rasp of timepieces being wound, the voice of parental
authority—"Come, young man, put up that book and get
to bed!" Then silence. By ten o'clock revelers straying home
from Mike Forrester's Happy Hour Pool and Billiard Parlor
saw only at rare intervals a lighted window, and spoke loudly
of emigrating to Indianapolis, where, it was understood,
were laughter and music—night life to meet all tastes.

Nights were for sleeping in Mayfield then; and, indeed,
in those early 'nineties the days were not much more exciting.
Life was simple and wholesome and placid, and the good

people of the town aimed to keep it so. Meeting casually under the maples that lined the streets they had time for prolonged social chats, for kindly inquiries as to one another's health and welfare. And if there was one with graying hair amid the group you were fairly sure to hear a complaint about the restless hurry of the new generation, a longing sigh for the amiable 'eighties, the gracious 'seventies.

Tom Meade quickened his step, for the clock in the tower of the new courthouse had struck the half-hour, and he had much to tell Jenny before they went to bed. The Republican rally had been a huge success, the opera house was crowded to the doors. Such rousing enthusiasm—but this was Indiana, where political argument was, to most men, food and drink. As for his own speech—and Jenny would first of all want to know about that—it had been enthusiastically received. He had done well, he knew it; with persuasive eloquence he had pleaded for the reelection of Mr. Harrison. Not an easy task, either, for there was little in the personality of the President to inspire an orator. However, the crowd had been with him, they had welcomed his sallies against Mr. Cleveland with loud approval.

Behind him, on the new brick pavement of the avenue, rang the rhythmic beat of a horse's hoofs. Turning, he saw old Bill Love's hack outlined in the moonlight. The nine-twenty was in from Indianapolis; some plutocratic citizen of Center Avenue was riding home in state.

The hack passed him and came to a stop in front of an ornate house, the finest in town, and the fare alighted just as Tom Meade came abreast. He recognized Jackson Perkins, president of the First National, leading citizen.

"Hello, Tom!" said Perkins. "Have a good meeting?"

"Great!" Meade answered.

"There's talk down in Indianapolis that Cleveland may come back," the rich man said.

"Don't you believe it," Tom reassured him. "You should have been in that opera house to-night. Looks to me like a Republican landslide."

"I hope so, I'm sure," replied Perkins fervently. "Good night."

As Tom Meade passed on he saw the banker carelessly bestow a coin on old Bill. Evidently Jackson Perkins thought nothing of two bits for a hack when he was tired. Oh, well! Tom reflected, he was only thirty-three himself. Lots of things could and would happen. Some day he, too, would be a power in May-field, have a great house on the avenue, come rolling home through the moonlight in Bill Love's hack.

He turned off the thoroughfare of the big bugs into his own street, Monroe. There, some distance down, stood the simple little frame house for which he was struggling to pay. Jenny-must have heard him coming, for the door opened and she stood there, sharply outlined against the yellow glow of the lamp within. Her figure was alert and slim, and the light at her back emphasized the rather alarming smallness of her waist, laced almost to nothing in the fashion of the period.

"Tom, I've been worried. It's nearly ten o'clock," she said.

"Never worry about me," he laughed, and kissed her. "I can take care of myself, I guess."

She caught the note of elation in his voice. She looked up at him eagerly.

"How did the speech go, Tom?" she asked.

"Like a house afire," he told her, putting modesty aside in the sanctity of his home. He tossed his overcoat on to a chair. "The best I ever made, Jenny, and that's a fact. I'll tell you how well they liked it—they're going to nominate me for prosecutor when the party convention meets next June."

"No! Oh, Tom!"

"It's the truth. Judge Marvin told me it's practically settled. Of course, I'll have to give up the street-railway job. But—county prosecutor! It's a big opportunity, Jenny."

"They're beginning to appreciate you at last. I've known all the time."

"Have you? Yes, I guess you have. Well, it takes a young lawyer a long time to get going, but once I've started—"

He followed her into the tiny parlor, a room of green-plush furniture, enlarged crayon portraits, hand-painted china, innumerable tidies. On the center table a large oil lamp was lighted, and close beside it sat his daughter, a fair, spindling girl of nine, spelling out an article in a woman's magazine.

"What? Clara, you still up?" he cried, surprise in his voice.

"I told her she could wait until you came," the mother explained. "I never dreamed it would be so late. Come, dear, kiss father and run to bed."

Clara rose and came to him. He took the magazine.

"What's this you're reading? 'The Girl with the Voice'."

"It's by a great opera singer," said Clara shyly. "Advice to girls who want to do like her."

"Oh, yes. Come on now. Up-stairs you go."

"I wish you'd go up and see if David's still awake," Jenny said. "You didn't kiss him when you left after supper, and he told me he was going to sit up in bed until you came. It would be just like him to do it too."

Tom Meade accompanied Clara up the short flight of stairs. In the little room sacred to his six-year-old son a night light was burning. He tiptoed in and bent over the bed. Evidently David was asleep. But as he was turning away the child stirred and opened his eyes.

417

"Hello, Daddy," he said-drowsily. "Want to have a boxing?"

"No, no boxing to-night. Too late," Meade told him.

But David would not be denied his nightly drama.

"I'm Corbett," he announced, for the recent bout in New Orleans had made a deep impression on the small boys of the town. Meade assumed his usual role of John L. Sullivan, and after a brief exchange of easy blows permitted himself to be laid low by the diminutive Gentleman Jim. Too sleepy to enjoy his triumph, David fell back on the pillow, his little fists clenched above his head. For a moment his father stood looking down at him; he wondered if David was getting a wrong idea of how battles may be won. Then, smiling gently, he kissed the boy and went down-stairs to Jenny.

Jenny had resumed her sewing. She was mending a rent in the lining of her sealskin coat, getting it ready for the winter. It was the pride of her life, that coat; so fashionable— the gift of Tom in one of his reckless moods. There were very few such coats in town. Mrs. Jackson Perkins had one—Mrs. Doctor Clark

"Well, Jenny," said Meade.

"Oh, Tom, I was just thinking. Prosecutor! That will be wonderful!"

"Yes, won't it?" He sat down and smiled at her pretty, flushed face. The future, with its infinite possibilities, opened again before him. "I tell you, my dear, it's something to look forward to!"

She sewed on.

"Who was at the meeting, Tom?"

"Everybody in town, I guess. I had quite a talk with Charley Nelson."

"How was he looking?"

"Not very well. Awfully thin, and—sort of transparent, almost."

"Mary is so worried about him. She was telling me the other day. She says he isn't feeling right. She's afraid he won't be here long."

"Too bad," said Tom. "By the way, he told me about Dan. It seems there was a big strike in Australia two years ago, and everything looked black for a time. But now, Charley says, Dan's doing mighty well again. Expects to be taken into that firm he's with. I forget the name—Holding and Somebody, I believe."

Jenny was looking at him accusingly.

"Tom, you've never written to Dan," she said.

"No, I haven't," he admitted.

"Really, it's too bad. And Dan your very best friend."

"I know—I agree with you. I was thinking about it coming home. Let's go up-stairs, and if you don't mind I'll stop in my den and have a try at it."

"Oh, Tom, I wish you would," said Jenny. "I always liked Dan so much."

Ten minutes later he was seated at a cheap oak desk in the room known as his den. On the walls hung pennants handed down from his college days, a group picture of his class at the law school, a crude copy of one of Mr. Gibson's drawings, done by Clara and presented with her love the preceding Christmas.

He lighted a pipe and took from the top drawer of his desk a small bundle of papers. On the top was an envelope somewhat yellowed by the passage of time. He removed it from the package and drew out the sheet of letter paper it contained. Although he knew almost by heart what was written there, he read it again:

"Holbrook & Bunting, Ltd.
Direct Buyers Sheepskins, Rabbit Skins, Wool, Hides and Tallow
189 Little Bourke Street, Melbourne, Victoria

"Dear Tom: Your letter with the news of your engagement to Jenny Fairbanks came in on the last boat, and I hasten to send my sincere congratulations. I always thought Jenny the prettiest cleverest girl in Mayfield, and you're mighty lucky to get her. As for you—well, I guess she knows what I think of you. May you have the long happy life together I'm wishing for you to- day.

"You asked for news of me. I'm still plodding along. Australia isn't so bad, even if we are a long ways from anything. I've never regretted coming out, though of course there are times when I get homesick as the devil for the old town, the old friends—you most of all. I guess I don't need to tell you what a letter from you means to me.

"I'm rushing this to catch the boat. Some time later I'll write at length about my life out here. This is meant to be nothing more than a friendly hail from this far outpost. Good luck, old man, and God bless you both.

"Your old friend, Dan Nelson."

The date on the letter was August 26, 1880.

Tom Meade got up and paced the floor of that tiny room. Eighteen- eighty—why, that was twelve years ago! For twelve years he had put off writing to his friend. In heaven's name, why? He who in his daily life was so punctilious, so prompt; he who never vacillated.

"I guess I don't need to tell you what a letter from you means to me," Dan had said.

Good old Dan, the boy with whom he had roamed the woods and fields about Mayfield, the inseparable pal of his youth. He had loved Dan like a brother, and yet he had let twelve years drift by.

He dropped again into his squeaky little desk chair and began an examination of the papers that had been tied up with Dan's letter. He never threw anything away. Here were the false starts he had made at a letter to Australia during those twelve years; the first one, written a year after he received Dan's congratulations :

"Dear Dan: I owe you a thousand apologies; but, as a matter of fact, I was so pressed for time, what with the excitement of—"

Why hadn't he sent that? As he recalled it now, Australia had seemed so far away. One really should have news—important news—to put into a letter that would be anywhere from forty to seventy days on its journey. And, wonderful as his marriage had seemed to him, there was no news in it for Dan; Dan had known he contemplated marriage. However, something else was impending, something of vital importance. He had been admitted to the bar, was shortly to go into Henry Brackett's law office. His name would be on the stationery. He would wait and write then.

His next attempt was, indeed, on the Brackett stationery.

"Dear Dan: I'm sure you will understand, but what with all the anxiety I have gone through owing to Jenny's illness—"

What illness was that? He tried to remember. Nothing serious, evidently. Like the first, this letter had never been finished and sent. Before its completion there was something new to look forward to. A baby—a son, he hoped.

The baby came—Clara. He loved Clara with all his heart, thought her wonderful, proposed writing Dan about her. He was only waiting to include in the letter another bit of news.

Old Judge Marvin had come to him and offered to take him into partnership as soon as he could break away from Brackett. Dan would remember Judge Marvin, would realize what a big step up this was, would rejoice with his old friend.

But Dan had never got the news. By the time Tom Meade had settled himself in the Marvin office and remembered his project of a letter to Dan another baby was imminent. A son this time, he hoped. To his great joy, David appeared, answering his dearest wish. He proposed to take Jenny, as soon as she was able, on a pleasure trip to Washington. A lively description of Washington, he reflected, would round off nicely his letter to Dan telling of David's birth.

The Washington trip followed, but for some reason now forgotten he held off writing to Dan.

Running through these incomplete records with their abject apologies, their ever-changing narrative, he perceived that there was always something in the air, something for which he was eagerly waiting—a nomination for mayor, which had finally eluded him; the winning of a big case;

his appointment as attorney for the new street-railway company.

Well, he reflected, the waiting must stop. All nonsense anyhow. He would write to Dan without any more delay; to Dan, in Melbourne, Australia. And with the feeling of a man who sits down to write a history of the civilized world he drew toward him a blank sheet of paper.

"67 Monroe Street, Mayfield, Indiana, October 25, 1892.

"Dear Dan: I don't know what you'll think of me, I'm sure. Believe it or not, I've sat down a score of times to answer that letter you wrote me so long ago—the one congratulating me on my engagement to Jenny. Yes, Dan, time after time, and always something held me up, sidetracked me. The truth of it is, of course, that I'm tremendously busy. My practise is growing all the while; and then, too, I'm attorney for the new street railway.

"But look here, I'm not going to bore you with a lot of stupid apologies. All I can say is that if you'll forgive me—which same you can indicate by answering this without delay—I'll promise to do better in the future.

"It was seeing your Cousin Charley at the opera house to-night that got me started on this. I had a little talk with him, and he told me how well you're doing. I want to assure you right here; Dan, before I go any further, that your kind wishes on our engagement were deeply appreciated at the time. Jenny and I have now been married eleven years, and all the happiness you bespoke for us has so far been ours. Jenny is still the prettiest girl in town—and the cleverest. What's more, she's not a day older than when you saw her last. Our daughter Clara is nine and David is six.

"As for my work, I've kept plugging along. Nothing very exciting has happened as yet, but I have hopes. As a matter of fact, only to-night—"

He stopped suddenly and read over what he had written. Stale stuff, every line of it. It seemed to him that in all these twelve years he had never had so little to put into a letter.

Once more his acutely materialistic sense of space asserted itself. Australia—the end of the world! Twelve thousand miles stretched between Mayfield and Melbourne, Monroe Street and Little Bourke. Thirty-two days of actual travel for this letter, provided it just caught one of the Oceanic Steamship Company's boats at San Francisco. If it missed it might lie over for twenty-eight days. There was a possibility that his letter might be sixty days on the way! A letter that traveled sixty days ought to carry news—real news.

And was he not, after all, right on the brink of something well worth writing to Dan? Prosecuting attorney—that was no trifling office. As good as settled, too, the judge had said. He visualized a new letter:

"Dear Dan: At last I've got something to tell you. I've just been elected county prosecutor by an overwhelming majority—"

Folding up the sheet of paper on which he had been writing, he added it to the package that had the yellow envelope on top. He restored the package to its old place in the drawer.

The little house was cold when he went out into the upper hall. He wondered if he had locked the back door. All the lamps were out, but the autumn moonlight shone faintly through the rooms. He felt his way cautiously to the kitchen, found the rear door securely fastened. Opening it, he stood on the stoop. The moon shone brightly on the modest garden where he had worked through the long summer evenings. Over the houses of his neighbors, over all Mayfield brooded peace and content.

He loved his neighbors, such simple, kindly, understanding people. He loved his town. In it, he told himself, he would climb high, become a power, make Jenny proud of him, give his children the best life could offer. He looked forward to big things.

When he entered the bedroom Jenny lifted her head from the pillow.

"Did you write to Dan?" she asked sleepily.

"No, not exactly. When I came right down to it, there was no news worth sending all that distance. And I thought if I'm to be prosecuting attorney— "

"That will be something to write Dan about," she agreed.

"Yes," said Tom Meade. "I thought I'd wait until that comes along."

His intentions were of the best. But it was eighteen years before he began another letter to Australia.

* * * * *

ON thanksgiving night, in the year 1910, the first snow of the winter fell in Mayfield. "The beautiful," as next day's Evening Enterprise described it, "cloaking in its mantle of white our fair and prosperous city."

Accuracy was the self-confessed aim of the Enterprise, and it was accurate here. The snow was beautiful. It was of the wet, clinging variety that lay where it fell—on telegraph wires, on picket fences, on the bare branches of the trees that lined Center Avenue, and on the cornices and window-sills of a house that stood on the avenue not far from the corner of Monroe, a great brick mansion of many rooms that advertised the wealth and dignity of its owner.

Tom Meade sat before the fire in the library of this house, with his family about him. That slender young lawyer who spoke for Harrison in the opera house in 'ninety-two was gone for ever; probably only Jenny remembered him.

For the years had added weight to Tom Meade's figure, grayed his hair. But they had not dimmed the twinkle in his eyes.

It had been an old-fashioned Thanksgiving, and he had enjoyed it thoroughly. The snow outside added the final happy touch; all his folks about him in this comfortable room. On his right sat Jenny, fragile, birdlike, pretty, still. On his left were David and Jean, David's wife. Behind him at the grand piano, Clara sat, singing, at his request, Kathleen Mavourneen. He listened, enthralled. There was in Clara's voice a soft beauty that always thrilled him, that exalted yet saddened him. He remembered what the great teacher in New York had said of Clara's voice.

Poor Clara, thin and faded and wasted—at twenty-seven! What a pity!

The last notes of the song died away through the silent house, and reaching out Tom Meade patted Jenny's hand where it lay on the arm of her chair.

"Don't be silly, Tom," she said, and they laughed softly together.

"What next?" demanded Clara, turning the pages of the ancient song book before her. "You choose, Father. This is your party, you know."

He moved his head in time to catch a look he was not intended to see, a questioning look from Jean to David which said more plainly than words, "Can't we break away now? Haven't we been here long enough?"

Tom Meade stood up.

"Guess we'd better let these children off, Mother," he said. "It'll be a hard drive back to Indianapolis through the snow. I think it was mighty good of them to come up here and spend Thanksgiving with us old folks."

"Speak for yourself," said Jenny quickly. "You know, David, ever since he passed fifty your father's perfectly absurd. You'd think he was a hundred. For my part, I'm never going to grow old. Never going to admit it anyhow."

"That's the talk, Mother," said David. "You stick to it." He got up and tossed his cigarette into the fireplace. He was a stout, rather florid-faced young man, decked out in clothes that were the despair of all the would-be snappy dressers in Indianapolis. "Come on, Jean, I guess we had better be drifting along. My carbureter acted sort of funny on the way up," he added to his father.

"Well, if we must," said Jean. She rose with seeming reluctance, a slim pretty girl, but like David a bit overdressed, a bit flashy. "You must come and see us soon—both of you. And—oh, yes," she remembered tardily, "you, too, Clara."

"Thanks," said Clara, without turning her head.

They went into the big oak-paneled hall, where the visitors donned their coats with more animation than had been theirs all day.

Tom and Jenny accompanied them to the side door. Under the porte-cochère stood David's car, a smart, blood-red racer, the sportiest model the year 1910 had to offer. Jenny was the recipient of two hasty kisses, after which Tom helped Jean to her place and even lent a hand to David, who had now taken on the look of a large fur-bearing animal.

"Well, folks " David began, his hands on the wheel. He

fumbled round in his mind for some kindly words of farewell, but words were never his specialty. He gave it up and turned his attention to starting the motor, which whirred instantly. "Listen to that!" he cried with enthusiasm. "It's a lalapalooser, this car! Well—well—we had a fine day."

The automobile began to move. Tom Meade, standing bareheaded in the shelter of the porte-cochère, heard "fine day" flung over Jean's shoulder. He watched them creep down the long drive, gaining speed as they went, then swing out through the great gate into Center Avenue. Bill Love's hack was not abroad on Center Avenue to-night, nor any other hack. At intervals a motor horn sounded shrilly through the storm and the lights of a passing car flashed momentarily over the snow.

"Come in, Father, you'll catch your death," Jenny said from the door.

He returned to the hall. Clara, half-way up the stairs, called her good night.

"It's early yet," Meade said. "You're not turning in, Jenny?"

"Of course not," she answered. He followed her into the library.

"Where's Cuffy?" he asked, referring to his aged colored butler.

"I told him to go to bed," Jenny said. "He wasn't feeling well—ate too much, I guess. You'd think he'd know better—at his age."

Meade laughed and began to pile logs on the fire.

"Well, it's been a happy Thanksgiving," Jenny went on. "I don't know as I recall many happier. I do hope they get back to Indianapolis safe and sound." She went over to the bay window and stood staring out. "It's dangerous driving in a storm like this. I wish I'd told David to call up when they get there."

Her husband came over and put his arm about her shoulders.

"Now, Mother, none of your worrying." He stood staring out across his lawn. It was a broad lawn, three hundred feet or more to the old Jackson Perkins place on the south, five hundred feet to the river in the rear. On it lay the Thanksgiving snow. "It's beautiful, isn't it, Mother?" Tom Meade said.

"Yes," she answered, "if only it would stay that way."

She was thinking, he knew, of what would happen to the snow to-morrow. For Mayfield was no longer the leisurely town of old, clean and calm. There were blast furnaces to the south, the west and the north, a hundred factories whose chimneys would in the morning belch forth smoke and soot. On the streets where Tom Meade had once known everybody many strangers walked, some of whom conversed loudly in the tongues of far countries overseas.

"The livest manufacturing city in Indiana," boasted the Enterprise.

He had kept his word; he had risen to power in Mayfield; but it was no longer his town; his town lived only in the loving memory of the middle-aged.

A cold wind swept in on them through the cracks round the window, and they returned to their places by the fire. For a long moment Tom Meade sat smiling at his wife.

"Well, Father?" she said.

"I was just thinking—that was a gallant thing you said, about never growing old. I believe you meant it too."

"Of course I did!"

"It's odd, Jenny, but to me you don't look a day older than you did when—when we were engaged. That Thanksgiving in 1880—do you remember?—just before we were married. The snow was three feet deep on the level, and when I went up to your house to Thanksgiving dinner they were racing cutters on Center Avenue."

"I remember. You were wearing a new stock. It was your ambition to look like Henry Clay."

"It was my ambition to look worthy of you—the prettiest girl in Mayfield, and the cleverest." He stopped. " T always thought Jenny the prettiest, cleverest girl in Mayfield,'" he repeated. "Who was it said that—in a letter, somewhere?" His mind groped back through the years. "Oh, I remember now! Dan Nelson said it in that old letter—that letter from Australia."

He paused, conscious of his guilt. He knew that Jenny's eyes were on him reprovingly.

"The letter you never answered," she said. "Oh, Father—"

"I know, I know. I'm ashamed of myself. It's been years since I even sat down to have a try at it. Though I've thought of it now and then, times when I've had a glimpse of Charley or seen a dispatch from Australia in the paper or—or something like that. I've even lain awake at nights and planned a beginning."

"But Dan doesn't know that."

"No, of course not. However, it salves my conscience. Why, only the other day I thought of writing him—that is, it was about two years ago, when we were on our way home from David's wedding. 'That letter from Dan Nelson congratulating us on our engagement,' I said to myself. 'I'll answer it when our first grandchild arrives.' It struck me that would be amusing."

"Father, Jean doesn't want any children," said Jenny softly. "I've known it for some time."

"I suspected it. Jenny, what's come over this new generation? I tell you, the world will go on the rocks."

"Don't try to change the subject," Jenny broke in. "We're talking about Dan Nelson's letter." She got up and went to his big mahogany desk, opened a drawer, took out a little package of papers. "I was cleaning out your desk the other day—you know you said I could—and I found this." She laid the package on top. "Come on, Father. No time like the present."

He walked over and took up the package.

He saw a letter postmarked Australia—faded ink on yellow paper.

"By gad," he said, "I supposed this was lost long ago!"

He sat down and began to read, while Jenny returned to her place before the fire.

Finally he looked up.

"Here's my last attempt," he smiled. "October 25, 1892. In the little house on Monroe Street." Into his mind flashed a picture of the room known as his den, the strip of rag carpet on the floor, the cheap oak desk, the creaky chair, the pennants and the Gibson drawing. He stared about him at the room in which he sat to-night, his big comfortable library with its lofty ceiling, its Persian rug on the floor, its soft, inviting chairs, its warm, rich, prosperous air. "We've traveled a long way since 1892," he said with a sort of awe in his voice.

"So we have," Jenny answered softly.

He read aloud the final lines of the letter in his hand: "'Nothing very exciting has happened as yet, but I have hopes. As a matter of fact, only to-night—'" He looked up and smiled at Jenny. "Only to-night!" he repeated. "Do you remember how thrilled we were, Jenny? County prosecutor! I was about to become county prosecutor!"

"It seemed almost too wonderful to be true," she smiled.

"It was true, though," he reminded her. He laid down the letter, a reminiscent mood seized him. "It all comes back so clearly. That night in June when the party convention adjourned, and I raced up the avenue to tell you I'd been nominated. You were waiting on the porch—happy times, my dear."

"Yet you didn't write to Dan."

"No. It was such a busy summer—remember? The summer of the World's Fair—and the panic. How big a dollar grew to look! I had to borrow from your father to make my campaign, and after election I was busier still; busy night and day, trying to pay back that loan, to meet the payments on the little house. We were pretty hard up, weren't we, Jenny? We might be hard up still if it hadn't been for Jim Wakefield and his horseless carriage."

"Yes," she admitted, "that was the turning point, and we never guessed at the time."

"I should say not! I was pretty discouraged, as I recall. It was in 'ninety- six, wasn't it?—yes, a July night in 'ninety-six. Hot as the devil in my little office above the Bon-Ton Store. And there was Jim Wakefield, all excited over his invention. I'd just drawn up the papers of incorporation for his factory, and I was hoping for a hundred dollars—fifty anyway. We needed money so badly. And then he told me he couldn't pay me—gave me those five hundred shares of stock instead. Jenny, I was pretty bitter when he left, though I didn't let him see. I'd have sold those shares for twenty-five dollars then—spot cash."

"Yes, and I'd have let you."

"Yet to-night David's riding back to Indianapolis in a Wakefield car, and those shares are worth more money than you and I can ever spend. Funny how things turn out."

"What came next, Father? The circuit court, wasn't it?"

"Yes. I was planning to write Dan about that. But by that time Jim Wakefield was paying me dividends; I was getting in on the ground floor in a dozen factories—I was on the make. Something seemed to say 'Bigger things coming—go on, go on!' And when I got to Congress—"

"You should have written Dan then—from Washington."

"I did think of it, but I was waiting for something definite, some brilliant speech, some impressive victory. And the first thing I knew my term was over and I was back here. Things here looked better than ever. In another year I had my first hundred thousand. I thought of writing Dan, but I held off. We were building this house—I decided to wait and write him about that." He rose and walked back and forth over the soft rug. "That was a happy night, Jenny—when they gave us the housewarming here. Everybody seemed so glad we were getting on. Not an envious word or look. And how proud we were of Clara when she sang Home, Sweet Home. That was when I began looking forward to great things for Clara."

He paused.

Jenny said nothing, but continued to stare into the fire.

"I wanted a big success for Clara," he went on. "I counted so much on writing Dan about her. A concert tour abroad—opera, maybe. But of course—it never happened."

"No," answered Jenny gently, "it never happened." She got up from her chair. "Father, you've waited long enough. You must write to Dan to-night."

"But it's so late."

"Nonsense! It's early. You said so yourself. No time like the present, Tom—for my sake."

"All right," he said amiably, "I'll do it."

She kissed him and moved toward the door.

"I'll leave you alone," she said, pausing there. "Don't you dare to come up- stairs until the letter's finished."

When she had gone he sat again at his desk. He was still thinking of Clara; Clara in New York, studying under the best teacher in the country; letters coming in from Clara's teacher, speaking sincerely, earnestly, in praise of her voice, urging that she be sent abroad; passage engaged, plans settled, himself and Jenny in New York to put her on the boat and say good-by.

He recalled now with something of the old surprise and pain that scene in the bare little parlor of the New York hotel suite. Clara had been rather apathetic, rather gloomy, ever since they met her. She was due to sail at three the next day. Suddenly she got up from her chair and came over to her father.

"I've got something to say," she began. "I think you ought to know. I'll sail to-morrow if you wish—I'll go on with my music—but it's against my will. I don't care if I never hear a note of music again as long as I live!"

He gasped. It fell upon him out of a clear sky. He had thought her devoted to her career, wrapped up in it.

438

Jenny and he questioned the girl gently. It seemed she was in love; in love with a young man named Harry Parker, who worked in a store at home, an utterly commonplace boy whose reputation was not of the best. Tom Meade was appalled. He had been barely aware such a person existed; yet here he was, entering his life, wrecking one of his fondest dreams. Though the hour was late, he went to the studio of Clara's teacher, asked the advice of that wise old Frenchman.

"No use to force her," the teacher said. "I have noticed. The heart is gone from her singing. We can not shape the lives of our children, wise though we may be. Let her follow her heart, which is no longer in the music."

So Clara followed her heart back to Mayfield, and they went with her. The day for her wedding was set, the trousseau bought, when suddenly, pale and tragic, she broke her engagement. The man for whom she had given up everything was not worth it, though just what act of his it was that enlightened Clara her father never knew. For months she walked about the big house like a ghost. Jenny and he hoped she could again take up her career, but as time went on they saw that Clara was finished with song.

The force of the blow was mercifully broken for Tom Meade—his son was left. David was in his first year at law school, struggling hard. Eagerly his father looked forward to the moment when David would come into his office, share his burdens, carry on the torch. "Meade and Meade, Attorneys at Law." He closed his eyes and saw the letterhead.

And then—it had happened only three years ago, and the sting of it was still sharp in Tom Meade's heart—David was expelled from school. A boyish prank, his father liked to call it. But it was the culmination of too many pranks, too long a list of failures, too little interest in the work.

"I'm sorry," wrote the dean of the school a bit brutally, "but I can see in your son no mental capacity whatever for the calling of the law."

In this very room David and his father had met, David alternately shamefaced and defiant. His father studied the boy. He was a bit florid for his years, a bit heavy. Could it be—a bit dissipated? Fiercely Tom Meade asked himself, was it his fault? Had he given David too much money to spend in college? He had had more than other boys—yes. But his father had only meant to be kind. Had he been too kind—ruined him with his kindness?

But David wasn't precisely ruined; he turned into an average, rather chuckle- headed citizen of the republic. He ate and drank a little too much, and his brain power did not carry him far past the sporting page. But he got along. He went to Indianapolis, secured the agency for the Wakefield car and was soon able to support himself. In another year he married Jean, spoiled daughter of a wealthy family, and Tom Meade began to dream of a grandchild.

Well, that was no use, either, it seemed. He glanced at the clock—eleven—he must get down to it. He felt no real urge to write Dan to-night, but Jenny was right—it was his duty. Besides, he had promised he would.

But what a job! After all these years! He arranged a blank sheet of paper before him and took up his pen.

"39 Center Avenue, Mayfield, Indiana. November 24, 1910.

"Dear Dan: I hold in my hand to-night a letter you wrote me in August, 1880, congratulating me on my engagement to Jenny Fairbanks. No doubt you have long ago forgotten it; perhaps you have forgotten me. If so, here's a line to remind you. Your old friend Tom Meade is still alive, and he's been planning to answer for a long, long time. By the Lord Harry, he's been planning for thirty years!

"Thirty years! Honestly, Dan, I can't find words. What can I say in apology? My silence constitutes a record, I suppose; yet it was only the silence of a man who was not content to scribble off anything and send it on its way. It was the silence of a man who, knowing how deeply you believed in him and his talents, wanted some big bit of news, some notable achievement to put into his letter to Australia.

"The odd thing is that as I look back that big thing seemed always just ahead, around the next corner. And so I'd go on. Sometimes when I turned the corner the thing was gone, sometimes it was there, but looking so much smaller, so much less important than I'd imagined it. And whether it was there or not, always there was another corner looming up, a bigger, better thing waiting there. And a voice that said, 'Go on! Go on!'

"I suppose that's life, Dan; always something to look forward to, to keep us moving on. It was life for me, a lawyer, and no doubt for you, a business man, and for all men everywhere.

"I've had a busy time of it. I've been pretty lucky and successful, as things go. After I was admitted to the bar Henry Brackett took me into his office— "

He set down his Odyssey—a page or more. The long list of his honors and achievements, the story of his investments, his financial rise, the high position he held in his profession—lecturer at the law school in the city, president of the State Bar Association, editor of The Bench and Bar of Indiana, in three volumes. He omitted nothing, it made an impressive history.

"Well, Dan, that's my record. I won't try to conceal the fact that I'm mighty proud of it. And now I want to hear about you. How have you got on? Write and tell me all about yourself.

"You wished Jenny and me happiness in that letter long ago. We've had it, Dan, thirty years of it, a pleasant life together. Two children—fine kids, both of them; nothing brilliant, of course, but mighty satisfactory as children go these days. How about you? Did you marry? It seems to me Charley said you did.

"Can you ever forgive me, Dan? Thirty years to answer your friendly hail! I can explain it to myself, but somehow when I try to explain it to you the words won't come. However, I believe you will understand. Thirty years, but all that time thinking of you again and again as I walked this town where we were boys together! A different town, Dan, a very different town.

"God bless us both, you said. God bless you, too, old friend, and write me soon. As ever,

"Tom."

He put the letter into an envelope and sealed the flap. On the outside he wrote Dan Nelson's name, then paused— "189 Little Bourke Street"—but that was thirty years ago. Dan had probably moved since then—several times, perhaps. He would have to save this letter until morning, when he would drop into Charley Nelson's hardware store and learn Dan's latest address.

For a moment he held the letter in his hand, thinking. It was not quite satisfactory somehow. None of the news it contained was recent enough to be interesting. After all these years of waiting it was an anticlimax. It had a sort of everything's-all-over, this-is-the-end tone to it. No, it wasn't quite what he would like to send, but still He put it in the top drawer of his desk.

The fire on the hearth was out, the room icy cold. He was shivering when he rose from his desk and went up-stairs. Jenny was sleeping soundly. He was careful not to wake her. He crept into bed, chilled through. In the morning he was too ill to rise. His old friend, Doctor Clark, came in and looked him over.

"How's your general health, Tom?" he asked. "You don't look well. I'm going to get you out on the golf course next spring."

"Nonsense!" snorted Tom Meade. "Chase a little white ball all over creation? No, sir; not me!"

"We'll fight that out in the spring," smiled the doctor. "For the present you do as I tell you. Stick close to bed. Jenny, I rely on you to manage him."

A week later he sat, a convalescent, in his library in the early evening. Cuffy announced a visitor—Mr. Fred Perkins, from next door. Perkins had taken his father's place in the bank and as a leading citizen. He rushed in, a short, bald, puffy little man.

"Hello!" he cried. "Glad to see you up. Just stopped a minute on my way home to dinner. I was down to Indianapolis to-day and had a chat with the governor. I've got news for you."

"Yes?" Tom Meade questioned.

"You know, of course, that there's a vacancy on the supreme-court bench in this state. Has been ever since

Marvin died. Well, the governor was telling me he's thinking of appointing you. He wanted me to sound you out."

"Appoint me? The supreme court?" Tom Meade's voice was trembling.

"Yes. You could serve Marvin's unexpired term and then run for it. You'd be elected. You're the best lawyer in the state and everybody knows it. I expect to see the governor again in a few days. What shall I tell him?"

"Why, tell him I shall be honored. It's a great responsibility, and I'd give it my best."

"Fine! Must run along now. Helen's waiting dinner."

Five minutes later Jenny entered the library to find that he had thrown aside the covers in which she had wrapped him and was pacing the floor in his bath robe.

"Now, Father " she began.

"Jenny!" he cried. "Big news! Fred Perkins was just here. The governor is going to appoint me to the supreme court."

"Is he really? Well, that's nice, I'm sure. Now come back here and cover up."

He permitted her to restore him to the chair.

"Jenny, I'm a proud man," he told her. "I won't try to conceal it. The crowning honor of my life. The thing every lawyer secretly longs for, and just when I thought I was about finished. But I'm not. I tell you, my dear, I've got years of usefulness ahead of me."

"Of course you have, Father," Jenny answered. "Would you like another glass of milk?"

Before she sent him off to bed she allowed him a moment at his desk. In the top drawer he found a sealed envelope with the name Daniel Nelson, Esq., written on it. Ah, yes, his letter to Dan—the letter with which he was not quite satisfied. Sort of anticlimax. But now—the supreme-court bench

"It's a matter of only a few weeks," thought the Honorable Thomas Meade. "Yes, I'll wait until that comes along."

It came along three weeks later, but it looked trivial and unimportant when it came, for Jenny was lying desperately ill in the big front room up-stairs and a dreadful fear was gripping Tom Meade's heart.

* * * * *

WINTER, as the Mayfield Enterprise remarked, had not seen fit to linger in the lap of spring. This was in the year 1921. He had been a timid, impotent fellow, anyhow, and he vanished, terrified, when April arrived with the earliest consignment of warm breezes from the South. By the first of May summer, too prompt to be entirely welcome, held the stage.

On the fifteenth of the month—early enough to constitute a record, as all golfers will recognize—winter greens were abandoned at the Mayfield Country Club. Three days later, just as the noon whistles were blowing in the smoky town, Tom Meade stood on the tee of the eighteenth hole ready to drive off.

Solemnly, as befits such occasions, he took a practise swing. He seemed, if anything, younger than he had been on that Thanksgiving when he had last attempted a letter to Australia. True, his hair was now almost entirely white, but his figure had improved greatly and his cheeks glowed with health. Golf is a grand institution.

He approached the ball as one who has received that inner message that the hour is ripe to strike.

"Don't forget the brook," said his caddie suddenly. He glared at the boy with an expression of acute disfavor. Surely the child should have known that the brook was the one thing in all the world he had no wish to remember now.

He drew his club back slowly and drove straight and far. The ball bounded on toward the water hazard that traversed the fairway about a hundred and seventy- five yards away.

"In the brook!" shouted the boy, with no attempt to conceal his satisfaction. He had the caddie temperament.

"Nonsense!" said Tom Meade. "Something wrong with your eyes, Son. It stopped this side."

An unwonted excitement shone in his face, for he was on the verge of a big moment. In the ten years during which he had been devoted to golf he had never gone round the course in less than a hundred strokes. But this morning, counting his drive in the final hole, his score was a beautiful ninety-six. If he made the cup in three his record would be smashed. He said a golfer's prayer as he went toward his drive.

The prayer was answered—his ball lay a good two feet from the brook. Pointing out to his caddie the error of going through this world a pessimist, he took his mashie and accomplished a magnificent shot to the green. His heart sang; it was his morning, beyond dispute his morning of glory. He would have something to tell his fellow judges when the supreme court met again.

The brook being safely out of his way, he stood for a moment regarding it kindly. His eyes followed it as it crept out of bounds under a rail fence, across a field and disappeared amid a clump of trees. Old memories assailed him.

"Used to go swimming in this brook when I was a boy," he told the caddie.

"Tha's so?" said the caddie.

"Yes, sir. Over there under those trees—only cool place round here in July and August. We used to come tearing up from town, running across the fields, undressing as we ran."

"Get arrested fer that," the boy warned him.

"Yes, I guess we would nowadays. There were five fellows in my gang—Spider Griffiths, Mike Forrester, Dan Nelson—"

He walked on for a moment in silence. "Remember once Dan Nelson thought he'd be smart. Hid my clothes, and I had to hang round those woods until dark. Anybody ever hide your clothes, Son?"

"Naw," responded the bored younger generation. "Here's yer ball."

It was ticklish business, those last two strokes. His heart almost stopped beating, but he managed them safely.

"Ninety-nine!" he cried. "Not bad for a man my age, eh, boy?"

"I seen the professional " began the boy.

"Yes, but I'm no professional. Here, give me the bag. I'm just happy enough to mark you 'excellent,' though you know mighty well you don't deserve it."

He went exultantly into the locker-room. Passing cronies heard the news. The club steward heard it and was properly impressed. His chauffeur, waiting to take him back to Center Avenue, also heard it.

"Under a hundred—the first time in my life!"

He rolled away from the club, over the bridge that spanned the brook. The boards rattled beneath his heavy limousine. Back into the sprawling city, down Center Avenue, through the big gates and up to his house. Somewhat old-fashioned now, his house, but still imposing and dignified.

Clara was waiting for him in the big hall. She managed his house, now that Jenny was gone. Thirty-eight and unmarried, Clara. Once she would have been that creature scorned in Mayfield, an old maid. But the world was changing, even May-field, and the unmarried woman was no longer looked down upon. Clara was finding life not so bad, after all.

"Hello," she said. "Lunch is ready if you are. Have a good time?"

"Did I?" her father cried. "Clara, went round in ninety-nine! What do you think of that?"

"Splendid!" she answered. "I'm so happy for your sake. I know it's been your great ambition."

"It was," he corrected. "Got a new one now—ninety-five or better by September."

After lunch he went into his library. The efficient Clara had a cheerful fire crackling on the hearth. He lighted a cigar and sat for a time in his favorite chair, at peace with the world. The cigar finished, he went over to his desk. Great piles of legal-looking documents awaited him. Ignoring them, he sat for a long moment staring into space. Then he began to rummage through the drawers of his desk. For about ten minutes he continued to search, then he abandoned the project—whatever it was. He laid out a blank sheet of paper and took up his fountain pen. He wrote:

"Dear Dan: [Pity he couldn't find that old letter of Dan's, but no matter, he didn't need it.] Well, Dan, here I am again after all these years. Thought I'd dropped of? the earth, didn't you? And no wonder. I certainly have been a failure as a correspondent, haven't I, old man?

"However, I know it's all right with you. I've been busy, Dan, busy as the devil with a lot of little things that, as I look back on them now, didn't matter much after all. Every day now—I wonder if you find it that way, too—every day the memory of those middle years grows fainter and fainter, and the old times, the days of my youth, seem more distinct and nearer.

"I was out playing golf this morning, Dan. Oh, yes, we have a golf links here now—you wouldn't know the old town. As I say, I was out on the links. They're north of town, on what you may recall as the old Marvin tract. Across the fairway of the eighteenth hole runs a brook the sight of which would stir memories in you, Dan, as it always does in me. It's the brook where we went swimming together as boys.

"Remember, Dan, that time you hid my clothes in the crotch of a tree and left me shivering half the evening in the woods? Pretty mean trick, my lad. I always swore I'd get even with you, but I don't know that I ever did. Remember the time we held Spider Griffiths' head under water because he said Republicans were skunks, and he almost strangled and scared us half to death? And the night Mike Forrester's mother came for him with a switch, and got hold of you by mistake in the dark and caned you good? And said, when she discovered her error, that she wasn't sorry, as she guessed you needed it. Maybe you did, eh, Dan?

"It's the truth, Dan, you wouldn't know Mayfield. It's big and dirty and prosperous; full of strangers too. There's a tire factory on the field where we played ball. Green Hill, where you and I went coasting, is now our most exclusive suburb, dotted with Italian villas and handsome colonial mansions somewhat the worse for soft-coal smoke. I was out there the other day and it reminded me of the time you broke your sled—your new one—and I could see you standing there in the snow with the tears frozen on your face and the red muffler round your neck, just as plain as though it was yesterday.

"I've got a colored man named Cuffy—he's over ninety, I guess. He was in here the other day complaining about the weather. 'We don't have weather like it was in the olden times,' he said. A nd he added, in a voice that brought a lump into my throat, 'Oh, jedge, I'se sholy longin' fo' olden times to come back.'

"I'm like Cuffy, Dan. I'm sholy longin' fo' olden times to come back.

"Why not come home for a visit, Dan? Nothing would delight me more. We'd tear down this town as it is to-day and build it up as it used to be. I'd take you over our golf course. It's a mighty sporty little eighteen-hole affair of more than six thousand yards. People tell us there's nothing in Chicago can beat it. I go round in just under a hundred—not bad for an old fellow, eh, Dan?

"Dan, I'd love to see you. Jenny would have liked it, too, but she's no longer here. She thought a lot of you, old man. She was always after me to answer that letter you wrote congratulating us on our engagement. I may be a little late now, but I want to tell you that we appreciated your good wishes. I guess your letter brought us luck and happiness. Certainly we had both. Thirty years together, Jenny and I—two children—life mighty kind. That's about all there is to tell.

"Well, Dan, excuse the delay, and write me all about yourself. Do you play golf? Got a course in Melbourne, I suppose. What do you make it in? Don't forget to tell me. Are you under a hundred too?

"Don't wait as long as I did. And, if you can possibly arrange it, come home, Dan, come on home. You've been wandering long enough.

"Your old pal, Tom Meade."

He was smiling softly to himself as he put the letter into an envelope and wrote Dan's name on the outside. A keen satisfaction filled his heart. Here was a matter that had long demanded his attention; it was attended to at last. Pretty good letter, too. Covered the ground thoroughly. Only dimly was he conscious of the forty-one years he had delayed; it didn't seem so long. Why, it seemed only yesterday that Dan was here!

He put the letter into his pocket, went into the hall and donned his overcoat. This time he would not delay an instant. He would go at once to Charley Nelson's hardware store and find out Dan's latest address.

"Mr. Nelson's out, Judge," said Phil Barclay, the clerk. "Be back in a minute, I expect."

"I'll wait," said Tom Meade. He sat down on a keg of nails.

"Say, Judge, have you seen these new golf balls?" inquired the enterprising Phil. Charley carried a side-line of sporting-goods. He came over with a box of balls. "The Green Flyer. Liveliest ball made. Guaranteed to carry ten yards farther than any other. Permitted by the golf authorities too."

"You don't tell me!" Tom Meade replied. He took up one of the balls and examined it critically.

"Better buy a box, Judge," Phil went on. "Cut ten strokes from your score as sure as fate."

Tom Meade restored the ball to its place.

"No, I guess not, Phil," he smiled. "I'm doing pretty well as it is. Went round in ninety-nine this morning. Not so bad for a man my age, eh?"

"Not bad at all," answered Phil, his enthusiasm tempered by his failure to make a sale.

The front door slammed. Tom Meade saw Charley Nelson coming toward him. A thin wraith of a man, Charley; transparent, almost, a man who seemed not at all well.

How many years had it been, Meade wondered, since Jenny told him how worried Mary was about her husband. Long, long ago. Now Mary was gone, and Jenny, too, and Charley was still abroad amid his hardware.

"Want to see me, Judge?" he inquired.

"Just a minute," Meade answered.

"Come into the office," Charley said.

He led the way into a little cubby-hole at the rear, just big enough to accommodate an aged roll-top desk and a fat tipsy stove. Mild as the day was, the latter held a rousing fire. Charley Nelson had always found the world a mighty chilly place.

"What can I do for you, Judge?" he asked.

Tom Meade took the letter to Australia from his pocket.

"I've written to Dan, Charley," he said. "I've written that letter at last. Here it is, sealed and stamped. I didn't have his address, though, so I thought I'd drop in and ask you—"

He stopped. Charley was staring at him solemnly.

"You can't send that letter, Judge," he said.

"Can't send it? Why not? What's happened? Dan isn't—"

"Dan's left Australia," Charley said. "He's somewhere in California now. I expect him here in about two weeks."

"Here? In Mayfield? Say, that'll be great!" Tom Meade's face was beaming. "Funny too. I was telling him he'd better come home—in this letter I wrote to-day."

Charley stared owlishly at the envelope.

"Well, you was a little late," he said. "Dan sailed from Melbourne last October. He's been spending the winter on the Coast."

"A little late," Tom Meade smiled. "Forty-one years. Yes, Charley, I guess I was a little late."

"I ain't sure that Dan won't settle down here," Charley went on. "He's alone in the world—wife gone, children married. He sold out all his interests over there. Yes, he spoke as if he might end his days right here in Mayfield."

"Where he belongs," answered Tom Meade. He sat staring dubiously at the letter in his hand. "Well, Charley, I guess I haven't any use for this, after all. Forty-one years to get it finished, and now—"

He opened the door of the fat old stove. Live coals glowed within. Slowly he tore the letter across and laid the pieces on the fire. He closed the door.

"Judge," Charley was saying, "you'll be glad to know that Dan has done real well out there. I guess he's worth a million or more. From what I hear—"

"There's just one thing I want to know," Meade said. "This is important, Charley, try to remember. Does he play golf?"

"I don't recollect," Charley answered. "He's a wool merchant, you know—the biggest in Australia—"

"You don't recollect! Think, man, think!"

"Well, I guess he did say something in one letter—oh, yes, he stopped in California to play golf. I remember now. Of course Dan never says much about the big success he's made. But in a roundabout way—"

"I wonder what he goes round in?" Tom Meade cut in on him again.

"Round what?" asked Charley, who was no golfer.

"Round the golf course—his score."

"Oh, his score. Land sakes, I wouldn't know that, Judge! But I guess anything Dan does he does well. He built that business of his up out of nothing. On the day he left Australia they gave him a dinner in Melbourne, and the leading men of the place—"

"Well, he ought to be good," said Tom Meade. "He's been at it all winter." He stood up. "You let me know when he's due, Charley, and I'll be at the station to meet him. I'll have him up at the club before he gets his breath." He smiled gently. "Dan and me playing round the old Marvin place once more," he added. "Life sort of moves in a circle, doesn't it, Charley?"

"I guess it does," said Charley Nelson.

Tom Meade returned to the front of the store and summoned the clerk to his side.

"What was the name of that ball?" he asked.

"The Green Flyer," said Phil. "Do you want—"

"Wrap me up a box of 'em," he ordered.

Phil smiled as he handed them over.

"Not quite satisfied with your score, after all?" he ventured.

"Not yet," said the Honorable Thomas Meade.

He had a number of errands in the town, and dusk was falling when at last he swung up Center Avenue on his way home. The box of golf balls was clutched firmly under his arm, his heels clicked a youthful tattoo on the stone sidewalk, his shoulders were thrown back, there was fire in his eye. Now and then he glanced up at the soft spring sky; he hoped to-morrow would be fine.

To-morrow and to-morrow and to-morrow! Looking forward still!

NINA AND THE BLEMISH

First published in The Saturday Evening Post, Aug 18, 1928

THE desert caravan in which Jim Dryden rode traveled only at night. Long nights they seemed to Jim, with the wind howling in his ears, the sage and the mesquite lying in a deathly hush under the pale unfriendly stars and the gray sand whirling ahead of him down that lonely stretch of macadam.

He stepped on the gas and glanced at his speedometer. Thirty miles—thirty-two. Vainly he sought to catch the whir of his motor above the roar of the wind. Was it running smoothly now? He hoped so. Dawn ought to find him close to his journey's end. For day and the sun's heat in that country meant that the precious cargo at his back in the truck would perish. He bent over and, skilful from practise, lighted a cigarette, his wrists guiding the wheel.

A romantic figure? The idea would have startled him— called forth that slow, surprised smile of his. A young man, lean and tanned, in khaki shirt and trousers, doing his job. Speeding on down the long road that leads by the Salton Sea; rumbling through little desert settlements where people awoke suddenly at the noise and knew that the Imperial

Valley was sending its cantaloupes up to the breakfast tables of Los Angeles.

To-night he rode alone; the caravan was far in advance. An exploding tire, faulty ignition—one thing after another had caused him to fall behind. He thought of his melons in the boxes and was worried. But that cold biting wind still swept in on him from the sandy waste land and brought him, oddly enough, comfort. Thank heaven for the wind. Better than the refrigerator cars in which the freight shipments traveled East.

His headlights caught a sign on the road ahead: Stop! U. S. Officers. One more delay. He cursed under his breath and threw on the brakes. Two sleepy immigration men with flash-lights and absurdly large guns greeted him as he leaped to the ground.

"Oh, it's you, is it?" said one of the officers. "So far behind the rest of the gang we almost missed you."

"Well, I guess I could 'a' lived through that too," Dryden grinned. "What can I do for you? Breakfast? I can give you a real nice melon, but I'm a little short on coffee an' rolls."

One of the men climbed on to the truck and his flashlight played over the crates. The Imperial Valley lies close to the border and smuggled aliens on the melon trucks are not unknown. Dryden watched him, a tired smile on his face.

"You're the most suspicious guys I ever met in my life," he commented. "Ain't you ever goin' to trust me? What would I be doin' with smuggled Chinks at a measly three thousand a head? Me, I ain't got no use for money."

"Is that so?" replied the other man. He dropped to the road and rolled under the truck, where his light flickered uncertainly.

"You be careful, Buddy," said Dryden. "If that gun o' yours goes off, you'll blow up all Southern California. What gets me is you guys goin' around with nothin' but a cannon in your belt. Brave, I call it."

The man on the truck jumped down. "Got a cigarette, Kid?" he inquired.

"Oh, is that what you was lookin' for?" Dryden proffered a package. "And me thinkin' all the time you was after the Chink I got curled up in a melon in that back crate. Will the cigarette be enough, or are you all out o' matches too?"

The officer took the sign from the road. "Go along," he suggested.

"I'll do that," Dryden answered, and swung on to his seat. He leaned over, harassed and sarcastic. "You must come and see me some time," he remarked, and the truck leaped off into the grayness that presaged dawn.

Dawn was a fact as he rolled into Indio. He went down the main street like the Limited on a falling grade. A friend waved to him from the doorway of a garage; he answered the greeting, but the scowl remained on his face. "A good-natured guy," he was often called, but the night had tried him sorely. The town dropped behind; the flaming sun peered over the wall of the hills, turning their dusky red to rose. The beauty of a desert sunrise filled the world. An old story to Dryden; he was thinking of melons.

As he approached the road that turns off to Palm Springs a battered little flivver came up behind and screeched by him, down the center of the empty highway. Dryden watched it idly—then suddenly his hand was on the brakes. For a glittering roadster had shot out of the Palm Springs road at fifty miles an hour. It struck the flivver amidships. There was a crash, a woman's cry, and Dryden stopped just in time on the edge of the wreckage.

He leaped to the ground. The solitary occupant of the expensive car was still at the wheel—a handsome girl of about twenty. Though she had been betrayed into a cry of fright, there was nothing of distress in her brown eyes now. She regarded Jim Dryden coolly, impersonally, as though he were part of a rather uninteresting landscape.

"Well, that was real pretty," Dryden said. "And what are your plans now?" More delay. He was inwardly raging. "Back away, if you know how it's done, and let's see what was runnin' this other car."

Her eyes flashed indignantly, but she backed off. A man disentangled himself from what was left of the flivver.

His hair was prematurely gray; he was thin and ill-looking, trembling all over. He said nothing.

"You hurt, Buddy?" Jim Dryden inquired.

"No—no, I guess not." The man's pale face twitched nervously. "But my car—it's—it's done for now, I guess."

Dryden looked at the wreckage. He was about to mention the junk heap, but hesitated. Some sixth sense told him that this was tragedy. "Don't you worry. The young lady's goin' to pay you for the damage. Say, Sister, do you always travel on to a main road at that speed?"

She had alighted and stood there on the highway. Slim, hat-less, with bobbed brown hair, the modern young woman at her best—or worst.

"Since when?" she inquired haughtily.

"Since when—what?" Dryden asked.

"Since when have I been your sister? It's news to me."

Dryden grinned. "My mistake. And lucky for you it is." Her manner, arrogant and self-confident, roused him. "If you was my sister you'd get a good spanking right now."

"Really? How interesting! And for what?"

"For coming round that corner the way you did. It wasn't good sense."

She shrugged. "This man was traveling on the wrong side of the road. You're probably not overly intelligent, but you know that much."

"Is that so? Kid, I don't know anything of the sort. I was the only witness to this smash-up, and I say it was all your fault. You ought to pay for it." Their eyes met. "And you will," added Dryden grimly.

She smiled—a superior, maddening smile. "Look at my fender. It's badly bent. There must be other damage too." She turned to her victim: "Will you let me have your name and address, please?"

"Of course," said the man nervously. "But I'm sure— I'm quite sure—it wasn't my fault. I may have been in the middle of the road. You see, I'd just passed the truck—"

"You was on the side," corrected Dryden. "I saw you."

"Your name?" persisted the girl coldly.

"Name's Sam Bristol. I'm living over at Green Palms."

Dryden looked at him suddenly. He could place this fellow now. He stepped to the roadster. On the steering wheel was the certificate of registration. Dryden took out a soiled bit of paper and a stub of pencil and copied off the name and address.

The girl turned. "What are you doing?"

"Never you mind, Miss Brockway," he answered. "You'll hear from us later. Got insurance, I suppose?"

"That happens to be my affair."

"Yeah? Well, we'll let you know how much you owe us. I guess your check will be O.K."

She came over and got into her car. "You seem rather sure of yourself," she remarked.

"The same to you, Kid," he answered. Again their eyes met. "One of us may have to back down," he suggested.

Her eyes defied him. "It's a little habit I've never formed."

"Funny," grinned Dryden. "I'm that way too. So long—until I see you again."

She turned the wheel and swept grandly off toward Indio.

Dryden stood for a moment looking after her. He shrugged his lean shoulders. "I know her kind too," he said, as one who boasted wide acquaintance among women. "Queen of the world, in her own opinion. Tourist, most likely. A few of 'em still hangin' round, infesting a pretty good state. From New York, I suppose."

"I'm from New York myself," said Bristol, with a touch of asperity in his voice.

"Yeah? Well, what you goin' to do, Buddy? What about this pile of tin?"

"Might as well leave it and walk back home," replied Bristol hopelessly.

"What? Say, now, don't quit on me! Leave it—hell! Hop on board my truck an' I'll take you into Banning. Fellow I know there runs a garage. We'll tell him to come an' get your car an' fix it up."

Bristol shook his head. "I haven't a cent in the world. The garage man would know it too—no credit."

"That's all right. He'll fix it up if I say so. An' we'll make that high-an'- mighty dame pay for the job."

"She won't," objected the other. "I could see that. More likely she'll send me a bill. She's that kind."

Dryden snorted impatiently. "Say, Buddy, I'm late as it is. Get aboard here an' let me handle this. Never saw the dame yet could put anything over on me."

Reluctantly the owner of the wrecked car helped Dryden push it to the side of the road, then climbed aboard the truck.

Again Jim Dryden and his cantaloupes were on their way. For a time neither man spoke. Bristol's face still twitched, his hands trembled.

"Pretty hard lines losing the old bus just now," he said at last. "They're doing a movie over by Palm Springs next week—a big war picture. I'd been promised a job as an extra—rive dollars a day, real money—and I wanted it pretty bad."

"War picture, eh?" Dryden's voice was filled with scorn. "The movies cashing in on the war again. Trenches an' actors in nice new uniforms—love among the hand grenades. It won't be your first time in the trenches—hey, Buddy?"

"How did you know?" Bristol looked at him. "Oh, yes—Green Palms—it's a sort of label, isn't it? It's true, I'm one of them. Gassed and a few bits of shrapnel. I've been trying for ten years to get right again."

"If anybody's got any call to make money out of the war, I guess it's you, hey, Old-Timer?"

"Maybe—but how am I going to do it now? No car to get to location. I promised two of the other fellows I'd take 'em along. Gosh, they'll be sorry!"

"Sorry about what?"

"About my not having a car."

"You'll have it. Quit kidding yourself."

"But the money—"

Dryden shot nonchalantly past a big limousine, leaving it just an inch of leeway. "I tell you that dame's goin' to pay. I was a witness, wasn't I? You leave it to me."

Bristol was silent for a moment.

Suddenly he looked at Dryden. "What was that name you called her?"

"Brockway—Nina Brockway. It was on the registration card."

"Palm Springs?"

"Yeah."

"Good lord!" Bristol's voice was awe-struck. "You know who her father is?"

"God help him, whoever he is."

"But he's Henry C. Brockway. You know what that means?"

"It means nothing to me, Buddy."

"Why, he's got millions—millions! Cleaned up in Wall Street. Somebody told me he was at Palm Springs. I used to hear a lot about him in New York. He's a big man."

"One man's pretty much like another out here," said Dry-den. "It don't matter to me who he is. Don't be so easy impressed, Buddy. You give me a pain in the neck."

Bristol relapsed into silence, thinking his New York thoughts.

They swept up before a Banning garage and the proprietor came out smiling.

"'Morning, Bill," Dryden cried.

"Hello, Jim. You're pretty late, ain't you?"

"I'll say I am ... Listen, Bill. This is Sam Bristol, a friend of mine. Some jazzy dame nicked him out by the Palm Springs road an' wrecked his car. Go out with him an' pick it up an' put it back in shape. He's got to have it by Saturday night."

"Sure will," agreed Bill.

"An' say, give him a statement," added Dryden. "The dame will pay it, an' if she shouldn't, I'm responsible."

"Oh, no, I couldn't let you " began Bristol.

"Hush up, Buddy," Dryden admonished. "You worry too much. I tell you I ain't seen the dame yet could get away with anything in my neighborhood. Now I gotta leave you.

These here melons is cryin' to be et." And he dashed away down Banning's main street.

* * * * *

IN the big house he had rented at Palm Springs, Henry C. Brockway was lying in a darkened room on the second floor, taking his afternoon rest. Three thousand miles were between him and Wall Street, that brief thoroughfare where he had picked up twenty million dollars, high blood-pressure, a neuralgic heart and a little asthma on the side. "Rest," the doctors said—"you must have rest." He lay there tense and unrelaxed, seeking to attain that rest, going after it like a born go-getter, but unlike the millions, it eluded him. He sighed.

He heard a car in the drive, and then the voice of his son-in-law, Arthur, Edith's husband, who had been playing solitaire on the veranda.

"Hello, Nina—back at last.... What's this, my girl? Another smash-up?"

Henry C. raised his head, alert and frowning. He waited for the voice of Nina, his younger daughter.

"Oh, pipe down," she said. "Father will hear and hit the ceiling again. Had a little accident, that's all." Henry C. crept silently to the window. "Some one got in my way, as usual."

"Who was it this time?" inquired the blase Arthur, glad of a bit of excitement at last.

469

"Who? What does that matter? Just a blemish—that's all he was. And another blemish got down from a truck and had the nerve to say it was my fault. They stick together, these blemishes do."

Wearily Henry C. put on his shoes, his coat. Going below, he followed his wayward daughter into the garage. He stood for a moment staring at the car.

"Again, eh?" he inquired.

"What do you mean—again?"

"You know what I mean. I'm sick and tired of it, I can tell you. Drive like a wild woman I've a good mind to take this car away from you."

"Now, Dad, don't get excited."

"Who wouldn't get excited? Every time you go out on the road No wonder they canceled your insurance.... It wasn't your fault, of course."

"Of course not."

"I don't believe you. But even if you were right, you couldn't prove it—not with your record. Well, by heaven, you'll pay for it this time—out of your own allowance! I've signed the last check for you."

"Neither of us will pay. I'll see to that.... Calm down."

"Calm down? That's good. Calm down—rest—keep quiet. That was the idea out here. But with you around—"

She frowned. "I'll leave if you say so. If I'm in the way here—"

"Now—now!" There was a note of panic in Brockway's voice; he was, oddly enough, fond of her. "I don't mean, Nina—you understand—I'm on edge all the time."

She glanced at him and her hard young face softened a little. He did look unutterably weary. "I'm sorry, Dad," she said in a quite different tone. "You're not to worry about this. I can handle it."

"I hope so. But controversy—wrangling—I don't like it. Somebody will be around to see me—somebody with a grievance—"

"Nobody but a blemish—nobody who matters."

"I wish you wouldn't talk like that," he said. "These people have as much right in the world as you have."

"Have they? Well, they're here, at any rate, cluttering it up, infesting the beaches, the roads, the cities. I get so sick of them—"

He looked at her keenly. "I was what you would have called a blemish once myself. Up from the crowd—that's where I came from. And I've never forgot—"

"I know. But surely you're not going to stand here in the doorway of the garage and tell me about those early struggles. I've heard all about them, Dad—believe me I have heard."

He sighed. "Did you get the mail?"

"I certainly did—the New York paper too. Now go up on the veranda and relax over the financial page. If the person who got in my way this morning tries to make any trouble I'll take care of him—I promise you."

"See that you do." He went up on to the porch and was shortly back on the New York Stock Exchange.

On the afternoon of the second day following, Nina Brockway looked out the living-room window and saw that a truck had stopped before the house. She was not the sort of person to be interested in trucks, but this one seemed somehow vaguely familiar. For a moment she was puzzled; then she saw Jim Dryden swinging up the path between the cactus plants.

The strain of driving in the desert caravan was not upon him now, and he walked as one at peace with the world. There was something rather attractive about his genial you-go-to-the-devil air; it must be admitted that—for a person of his class—he was strikingly good-looking. Nothing about him suggested that battle was in the air, but Nina Brockway sensed it and was ready.

Arthur was lolling on the veranda, an elegant figure. The pride and hope of a good but impoverished family, he had been a bond salesman until Edith, Brockway's elder daughter, had rescued him and brought him to this. Jim Dryden looked him over appraisingly. The appraisal was not very high.

"Hello," said the truck driver.

"How do you do?" answered Arthur coldly. "Deliveries are at the rear door, if you don't mind—"

"What of it?" said Dryden. "I ain't delivering anything, Son. I'm lookin' for Miss Nina Brockway. You can run along an' fetch her—if you don't mind."

Arthur glared at him but rose. He encountered his sister-in-law in the hall. "Gentleman friend to see you," he announced.

"I know," she said. "Just one of those blemishes I told you about. He won't be here long."

She went out on to the veranda, her head high, her manner haughty. Dryden greeted her pleasantly.

"Hello, Sister," he remarked easily. "Glad to see you. Afraid you might be out on the road somewhere. But you ain't—an' that's good news for anybody else happens to be goin' somewhere to-day."

"What do you want with me?" she asked. She looked straight through him at the cottonwood trees in the garden.

"Reckon you know what I want," he returned. He had been too harassed, too hurried, on that other occasion to pay much attention to her, but now he had leisure to look her over. He did so, casually, and without much interest. "Little matter of business," he went on, taking out an envelope. "Just saw Sam Bristol over in Banning. He tells me you sent him this—this bill for damage to your car." He grinned at her, and removing the enclosure from the envelope, tore it

473

carelessly across and tossed the fragments to the floor. "I got to admit, Sister, I admire your nerve. Wreck a poor guy an' then try to make him pay for it.... Well, that's all settled."

"You think so?"

"I sure do." He took a slip of paper from his pocket. "I just dropped in with the garage bill for repairs to Sam's car." She reached out a hand, but after glancing into her eyes, he drew his away. "Second thoughts, I'll hang on to it. All the tearing that's going to be done you just seen done. One hundred and forty-five dollars, Kid. I'll wait while you write a check."

"You'll wait for ever then," she replied, her eyes flashing.

"Well, no, I couldn't do that," Dryden explained patiently. "Got to be back at El Centro by dusk. I ain't got much time, you see. Would you mind stepping on it, Sister?" He dropped into a chair. "A. H. Bemis—that's the garage man's name. Just make it out to him."

"Never!" the girl said firmly. She remained standing; she was looking at him now, but there was only contempt in her look. "You're wasting your time. I've told you before—he was on the wrong side of the road—"

"Got to leave that to the witness," Dryden cut in, still with the grin that maddened her—"meanin' me. Witness being sworn, deposes that you came round that corner like hell fire an' lit into poor Sam. Damages assessed to you."

"Try to get them!" she said.

"Just what I'm doin'," Dryden answered amiably. "An', Kid, when I set out to do a thing, I generally stick—like a summer cold."

"If I may inquire, just what is it to you?"

"Sure—you can inquire. Won't you sit down? You make me nervous about my manners. Too tired to stand myself—on the road all last night. Don't expect to get more than three-four hours' sleep this evening. But what's it to me, you're asking. We'll, it's this way: Poor old Sam is sick an' livin' all alone in a shack on the desert. He hasn't got a penny in the world. He needs his car. Otherwise he just sticks to that shack—no games of pool in Banning, see? You come along an' knock his flivver to smithereens, an' when we try to talk to you, your manner is—well, out of my way, you scum. Sam may get out of your way, Sister, but I won't. Get that—I won't."

"Is that all you have to say?"

"Just about—except that I'm for justice. Too little of it in the world, the way I see it. Nights riding over the desert, I get lots of time to think—want to see more justice done.... Now please don't keep me waiting."

"I'm not keeping you," she answered. "You may go any time."

Henry C. Brockway came out on to the veranda, his afternoon rest broken once more. He stood there.

"An' who is this?" Jim Dryden inquired.

"My father," the girl said at last.

"Yeah? The big Wall Street man. Well, we don't see many of 'em on the desert." He looked Henry C. over curiously, but made no move to rise. "How are you, sir? ... Just a little matter of business between your daughter an' me. You see, she wrecked a car—"

"Your car?" Brockway asked.

"No—belonged to a friend of mine—Sam Bristol. I'm actin' for him."

"Why doesn't he come himself?"

"It's a fair question. But circumstances have made him sort of discouraged—meek. Me, I'm not like that."

"Not precisely," remarked Nina Brockway.

"You said it, Sister. Poor old Sam ain't got any fight left in him. It was all took out in France some years ago. Needs a friend—an' he's got one too. The damages to his car comes to one hundred and forty-five dollars."

"It was never worth that at the start!" flamed the girl.

Dryden nodded. "I know. Ain't it—er—terrible what these garages do to you? You ought to remember that when you hear that speed bug buzzin' round your head. Anyway, that's the bill, an' since your daughter was to blame for the accident, Mr. Brockway, I been askin' her in the politest way I know to pay it. If she won't, maybe you—"

Brockway shook his head. "No, this is her affair. She's been warned. If any one pays she must."

"That's the ticket," Dryden agreed. "Put it up to her. The proper way to raise a child, if you ask me."

The girl stamped her foot. "I'm not a child!" she cried passionately. "This silly interview has gone far enough. I was not to blame for the accident and I won't pay. I deny that this man Bristol's financial affairs have anything to do with it. He was on the wrong side of the road. Some of the rest of us are keen on justice too. And if you think I'm soft enough to pay because I'm sorry for him—"

Dryden stood up. "If I think that, I guess I'm all wet," he said. "Hard, ain't you, Sister?—wise. New York in your blood. All right. It takes all kinds to make a world. I got to be goin' now. But I hate to give up—for Sam's sake. I'm makin' a last request of you. Will you do something for me?"

"It's hardly likely," she told him.

"I'll be goin' back through here with the empty truck day after to-morrow. Meet me at the corner where you wrecked Sam's car. Make it two-thirty."

She was about to turn away, but something in his eyes

"Why should I do that?" she wanted to know.

"Just like to take you on a little jaunt—over to Green Palms. You'll do that much, won't you?"

"Oh, I see," she answered coldly. "You want to play on my emotions. You think that out of pity—"

"Well, you'll come, won't you?"

"I will not!"

He regarded her with his slow smile. "Well, that knocks me cuckoo. Guess I was gettin' too set up about myself as a judge of human nature. I thought you was surer of yourself than that. I thought you'd just know it wouldn't do any good an' would come along to prove it to me. But of course, if your hardness ain't any deeper than that—if you're a coward—"

"How dare you?"

"Oh, all right. Maybe I'm mistaken. Maybe you ain't such a coward as you seem. If that's so—prove it. Day after tomorrow—two- thirty—the corner where you hit Sam through your carelessness.... I'm sayin' good-by now. I've got to go."

He strolled off between the cactus plants, whistling a popular air. Without a backward glance at the house, he climbed on to his truck. The girl turned on her father.

"You were a great help. I thought of course you'd take my part. Your own daughter—"

Henry C. Brockway's eyes were on the retreating truck. "I sort of wish you'd pay it," he remarked.

"Never!" Her voice was near to breaking. "Not for you—nor for that—that appalling roughneck!"

"I rather liked him," said Henry Brockway mildly.

* * * * *

478

AT two-thirty on the second day following, Nina was waiting in her expensive car at the point where the Palm Springs road joined the main highway. Almost on the minute Jim Dryden appeared and brought his empty truck to a stop beside her. He leaned over, smiling his engaging smile.

"Good for you, Sister. You're surer of yourself than you thought, hey? Goin' to follow me over to Green Palms?"

She nodded. "Yes; I want a talk with Mr. Bristol. I prefer to deal with a principal, not with an agent—especially this agent."

"Suits me," agreed Dryden.

"I shall put the matter up to him," continued the girl. "The accident was not my fault and he must know it. Perhaps he is interested in justice too—in justice—not sentimentality."

"I'll lead the way," grinned Dryden. "Be a good kid an' don't hit me from behind."

They traveled on down the macadam and turned off on to a dirt road. The going became heavy, but Dryden did not slacken his speed. All about lay the eternal waste of the desert, treeless, monotonous, yet with a weird fascination. Mountain slopes, dark red and rocky and forbidding, walled in this arid corner of the world.

The winding road led at last to a discouraged little settlement: A number of cheap shacks, a desert inn with a pathetic attempt at a garden, a combined general store and post-office. Parking before the latter, Dryden addressed a group of young men who sat idly on a bench.

"Which is Sam Bristol's house?" he inquired.

One of the men pointed. "Right over yonder. He ain't in, though. Walked into Banning this morning to see about his car."

Nina Brockway parked beside the truck and stepped down into the dust of the road. Fresh and lovely in her white frock, a figure from another world, she created a mild sensation on the main street of Green Palms. The young man who had been speaking leaped to his feet, his eyes alight. Jim Dryden turned to the girl.

"Sam ain't in," he explained. "But come along. We'll have a look at his place anyhow. Maybe we can leave a note for him."

Without a word, she followed him to the little shack, built of lumber that appeared to be second hand. It boasted a tipsy veranda, on which was a cot with army blankets. Dryden pushed open the door. They entered a bare room with a kitchen table, a tottering chair, a wardrobe minus one leg, an oil stove. No need of the latter at this hour, for the room resembled an oven.

Dryden stood looking around. "Home, sweet home," he remarked. "Take a look at it, Sister. This is where your fellow New Yorker lives. An' he ain't forgot his old home town, I guess."

He pointed to the walls. All available space was placarded with pictures of New York, most of them carefully cut from rotogravure sections. The Woolworth Building, City Hall Park, Brooklyn Bridge, Fifth Avenue, the Library with the lions in front.

"Seems like New York's a disease people don't get over," Dryden said. "Me—I don't understand it. I was there once. Not for mine. A hard town. Every guy for himself. We ain't that way out on the desert."

Nina Brockway walked slowly about the room and Dryden followed at her heels. "Look familiar to you?" he inquired as she stopped to examine the photographs. "The limousine parade on the Avenue—been in it yourself, I suppose. Not driving, I hope. Does it make you homesick? Sam's homesick, he tells me. But you got it all over him. You can go back—he can't."

Still the girl said nothing. Dryden waved a hand toward the hot sandy world outside. "Yes, old Sam's here for life. Maybe that ain't so long, at that. But as long as he lives—just this. Goes to the movies now an' then—leastwise he did when he still had the car. Sees his old town on the screen. Times Square an' the signs—the Battery, Washington Square—the water front with the ships. To hell with it all, I'd say. But Sam, he don't feel that way. Born in the burg, he says. How about you? Born there yourself maybe."

He had forced her to speak at last. "I—I was born on Long Island," she told him.

"Yeah—Long Island," he nodded. "I know—I see movies too. Booze parties an' polo, hey? But a New Yorker, like Sam—You know his town. Madison Square—he was tellin' me he marched through there one time—when he come home from France. Maybe you was near enough to hear the music. The heroes, comin' home—nine-ten years ago. Nine-ten years—they make a difference. Out on the desert now, Sam is. Had a career once—the war smashed it. Had a second-hand flivver—an' you smashed that for him too. Everything smashed. Has to walk when he goes to the city—ten miles—if he can't get a lift."

Nina Brockway shrugged her shoulders. "What has all this to do with me?"

"I'm wondering," Dryden answered. He looked into her defiant young eyes. "Sam needs his car next Monday. Somebody who ain't forgot the war—somebody cashin' in on it—they're doin' a picture over by Palm Springs. Wants some of these disabled for atmosphere. It's a big chance for them. But they can't make it without the flivver."

"I'm sorry," said the girl coldly. She looked up at Jim Dryden, so earnest, so eager. Something about him—his sureness, his easy familiarity—maddened her. "I'm sorry, but he should have thought of that and kept on his own side of the road. Sentiment—pity—where have you been all these years? They went out of fashion long ago."

Dryden's smile faded. "All right. Hard as nails, ain't you, Sister? I been readin' young folks is like that, but somehow I couldn't believe it. I thought it was all a—a pose. I thought you'd take one look around here an' sign on the dotted line. I was plannin' to leave a note for Sam sayin' the garage bill was goin' to be paid an' he could get his car." The girl shook her head. "It would mean a lot to Sam, Sister."

"It means something to me," she answered. Her voice rose slightly. "It means something to me to stick by my guns—to—to beat you. You're so sure of yourself, so certain there's only one side to it—yours. You thought I'd be easy, didn't you? Well, I'm not. I won't surrender. A lesson to you. You need it."

Dryden nodded grimly. "Maybe I do.... Well, then it's all off. You won't admit you're wrong?"

"Why should I?"

"You won't pay that bill anyhow, without admitting—"

"That would be admitting it."

He turned away, walked to a corner of the little room. "Did you notice this?" he inquired.

She came over and he pointed to a crude sign, lettered with a shaky hand on a strip of cardboard and tacked to the wall: "This space reserved for a radio—if I get it," said the sign.

"Funny idea, ain't it?" Jim Dryden said. "A radio—if he gets it. That's the one thing in the world he wants most just now—something to help him through the evenings, he said. An' maybe when there's a big hook-up on—a reception to somebody, say—maybe he can hear New York, if he can't see it. Hear the crowds an' the music—" The girl turned suddenly away and walked to the window, where she stood looking out at the sun-drenched town. "He's figurin' this movie money might be enough, but of course " Jim Dryden stopped.

"Is there any reason why I should stay here?" the girl inquired.

"None that I know of." Jim Dryden shrugged hopelessly. She moved toward the door. "Well, I got something new to think of, nights on the road," he continued. "I've met dames a-plenty, but not many like you, thank God. I won't forget you, believe me, Sister."

The girl looked at him—a long look. "And I won't forget you."

"That's as may be. Don't matter to me one way or the other."

"You may tell your friend to sue me if he likes."

"Sue you? Say, quit kidding. Where would he get money for that? No, you're free of this thing. It's over now.

484

Go your way—an' I wouldn't have your conscience for a million dollars."

"It's not for sale." She paused in the doorway. "You've lost, haven't you?"

"It looks that way."

"I told you you would. If I've deflated that ego of yours a bit, then I haven't lived in vain. After this, perhaps you'll keep out of affairs that don't concern you.... Go back to your melons."

"I'm goin'. You've licked me, Sister. Run along." She crossed the sagging floor of the veranda to the yellow glare of the street. Jim Dryden stared after her, his honest face filled with wonder. "I didn't know they came like that," he muttered.

When he went back to his truck Nina Brockway was well on her way down the road.

* * * * *

THE season was late, it was very warm that evening after dinner in the living-room of the house at Palm Springs. Edith sat by a floor lamp, yawning over a book. Arthur was at the piano, improvising jazz. Rather clever at that sort of thing, Arthur was. Nina Brockway walked restlessly about. She stood at the window, staring at the snow of the cottonwoods drifting through the dusk.

Arthur burst into a roar of insane discords, banging the piano wildly. The girl at the window turned. "Oh, Arthur, for heaven's sake—"

"Can't help it." He gave the instrument one last vicious blow and got up. "I'm going mad. This quiet—this eternal quiet—it's getting impossible."

Edith threw down her book. "Surely we can leave before long." She might have been pretty had it not been for her constant expression of peevish discontent. Henry C. Brockway came into the room, smoking a forbidden cigar. "Dad, how long are we going to stay in this place?" Edith began.

Her father glared at her. "How do I know? When the weather warms up at home we'll go. It's a late spring—it always is these last few years."

"I want to get back to New York," complained Edith.

"New York!" Arthur threw himself into a chair. "Never knew what the place meant to me until I came away. Shows and night clubs—people again."

"Still, this is an interesting country," said Brockway.

"Too much Nature," Arthur objected. "A highly overrated commodity—Nature. Mountains and deserts and sunrises. Not for me. Ye gods, just think—if a fellow had to stay out here—a fellow who had known something better— like New York!"

Nina turned away from the window. "Some do," she remarked.

"Rather be dead," Arthur answered.

Brockway suggested bridge.

"Again?" said Edith. "Good lord, but I'm sick of it! However, I suppose there's nothing else."

They were at the bridge table once more. Arthur was dealing.

"By the way, Nina," Brockway said, "did you see that truck driver to- day?"

"I saw him." Her eyes were on Arthur's hands—the hands of a gentleman; no automobile grease about those well-manicured nails.

"Well, what about it? Is he going to make trouble for us?" Brockway wanted to know.

"He won't make any trouble." She was studying Arthur, as though busy with some vague comparison. "I've settled him."

"Fine—fine!" glowed Brockway. "I was a bit afraid of him. He looked so—so sort of competent. I'm glad he's out of the way.... What did you say, Arthur? Pass? I make it three spades."

They played their half-hearted game in the still hot room. Once, while her father dealt, Nina inquired languidly, "How much would a radio cost?"

"A radio. Who wants a radio?" Her father looked at her uncertainly.

"Nobody. I just wondered."

At ten o'clock the game broke up. It was Henry C.'s bed hour. His younger daughter stepped out on to the veranda, then to the road. She strolled on under ancient fig trees to the main street; it was deserted, the hotels closed for the summer. On she went until she came to the desert, gray under the stars. The moon shone on the storm-twisted pines that topped Mount San Jacinto. All about her were the intriguing little noises of the desert night.

The picture of Dryden, tall, nonchalant, grinning, filled her mind—driving a melon truck through scenery such as this—night after night—driving it up to Los Angeles— coming into the market before dawn. "Get lots of time to think, nights on the desert." What was he thinking to-night?

She went back to the dark house, through the door that was never locked, up the stairs to her bed. Too warm for sleep. She lay there in the darkness, staring at the ceiling. How much did a radio cost? They had thought she wanted one for herself. The Brockways never wanted anything except for themselves.

The morning came. She was out with Edith and Arthur, galloping across the desert on a horse, her sleek bob disarranged, her cheeks red with a color that was real. Not so bad, Palm Springs in the morning. After luncheon she took her roadster from the garage. Her father was on the veranda as she drove out.

"Please be careful, Nina," he called.

She waved to him reassuringly. "I will, Dad.... See you later."

She dropped in at the small local bank, then sped away to call on a friend who was stopping at a desert hotel near Indio. At five o'clock she drove again down the main street of Green Palms and drew up before Sam Bristol's shack. She found him cooking his supper over the oil stove; the small room was filled with the pleasant odor of frying bacon.

"How do you do?" she said. "You remember me?"

He gasped. The daughter of Henry C. Brockway calling on him! His New York mind could scarcely comprehend.

"Sure I remember you," he answered. "Don't see many like you out this way."

"I was just passing, and I thought I'd look in on you."

"That's—that's mighty nice of you. Won't you take the chair?"

She glanced round at the pictures on the walls. "We're both New Yorkers, it seems," she smiled.

"Say, I guess we are! You're looking at my pictures, ain't you? Sort of carry you back, don't they?"

"In a way—yes. Would you like to go back—really, I mean?"

"Would I?" His eyes lighted. "Say, I'm going too—just as soon as I feel a little better—that is, I hope I am. I don't know, though—could I get a job? It's been so long—"

"What sort of work did you do?" she asked.

"I was a clerk in a broker's office when the war came along. Sometimes, nights, I feel I got to go back—got to get one more ride in the Subway. I don't know, though—I'd be sort of afraid to tackle it. But if I could only feel the sidewalks of New York under me again " He stopped.

"Go on with your cooking, please. I don't want to interfere."

"You ain't interfering." He removed the frying-pan from the stove.

"I just came to say—I'm sorry about the car," said the girl.

"Why, that's all right."

"Not yet, it isn't." She hesitated. "I want you to promise that this is just between ourselves."

"Of course," agreed Bristol, flattered and puzzled.

"Not a word to that Dryden person—just between us two." She opened her purse and took out a roll of bills which she laid on the table. "One hundred and forty-five dollars, I think he said. But don't you dare tell him I gave it to you— tell him somebody paid an old debt."

"I don't get this," Bristol frowned. "You've paid it once. What does this mean?"

"I've paid it once?" It was her turn to be puzzled.

"Yes—you have, haven't you? The garage man called up the store this morning and told me to come for the car. It's out behind the cabin now. When I went in he said Dryden had stopped early this morning and given him the money. Dryden said he got it from you."

The girl stood up, a flush slowly spreading over her face. "I—I think I understand," she remarked.

"I don't," Bristol said.

"What does that matter? It's paid, isn't it? That ought to be enough for you." She picked up the roll of bills thoughtfully and glanced toward the corner with its hopeful placard. "Tell me—how much do you think a radio would cost?"

"Oh, I expect to get one for about " He paused. The red in his cheeks deepened. "No thanks," he said firmly. "I—I couldn't—"

She put the money back in her purse. "Of course not.... I—I rather wish I knew when Jim Dryden will be going through here again."

"I spoke to the garage man about that," Bristol said. "You see, I want to thank him. Bemis thought Jim would be through here late this afternoon. I'll have to put my thanks off for a day or two. I'm pretty tired to-night."

Nina held out her hand. "I hope you get to New York again," she said.

"I hope so too. And say, I want to thank you—"

She shrugged. "Don't thank me," she said. "Thank your busy little friend, Jim Dryden."

Her eyes flashing, her lips a thin determined line, she sped back to the main highway. Down it she went at forty miles an hour, scanning every passing truck with interest. When she came to the Palm Springs road she turned into it, swung about and drew up at the side just around the bend. There she sat, watching the procession of cars down the El Centro highway.

The dusk came; the mountains purpled and the yellow glare died on the acres of sand. But enough light remained for her to recognize Jim Dryden's truck when it came along, traveling at a terrific speed. Her intention was to shoot out ahead of him and thus attract his attention, and she almost made it. But his front wheel struck the rear of the roadster and there was another crash, a grinding of brakes and the sound of a strong man swearing loudly in the dusk.

He came over to where she sat limp and frightened at the wheel. "You!" he cried. "Good lord! Is this your daily accident at this corner, or what?"

"I only wanted you to stop," she said in a weak small voice.

"Well, I stopped, didn't I?" She got out of the car with no help from him. For a moment she stood there, and then began to sway.

He put his arm about her shoulders. "Brace up! What's the matter with you?"

"I—I don't know." Her voice was faint, far away. "I—I must be a little frightened."

"Fine business!" he remarked heartily. "It probably won't do you any good, but I'm sure glad to see you scared. You ain't hurt, are you?"

"I don't seem to be."

"A charmed life. But the Lord watches over children an' fools—an' when you get both in one package—"

"Look! There's a wheel off my car," she cut in.

"Yeah. That's all right. I got insurance—I'll settle for it. Your fault again, but I know better than to argue with you.... How you goin' to get home?—if home's where you want to go."

"I—I can walk, I suppose."

"Oh, hell!" he said wearily. "Twenty miles out of my way, but I suppose I'll have to do it. What did you want me to stop for?"

"I merely wanted to suggest that—you mind your own business for a change." Her spirit returned. "You had your nerve to give that money to Bristol and say it came from me!"

"Why not? I didn't want him to know what I know about you. The poor simp is from New York, an' he thinks all New Yorkers is perfect. Say, how did you find out what I'd done?"

"I—I went over to see him this afternoon—and—"

"—an' pay those damages? By heaven, you ain't as bad as I thought you was! You decided it was your fault?"

"I did not!" she answered passionately. "I just thought— it seemed to me— "

He patted her on the shoulder. "Don't try to explain it, Kid. I want to tell you, I'm sure obliged to you. You've sort of restored my faith in human nature. Now for Pete's sake, climb up on the truck an'—"

"Just a minute." She took her purse from the seat of the roadster. "I want you to take this—this money."

He removed it promptly from her hand. "You bet I'll take it. Things ain't so good on the ranch I can afford to toss money around. Thanks."

"You'd better count it."

"I'm in an awful hurry, Kid. Your word's enough. I'll just shove your car into the ditch an' you can send somebody over for it from Palm Springs to-night." She watched him as he laid strong, competent hands on the roadster and practically lifted it from the right of way. There was an odd look in her eyes. Strange things were happening there in the desert dusk.

He turned to her: "Now, Kid, on to the truck if you don't mind riding on that. Sorry I didn't bring the limousine."

She climbed up to the seat and he took his place at her side.

"It's a shame to take you out of your way like this," she ventured.

"It sure is," he agreed warmly. "I wish now I'd give you that spanking the other day." He shook his head. "You got to be more careful, Kid," he warned.

"Nothing has happened to me yet," she said.

"Who said anything about you? It's the general public I'm thinkin' of. Give 'em a chance for their lives."

"You—you don't care what happens to me?"—a plaintive note in her voice.

"That's no affair of mine." They swung round a turn between dusky red hills and the road to Palm Springs stretched ahead. Dryden stepped on the gas. "Sit tight," he advised. "I got to let her out now. Seems like I'm always late."

"I'm sorry."

"You ought to be. It'll be after midnight when I get to the ranch."

"Is it your ranch?"

"Yeah."

"Tell me about it."

"Nothing to tell. Three hundred feet below sea-level—reclaimed land. I like to reclaim things."

"Is that so?"

"Sure is. Having a hard struggle of it. Sometimes it just looks hopeless, an' then again it looks impossible. But we're makin' progress."

"We?" A sudden possibility loomed. Well, what of it? Why did her voice sound so stricken?

"Maw an' me," he explained. "Maw's an old-timer round here. Born on the desert. She knows this country like a book." He drove on in silence for a moment. "She'll wonder what makes me so late. Does a lot of worryin', Maw does."

"I—I've been trying to tell you—how sorry I am."

"What's the good of it? The damage is done."

Silence again. "Shall you be coming back to-night?" asked the girl.

"Not to-night. Too late—what with you an' all. But tomorrow night Say, what's it to you?"

"Oh, I don't know. I'll—I'll think of you—to-morrow night—on that windy road by the Salton Sea."

"Well, don't come dashin' round no corners into me; that's all I ask."

"You don't like me, do you? You—you hate me."

He gave her a fleeting glance. "No, Sister, you got me all wrong. I don't hate you. Only—"

"Only what?"—a ridiculous eagerness in the words.

"Well, I guess you won't care if I say it. It's just that you don't mean anything to me—one way or the other."

She clenched her small hands in the dark. Of course she didn't care. Why should she? "Oh," she said.

The lights of Palm Springs twinkled suddenly against the black background of the mountains. So soon—so soon. A sort of panic gripped her heart.

"Thank God, there's the town," said Dryden with deep relief.

She thought of the men—all the men who had followed her, who had tried to make love to her—the men who had meant nothing—nothing at all. If only she had been a little kinder to them

"Take the next turn to the right," she said—"the stucco house at the end."

"I've been here before," he reminded her. "You forget easy, don't you?"

"Do I?" Her tone was thoughtful. "I wonder."

He drew up under the fig trees. "Here you are, Kid. Jump down. I gotta be on my way."

She forgot all her pride. "Won't you come to see me—some time?"

"Come to see you?" He was amazed. "What for? You've paid the money. The only thing there was between us is settled now."

"I know, but—"

"Kid, I'm in an awful rush."

"Yes, but—but, Jim " She laid her hand on his arm.

He shook it off impatiently. "Blemish to you," he remarked. "Oh, I heard what you called me."

"I didn't mean it!" she cried passionately. "I didn't mean it I"

"It don't matter," he told her in a kind voice.

His words were like a sentence. It didn't matter! She leaped to the ground, and already the truck was starting.

"I'll never see you again!" she cried.

He leaned down, serene, impervious. "'Taint likely, Kid. Not if you behave yourself on the roads. That's my last word to you. Take it easy on the roads."

The engine sputtered and roared; the truck moved off, gaining speed as it went. Its red tail light grew dimmer and dimmer in the distance. She stood there a little while under the gray old fig tree that had stood there so many years.

When she went into the brightly lighted living-room her father looked up from his New York paper.

"What are you crying about?" he asked.

"I'm—I'm so lonesome here," she answered.

"Cheer up," advised Brockway. "I wired for our tickets to-day. You'll be back in New York before you know it."

Her eyes filled again. "Oh, Dad," she said, "I'm afraid I'll be lonesome there too."

She hurried past him and ran up the stairs to the shelter of her room.

BROADWAY BROKE

First published in The Saturday Evening Post, Feb 3, 1923)

YOU may have met them drifting along Broadway—men whose names were once in the lights, women who were the toast of the town. Something, they tell you, is gone from their theater; something they find it hard to define. But they who have followed it from Union Square to Madison, thence north to Herald and finally to Long Acre, feel that in each of the neighborhoods it deserted it left a little of its glamour, a little of its romance. They shake their heads and travel on, seeking one more engagement, one more opportunity to wrest a living from their profession before the final curtain falls. Unless you wish to encounter heartbreak, do not inquire too closely into their fate. It is an alien land through which they wander now, a "show me" country where the cry is ever for youth.

On a humid August afternoon Nellie Wayne was walking up Broadway—our Nellie of the magic voice. Your father will remember her if you do not. At the old Fourteenth Street Theater early in the 'eighties she first flashed on the town, and thereafter for twenty years her name was synonymous with beauty. Lady Teazle, Viola, Rosalind, Camille—it mattered not in which guise the young men saw her first, from that moment her portrait adorned their bureaus and her lovely face often haunted their dreams.

It was at that forgotten playhouse, the Standard, that she appeared in the comedies and melodramas written by the brilliant Charlie Farren. She was Charlie's wife then, and when the critics urged her back to the classics she only laughed, for to her Charlie's poorest line was better than Shakespeare at his best. Late in the 'nineties Charlie died, and in the hour of her sorrow she first began to realize that something almost as precious had left her, too—her stock in trade, her youth. One black morning a manager offered her a mother role, and though she at first indignantly refused, she took it in the end and so started down the long slope beyond the hilltop.

She was well down that slope this August afternoon, a woman of—well, no one could say precisely how many years; but sixty-eight is a good guess. A beauty still, her age considered; tall, with the carriage of a great lady and a face but faintly lined. Though her hair was snow white, a youthful sparkle lingered in her eyes. Yes, a fine figure of a woman, but lacking something—hope, high spirits, a real destination along this famous thoroughfare. Once, when she walked on Broadway, twenty blocks down, people nudged one another and turned to stare; but now in the cold, fishy eyes about her gleamed no faintest spark of recognition. Well down the slope, indeed.

A stocky, prosperous-looking man was standing on the corner of Forty-Fourth Street, gazing out across the alien tide that drifted by him; a gray-haired man who seemed lonesome on that crowded corner. Suddenly he chanced to see Nellie Wayne. His face lighted and he strode boldly through the horde of lesser creatures between and seized both her hands.

"Nellie!" he cried. She looked up, startled. Old memories of her golden past flooded her heart and her eyes filled with the quick tears of the artist.

"Tom! Tom Kerrigen!"

"Nellie, is it you? Fine and blooming as ever!"

To have some one step out of the mob and tell her that! Life was worth living, after all.

"Tom—where from? Whereto?"

"From Denver. I've been living out there since I closed here—ten years ago."

"In business, Tom?"

He shook his head.

"Retired." They walked along together through the Wednesday matinee throng. "I decided it wasn't any game for an honest man any more."

She glanced up at him, a little breathless, thrilled. It was wonderful just to see him again. Charlie's best friend, Square Tom Kerrigen, a dazzling figure on the old Broadway, a patron of the drama, front row on the aisle every opening night; Square Tom, whose establishment just off Fifth Avenue was the favorite resort of the men about town whose gaming instincts were active and who preferred to play where the game was fair.

"Nothing but crooks in my business to-day," Tom was saying. "The dirty outcasts of Europe—the scum of the earth. I saw it coming—no Americans left. Besides, I wouldn't pay tribute to any man living, in uniform or out. So I quit when it stopped being a gentleman's game. I dropped it. Denver was my old town—my daughter's out there. But I had to come back for one more look at the big street. And I'm sorry I did. I've spoiled it all." He turned to her wistfully. "Where's our Broadway, Nellie?"

She shrugged her shoulders.

"I don't know, Tom. Gone! Gone with the theater we knew—the theater that had traditions. Show business. That's what the drama is now—the drama of Booth and Cushman and the rest. Show business—a trade, like cloaks and suits." They walked on for a moment in silence. "I'm mighty glad to see you," she told him. "But I'm sorry you came back."

"I know—I suspected—but I got to thinking. So many old friends I had to see once more."

"And have you found them?"

"I've found you, and there's none I'd rather meet. But the others—lord, I don't know where to look for them! Once it would have been simple—a stroll up Broadway at the cocktail hour, from Martin's to the Metropole, and you met every last soul you knew. But now—"

"Not now," she smiled sadly.

"I shouldn't have come," he admitted. "But my memories brought me. Lord, Nellie, what good times we used to have! Nights after the show, in your old house on Twenty-Second Street, with Charlie at the head of the supper table—good old Charlie. Then afterward, when you'd sing for us, and the good talk lasting till morning, and Charlie following us to the door, holding us back, pleading with us not to go. 'The night's young,' he always said."

"Dear Charlie," she sighed. "Never wanted to go to bed. Never wanted to get up once he got there."

"I wonder what he'd think of our Broadway now." They walked along. "You—you're not working, Nellie?"

She looked away from him.

"Not for two years," she said softly.

"Oh!" He glanced at her quickly, then away. "Where you stopping?"

"I'm living with Grace." Gracie was her daughter, her only child. "We've got a lovely—a little apartment on Forty-Eighth, near Sixth Avenue. Gracie and young Nellie and I. Young Nellie's just turned seventeen."

"No, by gad! Well, if she looks like her grandmother at the same age—but there never could be another Nellie Wayne. What's become of Grace's husband?"

"Joe? Oh, he's on the road most of the time."

"An actor, eh?"

"Well, he's in vaudeville."

"Oh, I see! I don't recall his act."

"No?" She was silent a moment, as though debating something. "H'm—Karger and Chum. That's the name of it."

"Chum? Who's Chum?"

"He's—it's—it's a dog act."

Tom Kerrigen was too tactful to reply. He knew what the admission must have cost her. Nellie Wayne, Charlie Farren—all the glory, all the lights, all the applause—and the line ending in a dog act. The old gambler's heart was touched.

"You and Charlie made a lot of money once," he began, rather clumsily. "I—I understand you hung on to some of it. Enough—enough so that—you're all right, I hope, Nellie?"

"You know me," she answered, looking toward the street. Her head went up. "I'm all right, Tom, and thank you for asking."

"I'm glad to hear it. That was the impression I got from Lew Gorman. Lew made a lot managing you, and he's held on to it, believe me. By the way, he's in town. I met him on the train coming from Chicago. See much of him now?"

"Not for years," she said.

"Lew spends his winters in Hollywood, putting out a picture now and then just to pass the time. Tells me he makes good money out of them. A foxy boy, Lew."

"You don't need to tell me that. I'm going down here, Tom." They were at the corner of Forty-Ninth. "I thought I'd drop in and see Madge Foster's new piece."

"I'll walk along to the door," said Kerrigen. "Listen here, Nellie, why don't you take a fling at the movies? Something to keep you amused."

She turned on him, her eyes flashing.

"The movies! Are you serious? I'd die first."

He was surprised at the fervor of her tone.

"Well, I don't care much for the pictures myself," be began.

"I should hope not, after what they've done to our theater, our Broadway. Silly pap for fools. I hate the movies! There used to be a road to play to. Where is it now? There used to be gallery boys." Her voice softened. "Do you remember when I came back from England late in the 'eighties—my first night at the Standard, when they let down that banner from the ceiling—'The Gallery Boys Welcome Their Nellie'? The flowers and the tears and the cheering? Where are the gallery boys to-day? Oh, Tom, Tom, the movies have killed it all; the dignity and the glamour; everything that was human and lovable about the theater."

"I didn't know you felt that way," he said apologetically.

"I told you I'd die before I'd touch them," Nellie answered. "I meant it."

At the door of the playhouse Kerrigen invited her to dine with him that night, and she accepted. She would meet him, she said, in the foyer of his hotel, but he insisted on calling for her. Rather reluctantly she gave him the address.

"The fifth floor," she said. "A walk-up apartment. Or are—"

"Don't worry, I can make it, Nellie," he assured her with a laugh.

She went into the lobby of the theater. She was somewhat late, the place was deserted, the audience all inside. Through the front of the house as she entered spread the sudden coolness that instinctively greets the seeker for free seats. No, the man at the box office didn't know where Mr. McCarthy was—very busy somewhere, no doubt. Oh, sure, she could stand round and wait if she wanted to. Not much use, though. Mr. McCarthy probably wouldn't return.

With all the dignity she had she moved over to a corner. A beardless young press agent followed.

"Anything I can do?" he inquired. She explored her bag and offered him her card.

"I'd like a seat, please."

He read the card and glanced at her coldly.

"In the profession?" he inquired.

In the profession! Nellie Wayne! The insult set her heart thumping with indignation.

"My name is rather well known," she said haughtily, "to any one who matters."

Johnny McCarthy, fat, bald, genial, bounced out of the auditorium past the ennuied ticket taker.

"Nellie!" he cried. "You stranger!"

"Come here, Johnny," she said. "Come here and tell this young man whether I'm in the profession or not."

McCarthy's smile faded as he looked at the press agent.

"You lost your bib somewhere," he said. "Go back to the nursery and find it. Nellie Wayne in the profession? You poor bonehead!" The young man beat a hasty retreat. "They make me sick, these kids," continued Mr. McCarthy. "They think they invented Broadway. How many you want, Nellie? Are you all alone?"

"Just one, John."

He went to the box office and returned with the coupon for a good seat.

"How's all the folks?" he inquired.

"Oh, Gracie's well. We all are."

"I caught Joe's act over in Philly. The dog's good, but Joe sort of crabs it."

"You never liked Joe, did you, John?"

"I couldn't understand why Gracie preferred him to me. I always told you he was lazy, and now—living off a dog!"

"Joe's been a good son, John. Mighty kind and gen— and gentlemanly. By the way, I'm not working. If you hear of anything—"

"Oh, sure! I'll keep you in mind, Nellie. But it's not going to be a big year. Last season was so bad everybody's lying low." He looked at her pityingly. He had heard how, two seasons before when she was rehearsing a part, her memory had deserted her and she had been unable to learn the lines. All Broadway had heard; it was common talk for a time; and there was no engagement for Nellie Wayne; would probably never be one again. "The theater's been through some pretty tough times," he went on. "Worse than 'ninety-three, and they're not over yet. You can be glad you laid away your pile, Nellie."

"What? Oh, yes."

"Better go on in. Foster's entrance is about due. You'll enjoy her in this"—he lowered his voice—"she's rotten! But she still gets the crowd. Over a thousand in the box this afternoon."

"That's good," said Nellie, and went to her seat, where she spent an envious afternoon.

When she returned to the street after the matinee her spirits were drooping. She had meant to go behind and congratulate Madge Foster, but the task was beyond her.

Broadway was sizzling. Men had draped handkerchiefs about their collars; some carried their coats. The street is at its worst in August, though hope is in the air; high hope for the new season; a hit perhaps, recognition at last! Managers, authors, actors, pinning their faith to a new play, all the old failures forgotten—this—this is the one! Millions in it! Millions!

Rehearsals were still on, and round the stage doors of theaters not yet open for the season little groups of perspiring players awaited their cues. Nellie Wayne hurried by. The sight was almost more than she could bear. To be called again for rehearsal—the dim stage, the dusty piles of scenery, the empty auditorium, the droning voices, the kitchen chairs set to represent exits, and in the distance the first night looming, inspiring hope and terror too! Just once more—once more! She'd get the lines; she'd have them. That last trouble—that was the author's fault. His silly speeches didn't mean anything. Why should they hold that against her still?

With heavy heart she climbed the five flights to the little flat. Gracie was playing solitaire in the parlor—pale, colorless Gracie, who had come into the world without one spark of either parent's genius; Gracie, her inexplicable child, who now looked up from her game with a frown.

"Hello, you back?"

"Any word from Joe?"

"Not a line. I can't understand. You'd think the Orpheum in Frisco would answer my wire."

"You'd think Joe would answer." Nellie took off her hat and sat down in a rocker by the window. "No money order for three weeks—what does he figure you're going to live on? But then he's no good. I always said so."

"Now, Mother, I won't have that." Gracie pushed the cards aside. "Talking against Joe—and you living on his money for two years past."

"His money! That's good, that is! A fine time I'd have had of it on any money Joe could earn. The dog's money, you mean. And do you think I'm proud of it? Do you think I want to be reminded of it? Me—Nellie Wayne—supported by a trick dog in vaudeville!" She took out her handkerchief. "If Charlie Farren were alive to see me now—"

"Oh, Mother, don't cry! Things are bad enough as it is."

"I'll cry if I like. I met Tom Kerrigen on the street—you remember him. Your father's old friend."

"He's got money, hasn't he?" Gracie inquired.

"Yes, and he'll keep it for all of me. I'd die if he found out—I'd die. If he knew what I've come to—"

The door opened and young Nellie came in, a slender, sweet girl in a blue tailored suit. She had a newspaper in her hand, her eyes were big with excitement.

"Mother," she cried, "I got a Frisco paper! Dad isn't on the bill. The act was canceled."

"Why?"

"I don't know. It doesn't say."

"I can't make it out." Grade's face was blanker than usual. "What could have happened to him? Why doesn't he send us a wire?"

"You can starve for all he cares," Nellie Wayne said.

"That's no way to speak of Joe Karger," Gracie objected. "Every week regular he's come across—you know that. And never a word of complaint when you quit working—"

"Go on! Reproach me with it! Throw my misfortune in my face!"

"Well, if you'd saved a little of your money—"

"You know where the last of it went. Joe put it into those oil stocks. A fine business man he is! If he's paid my keep it's no more than he owes me!"

"Please," said young Nellie. "What are we going to do? That's what I want to know."

"The agent for the landlord was here," Gracie said. "He's given us two more days. I got that out of him. Heaven knows I'm not fitted for that sort of thing, but I managed it. There's no ice, and the milk has soured, and what more we can pawn I don't know."

"I told you not to buy that gray foulard," her mother reminded her.

"But it was marked down—a bargain. And I needed it; I really did. I'm not accustomed to going about in rags."

"If I could only get an engagement!" sighed young Nellie.

Nellie Wayne stared at her.

"What do you mean—an engagement?"

"She's been round to the agents," Gracie explained. "She thought—we both thought—"

"I won't have it! Baby on the stage!"

"Please stop calling me Baby," protested the girl. "I'm grown up. I've got to go to work some time. Why not now?"

"But not in the theater!" Nellie cried. "Look at me! Look at what it's done to me!" She stood up as though called upon for a speech. "Gave it my best, I did; made a name, a big name—none bigger. And what has it all come to? What's been the end? Forgotten, slighted, insulted, living on the earnings of a trick dog! That's the theater for you! I'd rather see you in your grave!"

"Well, it's all true, of course," Gracie admitted. She picked up the cards and shuffled them. "I've heard interior decorating is a splendid profession for women. If you could take that up, Baby—or even stenography—"

"Nonsense!" said the girl. "I'm going on the stage."

"Listen to her!" cried Nellie Wayne. "Gracie, have you no authority—"

"Oh, Mother, do stop!" Gracie was dealing the cards. "What ails you anyhow?"

"I'm upset." She sat down again and wiped her eyes. "Upset, and I can't help it. Seeing Tom Kerrigen and remembering the old happy days—and a young fool of a press agent asked me if I was in the profession! Me! That's Broadway for you—no gratitude, no memory. A star to-day and a has-been to-morrow. It's just as Charlie used to say—"

A knock on the door interrupted her. The three women sat for a moment, startled into silence.

"It might be the agent for the landlord," Gracie whispered. "He said he was going to put it up to the boss; maybe we're evicted. I could never hold up my head again." The knock came again, more insistent. "We'll pretend we're out— "

"We can't do that," young Nellie said. She walked boldly to the door and opened it: "Dad!" she cried.

"Hello, Baby!" Joe Karger came into the room, an overdressed, wise-looking citizen of forty, sleek and debonair, but with a weak mouth. "Hello, Gracie! How goes it? Ma, how are you?" He kissed them both.

Through the open door behind him trotted a small Irish terrier with a huge rhinestone collar about his neck— Chum, the vaudeville artist; three hundred a week, real money. Young Nellie dropped to her knees and put her arms about him.

"Joe, what happened?" Gracie cried. "We haven't had a word from you in three weeks. What you doing here? We thought you were booked solid through the winter."

"It's a long story," replied Mr. Karger, throwing his straw hat on to the table. "A long, sad story." He sat, but added nothing. Like all small souls, he enjoyed keeping others in suspense. It tickled his vanity.

"But, Joe, things are pretty bad here. The agent for the landlord—"

"Things are worse than you think," Joe assured her, and still he held back his news.

"Father!" pleaded young Nellie.

Joe Karger pointed to Chum, who stood trembling slightly and looking exceedingly guilty.

"It's the dog," said Joe. "He's laid down on us. He's quit us cold."

"What? What do you mean?" Grade's voice was terror-stricken.

"Old age, I guess," Joe said. "I never got his age straight, and it seems I was off a few years. Anyhow, out in Los Angeles one night, what does he do but forget his routine." He glanced meaningly at Nellie Wayne. "I'd heard of it happening to actors, but never to an animal act. However, he forgets it—balls up the whole turn—we're a frost. They

514

canceled me. I took Chum to a vet and he tells me the dog's too old; nearly blind for one thing—can't get my signals. This vet says there's nothing left but chloroform."

"Oh, no!" young Nellie cried.

"Well, I guess Chum wouldn't want to be a burden, Baby," said Joe. "I guess he'd understand."

They sat there in a circle, staring at the dog, these four grown people who had been living on his wages. And Chum looked back at them; looked anxiously from one to the other, a humble plea for forgiveness in his tired old eyes. He had sinned; he knew it; committed the deadly fault, lost the routine and crabbed the act. Yet there was his honorable past, his long years of service to the arts. Only in young Nellie's eyes could he find an answering spark of friendliness.

"Poor Chum!" she said softly.

"He was a good wagon, but he done broke down," said Joe.

Gracie's face, capable only of the simpler emotions, registered dismay. As for Nellie Wayne, she regarded Chum with renewed hostility. She had never been friends with the dog. To her he had been the symbol of her shame. She had hated him while she took her share of the money he earned. And now, to quote Joe, he had quit her cold. An icy fear gripped her heart. He had led her along a little way and then deserted her, and the great horror of these last years had descended on her at last. She was old and done for—broke, with not a ray of hope in sight.

"Joe, what can we do?" Gracie wanted to know. "We've spent pretty freely, with you booked solid over the Orpheum time. The rent's due, and the meat man wants his, and—and I don't see where we're going to end."

"Oh, we'll get along," said Joe the optimist.

"You—you got any money, Joe?"

"Me? Say, what do you think I am? Three weeks out of the bill, and my fare to pay from Frisco. This is a hell of a reception, anyhow!" Talk about money always annoyed him. "Ain't any of you glad to see me? I haven't heard you say it. You ain't, I guess. No, you'd rather have me out slaving, playing four shows a day, writing money orders. That's all you want out of me—money orders."

"Now, Joe, we're worried, that's all," Gracie said.

"Well, what the devil's the use of that? What does worry get you? Something will turn up. I can pawn that collar of Chum's for a few dollars. Then I'll look round. I'm going into business. Where I should have been long ago, with my talents. If I'd only gone into that broker's office when I had the chance! Oh, I'll find something. It's up to me of course. Nobody else will lend a hand."

"I'm going on the stage," young Nellie announced.

"Sure, you're old enough," Joe approved. "And you got what they want—you got youth."

"Mother doesn't think she ought to," Gracie began.

"Oh, is that so?" Joe turned and glared at Nellie Wayne. "And what has Mother got to say about it? What right has she to butt into our affairs? I haven't seen any of her money paying the grocery bills."

"Oil stock—that's where my money is," Nellie reminded him. "Going to be rich soon. That's what I was told when I handed it over to the person who got me into it."

"That's right, bring that up again!" growled Joe. "I was only trying to do you a favor."

A knock on the door interrupted him; and, opening it, Nellie admitted Tom Kerrigen. Mr. Kerrigen was in a gay mood, and if he found his old friend in surroundings that surprised him he gave no sign. Presently they all retired and left him in the parlor, while Nellie Wayne made ready for dinner. As she passed through the dining-room on her way Joe resumed their argument.

"Don't you try to interfere!" he warned. "If Baby wants to break into the profession it's no business of yours. Somebody's got to work round here. Somebody's got to support you, now that the dog's quit."

"Hush, Joe! Hush!" Nellie cried.

"Afraid your friend'll know, eh?" sneered Joe. "Well, I don't care who knows. You been sponging off that dog—"

"Father!" young Nellie cried. She alone could silence him; he subsided. The girl kissed her grandmother. "Have a good time," she said.

A good time! Nellie Wayne paused for a moment outside the parlor door, gathering her wits. Then she opened it and swept in as though it had been the entrance at rear center and the shabby parlor lay in the footlights' glare; swept in with her famous smile, her air of a great and vivacious lady. Tom Kerrigen went back thirty years at sight of her.

He took her to a quiet old restaurant, where the head waiter, a bent veteran of seventy, greeted them in a voice quavering with excitement:

"Nellie Wayne! Mr. Kerrigen! You remember me?"

They recognized in him a relic of their dead past. He had been a slender, blond young waiter at Delmonico's when that restaurant stood three blocks south of Union Square; a lad who haunted the theaters about Fourteenth Street, who worshiped at the shrine of Nellie Wayne. Only that afternoon she had wondered as to the whereabouts of her gallery boys, and here was one of them—wrinkled, feeble, one foot in the grave, but her admirer still.

During dinner he came again and again to their table with bits of old gossip, shreds of loving reminiscence. His open homage and the gallant attentiveness of Tom Kerrigen, looking very handsome in evening clothes, combined to make the evening a happy one for Nellie. Her cheeks flushed, her eyes sparkled, her troubles were temporarily forgotten.

They witnessed the last two acts of a modern play and agreed that the acting would not have been tolerated for a moment by Augustin Daly. When Nellie climbed to the fifth floor after her evening with the past she found the little flat silent and in darkness. A bed had been prepared for her on the couch in the parlor. She heard Joe snoring loudly in the room at the rear—the room she had been sharing with Gracie.

As she was stooping over to unlace her shoes a pathetic little creature crept in from the kitchen. Chum, unable to sleep, walking the house, conscious of something wrong, something that was his fault. He came up to her timidly, apologetically, and touched her bare arm with his nose.

But Nellie Wayne was back in the present now, the icy fear again in her heart. The dog's advances annoyed her.

"Go back! Go back, sir!" she whispered, and he meekly turned to obey. She watched him as he reluctantly left the room, dignified but hurt.

"Chloroform for you!" she said bitterly. "But for me—what? God knows!"

in the morning things looked a little brighter. Joe awoke in an aggressively optimistic mood. Everything, he announced, was all for the best. But for the dereliction of Chum he might have gone on indefinitely wasting his talents in vaudeville, when as a matter of fact he belonged in business, where he would shortly pile up an amazing fortune. He was a bit late starting, but he would show 'em now. He was through with the theater.

"Know a guy up in Columbus Circle sells automobiles," he said. "Three years ago he tells me I'm a born salesman. I'll just walk in on him this morning and ask when do I go to work."

After the meager breakfast Joe put on his hat and called to Chum. The dog ran to him eagerly, barking his joy, anticipating a happy stroll in the sunshine. Joe stooped and removed the rhinestone collar from Chum's neck.

"I'll see how much I can get on this," he told them. He winked. "Chum won't need it where he's going." And he went blithely out, leaving the dog whining his disappointment.

At six o'clock that evening Mr. Karger returned to them, wilted and again in the depths. His day had not been happy.

"Seems the car trade's all shot," he announced. "Nothing doing there. And the best I could do on Chum's collar was six measly ones. 'But look here, Uncle,' I says, 'them stones is set in sterling silver.' 'Six bucks,' he answers, 'and not a penny more.'"

"Oh, Joe," cried Gracie, "and the agent for the landlord coming back to- morrow! I told him positively—"

"I'm doing my best, ain't I?" Joe demanded. "What's the rest of you doing? Was you round to the agents, Baby?"

"Yes," said young Nellie. "They told me to call again."

"The old bunk! Ma, I don't suppose you got anything up your sleeve."

"I'd like to help if I could, Joe. I've got a sort of a plan—"

"Kerrigen?" he inquired eagerly.

"No, not Kerrigen."

"Well, Ma, he looks to me like your best bet."

"That's not the way he looks to me," said Nellie Wayne.

"Well, come on, folks." Joe stood up. "We'll dine at the automat. While the six last we live high."

Nellie Wayne asked to be excused. She had lunched well, she said, and had eaten a wonderful dinner only last night. The three went out and left her. For a long time she sat, staring into space.

She was thinking of Madge Foster. An old friend, Madge; they had toured together years ago, shared the same make-up box, the same bed in dreary hotel rooms. Madge was slightly younger. Nellie had given her her first engagement, shown her many a kindness in that dim past. Now that Madge was working, prosperous, she could not well refuse a little temporary aid to her old friend and benefactor.

Nellie sighed. It would not be easy to walk into Madge's dressing-room, and there amid the many evidences of her old associate's success and prosperity confess her own plight. Still, the situation was desperate; she must face the ordeal; she owed the sacrifice to Gracie and to Joe.

She arrayed herself in the best she had, and at seven-thirty was on her way up Broadway. The theater crowds were not yet on the streets; only occasional pedestrians, many of them actors hurrying to their work. Their work! With bitterly envious eyes she saw them turn off into narrow alleyways that led to various stage doors. Once she, too, had had a destination at this hour, had known the cheery greeting of the door man, had hurried to the star's dressing room and found her maid waiting for her in the bright interior, with the lid of the make-up box open under the mirror; the mirror lined with a hundred telegrams and messages, friendly words from camp followers of success.

She came to the alleyway beside the theater where Madge was playing, and turned in. An old man with drooping shoulders was loitering near the tall iron fence.

"Nellie Wayne!" he cried.

"Why, Frank Shore!" she said.

"Hello, Nellie! I ain't seen you since that week in New Orleans eighteen years ago. Remember? Bidwell's, in Canal Street—Charlie's piece, The Midnight Flyer."

"As long ago as that! Working, Frank?"

"Me? I ain't had a berth for three seasons, Nellie. I'm—I'm at the end of my rope. Been to the fund five times—I can't go again. Just—just begging in the street, Nellie."

Again the easy tears in her eyes. Frank Shore, an artist, a man who respected his profession, come to this!

"Wait for me here," she said. "I'll be along again in a few minutes."

She nodded to the door man, an old acquaintance, and crossed the stage, set for the first act, to the star's dressing-room. Madge Foster, resplendent in the evening gown she wore at the beginning of her play, greeted her effusively. She kissed Nellie on both cheeks and gushed with all the fervor at the command of a famous emotional actress.

"Nellie darling, this is a treat! Marie, a chair for Miss Wayne. Sit down, dearie—do. You're not in the way. Really, you're not. Where have you been keeping yourself?"

"Oh, I've been around," Nellie said. "How are you, dear?"

"Never better." Madge sat, too, a handsome woman, a magnetic personality, but with a face that bore the mark of many years of selfishness, of thinking only of Madge Foster. She leaned forward eagerly. "Have you seen me in this piece?"

"Yes; I was out front on Wednesday." A pause, while Madge waited impatiently for the laurel wreath. "I want to tell you—I think you're splendid, dear. Growing all the time."

"Thanks," said Madge. The implication that there was still room for artistic growth did not please her. "I don't know anybody I'd rather hear say that. I value your opinion, my dear, even though you're no longer working."

The shot went home. Nellie sat straighter in her chair.

"Of course, it's a wonderful part, dearie. Almost actor-proof."

"Oh, you think so?"

"But I'm glad to see you going so well, Madge."

Madge shrugged her white shoulders.

"If I was doing any better I'd be worried. Honest, Nellie, I get scared sometimes, the way things keep breaking for me. You wouldn't believe the money I'm drawing down! I told Levy it was too much, but he insisted."

"He would," smiled Nellie.

"And my children—all artists—all successful—all making big money. I ought to be a very happy woman, Nellie."

"You certainly ought, dear. Everybody's not so lucky. I met old Frank Shore in the alley."

Madge's face clouded.

"Is he still out there? You wouldn't believe, Nellie, what a woman in my position is up against. The appeals for help, the panhandlers—"

"I can imagine, dearie. I've been through it all myself, as you may recall. And I always tried to be kind—ours is such a precarious profession. One never knows what one's own finish is to be."

"Oh, I'm not worried about mine. Did you spend the summer in town?"

"Why, yes! You see, I didn't know what minute I might be called for rehearsal."

"Oh," said Madge, "I thought you'd quit."

Nellie's head went up.

"I'm trying to drop out, Madge, but they just won't let me."

"Really?" The tone was incredulous. "Well, if I'd known you were about I'd have had you down to my place in Great Neck. Like to have you see it, dearie. It's a darling little house—tiny, of course; I only paid fifty thousand for it. But that's enough about me. How about you, Nellie? How's Gracie?"

"Grade's fine, and very happy with Joe. Joe's doing well.
1 '

"Got a trick dog in vaudeville, I hear."

"Yes, temporarily," Nellie admitted. "He'd like to go out alone, but the dog's so popular. It would be a crime to refuse the money they pay him."

"Well, dearie, I'm glad to hear that," Madge said. "Must come in handy in your old age, so few engagements and all."

Nellie laughed lightly.

"Means nothing to me, Madge. I laid away my pile and I can take care of myself. I'd have been a fool if I hadn't—and me the best Rosalind of a generation, as Winter called me. Then there was Charlie's royalties—there's never been a playwright could touch him. Don't worry about me, dearie."

"I'm not worrying," Madge assured her. "How's that granddaughter of yours? It must make you feel old to look at her."

"I'll never feel old, dear; not while I've got my figure. Baby's well. Just at present we have all we can do to keep her off the stage. Every manager on Broadway is after her. I guess they figure she's a good deal like me."

"Oh, they want youth, Nell. Youth's the ticket. You can't get by without it." She glanced complacently at her mirror.

"That's why I always say you're such a wonder, Madge," said Nellie sweetly. She stood up, a triumphant figure, proud, successful, smiling. "I must run along. Just happened to have a free evening, so I thought I'd run in and offer my congratulations."

"Must you go, dearie?" Madge rose too. "Sorry the place in Great Neck is closed—like to have you down. Perhaps next summer—"

"That's mighty kind of you, Madge. Next summer, maybe—if I don't go abroad. I'm thinking of it. So many good friends in London. You remember my big hit over there. They write me to come—I don't know—"

"Well, it was good of you to drop in. Now don't be such a stranger." They kissed—to the outward view warmly, affectionately.

"Good-by," said Nellie. "Here's hoping your good luck continues, dear—as mine has." And with a gracious smile she swept from the room.

She crossed the stage—the old odors, the old thrill! She was extremely well satisfied with herself. But in the alley, where Frank Shore came shuffling toward her, she felt suddenly guilty.

"Well, Nellie, here I am." His quavering old voice was hopeful.

She took him by the arm and led him along.

"Listen, Frank. I can tell you what I can't tell many. I'm broke too."

"Nellie—not you!" There was real distress in his voice. "Oh, I'm sorry to hear that! It doesn't matter about me—I was never much, but you, Nellie, you were so wonderful!"

"Don't, Frank!" she said. "Don't, or I'll cry! It's the truth, I went in to borrow something from Madge Foster, but—I don't know exactly what happened. She started boasting, and I—I just couldn't do it. I couldn't tell her."

"Of course you couldn't," he said approvingly. "Don't you take any of her dust, Nellie. She's an amateur; a rotten little amateur compared with you."

"But I'm sorry for your sake, Frank. Here—here's a dollar."

"Can you spare it, Nellie? I'd rather not—"

"Nonsense! We old-timers—we must stick together. Get yourself a meal and a bed, just for auld lang syne."

"God bless you, Nellie! There was never one could touch you. An artist and a lady. I always said it. One of my proudest memories—I played with Wayne."

"Good-by, Frank, and good luck."

"Good-by, Nellie." He started to leave her, paused. Trained as he was in the old artificial comedies, the exit line did not suit him. "A meal and a bed," he added. "And dreams of the old Broadway where we were young together."

That was better, and he shuffled off into the crowd. Nellie turned toward home. The theatergoers filled the street, shining limousines drew up to the curb, expensively dressed people alighted. Inside, the orchestras were tuning up, the actors were strolling about in the wings; presently would come the rise of the curtain. The rise of the curtain!

Then on for that first sweet laugh, that first beloved ripple of applause.

She climbed wearily to the fifth floor and knocked. No answer at first, and then the sharp bark of Chum. Taking out her key, she unlocked the door and entered the dark passageway. Chum, overjoyed, frisked at her feet. She turned on the light and glanced down at him. He looked strange without his collar; but he wouldn't need it where he was going, and it meant six more dollars, the last he had to give.

There was a note from Gracie on the table—"Joe and I have gone to the Palace." How like them—the precious six fading fast! "Baby will be in soon."

Removing her hat, Nellie sat down by a parlor window—the one at the side that overlooked the alleyway of the theater next door. She could see far up the street the electric signs flashing in front of half a dozen playhouses, the dense throngs daring the August heat—the pleasure seekers.

The hour of eight! It was the hardest of all the twenty-four for her. Every evening at eight a feeling of restlessness overwhelmed her. What was she doing here, at home?

She leaned far out into the humid August night. A thousand memories assailed her, little pictures out of her past: a dress rehearsal that lasted till morning—and the greatest manager of all time on his knees before her in the dawn, thanking her for the genius she had shown; a big dinner table back stage, a Christmas tree in the center, and the great Nellie Wayne passing out the presents to her retinue; a moonlit night on Boston Common after the show, with Charlie Farren walking beside her, beseeching her to marry him; the dining-room of the house on Twenty-Second Street at midnight, dear, handsome Charlie standing at the head of the table, a champagne glass in his hand; a first night at the Lyceum, her dressing-room banked with flowers, flushed, excited people crowding in to acclaim her newest triumph.

Down below, through the open doors of the theater, she heard the orchestra tuning up. She began to speak, the magic voice choked and uncertain: old lines from forgotten plays, deathless lines from the classics, lines taken at random from the jumble for ever passing through her mind. Little wonder she could not learn a new role now. Up from below came a quick crash of music. The overture! Nellie Wayne was silent, and her head sank down on her arms.

Suddenly close beside her sounded a loud, sharp, excited bark. She turned, startled, and there stood Chum, every muscle alert, trembling with anticipation, his ears pointed, his absurd little tail wagging furiously. And then Nellie Wayne realized—it was eight o'clock for Chum!

He was not in this shabby little parlor—he was in the wings of a theater. The overture blared louder, and Chum's nervous bark rose above the music. He leaped against her, fell away, leaped again. It was time to go on. Time for his act.

"All right, Chum," she said. "Go to it!"

He tumbled into the center of the room as though into a spotlight's glare. Lie rolled over, played dead, did his drunken bit, walked on an imaginary ball, counted with sharp staccato barks as Joe had trained him. He had it all wrong, the routine twisted; but night had fallen, the orchestra was playing, and Chum was doing his act.

He finished as the music did and stood there before her, awaiting her applause. She saw him through her tears, his old eyes looking into hers. She reached down and gathered him into her arms.

"Chum! Chum, you darling! I understand! We're in the same boat now. We're old—old, and it's youth they want. We're finished, you and me. Our act's out. And Broadway goes rolling on. Poor Chum! Poor fellow!"

She sat by the window for a long time, holding the little dog in her lap. She and Chum were friends at last.

At nine o'clock, putting the dog on the floor, she rose with determination. She dashed cold water into her eyes, put on her hat and went to the door. Chum followed.

"You wait here," she said gently. "You just wait, Chum. Maybe we're not quite finished yet."

She went directly to Tom Kerrigen's hotel. A bell-boy discovered him lingering over his cigar in the dining-room. Nellie went in to where he sat. He leaped to his feet.

"Nellie, I was just thinking about you. This is fine! Won't you eat something?"

"No, thanks, I've had dinner."

"Just a little coffee then?"

"Thanks, Tom. I will have that." She sat in the chair the waiter held ready. "I'm glad to find you. I thought you might have gone to a theater."

He shook his head.

"I don't care much for the plays they have now. Sex stuff, and all that. I like 'em clean, Nellie—I always did. Clean, like Peter Pan." The old gambler closed his eyes. "I saw that twelve times, and whenever Maude Adams came to the footlights and asked us did we believe in fairies I shouted louder than any kid in the house. I'm afraid I'm too old-fashioned."

The waiter brought her coffee and disappeared.

"Tom," she began, "I've come to make a confession. The other day I let you think I was well fixed—had money. It's not true. I've hardly a penny in the world. I'm down and out. Broadway broke, they call it nowadays."

He nodded solemnly.

"I suspected. And it's a raw deal. You deserve better than this."

"It's happened, though." She smiled cheerfully. "And now, Tom, I've come to you for help."

"Everything I've got—it's yours." He leaned across the table. "I don't want you to think I'm taking advantage, Nellie—but do you remember? That time, before you knew Charlie, when I followed you to Philadelphia. You were playing at the old Seventh Street Opera House; stopping at that boarding-house that stood where the Bellevue-Stratford is now—what was the name?—oh, yes, Petrie's Rest. It was in the parlor there—I told you—I was crazy about you—"

She laid her hand on his arm.

"Don't, Tom!"

"I must! I'm still—crazy. Take me and you'll never want for anything again."

"Dear friend!" His anxious, ruddy face, his keen gray eyes, the absurd old- fashioned diamond stick pin in his tie—she saw all these through a mist of tears. "It can't be, Tom. That's for youth. We're only ghosts. And then—there's Charlie. It's just as though he still lived—with me."

He smiled bravely.

"Right you are, Nellie. It's as you say. But everything I have is yours, just the same."

"I don't want your money, Tom dear. I want you to do something else for me. I want you to help me get into—the pictures."

"The pictures! Why, Nellie, you said—"

"I know, but that was all wrong. We live too much in the past, Tom—we old people. The world moves, and we've got to move with it—or go down. And I'm not ready to go down."

"I should hope not!"

"Besides, I've got somebody to take care of now; somebody who's been taking care of me."

"Yes?"

"A dog. A dog named Chum."

He stared at her in wonder. "I want you to go to Lew Gorman, Tom, and sort of put the idea in his head—"

"Gorman, hell!" Tom cried. "I'll finance a picture myself, and star you. We'll get a good story—say, what's the matter with one of Charlie's plays? By heaven, that's the idea! You own the rights to all of Charlie's stuff, don't you?"

"I do," she told him. "I've been thinking about that myself."

"It's an idea! We'll take one of Charlie's comedies—or better still, a melodrama. Lew tells me melodrama is going strong now. How about The Midnight Flyer? I'll buy the picture rights from you—pay you ten thousand—fifteen—"

She laughed. "Is that an offer? Fifteen thousand?"

"It is—unless you want more."

"That's like you, Tom. But you needn't risk a penny. Keep out of this yourself. All you need do is run into Lew

Gorman casually and tell him you hear some one is thinking of making a picture out of The Midnight Flyer. Tell him I've refused fifteen thousand for the rights. I think that's honest, don't you?"

"Honest? Sure it is! My offer stands. Lew Gorman made a fortune out of you and out of Charlie's plays, and he has most of it yet. It's about time he split a bit with you. But do you think he'll fall?"

"I know he will. If I went to him and said I was broke and wanted to sell that play he wouldn't touch it with a ten-foot pole. But once let him hear some one else is after it, and—well, I know managers. He won't sleep till he owns it. You've got your lines down, Tom?"

"I sure have! I'll run into him accidentally early in the morning, and I'll call you before noon."

"You're a dear, Tom."

"And if Lew doesn't come through, my offer still holds good; any one of my offers—or all of them."

She smiled and rose.

"You're the best friend any one ever had," she said.

"Do you think so? Honest, Nellie?"

"I do, Tom." His broad face lightened. "And it's what Charlie always said."

"Oh, yes—Charlie." His smile faded. "Good old Charlie!" said Square Tom Kerrigen a little wistfully.

* * * * *

ANOTHER morning, with Joe cast this time in the role of pessimist. An evening at the Palace, where he saw a lot of acts the popularity of which he was utterly at a loss to explain, had soured his outlook on life. During breakfast his eye happened to light on Chum, munching at a bone in the corner

"Guess we'll say good-by to him to-day," Joe announced in a low voice.

"No, Dad—no!" cried young Nellie in alarm.

"Well I can't have him round here eating his head oft.

"Not to-day, Joe," said Nellie Wayne. "Give him another twenty-four hours, please."

"What's it to you?"

"It's a lot to me, if you must know.

"Beginning to appreciate what Chum did for you, eh? he sneered. "Maybe you'll thank me next."

"I do thank you, Joe. And Chum and I happen to be good friends now. Give him another day."

Joe regarded her curiously.

"You got something on your mind?" he inquired.

Nellie stared at him blankly.

"Not a thing in the world," she said.

But Joe was unconvinced.

"I believe there's something up with Ma, he said later to Gracie.

"She does look cheerful," Gracie admitted. "Though how she can feel that way, with the agent coming to-day for his money?"

"Oh, give us a rest on that!" Joe cried.

"That's all very well for you to say, but it's me has to see him."

"Well, string him along."

"I've gone the limit now. It's cash to-day or the street."

But Joe had jammed his hat on to his head, and the outer door slammed behind him. Baby, too, hurried off on some mysterious errand Nellie waited, an unaccustomed color in her cheeks. It was past eleven when a surly hall boy climbed the stairs to tell her she was wanted at the telephone on the first floor. She gave him the last coin in her purse-a quarter-and beat him down.

"Hello, Nellie, that you?" Good old Tom—it was his voice. Her heart almost stopped beating with suspense.

"Well, Nellie, I sat round Lew's hotel for two hours this morning, and oddly enough I happened to run into him. I just casually mentioned that offer you had for Charlie's play and the shot went home."

"He fell, did he, Tom?"

"Sure did! You must have heard the thud up where you were. He wants to see you before noon. He's leaving to-night for the West. The lad's all het up. I told him I'd do my best to get you round there, though it looked pretty doubtful to me. He's got a desk in Shane's office—you know where that is. Now be careful, Nellie. Remember your big offer. And besides, you've got so much money you don't care whether you sell or not."

"Leave him to me," answered Nellie. "I can handle Lew. I know him of old."

"All right, Nellie. Let me know what happens. Good luck!"

"Thanks, Tom. God bless you!"

She hurried back to the flat for her hat, but said nothing of her business to Gracie. The thing might fall through, and in that case she would bear the disappointment alone. A few moments later she was out on the hot street.

Shrewd little Lew was waiting, but greeted her with an assumption of great carelessness. At sight of his placid poker face she remembered what she was up against, and knew that she would have need of all her cunning.

"Hello, Nellie! It's great to see you again. Where you been hiding? Minna was saying only last night, 'Why don't we ever see Nellie no more?'"

"How is Minna?"

"She's fine, thanks. We're going West to-night. Just wanted to see you before I went—say hello, for old times' sake."

"Well, Lew, I'm glad to drop in. But I've an engagement at the Claremont for lunch—"

"Oh, I won't keep you. Why don't you come out West sometime and visit us?"

"Thanks, Lew, I'll think about it. But Broadway still looks pretty good to me."

"That so?" He took up a paper knife and toyed aimlessly with it. "Anything on your mind, Nellie?"

"Not a thing."

"Humph! Feeling well, ain't you?"

"Never better."

"That's good." He stared past her out the window.

"Did you want to see me about anything in particular, Lew?"

"Oh, no; no, I guess not."

She rose.

"Well, give my love to Minna—"

He rose, too, stifled a yawn.

"I sure will. Mighty good of you to come in." He followed her to the door; her hand was on the knob. "By the way, I hear you're selling some of Charlie's stuff to the pictures."

She laughed a little scornfully.

"Oh, I don't know. They're after The Midnight Flyer. They say there's a wonderful picture in it, but I haven't made up my mind. I don't need the money, you know."

"So? How much do they offer you?"

"Oh, not much—fifteen thousand."

Despite his best efforts an expression of pain crossed Lew's chubby little face.

"They're kidding you," he said warmly. "There ain't that much money in the business any more."

"Well, it doesn't matter," Nellie answered. "I don't believe I'll sell, anyhow. I hear prices will go up later."

"Don't you believe it. Prices have reached the peak and they're going down every minute we stand here. I know, because I've been dabbling a bit in the movies myself."

"That so, Lew? Well, I'll go along." She opened the door.

"Wait a minute, Nellie. Come back here and sit down." She hesitated, seemed reluctant, but obeyed. She was wishing she had borrowed Baby's wrist-watch for this encounter. Lew sat down too—on the edge of his chair. "Now look here, Nellie," he began. "It seems to me that if anybody makes pictures out of Charlie's stuff it ought to be me. I produced all his plays and I loved him like a brother. I'd have been down for a slice of the picture money, only, of course, in those days there was no such thing."

"Well, I guess that was the only bet you ever overlooked, Lew."

Lew ignored this.

"If Charlie was sitting in that chair now, do you know what he'd say, Nellie? He'd tell you if you sold to anybody you ought to sell to me. He'd say, 'Think of all Lew done for us, Nellie.'"

"And made a million doing it."

"A million! How do you figure that? I'm a poor man, Nellie?"

"Maybe I could lend you something, Lew. Was that what you wanted?"

"It was not." He looked her firmly in the eye. "I want the rights to The Midnight Flyer. But I'm not paying any fifteen thousand, and don't think for a minute I am."

"Well, then, you're outbid, Lew." Again she stood up. "I really must go."

"Come now, Nellie, listen to reason. I tell you somebody's been kidding you. Such prices ain't paid any more. Who made the offer, anyhow?"

"Tell Minna I'm sorry not to see her—"

She was moving toward the door. He followed at her heels.

"I'll give you ten thousand, Nellie."

"I was always so fond of Minna."

"Twelve thousand—for Minna's sake. You wouldn't rob Minna's husband?"

"This engagement of mine is for one o'clock—"

"Nellie, have a heart! For auld lang syne—"

"For auld lang syne you can have it at fifteen. I'll not ask you to go above these other people, though it's hardly fair to them."

"Nellie! Don't old times mean nothing to you?"

"Not where money is concerned, Lew. I'm like you that way. Now make up your mind, for I'm going."

"All right—go! Ungrateful! Nellie, I hate to say it, but you're ungrateful. Charlie wouldn't like it."

"Charlie wouldn't be so easy." She opened the door. "Good-by, Lew."

"Fourteen thousand dollars!"

"Good luck on the Coast!"

"What do you think you're selling—Ben Hurt"

"I'm not selling. You're trying to buy, that's all. Acting like a piker too. The Midnight Flyer—the most popular play of its generation!"

"Yeah. And everybody dead that ever heard of it."

"There's a few of us left. You must have heard of it, Lew. You cleared four hundred thousand on it. My love to Minna, remember."

"Minna—Minna! Minna's heart would break if she heard you. Fourteen thousand five hundred and not another nickel!"

Nellie came back into the room and closed the door.

"Sold!" she cried.

"I should think so!" wailed Lew. "And me bankrupt!"

"On one condition!"

"What now? Nellie, how you have changed!"

"I play in the picture."

"You—-you—in the picture! At your age! What you thinking of, Nellie? We got to get a young girl for your part."

"Of course. I'm not insane, Lew. I play the grandmother."

"Oh, the grandmother! Well, that's all right. Only naturally you understand we don't pay much for a little part like that."

"You'll pay me! Think of what my name will mean! Nellie Wayne and The Midnight Flyer billed together again! All over the country are millions who will remember—"

"Millions—yes—in the graveyards."

"No, on their feet, going strong, like you—and me."

"Well, you're going strong. I'll admit that, Nellie. All right, we put it in the contract—the grandmother part. A hundred and fifty a week."

"Three hundred!"

"Nellie, you robber!"

"Take it or leave it! What say, Lew?" He was muttering to himself.

"I ain't saying—I'm choking. Maybe I can do it—if I close my eyes when I sign."

"Nonsense! You'll get it all back, and a lot more. If that wasn't so I'd be on my way to the Ritz now."

"The Claremont, you said," he reminded her.

"But I'm to pick up some friends at the Ritz."

"All right, Nellie. Sit down. I'll go and dictate a contract."

"You be careful what you dictate. I can still read, Lew."

He left her. She sat erect in her chair, her eyes shining. She had not looked so beautiful in years. The joy of battle was in her heart, the thrill of victory. If Charlie knew—but perhaps he did. Perhaps he had been at her elbow, fighting too. Clever Charlie! Dead more than twenty years, but supporting her still; supporting her by his wit and industry; saving the day for her when all seemed lost. That was the theater—the dear theater. The hits never died.

"How you want the money?" Lew called.

"Give me your check for two thousand now. I'll take the rest when we get to Hollywood."

He came back to her presently with three copies of the contract ready for her signature—and the check.

"How soon can you start?" he wanted to know. "Why not go along with Minna and me to-night? You can get ready—an old trouper like you."

"I'll be there. When and where?"

"The Pennsylvania Station at eight. I'll buy your ticket."

"Thanks."

"And you can pay me on the train," he added hastily. He blotted the signatures. His spirits appeared to be rising. "I'm going to give this thing a whale of a production, and if it goes over I might try one or two more of Charlie's pieces. But I ain't paying such prices again."

"We'll discuss that later," she smiled.

"You better settle down out West," he suggested. "I'd have work for you now and then, and you could pick up something occasionally in the other studios. You got a name, Nellie—a big name. I know, because I give it to you."

"Thanks, Lew." She folded the check. "I'll think about that."

"Me and Minna will look for you at the train." He followed her to the door. "Maybe you think I'm close, Nellie; but if I am I got a reason. All my life something's been hanging over me—a fear—an obsession. I got it watching the other managers. One by one I seen them go Broadway broke, and I been afraid; afraid it would get me too. It wouldn't be any fun, Nellie, being broke and old in this game."

"No, I guess it wouldn't, Lew," she answered gravely. "See you to-night at the train."

She traveled the short distance back to the flat as blithely as a girl of twenty. Five flights up suited her mood.

She pushed open the door. Something struck her at once—a silence, a disappointment—something gone. Chum! Chum, who frisked about the feet of all who entered there.

Gracie sat by a window, languidly scanning the department-store advertising in a morning paper.

"Where's Chum?" Nellie demanded.

"Hello, Ma! Chum? Oh, Joe came back and we made up our minds it was time to part with poor old Chum. So Joe took him down to the vet—"

Nellie's heart sank.

"What vet? Where?"

"Meyer, I think the name was. Somewhere on Tenth Street—East Tenth—over near the river. Ma, where you going?"

"Out!" Nellie was at the head of the stairs.

Gracie followed. "The agent was here," she called. "He's coming again at three."

"Let him come. It's all right, I'm working," Nellie replied over her shoulder, and left the dazed Gracie far behind. She ran over to Broadway and signaled the first taxi she saw.

"Never mind the speed laws!" she cried, climbing in. "Matter of life and death!"

"Where to?" inquired the driver, naturally curious on that point.

"East Tenth. I don't know the number. Near the river. We'll find it somehow. We've got to find it!"

The car started. Nellie was angry now. This was like Joe—a little opposition and he was off, couldn't wait; wanted to show he took nobody's orders. Well, she had the upper hand now. The check in her purse gave her that. And little Joey would step round. The taxi crept in and out of the traffic; at every enforced stop her spirits sank.

On East Tenth luck was with her. She looked out the window of the car and saw Joe plodding along—alone. She directed the driver to draw up to the curb, and before the taxi had quite halted she leaped to the sidewalk and confronted her son-in-law.

"Where's Chum?"

"Ma, what are you doing here?"

"Where's Chum? Answer me!"

"I left him in there." He pointed over his shoulder. "They'll take care of Chum."

She ran past him and through the open door of an ancient brick stable. The darkness blinded her for a moment—and then she saw a thin streak of white coming toward her, heard a familiar bark. Nellie Wayne knelt on the dirty floor and opened her arms.

"All right, Chum. Everything's all right. You're not staying here. You're going with me."

Joe came forward, officious.

"Now, see here, Ma, I won't have you butting in. Chum will be better off. And I can't afford to have him round eating his head off."

"Forget it, Joe," she advised. "After this Chum belongs to me."

"To you? That's good! How you going to take care of him?"

She stood up and took a pink bit of paper from her purse. "Read that," she said. It was the simplest explanation.

"Two thousand!" Joe gasped. "From Lew Gorman!"

"Yes, and there's a lot more still coming to me."

"What's he going to do—star you?"

She did not reply, but knelt again and took Chum in her arms. An old, unshaven man shuffled out of a smelly office.

"All right, Doc," Joe told him. "We changed our mind about the dog. You can give me back the two dollars." The old man objected with surprising vehemence. He was, he said, ready to do his part.

"Come along, Joe," Nellie called. "You can ride with us if you like."

Joe hesitated between his two and Nellie's two thousand, but only for an instant. He followed her and meekly climbed to her side in the taxi.

"I don't get this," he said.

"I sold one of Charlie's old plays to Gorman for a picture," she explained. "And I'm going out to Hollywood to act in it."

"In the movies! You, in the movies!" Joe threw back his head and laughed loudly. "After all you've said against them—"

"Well, I can change my mind, can't I? I see my mistake. It's up to me to move along with the times. You can't just stand round mooning about the good old days. If you do you're sunk."

"Now you're talking sense," Joe approved. They rode on in silence for a time. "A fellow was telling me that copper's the thing," he went on presently; "a fellow who works in Wall Street. 'Just put a few thousand in copper,' he says, 'and'—"

"Listen!" cut in Nellie. "All the money I used to have hated me, Joe. It left me right away. But this is friendly money. It's going to stick around."

"Well, I was just suggesting—"

"I'll pay the rent and give Gracie five hundred to tide along until you get work. Then I'm going out to California and buy a little bungalow—a little home for Chum and me; a place where he can lie round all day in the sun, or maybe chase butterflies if he feels ambitious. Do they have butterflies out there?"

"They got everything," said Joe.

"I'll pick up a bit of work now and then. And what's left over after buying the house goes into bonds—government bonds. My home will always be open to you, Joe—to Nellie and Gracie—/just the way yours was to me. Only there won't be any agent for the landlord in the cast."

"Well, I done my best," he said.

"That's all right, Joe. You did, and I'm mighty grateful. And there'll always be a welcome for you out West."

"Somehow, I can't see you leaving Broadway," said Joe.

"Why not? My Broadway left me long ago."

She stopped the cab at a bank not far from the flat and sent Joe home with Chum. A cashier, who knew her well, translated Lew's hieroglyphics into a magnificent roll of bills. She rode in triumph back to the walk-up apartment.

In the parlor Gracie and young Nellie were bending anxiously above a black silk dress, over which Gracie was waving an uncertain needle. Nellie went to them at once and seized the garment.

"What's this?" she wanted to know.

"Ma, Joe says you got an engagement."

"Yes; but what's this?"

"It's mine," young Nellie answered. She seemed breathless with excitement; her big brown eyes were glowing. "I've got a part too! Levy's rushing me into his new comedy—a maid role, only a few lines, but a beginning. The girl who had the role was fired, and we're trying to make her costume over to fit me. The dress rehearsal's to-night."

Nellie Wayne stood silent, staring at the costume with a sort of contempt.

"Nonsense!" she said suddenly, and tossed it into a waste-basket.

With a little cry young Nellie rescued it. She faced her grandmother, trembling, flushed, determined.

"How dare you?" she cried. "How dare you interfere? It's my life, I can live it as I please. I'm going on the stage. You had your day, you had your fun; you can't stop me. I'm going on the stage, I tell you! I love it! I want it! I'd die if I didn't!"

"Baby!" Nellie put her hands on the girl's slim shoulders. "Baby, that wasn't bad at all. A little more voice, perhaps—a little more authority—but that will come in time; when you've lived longer—suffered. Going on the stage! O f course you are! But not in that dress. Come with Nellie Wayne and she'll buy you the best in town."

Young Nellie wilted.

"Oh, I'm sorry! Excuse me! But I thought, after what you said—"

"What did I say?"

"About my acting. You said you'd rather see me in my grave; that Broadway was a dreadful place—no gratitude— no heart—"

"What rot, Baby! You're dreaming! I never did!"

"But, Mother," protested Gracie, "I heard you myself!"

"You're crazy, both of you! I may be getting old, my dears, I may be fifty"—Gracie looked at her—"or thereabouts, but I fancy I know what I said. Would I belittle the profession that gave me so many happy years? Would I smirch the memories I've got by wild talk like that—me, the best Viola of a generation? I should hope not! Of course, Baby's going to act! I want her in the profession—carrying on the torch—but not in one of Levy's hand- me-downs; not while Nellie has a roll of bills like this." She opened her pocketbook; they saw and gasped. "It's your father, Gracie. It's from him. Dead and gone, but helping us still. Now, Baby, get your hat. If your dress rehearsal's to- night we must rush. Besides, I'm off at eight myself."

The girl disappeared into her room. Nellie walked the floor, beaming, happy.

"A maid's part! To think of it, Gracie! I had a maid's part my first engagement too. What was that line? 'My lady, the curate is waiting for you in the garden.' Our Baby! She's got the spark, Gracie! Did you see how she flared out at me?"

Gracie put her hand to her head.

"So many things are happening," she complained.

Nellie explored her purse and threw a handful of bills on the table.

"There—some of it's for the rent man, with Nellie Wayne's love. Give the janitor ten dollars and tell him to bring my trunks up from the storeroom. We'll have to spend the afternoon packing." Young Nellie reappeared. "Come, child, I'll take you to Madame Claire. It's a rush job, but Maggie will do it for me. And oh, Gracie dear, call up the Walden and engage a table! I'm giving a farewell party tonight. Better say six o'clock. I mustn't miss my train. And order it, too, will you, so we shan't be kept waiting."

"What—what shall I order?" asked Gracie.

"Oh, I don't know. Just shut your eyes and spend, Gracie. It's Nellie Wayne's good-by."

* * * * *

THE dinner was over and they emerged from the hotel. Nellie Wayne, erect and blooming—booked again! Then Baby and Gracie, Joe, carrying a florist's box, Tom Kerrigen with Chum in his arms.

"Now, Gracie, I want you and Joe to go with Baby. Her first dress rehearsal—you've got to be there. Tom will take me to the train."

"All right, Mother, if you wish it."

"Did you order the taxi, Tom?"

"Here he is, Nellie."

"And he's got the top down. That's good! I'm not going to say the word, Gracie; such a sad word; just au revoir."

Joe proffered his box.

553

"So long, Ma. A few roses—from the three of us."

"Oh, Joe, you're too good to me!"

"Your money paid for them," said Joe humbly.

"Your kindness bought them." She took the box. "You and Gracie must visit me—"

"We'll be there," Joe promised. "Fellow in Los Angeles wanted me to go into the real-estate game with him. Maybe you'd better hold off buying that house— "

She smiled, pressed his hand, turned to her daughter.

"Well, Gracie—what you crying for? You've seen me start on the road a thousand times. Baby"—she put her arm about the girl—"you're in the profession now; the greatest profession in the world. Respect it, give it your best, no matter what's in the box. That's the first rule—the only one."

"I'll never forget," young Nellie said, "what's behind me—you—and grandfather. I'll never forget this afternoon— buying the dress—my first costume. You'll be proud of me."

"God bless you, dear. You're on your way. A great star—I'm sure of it. How happy Charlie would be to see you tonight!" Her voice broke. "Run along now, please, the three of you."

She stood looking after them until them were lost in the throng on Broadway. Her eyes were wet.

"We'd better start," Tom Kerrigen said gently. "The taxi's waiting."

She turned to him.

"I wanted this last ride with you, Tom, down our old street together. Tell him to drive to the Pennsylvania by way of Union Square. I guess there's time." He helped her into the cab and deposited Chum in her lap. The dog was restless, excited—the lights, the crowd, eight o'clock again. "There, Chum, old fellow," she said, "calm down. We're not showing to-night; we're off for the road; booked solid into the hereafter—and it's a long sleeper jump."

The cab swung into Long Acre, into the dazzling square of the electric signs. The new Rialto—all glitter and no heart. They crossed Forty- Second Street, and the White Way grew darker. They were moving on into the past.

The Empire was left behind, and then the Knickerbocker. No more playhouses, no more in reality; tall loft buildings towering overhead—Feinberg & Morris, Ladies' Waists; Max Hirschfield, Artificial Flowers—and then the big grim department stores of Herald Square.

No more playhouses in reality, but a dozen or more in their dreams. Famous temples of the drama, torn down and forgotten. The Herald Square, the Bijou, the Standard! Nellie Wayne in Charlie Farren's Latest! Wallack's and Daly's. Nellie Wayne in As You Like It! Prancing horses at the curb, fine ladies and fine gentlemen descending, silk hats gleaming above the crowd. The crack of cabbies' whips. Carriages at eleven-thirty sharp! They were in Madison Square.

"Did you see what I saw, Tom?"

"Ghosts, Nellie; a thousand ghosts. I'm going home tomorrow."

"We're ghosts, too, Tom. The stage is set for a new piece and here we are mumbling the old lines, the lines nobody wants to hear."

"Over there at the Hoffman House I saw Charlie that last night. He said he wasn't feeling right."

"Tell the driver to turn down Twenty-Second. Never mind Union Square. I've seen enough."

"You shouldn't have come this way, Nellie."

"Nonsense, Tom! I came on purpose. It saddens me, but it makes it easier to go—to go and never to come back. There's nothing to come back for."

Into the dark of Twenty-Second the taxi swerved, and Nellie laid a hand on her friend's arm.

"Have him stop just a moment, Tom." The bored driver obeyed.

They had come to a halt before a battered old brick house almost obliterated by time—a weary old house given over to trade. Alien names decorated its front. Talk of blouses and whalebone and leather goods. Wholesale only. On the first floor a lunchroom, closed for the night.

"Do you remember my garden at the rear? The hollyhocks? And the canary in the dining-room window—the canary that used to wake and sing when we came home after the play?"

"Sometimes I'd get here first, Nellie, and I'd sit on the steps and wait for the sound of the horse's hoofs. And then the shining news hansom with Reilly on the box passing the gaslight on the corner—and Charlie on the sidewalk, helping you down?"

Silence for a moment.

"Tell him to go on now, Tom," she said softly.

The rattle of a protesting engine followed, and they moved away.

"That's all over and done with," Nellie said. "We're just old useless props cluttering up the scene. It will be different out West. Thank heaven, I've still got work to do!"

"That's right, Nellie." They rode along. "I—I'll be spending the winters down near you. I'll see you now and then."

"I'm glad to hear that, Tom. The best friend anybody ever had. Wasn't it strange how clearly we seemed to see him—there in front of the old house? Charlie, I mean. Did you see him too?"

"Yes," said Kerrigan, "I saw him."

"His name will be on the billboards again, all over the country, just the way it used to be."

"So it will."

She took something from her purse.

"Tom, I want you to look up an old actor—a character man named Frank Shore. Give him that and tell him I'm going to find him a berth out on the Coast."

"I'll do it, Nellie."

They were speeding up Seventh Avenue; the station was close ahead. Nine blocks off the lights of Long Acre were flaming. Nellie Wayne lifted Chum where he could see.

"Take your last look, Chum, old fellow. We're saying good-by." Chum's tired old eyes swept the yellow horizon and he barked a rather faint farewell.

"Sorry, Nellie?" Kerrigen asked.

She shook her head.

"Not very sorry. One thought keeps running through my mind. Whatever happens, I'll never be Broadway broke again."

The taxi swung suddenly into the tunneled drive at the south end of the station—the long dim tunnel where the lights of Long Acre were just another memory.

THE END

www.ingramcontent.com/pod-product-compliance
Lightning Source LLC
Chambersburg PA
CBHW031022030726
47497CB00004B/957